ALL THE WAY OUT

ALL THE WAY
BOOK 2

HENSLEY AMETHYST PARK

This story is a work of fiction. Names, characters, places, and incident are either products of the author's imagination, or are used fictitiously. Any resemblance to actual persons, living or dead, businesses, events, or locales is *entirely* coincidental. The author makes no claims to, but instead, acknowledges the trademarked status and trademark owners of the word marks mentioned in this work of fiction.

No part of this book may be used, resold, reproduced, shared, transmitted, sold, exchanged, photographed, digitized, printed, or otherwise copied in any manner whatsoever without the express prior written permission of the publisher and or author, except in the case of brief quotations embodied in critical articles and or reviews and other such non-commercial uses as are permitted by United States Copyright law.

If this work or any part of it is being shared, plagiarized, or copied in any way, please report it to us via www.myswoonromance.com. Please report grammatical errors and typos to us via www.myswoonromance.com.

Copyright © 2023 by Hensley Amethyst Park

ALL THE WAY OUT by Hensley Amethyst Park, part of the ALL THE WAY Series by Hensley Amethyst Park

All rights reserved. Published in the United States of America by Swoon Romance/Georgia McBride Media Group in Raleigh, NC 27609

ePub ISBN: 979-8-9890618-2-2

Trade Paperback ISBN: 979-8-9890618-3-9

PRAISE FOR ALL THE WAY IN

"Mitchell is the hottest billionaire boss MC I've read it a WHILE. This book earned 5 stars from me & 4 spicy peppers!" —Jordan R

"Mitchell, God where do I even begin with him😅. This man has the mouth of a f***ing sailor because he just can't keep the filth inside..." —Tali

"Mitch & Mirabella!!! OMG 😵‍💫🔥😵‍💫 I love billionaire romance novels and this is the new standard!" —Theresa

"Humor, sass, and some spice." —Hillary

"I give this a solid 4/5 and 2/5 spice! This was so so good even though it is a slow burn it's so worth it!" —Abby

"The tension between these two was insane." —Victoria

"This is a quick steamy billionaire romance with absolutely unhinged characters. It was very over dramatic in the best way possible." —Sariah C

"The things that came out of his mouth was filthy and hot. A one night stand that leads up to some good banter and leaves you wanting more." —Cami29

AUTHOR'S NOTE

Dear Reader,

I'm overwhelmed by the reception, reviews, and love you guys gave ALL THE WAY IN. You posted reviews, DM'd me, emailed me, and reshared, liked, commented, and paid attention to my social media. Some of you even offered me advice. To show my appreciation, here is Book 2, ALL THE WAY OUT. It's noticeably longer than ALL THE WAY IN because you guys deserve more Mirabella and Mitchell!

This book, ALL THE WAY OUT, was a true labor of love. I'd thought Mirabella and Mitchell's story was complete with ALL THE WAY IN. But a dear friend convinced me that they had more to say, and that it deserved to be read by you!

Instead of worrying about manuscript conventions or being a slave to chapter lengths, I wrote and wrote and wrote. I wrote the story I felt Mirabella and Mitchell needed me to. And despite cutting quite a lot of words, this book is LONG. The first chapters are comprised of some of the longest chapters in the book. Not to be outdone, Chapter 12 is also rather long. This book is very emotional. I was emotional when writing it, and it contains **all the words** (see what I did there?).

These characters are extremely flawed. You may not always agree with or like their decisions. Some readers may find certain activities and events mentioned in this story as triggering, including mentions of drug use, possessiveness, abandonment, death, sexual assault, family tragedy, terminal illness, touch deprivation, gagging for sexual gratification, affection deprivation, imprisonment, addiction to pornography, physical assault, mental illness, generalized anxiety, graphic violence, toxic family dynamics, and threats of physical violence.

ALL THE WAY OUT features explicit sexual content, adult situations, exceptionally strong language, and cursing.

I really hope you enjoy this sequel! I wrote it for you!

With love and appreciation,

Hensley Amethyst Park

Don't settle. You deserve it all

ALL THE WAY OUT

She's said too much. Now, it's his turn to talk...

ALL THE WAY 2

CHAPTER ONE

MITCHELL MAGELLAN

It was one thing after the fucking other at Magellan Media. A federal criminal indictment against Peter Trenom was expected to be handed down from a Grand Jury. For what? I had no fucking idea. To make matters much worse, I had to rely on Gina Abruzzi-Torres for counsel and Aunt Meg had gone all Mama Bear on me, in an effort to protect Peter's grown ass.

After the event in London, my star in the media and entertainment businesses was at peak brightness for about five damn minutes. But the Board became increasingly concerned as Brennan Enterprises' new billion-dollar-product, AKA Mirabella Castle, was rapidly gaining interest from licensing partners looking to hitch their star to her particular brand of Feminism.

Not long after said event, Hyacinth Rose and her team of merry brand marketers landed deal after fucking deal and announced them in the trades. The media took to pitting our two companies against one another with Mira in the middle, claiming she had managed to "reignite a decades-old rivalry" between us.

They further lauded Mirabella's botched interview and subsequent social media success as the catalyst that had awoken two sleeping giants.

One article said, "... and it only took a twenty-one-year-old woman to remind these once formidable rivals what's worth fighting for, as each had become complacent in recent years." Next to it was a picture of Godzilla versus King Kong.

And, while I was happy for Mirabella, her success with Brennan Enterprises was bad for my business *and* my sex life.

We saw one another whenever we could in this hotel or that one, and I sent Mirabella to work with a fucking smile on her face and my dick on her breath. But in the past few weeks, it was all phone or video sex, and if I was being honest, it wasn't fucking enough. If things didn't change, we were going to have a problem.

"Mitchell, we need to stay focused." Aunt Meg noticed me checking my phone for texts from Mirabella and tossed me an annoyed look. I had to pull back a smile after reading the message. Pocketing my cell, I shook my head and pinched the bridge of my nose. When she had my attention once more, Aunt Meg added, "we are going to want to issue a statement in full support of Peter."

"Yes. We can do that, if not from me then definitely from Magellan Media once the indictment is handed down."

She looked at me like I was still that child she would let eat chocolate ice cream for dinner when I was six.

"That's not convincing enough. We need to demonstrate that Peter has your full and unwavering support."

I sighed way longer than I should have while Aunt Meg, Phillip Braxton, Peter Trenom, and I huddled around the kitchen island on the landline phone Aunt Meg insisted on keeping exactly for situations like this.

In a past life, we would have made a formidable team, one that nobody would dare have messed with. But Peter Trenom had put us all at risk, and this duplicitous motherfucker had the nerve to be mum about exactly what he had done.

Now, the Feds were crawling up my ass and my Aunt Meg was

covering for her on-again-off-again lover in the biggest case of "I didn't see that shit coming" since Mirabella Castle invaded my life.

Luckily, Braxton got the jump on the situation a few weeks ago. He came to tell me about it at RayRay and Christina's party. I had to remain calm and pretend like he was delivering a gift for the baby. To keep up the ruse, he'd even held Christina for a few photos when the photographer mistook him for a family member.

We'd managed to keep things quiet until the media started sniffing around. Clara was the first person to alert me to the lengths reporters were going to for a scoop. She'd been stopped outside of the building by a woman who offered her five thousand dollars for some dirt on Peter.

"I almost took it too, Mitchell. Peter Trenom has been nothing but rude and entitled since I started," she'd said. "Unlike the other execs, he never bothered asking me about my kids or wishing me a happy birthday. I just hate that his poor wife and kids have to go through this."

This fucker continued sipping his tea, casting his eyes down, avoiding the rebuke in mine. I should have thrown his ass to the wolves for how he treated Clara alone.

"Gina, are we prepared to make a statement?" I asked, hoping she could oversee things from London. If I had to endure her in person, I might just fucking lose it from that stunt she'd pulled with Mirabella and the subpoena.

"How can we make a statement to the press or our staff without knowing what the indictment is even for?"

As usual, Akila Norris was spot on.

"Akila's right. We need more details about this indictment, unless you want to tell us what the fuck you did, Peter?" I said, my gaze of disbelief and disappointment landing squarely on the Judas standing across from me sipping a fucking "calming" herbal tea.

Aunt Meg placed a hand on Peter's arm as if to say, "Ignore Mitchell."

"I think we can say something like, I, *together with the Board of Magellan Media are shocked and disheartened by the actions taken by the FBI, the SEC, and the U.S. Attorney's Office against Peter Trenom today.*

However, we plan to cooperate fully with the investigation, and look forward to its speedy resolution. In the meantime, in order to protect the integrity of our company and the relationships we have with our customers and partners, we will be removing Mr. Trenom from his position on the Board, replacing him with Megan Magellan, effective immediately."

Gina had clearly prepared to respond to the indictment even before we'd received word there was going to be one.

Even though I wasn't exactly sure I cared what Gina thought about this very thing, I said, "That sounds great. Meg, are you OK with that?"

Peter seemed like he was about to chime in when she responded.

"Well, we need to have the Board vote, but yes."

Peter opened his mouth to speak but I quickly corrected my aunt before he had a chance to. Nobody gave a shit what that motherfucker wanted, thought, or had to say. His job was to shut up, appear contrite, and not do or say anything that could make matters worse.

"We don't technically need their vote. The bylaws call for me to name an interim replacement in the case of any sort of civil or legal action against a Board member without the need for a vote."

"Mitchell's right," Gina said. Under normal circumstances I would have preferred not to need Gina's fucking two cents. But given the severity of what we were facing, I appreciated it.

As if annoyed with the lot of us, Meg shook her head and placed a supportive hand on Peter's arm again. Right then, the dynamic of their relationship became clear. She was in charge. Peter was subdued. Brought to heel for doing something that was potentially unforgivable, criminal even. And now, he was more upset about what it would mean for her than his own damn wife and kids. To save face, he stood silently next to her, allowing her to take point on strategy, in case she might be able to fix his very public fuck up.

"Braxton, let me know what you find out about this indictment. I want to be informed of everything they think they have and when the indictment might be coming down. As usual, money is no object."

Braxton had been strangely quiet during this meeting despite having a shit ton to say to me about it in private.

I got the distinct impression that whatever role Braxton had served under my father, that he had done so with far more discretion than now. Under my leadership, he was front and center in just about every major situation, and I was sure he hated it.

"Of course, Mitchell. I'll get right on it."

When Braxton left, only the official Magellan Media employees remained, so I spoke freely, perhaps more than I should have.

"We can't afford more scandals or negative press."

Just then Aunt Meg placed a comforting hand on Peter's arm as if to say, 'he's not talking about you' when in fact I was talking about him exactly.

"Let's just make sure we know everything they know. Gina, I'm sure you've got much on your plate already. So, I've hired outside counsel from Kain, Carpenter, & Maguire to take point on this," I said, feeling like a fucking boss. "If I need you, I'll let you know."

Giving her zero time to protest, I said, "Akila, I need you here in New York. Plan to stay a few weeks. Have Cindy put you up at The Mark. We need to start making some personnel changes."

"Ok, Mitchell. I will fly out tomorrow morning."

"Akila, I need you here tonight. I'll send a jet."

"Oh, ok. I'll start getting prepared. Do you need me on this call further?"

"No. Thanks. See you soon."

Then I turned my attention to Peter Fucking Trenom. This motherfucker shifted his weight from one leg to another and then eyed me defiantly, like he wanted me to know that I had no power in my aunt's house. I guess he'd missed the memo; I was the fucking boss now. And whatever shit he pulled when my dad was alive wasn't gonna fly here.

"Peter, I can't have you hanging around here anymore now that Aunt Meg is Board President. Go home to your *wife and family* and don't fucking skip town."

Neither he nor my aunt spoke, both looking shocked and dis-fuck-ing-missed.

"Thanks for your time, everyone," I said before disconnecting the call. And when I was certain everyone had hung up, I turned to Peter again and said sternly, "What the fuck did you do?"

"It's not what you think or at least how it seems," he said, looking from me to Aunt Meg.

"Enlighten me, Peter." I was losing my fucking patience.

"It was just ill-timed. Just unfortunate timing given the circumstances. No one could have foretold what would happen, Mitchell," Aunt Meg chimed in, speaking for his sorry ass. I can't believe I had considered him a father figure at one point.

Just then my phone dinged. I pulled it out of my pocket and read the text message.

> BRAXTON: Indictment coming soon. They have Peter on offloading Magellan stock the week before your family's accident and again the day before. They have audio and video evidence of insider trading.

> ME: Stay on his houses, apartments, and other known dwellings. Don't let them get ahead of us. I assume SEC will bring separate charges?

> BRAXTON: Fluid situation. Will update as I get info.

"Does anybody want to tell me what's going on?" I looked from Aunt Meg to Peter.

"Mitchell, I advised Peter to retain counsel and not to say anything to anyone, including you."

"You can't be serious."

"Don't talk to your aunt like that, Mitchell. She knows what she's saying, and I am taking her advice. She's just trying to protect me. And you too."

The only reason I didn't grab a knife from the nearby drawer and slice that fucking asshole's neck right then was the thought of staying out of prison.

"Meg, you haven't practiced law in over twenty years. Don't you think it's a conflict of interest for you? For Magellan?"

"I haven't said anything that can hurt us, Mitchell. But anything he tells us can be the subject of a subpoena in the future. We can be called on to testify about what he told us. So, it's better that he talks only to his retained counsel," Aunt Meg said like a true lawyer, albeit a commercial real estate one.

She made sense but I was fucking pissed at her for trying to protect her lover even though his ass had a wife and kids. Wasn't he recently featured in *Family Man* magazine? When I saw that shit, I nearly put my hand through the nearest window. There was a fucking two-page spread of a photo of him in his cricket outfit with his grandkids running across the expansive lawn of his Long Island mansion.

Just then, Preston came into the kitchen with headphones on that I hadn't seen him with before. I took a deep breath so I could center and not be cross with him despite my shitty mood.

"Mitchell!" His big smile immediately fixed my attitude. Preston was a daily reminder of both the fickleness of life and its beauty.

I dapped him up and pulled him into a bro hug for longer than I normally did. Preston was the kind of person you wanted to spill your feelings to because you knew he wasn't going to judge you. That he would be there just listening, even if he didn't one hundred percent understand the nuance or complexities of what you'd said.

"Hey, Pres. Are those new headphones, Brother? I like 'em." If today hadn't been so fucked up, I would have spent more time with him.

He removed his headphones from his ears, and put them on mine. This motherfucker was listening to *WAP*.

"Nice, Pres. I like that song. Reminds me of Mirabella." I was unable to stop the smile that spread across my face.

He grinned and pulled his headphones off my head, then stopped to look at me.

"What's wrong, Mitch? Is Mitch a sad motherfucker?"

He was intuitive, empathetic, and the only person I let call me 'Mitch.'

My thoughts quickly turned to that time Mirabella had jokingly called me 'Mitch' during our first date in London at the Shard. I pushed the thought away and turned my smile into a scowl befitting my current situation.

"Yes, Pres. I'm a sad motherfucker today."

Aunt Meg shook her head at me, silently chastising me for teaching Preston a library of vulgar words. "But next time I come visit, me and you will do something, just the two of us. Ok, Bro? I have to go now. I'm sorry. I'll see you soon, ok?" I said, waiting for Preston to hug me because one of his quirks was he didn't like to say goodbye. He'd hug you when he first saw you but getting him to do it on your way out was a lot harder.

Preston seemed to contemplate what I had said, and then put his headphones on, and walked away. On his way upstairs, he yelled, "Go fuck yourself, Mitch!"

I laughed, gathered up my phone from the white marble center island, and gave Peter Trenom a look he could not mistake for kind.

"Say your goodbyes. Don't leave town," I said before nodding to Mr. Feer who'd spent the entire time nosing around quietly while pretending to dust. I walked out of the kitchen, feeling a little less annoyed the closer I got to the front door. And when I was outside, I realized I hadn't said goodbye to Aunt Meg.

Let her fucking stew in it, I thought.

As always, Brendan was waiting, this time in the Maybach.

"Hey," I said as I opened my own door and got in. My phone rang, and I was hoping it was Mirabella.

As we pulled out of Aunt Meg's long driveway leading to the giant iron gates, I answered the phone.

"Magellan," I said as my new form of 'hello.'

"Mr. Magellan, hi it's Sherilyn. Um, there are some people here, sir. They say they have a warrant. I don't know what to do."

FUCK!

"What agency are they with?"

"Sir?"

"Where are they from? FBI, SEC? U.S. Attorney's Office? NYPD?"

"I'm not sure, sir," she said in a timid and uncertain voice. She'd only been my personal assistant for three months. And even though Cindy and Clara were still there, Sherilyn was now managing my day-to-day. And if I was being honest, she wasn't a fit. Mirabella? She would have already had it handled. She would have known what to do if for no other reason that she was intuitive and had great instincts, whereas Sherilyn had office skills, but she had little common fucking sense.

"Ok, listen, I'll be there in forty minutes. Just hold tight and don't talk to anyone. Call Gina Abruzzi-Torres and let her speak to the agent in charge."

"Ok, sir. See you soon," she said before hanging up.

I dialed Cindy's cell.

When she picked up, I said, "Cindy, please make sure Sherilyn is doing what I asked her to. Please call Kain, Carpenter, & Maguire and tell them to get someone down there ASAP."

"Of course, sir. Is there something I should know, sir?"

I wanted to tell her everything was going to be ok, but in all honesty, I didn't know whether it would be.

"Cindy, keep focused on making sure those officers and agents have whatever they need, that we appear to be cooperating, and that someone from Kain, Carpenter, & Maguire gets there."

"Yes, sir. Is there anything else, sir?"

"Yes. Turn off the executive floor elevator."

"But, sir, if I do that, there will be no way for all the agents to get up to or down from the fiftieth floor," she said, ever the worrier.

"Cindy, they can take the stairs."

"Ah, yes, sir." There was a smile of recognition in Cindy's voice now. I think she was proud of me for devising a plan to make it difficult for the agents to conduct their task if they had to walk up and down that many stairs.

"Also make sure Mr. Coster supervises any and all searches of *my* office *himself*."

"Sir, Mr. Coster is out of the office today." Cindy sounded apprehensive.

"Call his ass at fucking home or wherever the hell he is and tell him I said to get his ass to the office ASAP."

"Yes, sir. I'm messaging him now."

"Who's next in charge in Security?"

Cindy was click-clacking on the mechanical keyboard Mirabella had convinced her to get.

"It's Andrew Denowitz, sir. I'm messaging him now as well."

"Thanks, Cindy. Please keep me posted."

I hung up, a head-splitting fucking migraine brewing.

I grabbed a bottle of water from the drink fridge and dug around in the first aid kit for some Tylenol.

As I downed two extra strengths, my phone vibrated.

What fucking now?

It was Mirabella.

"Hey, beautiful," I said, truly wishing I could be with her right then. My head felt like it was in a vise, and I really did not feel like talking to anyone.

"What's wrong?" She was intuitive and no doubt hearing the tension in my voice.

I sighed, debating whether to tell her everything. But Mirabella didn't want to hear about my corporate fucking nightmare.

"I miss you, Mira."

"I miss you too. I've been so tense; I got a massage yesterday. Today, I'm in the hot tub." She spoke as though she didn't know how badly I wished it had been me to lube her up and give her a massage. Because if it had, I would have given her a full body massage, making sure to adequately rub and caress her all around her pleasure center until she begged me to be inside her. And don't even get me started on the hot tub.

My thoughts were running away with me. I was getting hard thinking of rubbing oil all over Mirabella's perfect caramel skin.

"You feeling better today, Baby?"

"I'd be feeling much better if you were here." Even though I know she said it to comfort me, it made me feel so much worse.

"Me too. How's the tour?"

I had a million fucking thoughts running around my head right then, all competing for my attention. And now, my erection was completely gone. Jesus. I didn't want to be the kind of guy who let work fuck with his sex life.

"It's been busy. So many people want to meet me; it's very strange."

"You're a social media star now." I tried to sound supportive and encouraging when all I wanted to do was relieve all this fucking tension with a blow job. Blow jobs were easy. I didn't have to do anything but sit back and receive. Jerking off was too much fucking work. It required concentration, a good imagination, and fucking energy. And intercourse required the most work of all. *What is she thinking? Am I hitting the spot? Does she like it? Can I make her come? Can I hold out until she does?*

"It's so weird," she said, and I knew she meant it, that she wasn't getting a big head from all the attention and hero worship.

Just then my phone beeped. The call coming in was from Braxton.

"Mirabella, I need to take a call from Braxton. There is so much shit going on. I don't know if you'll see it on the news there, but I really have to take this."

"Ok. Well, I just wanted to say hi and to tell you I . . . I miss you."

I felt like such a heel hanging up on Mirabella to talk to fucking Braxton, but I needed to boss right now.

"Thanks so much, Baby. I miss you too, so fucking much."

"Braxton," I said when I'd hung up from Mirabella and accepted his call. "What have you got?"

"Mitchell, it's not good."

"What is it?"

"They have video and audio footage that could cause us major problems. They have been surveilling Magellan Media since before the airplane crash."

"What? Why?"

"Someone's out to get you, and they were out to get your father before you. Somebody wants to take down Magellan Media."

Fucking Brennan was the first thing that popped into my head, despite Aunt Meg's warnings not to look to placing blame on him until we could prove it.

"What the hell are you talking about, Braxton? First you tell me someone may have accidentally killed my family while botching a hit on Robert Brennan, now this?"

It was too damn much. The urge to say fuck it all, grab Mirabella up, and fucking go live on an island somewhere pecked away at my skull. For a second, I actually entertained the idea.

"Sir, they have video footage and audio of *all* the goings on inside all of the offices on the executive floor."

Jesus Christ. That means they have audio and video footage of every single time I jerked off or got a blow job in my office. I could not let that shit get out.

"How can that be? I mean, even if it is, the police can't use it," I said, hoping I was right.

"Maybe not, but these people aren't police. Someone is extorting you."

"Braxton, what the fuck are you talking about? Who is extorting me? And what do they want? How much do they want?"

"I don't know. They haven't made any demands yet. Haven't asked for any money. But whoever it is, they are the ones who leaked information about Peter Trenom to the FBI and the SEC. They've made their move and now they will wait for you to make yours."

"I'm not following you."

"This person, whoever it is, they're fucking with you. They're playing chess. They just made a move, a pretty significant one, I might add, and now it's your turn. They want to see you rattled. They have already told you what their move is going to be. They're ready and able to release some pretty damaging footage. It seems you've made an enemy in your short tenure as CEO of Magellan Media."

I shook my head, trying to piece together what Braxton meant. Surely, I hadn't yet made any corporate enemies.

"And do we know what information they gave the Feds?"

"Seems they have evidence that shows Peter offloaded Magellan Media stock two days prior to the plane crash but also doing so long before then. Apparently, Peter's been enriching himself and his friends with insider info for some time."

Holy Shit.

"What kind of evidence?"

"Well, they're looking for the paper trail. That's why they have a warrant and are tearing up your offices at the moment. But like I said, they have audio and video they may not be able to use in court," Braxton said, confirming my worst fears about Trenom. This motherfucker was not only stupid enough to do what he had done but he was stupid enough to leave evidence. Surely, he was smarter than that?

"That's what Aunt Meg meant when she said it was a coincidence then. Ok, what else? Because I get the distinct feeling that there's more," I said, trying not to lose patience with Braxton's slow ass.

"Sir, it is believed he recommended that all his friends do the same. And right now, the SEC and the FBI are trying to get those friends to drop a dime on him, to testify against him. My informant says there's a particularly good chance that these people who were once loyal to Peter may cut deals to save their own asses."

"That's what I would do if I were them."

"Of course, you would. But, Mitchell, why would Peter Trenom allow himself to be so easily caught? Doesn't that seem odd to you?"

I texted Cindy while listening to Braxton, asking her to get me a list of all major stockholders who dumped stock seventy-two to forty-eight hours prior to the crash.

"No one ever thinks they're gonna get caught, do they?"

"More importantly, Peter doesn't need the money, so why do it to begin with?"

His penchant for delayed gratification and answering a question with a question was getting annoying.

"Peter is one of the largest shareholders we have. His wife's family has more money than all of us."

It was not only shocking what Peter Trenom had been accused of, but utterly unlikely. Peter had replaced Robert Brennan as my dad's best friend and had been like an uncle to Alex and me. His on-again, off-again relationship with Aunt Meg made him a near-permanent fixture at Magellan events even after he married that computer chip heiress. I know my dad admired him and, worse, trusted him. I did not want to believe that my dad had been wrong about both Robert Brennan and Peter Trenom.

"You know, your father really liked Trenom. Took him into his confidence on a lot of things, despite my misgivings and his relationship with your aunt."

"Really? Why wouldn't Dad listen to you? Clearly you were right."

"Your father paid me for my actions not my words. Sometimes he heeded my advice, sometimes he didn't."

"I thought you said my dad was smart. How come he couldn't read Trenom or Brennan? Why did he have such a blind spot where they were concerned?"

"Mitchell, your father was a prideful man. He usually read people rather well. Peter was a family-oriented person, dedicated to his wife and their kids; at least he was in the beginning. Perhaps your father envied that. Perhaps he admired how Peter Trenom could manage it all."

The implication of failure as a family man on my dad's part wasn't lost on me.

"Well, apparently he couldn't since he was cheating on his wife with Aunt Meg."

"Remind me to tell you about that argument one day. Ooooo-weee! Your Aunt almost came to blows with your dad over that man."

"What? She stood up to Dad over that fucking loser?"

"Yep. And yet, your father appreciated Trenom's way of looking at the world, and he was one of a handful of people your dad actually took advice from. And Meredith? She and Trenom's wife were good friends. Your father and mother did couples' nights and trips with Peter and Cynthia," Braxton said, proving once again how well he'd known my parents.

I couldn't picture my dad on a couples' trip. Surely Braxton was making shit up to entertain me at this point.

"I'm not my dad. He was foolish not to listen to your concerns about Peter Trenom."

"It was the only time your father didn't take my advice, and it came back to bite him in the ass."

"What advice would you give him now if he was still here? What advice do you have for me?"

Braxton hesitated, and I hoped it wasn't because he didn't think I was equipped to manage this situation and therefore the advice he was about to give me would be vastly different than what he would have given my significantly more experienced father.

"Well, Mitchell, my advice to you is: be careful who you trust and start cleaning house at Magellan Media."

"Cleaning house?"

"Firing anyone remotely connected to Peter Trenom."

"I'm way ahead of you. I have already asked Akila to come from London. I can trust her," I said, feeling good about having already made that decision without anyone's advice.

"Good. Good, and Mitchell, I would have told your dad something else, so I'm telling you too."

"What's that, Braxton?"

"There is a real possibility that Peter offloaded stock because he knew the crash was going to happen. And if Peter Trenom knew your parents would be killed in that accident, then the crash was no accident. It wasn't a botched hit. It was simply a *hit*."

CHAPTER TWO

MIRABELLA CASTLE

I couldn't believe my eyes. Ben texted me an invitation to opening night of his new play called *The Man*, playing at the Connelly Theater in the East Village. It was a step up from his last play at a venue that could only seat fifty people. The description read, *A man's journey of forgiveness, love, and loss as told through his paintings found by his daughter after his death.* Starring Carol Simms, Mel Shine, and Kim Feldman. And the media 'partner?' Magellan Fucking Media.

Deep breathing had never worked for me. My grandmother suggested it after the shit that went down with Mitchell and the canceled interview. She said I should have tried that rather than acted as I had. She even went so far as to suggest that God himself was not pleased with my behavior. But the damage had already been done. Besides, it had gotten Mitchell's attention. It had gotten the world's attention.

Now, I was doing everything I could not to blow this out of proportion, not to make a scene. So, I closed my eyes and counted to ten. Then I counted to twenty from one again. I inhaled deeply until I was dizzy, then exhaled short breaths a few times.

My rage was slowly taking me over. It wasn't clear to me, which was more upsetting, that Ben had taken the time to text me an invitation to his damn play, that I hadn't yet blocked his phone number, or that somehow, he had managed to get Magellan Media to sponsor it. Neither made any sense. Neither of those things was positive. After the way Ben had dumped me over text, I never expected to see or hear from him again. Seeing the invitation brought back so much pain. It awakened in me emotions I didn't even know I had about our time together. Emotions I had managed to keep in check and bury until now.

My relationship with Mitchell was healing for me, in so many ways. He was so good for me. I was learning to trust. To accept. To be myself with him. I was learning to let go. And then this shit happened.

The thing about me is that I was the kind of person whose mental and emotional stability was quite fragile. Things that were perhaps no big deal to others could be overwhelming to me. Little things could send me into a downward spiral of self-doubt, fear, rage, and anxiety. It was not the kind of thing that deep breathing or journaling could solve. It required medication, therapy, rest, hydration, positive affirmations, and surrounding myself with supportive people who could encourage me and lift me up. At least that's what my doctors had said.

I needed to get ahold of myself. Mitchell had texted to say he was a few minutes away. God, I fucking missed him. But this shit? This shit I couldn't let go. And while I wanted desperately to squash it, to suppress these feelings for long enough that I could enjoy being with him, feel him against me. . . *Oh God*. I could not stop the fucking absolute rage building in me.

And being on tour meant my irregular schedule resulted in missed medication and not taking the time for myself that I needed in order to remain healthy or mentally and emotionally stable.

Being with Ben had broken what little of me I had built up and coaxed back to healthy. Our relationship broke me in all the wrong places.

I had allowed myself to endure a humiliating, sexually stifling, and all together horrible relationship. I let him convince me that I was the reason he was addicted to porn. The reason he couldn't stay hard long enough to penetrate me. The reason he made me feel like I was unsexy and unattractive. Ben made me feel completely and utterly non-sexual to the point where I would just bury any sexual desire or thoughts or needs.

Suppression was the name of the game when I was with Ben. He had made me feel wrong and dirty for wanting sex. He'd made me feel needy for wanting to hold hands. He'd made me feel clingy for wanting to cuddle. I'd spent nearly two years allowing Ben to strip away any and all pieces of me that made me lovable, touchable, desirable.

And when I thought I had gotten a handle on my outburst on the day of my failed interview, my therapist unleashed this gem on me.

"Perhaps you called Mitchell Magellan out in a desperate attempt to get a man known for his sexual exploits to take notice of you. Maybe your rant on social media was more than just revenge, maybe you were unwittingly trying to get him to notice your sexual self."

"Are you saying that I was subconsciously throwing myself at Mitchell Magellan? That's absurd."

But when his expression didn't change and instead, he raised an eyebrow to signal that he was doubling down on his assertion, all I could do was sit back in my chair and stew in his statement.

My anxiety, anger, and frustration at the situation got worse as the minutes ticked by. I was no longer obsessing about how I looked or whether I had chosen the right outfit or even whether I should have flat-ironed my hair. When the knock on my hotel door came, something in me wanted to explode but when I opened the door, all my plans to unleash fury immediately disintegrated.

Mitchell.

He looked so fucking good, and the expression on his face told me he felt the same way about me. Right then, he spoke with his hungry eyes saying something between I'm-going-to-fuck-you-so-fucking-good and I-missed-you-so-fucking-much and I-might-come-just-looking-at-you. Then, I had a choice to make. I could let Mitchell Magellan do what he had come to do, or I could tell him what was on my mind.

"Fuck," he said. There were so many different meanings behind that one word, and every single one of them ignited a fire low in my pelvis. Mitchell smiled, dropped his bags, and swept me up into his arms. "Baby," he said, holding me close and also looking at me like he hadn't ever seen a more beautiful sight, "you feel so damn good."

"Mitchell," was all I could manage in that moment. Being with him right then felt surreal, magical, and absolutely incredible. When I said his name like that, he blinked slowly, his long eyelashes tickling his skin.

This man felt good, too good. The way he smelled was delicious enough to make me acutely aware of how my body was responding to the assault on my senses that this man was perpetrating. And the look on his face? If I had been wearing any panties, I would surely have dropped them by now.

"I missed you," Mitchell said, staring at me. The fact that he hadn't yet kissed me was almost too much. Perhaps he too was remembering that night in my apartment when I'd asked him to come over. Although we'd both been worked up on the phone, I became shy and unsure of myself sometime between when he said he was coming to Queens and when he arrived.

Now though, my body hummed with desire for him. There was no way he didn't feel it. The air charged way the hell up. Michell Magellan was in the building, and my entire body was called to attention and awaiting instructions from its master.

"I missed you too." My breathing was shallow.

Whether it was his proximity or my own sexual starvation, my entire body was now on fire. I was literally burning up for this man. I allowed him to hold me to him while I awaited his next move, finding it difficult to control myself now that he was physically here. All those nights of phone sex, touching myself thinking about him, and dreaming of when we could be together had served only to make me feel rabid and out of control.

Despite the grueling schedule Brennan Enterprises had me on, when I wasn't working, I was thinking about him, texting him, or planning when I could talk to him next. I wrapped my arms around his neck and pushed my body against his with my phone still in my hand. And then, as if that was the signal he'd been waiting for, he kissed me.

Mitchell took his fucking time, kissing me slowly and deliberately at first, keeping his mouth on me a little bit longer with each kiss. The anticipation of how long he'd kiss me for next made my heart bang ferociously against my chest, reminding me of the climb of a rollercoaster that happens before the drop.

He walked forward into the doorway, pushed his bag in with his feet, and closed the door. This man expertly never broke contact with my mouth, his tongue now eager and searching, as the tent in his pants hardened against me. I ached for him, feeling needy and neglected.

Just as my back was nearly up against the wall, Mitchell must have sensed that something was off because he pulled back to look at me, concern in his eyes.

"Mira, what's wrong?"

I pulled out of his embrace as his expression turned to confusion. Trying not to be distracted by how hard he was in his sweatpants or the ache between my legs, I distanced myself from him, and said, "What's wrong? How about what the fuck is this?"

I shoved my phone at him a little more dramatically than I had intended to. On the screen was the offending text. He almost dropped it because I didn't even bother putting it in his hand all the way.

Mitchell stared at the phone, a confused look crossing his face. When he was done reading, he said, "Mira, please. Let's not do this right now. I have no idea how this came to be. I don't personally have a hand in corporate sponsorships."

"How can that be when it has your fucking name on it?"

His face was sad then, but his eyes were filled with desire. It was as if he was tired of wanting me and needing me, and now that we were finally together, I'd put another obstacle between us, and it was too much. This man looked like he needed release so fucking badly in that moment. All I could think about was that somehow my ex-boyfriend and my new boyfriend got together to do business, and no one thought to mention it to me.

The idea that they might have compared notes. That Ben might have told him how needy I was and how I was bad at sucking dick made me sick to my stomach. Picturing the two of them talking shop about me . . .

I began to back up and away from him.

"Mira, please. We can talk or fight about this later, but I fucking need to touch you right fucking now. Please. Let me fucking touch you," Mitchell said.

"Ok, I need to pee first." I sprinted to the bathroom, unable to face him. Wild and intrusive thoughts left me wondering what Ben might have told him about us. Wondering what Mitchell had thought when he met Ben. What it made him think about me.

I ran from Mitchell right then because I was embarrassed by the idea of my old life and my new life colliding. That if Mitchell understood who I was before I met him, the girl who allowed a man as mousy as Ben to destroy her, he would never respect me. Want me.

And, if I had let him touch me, I would have never been able to hide the truth from him. He would have known my heart. He would have known I was falling deeply in love with him. And I could not allow myself to fall so deeply for such a man.

On paper, we were completely incompatible with nothing at all in common. And yet, there was no denying the heat between us. That rabid desire. The thing is though, I had no idea what was normal and what wasn't. I had no idea whether what I was feeling was real or whether it was due to being out of touch with my own body and its needs and being sexually and emotionally shut down.

Thinking he might have been listening at the door, I forced myself to pee. I wanted to go to him, to tell him everything I was feeling. To be with him and allow myself the pleasure of his company. Mitchell had flown for hours to be with me. How many women could say that? One. Right now, I was the only woman he was interested in. At least that's what I told myself as intrusive thoughts tried to wreck this for me.

I forced myself to remember the conversation we'd had last night and the reason why Mitchell was here.

SOMETIMES, my calls with Mitchell were done at ungodly hours after long days of appearances and interviews because it was the only time we could talk. We'd decided at one point that we'd rather talk, even if we were exhausted, than not.

So, when Mitchell wanted to have phone sex, I couldn't do it. I was so drained; I just didn't have it in me.

"I can't," I'd said last night when Mitchell wanted me to touch myself on camera for him.

"Mirabella, I need to see you touch yourself," he'd said, his voice husky, deep, and pleading.

"I can't; I have to get up in three hours," I whispered into the phone, exhausted from the non-stop schedule of appearances Brennan Enterprises had me on and from having been on the call with Mitchell for the past hour.

"I miss you so fucking much. When can I see you?"

"I miss you too," I said, feeling overwhelmingly sad and lonely after hearing the longing in his voice.

"I don't know; this schedule is really tight," I said.

"Fucking Hyacinth is determined to keep us apart. Rock stars have more breaks in their schedules than you. Not that you aren't a rock star, babe," Mitchell said, his tone first angry and then playful.

"Yeah," I said.

"Mirabella," Mitchell said, and I could tell he was feeling turned on again.

"Yes?"

"You know what else is tight?"

I played along because he liked that.

"No. Tell me what's tight, Mitchell."

"My girl's pussy. It's so fucking tight I might come thinking about it."

I smiled a lazy, sleepy smile. I loved that he thought of me as "his girl."

"I wish I was with you right now," I said, wishing I could curl up into his arms.

"What would you do if I was with you, Baby?"

"I'd curl up under your armpit and go to sleep," I said, no doubt disappointing him.

"Oh no; are we that couple already?"

"No. I'm sorry. I'm so fucking tired."

"I know, Mira. What can I do to help?"

"Just stay on the phone with me until I fall asleep," I said, turning over onto my side, and hoping it would help.

"I wish I could see you right now, Mira. I would help you fall asleep." Mitchell had the sexiest frustrated voice.

"I know you would." Pressure built between my legs at the suggestion.

"What are you wearing?" He was teasing me now.

"NOOOOO! Not that question," I said covering my face with my pillow as if I wasn't alone.

"Lemme guess," Mitchell said in a sexy teasing voice. "Black lace lingerie with cutouts where your boobs are, and a black lace thong?"

"Oh my god, how did you know?" I teased back, somewhat alarmed that Mitchell had seemingly conjured that outfit up from his mind so quickly and the fact that it was the complete opposite of how I was actually dressed.

"Is that how you want me to dress for you?"

"Are you offering?"

"I'm not sure. Is that something you like?" I said in a small insecure voice.

Mitchell hesitated, and he only did that when something I said or did threw him off guard.

"Mirabella," he said, like he always did when he wanted me to pay attention to what he was going to say next.

"Yes."

"I *fucking love* your body. You are a fucking knockout. The idea of you makes me hard. There are times when I'm around you and you look at me a certain way or say a certain thing, and I'm not sure I can fucking stop myself from coming in my fucking clothes. I am so turned on by you. With clothes. Without fucking clothes. The bottom line is, I need you so fucking badly, and I can't fucking decide if the day I met you was the best or worst day of my fucking life."

There were only a few times in my life as an adult where I have been speechless. And this was one of them. Mitchell sounded tortured, turned on, frustrated, and a little sad.

"Mirabella," he called me again, like he was calling my body to attention. My vagina clenched with need as my clit throbbed against my slick panties. I didn't have the heart to tell him that I was wearing baggy sweats, fuzzy socks, a sweatshirt, and a hair bonnet to bed.

"Mitchell."

"Are you wet for me, Baby?"

"I . . . I don't know," I said, my voice barely above a whisper. For some reason, I was feeling embarrassed.

"Why don't you put your hand inside your panties and find out." His voice got deeper.

"Mitchell," I said it as sexy as I could. "I can't." I was trying to keep the smirk out of my voice.

"Why not?" He sounded even more frustrated. I knew he was touching himself. I wanted to watch him doing it.

"Because I'm not wearing any panties," I said knowing full-the-fuck-well I was.

"Fuck . . . Mirabella."

Mitchell sounded like he was about to lose his shit.

I put my hand inside my pink panties, placed a finger inside me, and was surprised by how turned on I was.

This. Fucking. Man.

"Mmmmmmmmm," I said. "I'm so ready for you." I pushed my finger deeper inside my vagina, surprised by how incredibly soft and warm it was in there. Quickly grabbing at my needy breast and squeezing my nipple harder than I normally like for it to be squeezed, I was into it. I began rubbing my engorged clit.

"Tell me what you're doing, Mira," Mitchell said, his breathing heavy and quick.

"I have my middle finger inside me, my thumb on my clit, and I'm squeezing my nipple." I hoped that sounded sexy to him.

"You're so fucking seductive, Mirabella. Which nipple are you squeezing?"

"Your favorite," I teased.

"Ah, the left one," he said teasing me back.

"When I fucking see you, not to worry, I'm going to give each nipple equal fucking attention." Mitchell was clearly riled up.

"You better."

My voice strained. I was building to my climax.

"What about you? What are you doing?"

"Fuck, Mira, I'm imagining you beneath me on your stomach as I fuck you deeply and slowly from behind."

"I love when we do it that way."

Remembering the last time (which was the first time) we had done that position, my breathing was jagged now. I fucking loved it when he put his weight on me, his chest smashed against my back pressing me into the bed. He put his penis all the way in so fucking slowly, and it had me moaning against the mattress and gripping him so damn hard. I started moving on him, and when I did, my clit rubbed against the mattress creating the perfect amount of friction. When he realized what was happening, he said, "You think I'm gonna let the mattress have all the fun? Lift up a little for me, Baby. Let me rub your clit."

I almost lost my fucking mind. Mitchell had me coming so hard on him, that I found myself joining in his fantasy now, as I worked up to my release.

Mitchell's breathing became heavier and quicker.

"How's your pussy feel right now?" He liked to ask me that when we were having phone sex and he was about to come.

"It feels so fucking good, but I wish you were the one inside me." I felt deliciously frustrated right then, never really able to get my body worked all the way up like he could.

"I will be . . . fuck, Mirabella."

I could tell he was holding back, waiting for me. He wanted us to come together.

"Yes, Baby," I said, calling him what he likes to call me.

"Fuck, I'm gonna come, Mira."

Imagining Mitchell coming undone in his bed in Chelsea, spraying his streams of cum all over his expensive sheets while thinking about us had me coming too, clenching and soaking my own finger.

"I'm coming too," I said, moaning and grinding and humping and wishing I was with him.

As I gently removed my finger from inside me, I reached over to the nightstand to get a tissue to clean myself with.

We had this ritual that whenever we had phone or video sex, we would quietly clean ourselves before continuing to talk. Now, Mitchell was taking an awfully long time.

"You ok over there?" I asked.

"Sorry; just cleaning up. I kind of made a mess," he said, half-laughing.

"Maybe you need to do it into a sock or something." Only after I'd made that suggestion did I begin to feel silly and immature. Mitchell was a grown-ass man. Men don't jerk off into socks.

"Mirabella Alexia Castle, as long as I have you, I will never jerk off into a fucking sock again," Mitchell said.

I laughed.

"Speaking of which, can I ask you a question?"

"Uh oh, what?"

"Remember the night we first met?"

"How could I *ever* forget?"

"Remember you told me that you jerked off in the car when you left my apartment?"

"Yes."

"Was that true?"

"Yeah, why?"

"Where did you, you know, put it?"

"Where did I put what, Mirabella?" Mitchell teased.

"Your cum," I said quietly, like I was afraid one of the guests in the other five hundred hotel rooms might hear me say the word and know I was talking about sex.

"Not my proudest moment, I'm afraid. I came all over the fucking car."

Something about the visual of Mitchell being out-of-control turned on by me that night got my pussy clenching again as I imagined that I could do that to him.

"No fucking way."

"Way."

"And what about Brendan?"

As sexy as that image was, my thoughts turned to his poor driver who might have had to clean up after him.

"I'm not a fucking horrible boss, Mirabella. I had someone come clean it. I couldn't ask Brendan to do that."

"But, why? Why didn't you just put it in something?"

"Jesus," Mitchell said, and I knew what that meant. He was calling on the Lord for strength because I had gotten him riled the fuck up again.

"What?" I said, playing his fucking game.

"I fucking wanted to put it in your mouth," he said in a deep, husky, sexy voice that had my loins stirring and my nipples aching.

"Why didn't you?" I said, taking a chance and fucking with him since we were so far apart.

"Mira-fucking-Bella."

Mitchell was turned the fuck on.

"Yes," I said, getting breathy myself.

"I'm this close to calling Pilot Cole and telling him I want to be wheels up in the fucking morning."

I could tell he meant it, so I had to think very carefully about what I would say next because Mitchell was the kind of man to do whatever he wanted. And if he wanted me, he was going to come, and fucking take me.

"I . . . I'm off all next weekend," I said, chickening out.

"Oh, so now you're off next fucking weekend? And you're just telling me this now? Why the fuck didn't you lead with that, Mirabella?"

Shit. Now I felt guilty and conflicted.

"I was going to invite RayRay and Mena out for the weekend, but you can come too if you want."

Shit. I didn't intend for it to come out how it must have sounded to him.

"I can come too if I fucking want?"

I think Mitchell was mad. I wasn't sure what to say.

"Mitchell?"

"What?"

Shit. He *was* mad.

"I'm sorry. I didn't mean it like that. Like you are an afterthought, it's just—"

He cut me off mid-apology.

"You want to make it up to me? Tell me you want me to come there and put my dick in your fucking mouth, Mirabella."

Mitchell," I said, my mouth getting dryer, my arousal peaking.

"Don't fucking 'Mitchell' me. You have been wanting me to feed you my cock since the night we met."

"I . . . I . . ."

"Fucking admit it, Mirabella."

"Yes!"

Mitchell pushed and pushed. He had been doing so since the day we'd met. Now, he got what he'd been wanting. An admission. I was unable to fucking deny it. I felt like I was going to explode. I was a ball of need, desire, want, frustration, and sadness right then. I hated the way I felt being away from him for so fucking long.

"Fuck, Mirabella."

He was breathy. I imagined him sitting in bed trying to keep from touching himself.

I wanted him so fucking badly.

I was tired of having orgasms but never feeling satisfied. I needed him on me, inside me, next to me.

"Mitchell." My voice dripped with need.

"Don't be afraid to tell me what you want."

"I'm embarrassed."

"If you would have asked me that night, I would have fucking taken you to my apartment and worshipped you."

"I'm not like that. I wouldn't have asked a total stranger to fuck me."

"Mirabella, I would have made you come so much."

His voice was soft now but also somehow deeper, needier, sexier.

"Mitchell."

"Mirabella, if I'd had you at my apartment that night, you would have been spent, unable to handle any more pleasure. And just when you thought it was over, I would have fed you my fucking cock and come deep down your fucking throat. And you would have taken it. Every fucking drop. Because I know how badly you wanted it."

Mitchell broke me. He knew me so damn well. Even that first night in my apartment, he knew me. He knew what I needed and what I wanted.

"Why didn't you? Why didn't you just touch me?"

My voice came out high-pitched, almost like a cry.

"Mira, I'm so sorry. I would never touch you without your permission. I didn't know how badly you needed me to fucking touch you. But I can now. Tell me what you need, Mirabella. Is our sex not good?"

"It's . . . you're amazing. Everything we do is so fucking amazing. But I just . . . really miss you. The phone and video sex are ok, but they're never really all the way satisfying. I don't know. I feel stupid now. I don't know what I'm saying."

Feeling overwhelmed with emotion, I gulped back tears.

"Tell me what you need, Mirabella."

"You," I said, practically crying. "I need you. I need you to do all the things you've wanted to do to me since the night we met. No holding back," I said, no longer afraid to ask him for what I needed.

"I'll be there tomorrow, Baby."

And now, as I hid from him in the bathroom because I was a mess of emotions, anxiety, need, and insecurities, I wondered if Mitchell was on the other side of the door regretting coming to see me.

CHAPTER THREE

MITCHELL MAGELLAN

LIKE MOST NIGHTS WHEN WE WERE APART, I DREAMED ABOUT Mirabella. It was the fuel I needed to get through the time without her. And, if I didn't have so much shit going on at work, I would have blown it off and spent her entire tour tagging along like a fucking groupie. And when she was done working, she could expect to find me waiting for her, my dick hard, so I could help her unwind from a long workday.

But it was difficult to find even a few minutes to call her, let alone time to go to her, to be with her in person. Besides, we both took our work very seriously. Neither of us was the type to play hooky just to spend time together. My thoughts turned to my brother right then. Who the fuck was this guy I was becoming? Alex would most definitely give me shit about being a fucking suit. And yet, he could not have left me at a worse time.

Magellan Media was in shambles. Still, during our limited call times, I focused on Mirabella's tour and what was going on in her life because if we had talked about me, she would worry. And I knew if this situation got worse, it was quite possible that she would get wind of the video and audio recordings of me getting blow jobs in my office. But after talking to Mira and hearing the need in her voice, I had to go to her. I needed to see her. I had to give her what only I could.

When Aunt Meg heard I was skipping town in the middle of this shitstorm, she was furious. But if I didn't see Mirabella, even if I had to turn around and go right back home, I was not going to be fit for anything.

I had wanted to arrive before Mirabella got back from her public appearance but filing this last-minute flight plan was, well, too last fucking minute. So, for the second time in my life, I had to snag a commercial flight. I laughed to myself thinking about how Mira would have called my frustration 'rich people problems.'

It was spontaneous for sure, something Anna had warned me about giving in to. So, in order to keep her off my back, we had a session in the car on the way to the airport. And when she pressed me for how long I would be gone, I had no response to give. If Mira would let me, I'd stay with her forever.

Acknowledging that fact made me realize something. Mirabella was making me weak. My need for her was making me hasty. Being unable to do without her was making me vulnerable. Fucking intolerable. Several times since she'd been gone both Cindy and Clara commented on my "attitude." They'd implied that I was acting 'out of character.' Even they knew something was wrong.

So, when I'd messaged to say I was going out of town, I imagine they were relieved to see my cranky ass go. And even though I didn't tell them where I was headed exactly, I'm certain the minute I was gone they gossiped about it.

I laughed to myself thinking about how much my mood will have improved when I returned, having had several doses of a particular medicine only Mirabella Castle could provide.

Thinking about the things Mira and I were going to get up to had me distracted and fucking hard. And the closer my driver got to her hotel, the harder and more impatient I became. I texted her when my plane landed.

> ME: Landed, Baby. See you soon

Then when I was about ten minutes out, I texted again.

> ME: I'm ten mins away. Are you ready for me?

> MIRABELLA: Are you fucking ready for me, Mr. Magellan?

I'm not gonna lie, my girl's text got me worked all the way up. My baby was flirting.

I'd had plenty of time on the plane and in the taxi to think about what I wanted to do when I saw her. I thought about just walking in and putting my hand inside her panties. I considered telling her to get on her knees and not saying anything else before feeding her my cock. Maybe I would kiss her. Like really fucking claim that mouth. But none of those ideas seemed right. So, I put it out of my mind, thinking I would know what to do when I saw her.

This is how it was when we hadn't seen one another for a while. It was how it was that night in London. I was overthinking it. Around Mirabella, I was off my fucking game. But it wasn't just me.

Sometimes when we've been apart, Mira was really shy when we were finally together again. I'm not sure why but we could have just had the filthiest call, the raunchiest text session, or the most X-rated video chat, and when I saw her in person next, she would be coy, unsure, uncertain. Used to her now, I had to take particular care to warm my girl up. To remind her of how fucking beautiful she is. How very fucking sexy I find her.

I was horny as fuck. I missed what Mira's body did for me. But I also really missed Mirabella. I missed looking at her, listening to her talk, making her laugh, just being around her, and with her. I missed sleeping in her arms at night. I missed the feeling of her hands in my hair. I missed watching her move about the world when she had no idea that I was looking. I missed my best girl, and I couldn't wait to feel her put her arms around my neck.

When the taxi driver parked in front of Mira's hotel, I nearly jumped out of the car and skipped in-fucking-side. And as I passed the front desk and made my way over to the elevators, I had to stop myself from getting too noticeably excited. The fucking anticipation of seeing her was just about killing me.

Shit. *Am I nervous?*

When we first met that day of her ill-fated interview, I remember thinking all the way on the car ride to Queens about her. Fuck if I wasn't nervous when I met her roommate Mena at the door to her apartment after sneaking in behind a food delivery guy, glad I didn't have to ring the outside buzzer and request to be let up.

I replayed it all in my head as I walked up five flights of stairs to her apartment. How surprisingly hot she'd looked when I saw her in the reception area. What she'd worn. How she'd looked at me, her expression curious, pleading, panicked, sexy. Now, after having had her in my bed, in my mouth, on my fingers, and having been buried deep inside her, I still could not get enough.

Thinking about that day now, and all the days that have followed, I don't know how I had managed to get so fucking lucky. How I had managed to convince that woman to let me kiss her. Lick her. Touch her. Fuck her. I was a lucky bastard, for sure. One thing was certain, whether driving in the middle of the night or flying across continents to see her, my lust for Mirabella had grown into something deeper.

I entered the elevator, pressed the button for the sixteenth floor, and checked my look in the mirror-like metal of the interior. I wondered what Mirabella would be wearing. That white tank top she knows I like? That blue sundress she wore to The Guggenheim a few weeks ago? Maybe that gray bodysuit I stripped her out of the day before she left. Fuck, that was sexy.

I then wondered if she'd let me buy her clothes without finding it too controlling. I fantasized about taking her shopping and watching as she modeled all the choices. Thoughts of Mira had me breathing harder and needing to adjust my pants in case someone else got in on my way up.

When I exited the elevator, I read the wall signage to see which direction to would find her room. Of course, hers was farthest away from the elevator, the long walk only serving to build my anticipation even more. She seemed to enjoy seeing me in sweats, especially with a bulge in them, and damn if I wasn't going to give my girl exactly what she fucking wanted.

Even though I knew what she liked sexually, after having her in my life for months, I was no closer to understanding Mirabella than I was on that first night. She was the kind of woman you had to be careful with. She didn't always respond predictably. And while that made for a sexy and interesting sex partner, it could sometimes lead to messy interactions outside of the bedroom.

She'd been hurt in her past, and I was left cleaning up after sloppy and unappreciative motherfuckers who had no idea what to do with a woman like Mirabella and who didn't fucking deserve to be in the same room with her, let alone the same fucking bedroom.

Nonetheless, I was ready for her. And after finally reaching her room which was tucked away in the corner of the hallway and knocking on her door three times like the Big Bad Fucking Wolf, the time it took her to open it felt like a million goddamn agonizing minutes.

But when I saw her, all the fucking anticipation, outfit planning, commercial airline flying, stuck in a middle seat, in-car therapy session, jerking off in my bed and in the shower and in my fucking office, was worth it. Mirabella was a fucking knock-out, her bouncy natural hair looking like it wanted to bounce incessantly up and down as I fucked its owner's mouth.

I couldn't tell you where the time went. One minute I was on her, my mouth and hands claiming, sucking, kissing, and licking. I pressed and rubbed my erection against her with all the fucking need that had built up over the past few weeks, showing off my size.

But then, things went horribly wrong. The moments that followed were a blur. Next thing I knew, Mirabella was in the bathroom avoiding me, and I was standing outside the door feeling like the biggest piece of shit to ever exist. The minutes ticked by excruciatingly slow. I didn't know if she was in there crying, raging the fuck out, or thinking about leaving me.

The thought of not being with Mirabella, not having her in my life was enough to fucking break me. It was enough to make me contemplate punching a hole through the hotel's floral papered walls.

Smashing something seemed like a fucking great idea right then. Anything to get Mirabella to come out of that fucking bathroom. But somehow, I managed to hold it all together, barely, for the sake of Mirabella, me, and now Magellan Media because everyone knew we didn't need another fucking scandal or any more bad publicity.

I hadn't even had a chance to tell Mirabella what was going on with me. Between all the conversations at odd hours and missed calls, we'd barely had time to talk about anything other than what a bitch Hyacinth was and how badly I needed Mirabella to come for me. And over the past three weeks, in all that was going on, all of the emotions that had rushed to the surface for me, including conflicted feelings about Aunt Meg and Preston, something else emerged that felt as undeniable as it was fucking terrifying. And, if she would have let me, if she had opened the door, I would have told her so. I would have told Mirabella that I could not live without her.

When she finally came out, the restraint I had to practice was like nothing I have ever had to fight through before. Even that night in London, when she had spread her legs for me and told me to come to her, it wasn't this bad. Perhaps it was because she was drunk, and I would never have taken advantage of a woman like that. Or perhaps I knew if I did— because I surely could have—she would have never forgiven me. Still, that felt like a walk in the park compared to now.

"Mirabella," I said, unable to form more words than that as she stood in the doorway of the bathroom, naked, one arm across her chest, hiding her beautiful breasts from my view and one hand covering her deliciously soft mound. Her fucking beauty was too much for me in that moment. The gift of her in my life was something I was one hundred percent not deserving of. And yet, there she was, exposed, offering herself to me, even though I was nowhere near good enough for her. And right then, all my resolve left me as I accepted that I would never again be able to ever let her go.

She began to speak, some sort of mild apology, I presumed. But it didn't fucking matter. I didn't want to fucking hear it. I shut her up by putting my index and middle fingers in her mouth, slowly sliding my fingers all the way to the back of her fucking throat.

It was my turn to fucking talk.

She must have known I was not all that pleased with her antics by the way I finger fucked her mouth. That there was going to be hell to pay for what she fucking pulled because I was quiet now, watching. Seeing how far I could put my fingers down her throat before she gagged.

Surely, she knew I was tired of her shit by the way I was handling her. Mirabella was going to fucking get it, and it was me who was going to give it to her spoiled ass.

I worked her good, alternating between taking my fingers from her mouth to her needy fucking nipples, wetting them with her saliva and sucking on her glorious full tits. She panted heavily, the sound of her little moans filling the room and fueling my madness. God, I missed her.

My body moved against Mira's instinctively as if of its own free will. The softness of her vanilla and honeysuckle-scented skin caused me to falter in my resolve to punish her. And for a split second, I considered how good it would feel to give her all of me right then.

"You want to be mad at me, Mirabella?" I whispered against her ear, causing her to tremble. The familiar feeling of being out of control when I was with her like this enveloped me. "You want to fight because you fucking need me, and you don't know how to ask for what you want? Fine."

My dick twitched in my pants, reminding me that it was still captive inside my underwear. *Jesus.* We wanted to be inside her. I licked at my fingers, still in her mouth. As if she had no other choice, Mirabella licked me back, first on my tongue, then my cheek, and then against both my lips.

Fucking. Hell.

Overcome by Mira's attention, I claimed her fucking mouth, licking and sucking on her tongue like I couldn't live without it. And right then? I fucking couldn't.

Jesus. Pre-cum seeped out of my cock, drenching me in front. I needed to come, and my baby must have known.

Mira put her hands in my hair how I like. I rewarded her with two fingers to her tight, hot, pussy, allowing them to run slowly over her clit on the way down to her slit. My girl moaned in my mouth spurring me on. Never breaking contact with her lips, I continued to crush my face to hers, turning my head this way and that to get more. Deeper.

Mirabella moaned and shook and vibrated against my fingers, moving her entire body into me, trying to get closer and closer, like she was trying to become a part of me. She was so fucking needy, and so was I. We'd been untouched for weeks.

How was it that I had let Mira get so far gone that she would fuck my fingers with her whole body? What kind of man allowed his girl to get this way? So pre-occupied with the shit going on at work, I hadn't been taking care of her. And yet, she allowed some bullshit to get in the way of us, of our fucking pleasure.

"You can be mad, and we can still fucking make one another feel good. But you act like you don't fucking want me. Mira." I pulled my fingers out, admired how they glistened from being inside her, and put them in my mouth to taste.

I moaned at his delicious she was. "It doesn't taste like you don't want me."

That shit seemed to surprise her because the look on her face was to die for. And when Mira was satisfied that I had licked all of her off me, she grabbed my fingers with her free hand and placed them back inside her. Deep down to the fucking knuckles. *Fuck.*

Then suddenly, Mirabella did something I was not expecting. She reached into my sweats, into my underwear, and ran her hand across the tip of my dick. And when she had collected some pre-cum, she sucked it off her fingers.

Fuck if my dick wasn't spazzing and twitching by now.

Jesus.

"You mad at me?" I was out of breath already as she began stroking and teasing my cock, eyes fixed on me with a challenge to resist her. My balls felt like bricks. Mirabella was making it exceedingly difficult to enact my punishment on her, and I bet she knew it.

"Yes," she said breathlessly as she ground against my fingers some more.

"Fucking take it out on me in the bedroom, Mirabella."

I hoisted Mira, eliciting a gasp from her fuckable mouth and a look of absolute surprise. Before she could protest, I flung her over my shoulder, and carried her to the bed, rubbing on her ass while doing so. God, I wanted to spank it. And bite it. And fucking shove my tongue inside it.

"What are you doing?" Her voice was shaky.

"What am *I* doing? I'm getting you ready."

After pulling her down so that she and I were level, I tossed her slender body onto the bed, and quickly began taking off my clothes. Keeping my fucking hungry eyes on her and loving how her tits bounced in tune with her hair, I licked my lips in anticipation.

"Open your legs; let me see."

Mira rubbed her thighs together.

"Mitchell . . ."

"Don't fucking 'Mitchell' me, Mirabella. Spread your legs. Let me see if you're ready for me or if I've got more work to do."

She positioned herself at the head of the bed and leaned against the headboard with her legs open and knees bent so that her feet were flat on the mattress.

God. She was so fucking beautiful.

Any other time I would have broken my legs to get to her. But I decided to wait. I needed my fantasy today. I missed looking at her.

I stroked myself through my briefs, watching her watch me, the anticipation causing her chest to rise and fall rapidly.

"You know what?" I said as I moved onto the bed and crawled between her legs. I leaned down to touch her. To smell her. "If you hadn't run and hid in the bathroom, you could have had three orgasms already."

Her breath caught in her throat as my words registered.

It was all I could do not to push into her mouth right then. Instead, I met her stare, freed my cock, gave it a few careful strokes, and watched my girl rub her thighs together again because she loved watching me.

I got on my knees so I could anoint her flawless lips with my swollen tip. And when she ran her tongue across her bottom lip, I tapped my cock against it and then squeezed pre-cum onto her tongue.

Fuck.

The promise of Mira's tongue on me was too much. A moan I had tried to hold back escaped my mouth. Mirabella Castle was determined to be the fucking death of me.

So. Fucking. Sexy.

Just then, Mira did something I wasn't expecting. She put her hand between her legs while looking into my eyes.

Jesus.

She pulled a drenched finger from inside her and rubbed it on my tip, combining her pre-cum with mine.

Mother. Of. God.

Suddenly, I was subdued. It felt like I was the one being punished now. "Will you lick it for me, or are you planning to just play with it?"

"I thought you liked when I play with you."

"I do, Baby. But I want to see you take it down your throat. Can you show me how much you love sucking on me?"

Mirabella didn't say a word. She lowered her eyes to my engorged and dripping cock and began to lick it from tip to base, while dragging my underwear all the way down.

Unable to keep my hands to myself, I rolled her left nipple between my fingers, relishing in the feeling. Her body responded immediately with a shiver. Mira was a glorious site as she groaned and moaned and wound her hips all while taking my cock deep and slow, occasionally jerking me off and sucking and licking on my tip.

I was about to lose my shit.

"Mira," I said, quickly deciding on a change of plans. "Come here," I said as I helped her up and into a position where her tits pressed against the headboard. I didn't fucking wait until she found her footing. I couldn't. I pushed myself inside her from behind.

Jesus.

Mira and I both moaned, the euphoric feeling of that first thrust hitting us both.

She was so tight; I nearly didn't fit all the way at first.

Fuck.

Holding onto her hips, I pushed in some more as she very slowly adjusted to the size of my swollen penis. When I was *all the way in*, I steadied myself there while she clenched me. Right then, there was nowhere else I wanted to be, nowhere else I had ever been, and nothing else that existed except for Mirabella's hot, sweet, and tight pussy.

"Fuck, Mira. How do you fucking make me feel like this?" I said as my cock twitched and fucking vibrated deep against her wall how we both liked.

"Mitchell," she breathed out. She was so fucking cute, pushing back on me, trying to get me even deeper. She needed me to give it to her like this. To own her and to fucking shove my cock inside her until she couldn't take any more of me.

I leaned her back a little and bent her over slightly while holding onto her neck. Then, I very slowly pulled out. How it felt to ease out of Mirabella's hot, tight, core was like nothing I had experienced before I met her. She clenched me so hard, almost pushing me out as I went. It was sweet, slick, sticky, juicy torture. The only thing better, was driving back in.

But when I reached that sweet spot we both loved, I stilled.

"Mitchell, please. Fuck me."

Shit.

"You need me, Mirabella? You need this?"

She was trying to move on me again, but I was holding her hips in place.

"Tell me you missed me, Baby."

"Mitchell..."

Mira was whining now. My girl was so pitiful. Her pussy clenched and soaked me, and if I was being honest, I could have come just from that.

Lucky for her, I was going to fucking be relentless. I was going to give my girl all of me. I was not going to be gentle. So, I leaned over to whisper in her ear, "I flew six hours so I could be inside you just like this. This is what you fucking do to me."

Not even pulling out at all, I fucking shoved myself so deep inside her so hard that she gasped, grabbed the headboard, moaned a deep guttural moan, and then said, "Like that, Mitchell."

Pumping deep and hard and fast, I watched as Mira's ass jiggled and her hair bounced up and down. I was overcome with greed then. So, I leaned forward so I could touch her tits, wanting them both at the same fucking time. When she tilted her head to the side, ecstasy on her face, I became rabid. I licked and kissed her neck while she moaned and made very sexy sounds.

Mirabella was about to come, and fuck if I wasn't going to as well.

I stilled inside her again, hoping to prolong the feeling. I didn't want to come just yet. I wanted her some more.

"Mitchell," she breathed out.

Fuck.

I was out of time, so, I reached under her, finding her little swollen clit. I only needed to touch her lightly before she said, "Oh, God, Mitchell, I'm coming. Shit. I'm coming so fucking good." Mirabella came, choking the fucking life out of me. And the way she gripped me and said my fucking name had me coming too, shooting my long overdue load deep inside her.

MIRABELLA WAS MOST beautiful in the few minutes after she came for me; that fucking afterglow was everything. And to know it was me who'd made her feel like that? It was king making.

"Why didn't you tell me about Ben?"

Fuck. Mira.

"Mirabella, I really don't want to talk about your ex-boyfriend right fucking now."

"Why didn't you tell me?" she said, more insistently this time, scrunching up her face in that way she can when she's not about to let me get away with not responding but also not mad enough to spit fire.

I shook my head. She wasn't going to let this shit go.

"He came to me. Mena made the introduction. I thought you would want me to help him." I thought that would settle her, but the expression on her face didn't change. "So, I sent him to the person who manages that. Until today, I never fucking thought about it again."

"You thought I would want you to help my porn-addicted ex-boyfriend fund his fucking Off-Off-Off Broadway play?"

What the actual fuck? Now *I* wanted to talk. About Ben.

"Ben had a porn addiction?"

"That's not the point," she said, now seemingly sorry she had mentioned it. This guy really was a no-good piece of shit. How he had managed to land a woman like Mirabella, I will never fucking know. If she tells me he had a huge dick, I'm going to fucking shoot myself.

"I don't think you understand what he did to me. I'm so fucked up because of him."

Mira looked to be on the verge of tears, but she was being brave.

Shit. I wanted to hear what she had to say but I really didn't want that motherfucker taking up space between us right now. I swear to God. I was this fucking close to not only pulling his sponsorship but arranging to ruin that fucker.

"I asked you before if he hurt you. Tell me what he did."

I cupped her chin, dying inside from seeing the pain on her beautiful face caused by a guy who couldn't handle how fucking amazing she was and so he tried to kill the light inside her. Tried to make her less than, like him.

"He did hurt me. Not physically. He fucked with my head. He made me feel like I was wrong for wanting to have sex. That I wasn't sexy at all. Not worth holding hands with. Forget it. I don't want to talk about him."

I didn't want to hear about how much sex she wanted to have with this fucking guy.

Mirabella began to get up from the bed. She was going to do what she always does when shit got real. She was going to fucking run. And, as much as I didn't want to hear about it, I needed to let her get it out once and for fucking all or, she was never going to trust me because of that piece of shit.

"Mirabella, please. Don't go. Let's just talk. How did you find out he had a porn addiction?"

She looked down, like she was thinking about whether she wanted to talk about this or not. But when she looked back up at me, the pain in her eyes nearly fucking broke me.

"Whenever we tried to have sex, he couldn't stay hard enough for penetration. And of course, the more we tried and failed, the less into it I was. He would say he was tired or that he was so comfortable with me that he was just too relaxed to keep an erection. Sometimes he would say it hurt him to try because I wasn't wet enough. But I wasn't wet enough because he never really tried with foreplay. He just expected me to be hot and ready."

I didn't want to imagine Mirabella being all worked up and wet for another man or worse wasting her energy on a guy who was trying to get hard enough to fuck her. I didn't need either of those fucking images in my head. But this shit was intriguing.

"Can I ask you something?"

"Yes," she said, reluctantly. She broke character right then, distracted by my mouth.

Fuck yes.

I took my time licking my bottom lip, hoping to disarm her. Then, when I saw a slight change in her breathing, I ran a finger across her bottom lip, then her top one. I blinked slow, like she liked, allowing my lashes to rest lazily on my skin before raising my eyes to look into hers.

Mirabella smiled, my slow seduction working. God, I loved looking at her. I loved talking to her. I loved listening to her. *Fuck.*

Unable to resist, I planted a chaste kiss on her delicious mouth. I had to stop myself from shoving my fingers in her mouth again.

"You must have had your pick of guys. Why Ben?" I traced her left eyebrow slowly.

"I don't know. We talked one night at Iggy's show. He seemed ambitious. Talented. Smart. He had plans. He was creative."

"So, it wasn't like a physical attraction to him?"

"Not at first."

"He didn't make a move the night you met him?"

"No."

"Please tell me it wasn't you who made the first move."

"It was. I did. Oh, God; this is so embarrassing."

Mira hid under my armpit. And while I considered this fucker could have had a medical problem, I still couldn't imagine being unable to get hard enough to fuck Mirabella, and I hoped to God I never find out what that feels like.

"You said he wasn't really hard. Were you wet?"

She stopped breathing. I pulled her out from under my arm so I could see her.

"I don't want to talk about it."

"Mirabella, please just tell me. Did he make you wet? Like when he touched you? When you thought about being with him?"

"I didn't really think about being with him like that. I just kind of like wanted his company. And as far as touching me? He wasn't very good at it."

I pulled my smirk back. This guy was bad at every fucking thing.

"So, you were lonely."

"I guess. I mean what's the point of having a boyfriend if you were always alone?"

The idea that Mirabella was stuck with a loser who couldn't satisfy her both made me livid and turned on. Still, something told me there was more to this story than Ben being a loser and me being a stud.

"You didn't want to fuck him?"

I must have been making an incredulously confused face.

"Not like how I want to fuck you."

Now I was the one smiling. I might have even been blushing. Damn my girl got me just then.

"Tell me about the porn."

Mirabella gulped. "I caught him jerking off to porn in my bathroom. He said he never had a girl who wasn't wet for him, and it was a turn-off," she said, in a quiet voice.

This motherfucker was blaming Mira for not being wet enough for him.

"What did he do when you caught him?" I said, trying to retain my composure.

"He told me not to worry, that he was jerking off to Black girls. Can you believe that?"

"What a dumb and inconsiderate motherfucker," I said, unable to believe this guy myself.

Mirabella and I had never actually talked about race, other than when she told me her dad's white. She had an eclectic mix of friends who spread the ethnic spectrum but judging by her relationship with Ben and now me, I assumed she was into white guys.

"Would it have bothered you if the women he jerked off to were white?" I never in a million fucking years thought I would ever have needed to ask my girlfriend how she felt about the race of the women her ex-boyfriend jerked off to instead of fucking her.

Mirabella seemed to hesitate as she thought about my question or her answer.

"No. I didn't think of it that way. I thought it was me, that I just wasn't sexy enough," she said before casting her eyes down.

"Have you ever been with a Black guy?"

Mira's head shot up, eyes on me.

"What kind of question is that? Have you ever been with a Black girl?"

I struck a fucking nerve.

"Yes."

Mirabella was trying to pretend like she wasn't surprised to learn she wasn't the first Black woman I had been with.

"No. I've never been with a Black guy."

"Why not?"

"Black guys don't ask me out."

"I find that hard to believe."

"What's that supposed to mean?"

"I think you give off 'I only fuck white boys vibes.'"

Mirabella grabbed a pillow and began beating me with it.

"You should be glad I only fuck white boys!"

I crouched, feigning injury under her attack, loving how her tits bounced as she got on her knees and spread her legs for more traction.

I fucking hated that Mirabella had a past like that, not to mention one so painful. It was a selfish thing to be sure since I had the past to end all fucking pasts. But she had never asked me about mine. I assumed she didn't really want the details of all the many sexual encounters I'd had. The kinds of things I had done with other women.

But this moment with Mirabella made me realize that it wasn't right to hide from her. She had a right to know me, including the good, the bad, and the very fucking ugly. And if she had asked me, I would have come clean. Because the amount and kind of sex I've had is probably nowhere near what she can imagine. It's far fucking worse.

I grabbed her to me, mid-pillow attack, and held her.

She was panting heavily, having exerted all of her energy pillow-beating me for teasing her about what she likes. I pulled her to my eye level.

"Mirabella, look at me."

Now she was back to being shy and small and lost and sad. Admittedly, it was a huge turn-on.

"I'm embarrassed," she said, as a few tears suddenly fell.

"Mirabella, don't you see what you do to me? How you fucking make me feel? Just looking at you with all your fucking clothes on gets me all the way turned on."

That douchebag had really messed her up. She didn't trust that I was being genuine and not just saying whatever to get her to let me fuck her. Mirabella put her head down again, trying to hide her shame.

I pulled her chin up so I could look into her eyes.

"If that fucking asshole didn't see you, it's his loss. You are a fucking knock-out, Mirabella. And it's not just your body. It's your essence. Your personality, how you carry yourself. How you speak. I can't get enough of you."

She was quiet. Mirabella was pensive, in deep thought seemingly despite keeping her eyes fixed on me.

"Mira, if this is too much for you, I'll pull the funding right fucking now."

"No," she finally spoke. "What's done is done. Just next time, can you not assume what I will want or think; can you just ask me? I wanted to put Ben behind me. I wanted to be free of the shit thinking about him stirred up in me. I like who I am when I'm with you, and I want this to just be for us."

I thought about what she said, and now that I was hearing it, it made me feel like a fucking heel. I had inadvertently allowed Ben to weasel his way into our fucking bedroom by trying to impress her and show her that I can put my personal feelings aside in order to help someone.

"I'm sorry, Mirabella. I really am. I had no idea you guys had such a painful history, and that he wasn't man enough to take care of you the way he should have, the way you deserve. But I'd be lying if I said I wasn't happy that you're no longer with him. That I get a chance to earn you now."

Mira looked down as more tears fell, and for a minute I was back to wanting to snap that motherfucker's neck.

Instead, I did the only thing that would make us both feel better. I kissed Mirabella with all the need, longing, and desire that had built up in me since I saw her last. And I hated every minute that followed because I would have to leave her soon and go back to New York.

CHAPTER FOUR

MIRABELLA CASTLE

When I was away from Mitchell, even for a little while, I missed him terribly. Thought of him constantly. I wondered what he was doing and whether he missed me the same. Mitchell Magellan even had me daydreaming. But despite all attempts to deny my rapidly escalating feelings, I was in fact obsessed. He was my every waking thought. It didn't help in the least that my job was to talk about him.

Mitchell was a really busy man, and yet, he had dropped everything to come to me. The almost ten hours we'd spent together last weekend were exactly what we both needed to tide us over to when my tour was finished, and we could be together as often as we liked. Still, I hated needing him. I hated feeling so off kilter when we were apart. I hated that I cried when he left.

These types of all-encompassing emotions made me feel like I was suffocating from the inside out. Like I was becoming less of me and more of what I despised in others. It was as if I was losing brain cells, becoming the smart dumb girl who falls for exactly the wrong man, just like my mom.

From an early age. I learned to be independent. My father had an entirely new family while still technically married to my mom. He cut us off financially and emotionally when he was found out, I suppose to punish us for existing. My mom worked all the months that followed, because she no longer had my dad's income or support. All the while me and Jared were basically left to our own devices at eight and ten-years-old, respectively.

Before things got totally out of control, and after the state got involved, Grandpa and Grandma Wright stepped in. They offered to help Mom by having Jared and I move to Kentucky and live with them.

From then, I decided that I never would depend on a man. I vowed to never marry. I would do whatever it was that had to be done by myself and for myself. I hated asking for help, or worse, needing it. For the longest time, it worked. I had managed to make it all the way to Harvard. Then one day, I just collapsed emotionally and mentally under the pressure of living like that.

Even though I'm older now, those scars run deep. Every day felt like I was getting that much closer to caving under the weight of keeping it together and not breaking in front of Mitchell. That if Mitchell found out that I was not really the strong woman I pretended to be, that he would walk away from me. That maybe he should in fact walk away. So, when things got rough, I ran before he could have a chance to leave me like my father had done to my mother. Before he found out what was hiding beneath all of this bravado and hair.

It was quite unsettling to be falling for Mitchell Magellan, of all people. And the entire time we'd been together last weekend, I'd allowed my insecurities, uncertainties, anxiety, and my tendency to self-sabotage mess with my head. Enjoying my time with him, how he made me feel, seemed like a luxury I could not afford and wasn't deserving of.

Now, a week later, I was looking forward to celebrating the end of this tour with my friends and preparing to go back home. And, if ever there was a way to end an exhaustive multi-week tour, a weekend with RayRay and Mena in Lisbon was it. They'd arrived on Thursday, and we'd plan to leave together on Sunday.

At the Friday night wrap party Brennan Enterprises had thrown for me, their licensing partners, and the media, I hung with Will, Maisy, Hyacinth, and a slew of other staffers who'd flown in for the occasion. And when most of them had gone and we were away from cameras and prying eyes, my friends and I could finally be ourselves.

"Wow, Brennan Enterprises really went all out," RayRay said, after checking in on Christina. RayRay had asked his mom to join us on this trip so she could look after Christina while the adults partied on Brennan Enterprises' dime.

"Everything OK?" I said, when RayRay returned to our booth.

"Yeah, Mom is in her glory. They are watching cartoons and eating ice cream," RayRay beamed. "Where's Mena?"

"Bathroom." I took a sip of my fruity drink.

"Did you mention the thing with Ben yet?"

"Not yet. Didn't seem to be the right time."

RayRay gave me a look like, 'Since when do you give a shit about timing?'

Needing to change the subject, I said, "I'm so glad this tour is over. I never thought I would be so happy to see my apartment again."

"Well, things have certainly changed since you've been away."

I could only imagine how much was going on while I was doing meet and greets, guesting on morning and nighttime talk shows, and generally being a media darling overseas.

Just then, Mena came back to the table with a bottle of champagne and three champagne flutes.

"Time to toast Mirabella," Mena said in a sing-song voice and wearing a giant smile.

"Fuck yeah it is," I said.

Mena popped the cork, and for some reason, we all screamed. We each presented Mena with our glass to fill, and like typical Mena, she overfilled them all. When she finished, she raised her glass in the air, and so did RayRay and I.

"You've come a long way in six months. You went from being nearly homeless Mira to Mitchell Magellan's reject, to a fucking superstar, to Mitchell Magellan's main bitch, and I for one am proud to say I knew you when. And, I would be more than happy to have our bedroom all to myself if you and Mitchell ever decide to make things more permanent. Congratulations on a successful tour, Mirabella. Cheers!"

We all clinked glasses and took sips of our champagne.

"Ok, it's my turn." RayRay beamed like a proud parent.

I smiled widely, loving how crazy good my life was right then. And even though I was upset with Mena for that shit she'd pulled with Ben and Mitchell, having her and RayRay there meant more than either of them could know.

I'd earned a lot of money since Brennan Enterprises made me their billion-dollar brand. With each new licensing deal, I was paid an advance of around five thousand dollars. And now, I had six deals in place. They were paying me a one-thousand dollar a day *per diem* while I was on tour, and that included weekends. Plus, I still had my base salary of forty-five thousand dollars. And to top it all off, each time I made a public appearance, I was paid five thousand dollars. On this tour, I'd made a total of seventeen personal appearances. It wasn't Magellan money, but it was more than I had ever made before.

This new financial freedom enabled me to fly Mena and RayRay out and pay for RayRay's mom and Christina to join us. And now, while I waited for RayRay to collect his thoughts and make a speech, it felt like that humiliating day at Magellan Media was so long ago.

"My baby is growing up," RayRay said with a bright smile and watery eyes. Mena batted her eyelashes and wiped away a fake tear in mock sadness. I smiled at them both. "Seriously, B. I'm so damn proud of the lemonade you made out of those goddamn lemons. Enjoy your rapid rise and well-deserved success. And thank you for bringing us out here to celebrate with you. We love you, B! Cheers!"

I raised my glass with a heart full of gratefulness and joy. My phone vibrated in my real Gucci bag. I ignored it, even though it might have been Mitchell, clanged glasses with my dear friends, and then downed all of my champagne. And since this was now her job, Mena refilled our glasses and kept doing so until the entire bottle was empty.

Now that we were all together, I told them about last weekend with Mitchell, leaving out our fight about Ben. Next, Mena and I listened to

RayRay reenact hilarious stories about his co-workers. Then, Mena shared news of Dino's latest restaurant happenings, alluding to some potential shady dealings RayRay and I were intrigued by. As we drank and listened to one another's tales, things felt right, like how they should be exactly. I felt good, happy, and hopeful even while I pushed intrusive thoughts from my mind.

But after five glasses of champagne, I was ready to fucking fight.

"So, Mena, you want to tell me why you thought it would be a good idea to introduce fucking Ben to Mitchell so he could ask him for money? Your family's rich, why didn't you ask your parents for the money to give to Ben then?"

RayRay made a face like, 'Oh shit; here the fuck we go!'

Mena looked utterly shocked, maybe even a little embarrassed.

My phone buzzed again. I ignored it.

Mena glued her eyes to mine, readying her response.

RayRay cleared his throat, and said, "I'll go get us some more drinks."

When RayRay left the booth, Mena spoke.

"First of all, I'm really sorry, Mirabella. I had no intention of doing anything that would hurt you. But I saw Ben one day in Chelsea with his new girlfriend, and shit . . . I mean, do you care that he has a new girlfriend? I mean you and Mitchell are together. You guys *are* together, right?"

I rolled my eyes, annoyed at Mena for being so damn inconsiderate of me and Mitchell. She never even liked Ben. And when I told her about him jerking off in our bathroom, she'd begged me to report it to the police. Now, she was fucking looking at me like the doe-eyed innocent friend who was just trying to do the right thing, only by Ben and not by me.

Mitchell had said, about the same incident, that he had been trying to do what he thought I would want. Is that how they saw me? Sweet, innocent, Southern good girl Mirabella? *Do unto others? Turn the other cheek?* Had I not shown them the *fuck around and find out* me enough?

"I just don't understand why you felt the need to help Ben by way of Mitchell. Having my current boyfriend and my ex-boyfriend be business partners isn't something I would have wanted. You had to have known that. And after how things went down with Ben—he broke up with me over text, for crying out loud—I was just hoping to rid my life of anything having to do with him." Could she not understand how her kindness to Ben affected me?

"I'm so sorry, Mirabella." Mena looked genuinely remorseful. "If I could take it all back, I would. But he came over to my table at dinner and asked me for your new number. Apparently, he had been trying to get in touch with you."

"What the hell for?" I wasn't interested in ever speaking to him again.

Just then, RayRay returned with a round of shots. Just what I fucking needed. We all clinked glasses and downed our shots.

"He said he wanted to ask you something," Mena said, with a can-you-believe-that-motherfucker look.

"Oh my God, Mena. What else did he say? Get to the part where you thought it was a good idea to give him Mitchell's number." I was suddenly drunker and even more annoyed. Mena, on the other hand looked pretty defeated.

"I guess I wasn't thinking."

"The only reason I gave it to you was in case of an emergency. Like if I was with him and if you needed to get in touch with me or if something happened to me and you needed to call him to let him know. Not to give it out to my ex-fucking boyfriend!"

I really needed another shot.

"I know. I know. I just... He was talking fast and giving me this sob story about his new play, and how if he could talk to someone at Magellan Media about sponsorship. And I was like, I don't know anyone at Magellan Media, sorry. And then stupid fucking Dino was like, well you know Mitchell Magellan."

"So, it's Dino's fault you couldn't keep your damn mouth shut, then?" RayRay said.

Mena looked from me to RayRay and then back to me as if any of what she'd said made any darn sense.

"I'm really sorry. I honestly just gave him Mitch's number so he could leave me alone," Mena said, looking defeated.

"Mitch?" I said. "I don't even call him that."

"So, if you two are done and speaking of Mitchell Magellan," RayRay said, sitting forward.

"What?"

"Have you talked to him lately?"

My anxiety was on alert. I had just spoken to Mitchell by phone two days ago and we'd texted yesterday and this morning.

"Yeah, why?"

When I looked at Mena, she said, "Do you Google him?"

My heartbeat drummed in my ears and kicked against my chest now. *What the heck was this all about?*

"No, I don't Google him. Who does that?"

RayRay took out his phone, typed in some words, scrolled, then handed it to me, and said, "Maybe you should."

I grabbed the phone from RayRay.

So many articles . . .

Scroll

Peter Trenom indicted on federal securities charges

Scroll

Mitchell Magellan refuses to comment on FBI investigation at Magellan Media

Scroll

Megan Magellan named interim head of Magellan Board

Scroll

Magellan Media to sponsor The Man play by upstart playwright Benjamin C. Rothenburg

Scroll

Mitchell Magellan named to RAVE's Top Thirty Under Thirty list

Scroll

Magellan Media under scrutiny with the FBI

Scroll

U.S. Attorney says case against Magellan Media going forward

Scroll

Feds seize audio, video, paper, and digital files from Magellan Media

Scroll

Mitchell Magellan issues statement on Peter Trenom indictment

My stomach did somersaults. Mitchell had so much going on but had neglected to mention any of this. He spoke often about how hectic things were at work and how stressed he was. When I would ask if he had wanted to talk about it, he would always refuse. He only wanted to hear how my tour was going, to talk dirty, and to have phone or video sex.

I suppose that made sense. We weren't really in a relationship. We hardly ever did anything outside of the bedroom. We didn't go on dates. He didn't want me to know him. He didn't want to share his life with me. His feelings with me. His problems with me.

I must have looked sad when I handed RayRay back his phone.

"Shit. He hasn't talked to you about this, has he?"

I was on the verge of tears, so I just shook my head, "No."

The fact that I was the only person at the table who didn't know what was happening with Mitchell made me sad and embarrassed. Part of me was mad at myself for not pushing him to talk like I had tried to get Ben to. I just figured if he had wanted to open up, he would. Maybe I was just not the kind of woman men wanted to talk through their stuff with.

"I'm sure he has his reasons, B," Mena said. "Could it be he didn't want to worry you during your tour? Maybe he wanted you to be able to focus on your work and all you had to do. Now that it's over, I'm sure he will be more open and forthcoming, right, RayRay?" The uncertainty in her voice exposed how she really felt.

RayRay made an 'I don't know' face.

"Ok, let's talk about something else, ladies. I don't want to talk about Mitchell or what he is up to." My voice said one thing and my tone and demeanor said another.

They both had looks of pity on their faces.

"Guys, come on, we're celebrating, and this does not look like a celebration!" I said. "RayRay, tell me about my goddaughter. How's fatherhood?"

RayRay's whole demeanor changed, and his face lit up when I

asked about Christina. "She is amazing, but she is spoiled as fuck!"

"And who spoiled her, because I certainly have not been around to do that?" I said, knowing the answer already.

"Well, my mom of course. Mena, I'm looking at your ass. And . . . Mitchell."

Mena shrugged her shoulders and shook her head.

"Mitchell?" That surprised me.

"Yeah, I was in a childcare bind one day, and Mena couldn't watch her, and my mom couldn't get to Queens in time, and Billy and Camille were at work. So, I called the only other person I trust her with."

RayRay eyed me like I should have known that already.

"And what did Mitchell do?"

"He had me bring her to Magellan, and he watched her for four hours until my mom came to get her," RayRay said. "Look, he sent me this video."

I scooted closer to RayRay when he turned his phone around to show me a video.

"Say hi, Dad. Uncle Mitchell is spoiling me. He fed me ice cream for lunch." Mitchell held Christina while sitting on the couch in his office, looking hot as fucking hell in a black suit with a white shirt, black vest, and a gray tie. His jacket lay strewn across the arm of the couch and his sleeves were rolled up. He was letting Christina play with his Audemars Piguet.

The smile on his face was one of pure joy. And for some reason, I think my fucking pussy clenched looking at Mitchell holding a baby.

"Hello, Mirabella!" Mena waved her hand in front of my face. "I think your fucking uterus just licked the phone screen."

I couldn't take my eyes off Mitchell.

"Let me guess," RayRay said, "he didn't tell you about that either."

RayRay shook his head, most likely thinking I was going to rip Mitchell a new one.

But as my phone buzzed again, I was hoping the message was from him. Not because I wanted to read him the riot act but because I missed him.

I checked my phone as RayRay put his back on the table facedown.

> HYACINTH: Wonderful job today. Congratulations again. Did you decide if you're taking Monday off?
>
> MAISY: I think I have your AirPods
>
> GRANDMA: I hope it all went well for you today! I'm so proud of my girl.
>
> JARED: Thinking of coming to visit end of next week. U gonna be around?
>
> MITCHELL: How'd it go today, Baby?
>
> IGGY: Been trying to reach Mena. Really need to talk to her.
>
> MITCHELL: Call me when you can. Miss you.
>
> IGGY: Are you with Mena?
>
> SHAYLA: Is Mena with you?

"Mena," I said, "Iggy's been trying to reach you for some reason."

Mena picked up her phone. "Yeah, my battery has been dead for like two hours."

"Oh, want to call him from my phone?"

"Oh sure, thanks," Mena said, taking my phone and dialing Iggy at the same time that the night's live band took the stage.

"What? Iggy, I can't hear; I'm going to take it outside." Mena put a hand over the phone and told us that she was going to take the call outside, as if we didn't hear her tell Iggy that.

When Mena left the table, I moved all the way next to RayRay.

"So, Mitchell can add babysitter and uncle to his resume, huh? Unbelievable."

RayRay moved even closer as if we were sharing some conspiratorial secrets. Or, maybe he just missed me.

"You should have seen him with her, B. He's a natural. And he gets annoyed if she doesn't call him 'Uncle Mitch,' you know? He's really taking this whole found family thing very seriously. Did he tell you he offered to pay for her to go to daycare and private school? He set up a trust fund for her."

His expression sat somewhere between pride, disbelief, and elation.

"Holy shit. Are you serious? I had no idea. Mitchell seems to have been quite busy while I've been gone. I love that he's in a position to secure her future, and now you don't have to worry."

"You did good with this one, B. Really. Mitchell Magellan is the real deal."

Just then, Mena came back to the booth with tears on her face.

"What's wrong?" RayRay said.

Mena bit her lip, and said, "My mom. She's been in an accident. She died."

RayRay and I jumped up at the same time, exited the booth from opposite ends meeting up to pull Mena into a hug.

"It's gonna be ok, Mena. We can leave tomorrow instead of Sunday."

I took my phone from her hand to check the time in New York. It was two-thirty in the morning in Lisbon. So that meant it was nine-thirty pm in New York. I typed my message.

> ME: I need a HUGE favor.

> MITCHELL: Hey, Beautiful. Everything ok?

> ME: What are the odds you can charter a plane from Lisbon for me, Mena, RayRay, Christina, and Mrs. Ellis? We need to get home ASAP.

> MITCHELL: Why? Did something happen?

> ME: Mena's mom died.

> MITCHELL: Oh shit. Ok. Lemme see what I can do.

> ME: Thank you so much.

> MITCHELL: Of course, Baby.

"I texted Mitchell to see if he can get us on a flight out in a few hours. He's going to let me know as soon as possible."

"I ordered a car; it'll be here in five minutes," RayRay said, holding onto Mena who looked like she was in a trance.

"Maybe you should sit down, Mena, until the car gets here," I said, gently pushing her into the cushion of the round booth's bench. I turned to RayRay; neither of us knew what to say. Mena was closer to her dad than to her mom until her dad cheated on her mom with a man he claimed to be in love with. She and her mom had gone on a 'fuck men to hell' trip, and came back closer than ever. She'd met and started dating Dino shortly thereafter.

Minutes ticked by before the car arrived forcing us to listen to the crappy band that was singing American country music. And even though I didn't get any vibrating message alerts, I kept checking my phone to see if I'd missed texts from Mitchell.

"Let me see where this damn car is," RayRay said as ten whole minutes passed since he had ordered the car and gotten confirmation that it was five minutes away. When he checked his phone, he said, "Shit. He's outside."

Just then my phone dinged.

> MITCHELL: Baby. I just sent flight details to your email.

> ME: Thank you soooo much.

> MITCHELL: A car will pick you guys up at 4:30AM. Your flight will leave at 6AM. You will be back in New York by 7PM NY time. When you arrive, I'll have cars on the tarmac waiting to take everyone where they want to go. Except for you.

> ME: I think I should go with Mena.

> MITCHELL: You're coming with me.

> ME: *typing*

> MITCHELL: Whatever you're trying to say, save it. I'm gonna fuck you in the car.

CHAPTER FIVE

MITCHELL MAGELLAN

It was going to be a long fucking Friday. Like securities fraud and FBI investigations weren't enough to keep me busy, we had layoffs planned for later this afternoon, and I was already on edge trying to free up some time now that Mira's tour was finally over, and she was coming home on Sunday.

Braxton hadn't made any headway on whoever the hell was trying to blackmail me with audio and video they had of my office extracurricular activities. Still, he'd recommended that I set aside a couple million dollars in cash in case we needed it at the last minute. And when I asked him to be more specific, he said, "Mitchell. Your father always had at least five million in cash ready to move."

It sure sounded like my dad and Braxton were into some heavy shit. But this looming threat of exposure was weighing on me. Yet, embarrassment was the least of my concerns. Sure, people would make memes, women would crucify me in the press, and the Board would probably call for my resignation once and for all. Given my very public past, I don't even know how many people would really be surprised.

But faced with the real possibility that what Braxton had suggested was right, that someone was simply trying to embarrass me, it was Mirabella I was worried about. She hadn't really asked me about my past. And about sexual things, she wasn't all that experienced, or at least she wasn't until she fucking met me.

And while I hated to think of her with other men, at least the one I knew about was a complete fucking loser incapable of satisfying her. He projected his inadequacies onto her, so he didn't have to face himself at the end of the fucking day. The Mirabella I had been with bore little resemblance to the one she had described to me. The passive girlfriend content to live her life in the background, suppressing her most primal needs for a mouse of a man who couldn't give her what she needed. That Mirabella didn't know her worth.

So how the fuck was I going to explain to Mirabella in any way she could accept what was on those tapes? How was I going to explain my behavior?

Mirabella believed in right and wrong and black and white. In her world, there was little room for ambiguity or gray, let alone morally gray or blurred lines. When she'd confronted me both in person and online, she'd spoken about integrity. She said she should have been able to take me at my word and trust that I would keep my appointment with her. She'd lamented about how even though I'd seen her that I'd used my assistants, Cindy and Clara, as shields to hide from her.

And you know what? She was one hundred percent right. At the sight of her, I cowered. Bowed to the power of the look she had given me that morning. *Prince of the City*, my ass.

If someone actually released video of Marissa from Accounting going down on me while I was supposed to be interviewing Mirabella, it would break her to see it. To hear it. Something like that would be explosive for Magellan Media, damaging to me, and utterly humiliating for Mirabella. *I cannot let that get out.* So, whatever that motherfucker who was extorting me wanted, I was going to have to fucking pay it. And if it turned out that somehow Robert Brennan III had anything remotely to do with it, I was going to put that fucker down once and for fucking all.

And because I felt like I was on borrowed time, being with

Mirabella was even more important. So, on Sunday, I planned to pick her up from the airport and do things to her in the car on the ride home. Then, I wanted to take her to my apartment and draw her a bubble bath in which I planned to join her. After, I wanted to hire a chef to make us an amazing dinner to pair with some of the wine Emilio had picked out for us in London. After that, I wanted to take her to bed, make love to her, and then hold her in my arms until she fell asleep.

But if I was really being honest, the real reason I was on edge had little to do with being extorted or the fact that Peter Trenom had been indicted, or even that the FBI and the SEC had been sniffing around in my dad's affairs. I was anxious because I had planned to ask Mirabella to move in with me.

I SAT in my daily stand-up meeting with Sherilyn, Clara, and Cindy. This one was going to be a long one.

"Sir, I cleared your calendar like you asked with the exception of the Security Leadership meeting with Coster and Denowitz," Sherilyn said.

"Thanks, Sherilyn. I want to update the emergency call list to remove Peter Trenom and add Jared Castle and John Raymond Ellis, Jr."

"Sir?"

"The list of people who can reach me no matter what and without exception. I want Trenom removed, and those two names added, please."

"Sir, Jared Castle?" Clara said, looking from Cindy and back to me, as if I had misspoken.

"Yes, Clara. Jared Castle. He's Mirabella's brother. And while you're at it, please also add Martin and Anabella Castle. I'm sorry. I mean Martin Castle and Anabella Wright, her parents. Her mother goes by her maiden name. Also, Miabella Wright, Mira's grandmother. Add Mena Kathri too."

It must have sounded strange because the list of emergency

contacts for me only had two names on it since becoming CEO. Now, after meeting Mira, the list grew weekly. I had even put Will and Maisy on there in case something happened to her while she was touring.

Even still, my relationship with Mirabella was one of those open secrets. After my dustup with Robert Brennan and our subsequent "talk," we no longer needed to sneak around so much. It wasn't like I'd planned to shove my relationship with Mira up Brennan's ass. I understood what a valuable asset she was for him.

So, I'd agreed to keep things between Mira and I quiet, to stay out of the public eye, and to be discreet in exchange for my temporary silence about Preston and how exactly he came to be. That's what I'd told Robert Brennan to get him to drop the charges and the lawsuit against me. But I really did it for my mom, to protect her memory. I had also intended to save Preston the scrutiny and pain of that revelation, and I didn't want to shit on Mira's success. Now, I wasn't so sure I'd made the right decision.

"I'll make sure it gets updated," Clara said, as I considered coming clean with Mirabella. To tell her the truth of it all. To make her understand how I really feel about her working for Brennan Enterprises.

"Thank you. What's the latest on the investigation?"

"Kain, Carpenter, and Maguire sent over their report last night, so it should be in your inbox," Clara said. "But to summarize, in case you've not had a chance to review it, they feel there is convincing evidence against Mr. Trenom, and they would like you to distance yourself as much as you can."

"Is that it?"

"No, sir. They said the investigation, as a result of the recent search warrant execution, may have uncovered something troubling related to your father, sir."

My throat tightened, as I inhaled deeply and braced myself to absorb this new potential blow. I massaged the bridge of my nose, and went to pour myself a bourbon despite it being nine-fucking-am.

"Is Akila Norman in the building?"

"I'll find out, sir," Cindy said.

"Have her come see me when you find her, please," I said.

"Sir, I have just messaged her," Cindy said as if she had carried out a difficult task on my behalf.

"Thank you, Cindy," I said.

"Any calls from Phillip Braxton?" I asked, because I found it odd that I hadn't heard from him in a few days.

"No, sir," Sherilyn chimed in.

"Did you send the quarterly competitive analysis report on Brennan Enterprises? I want to know how their *Mirabella Castle* tour went in terms of numbers."

"I spoke to Mark in London; he said he would be sending it over at the end of next week since the tour ended yesterday," Clara said, clearly expecting that I was going to pressure Mark to deliver it sooner rather than later.

"Please have him deliver it by Tuesday end of business." I instructed Clara to deal with staffers on actual work product most often because there simply wasn't much to be done as the Manager of the Executive Floor anymore. She seemed to thrive in this new role, and I needed to make it official. And, since I had never promoted anyone before, I decided to do that now.

"Clara, I'd like you to take on more staff engagement and management of work product and delivery communication from now on. You're excellent at it, and it makes me feel better knowing you are on top of these things. From what I hear, the staff enjoys collaborating with you, and they respect you."

Clara looked shocked, though she should not have. She was talented, skilled, and effective.

"Thank you, sir."

"You are very welcome. Akila will meet with you by tomorrow to further define the role and your new salary," I added.

"New salary, sir?"

"Yes, Clara. I'm promoting you to Chief of Staff to the CEO," I said with a smile I hoped expressed my gratitude.

"Oh my, thank you, sir. Thank you so much, Mr. Magellan," Clara said through her electric smile.

"You're very welcome, Clara."

I turned my attention to Cindy who was doing her level best not to appear shocked or envious.

"Cindy, in a similar vein, you have proven to be not only a tremendous asset to my father but also to me. The way you've overseen and are handling all of the investigation and search warrant stuff has been nothing short of amazing, and it has allowed me to focus on what I need to, knowing that you have things handled. Your loyalty and effectiveness mean a lot to me. I am promoting you to Vice President of Operations for the Executive Team. Similarly, Akila will also be meeting with you to discuss the role further and your salary increase."

"Sir, I don't know what to say, so, I'll just say thank you," Cindy said, tears in her eyes.

"You are very welcome, Cindy. Now, Sherilyn will report to Cindy directly, and Clara will no longer report to Cindy, but directly to me. Of course, Cindy, you will continue to report to me," I paused in case anyone had questions or concerns about the new arrangement, none of which I had actually talked to Akila about yet.

"Sherilyn, you will continue to handle day-to-day calls, emails, and inquiries for the office of the CEO as well as any requests for me to speak, appear somewhere, participate in something, and or to give a statement. Other than "No comment," you'll run any and all potential comments first through Cindy, then through legal, then through Abigail in PR, and finally through me."

Sherilyn looked like she'd swallowed a bee.

"I know it seems like a lot of red tape but it's important. You'll also manage my calendar including meetings, engagements during office hours, and any events I am supposed to attend relating to Magellan Media. We've been treating you with kid gloves and easing you into this role since you began, but now is the time for you to fully step confidently into your position and shine," I said.

I offered her an encouraging smile.

"I can handle it, sir. I can handle you, sir," Sherilyn said, and if it had been six months ago, I would have been tempted to kick Cindy and Clara out to see just how well Sherilyn could fucking handle me. I pushed that thought way fucking far away. It had no place in my mind or heart now that I was with Mira.

"Ok thanks for your time, ladies. That's all."

And when they had all left, I allowed my thoughts to turn briefly to Mirabella.

I had only been with her once in the entire four weeks she had been away on tour, and that had almost been soured by the fact that I had agreed to support her shitty ex-boyfriend's Off-Off-Off Broadway play, a mistake I will never make again. It wasn't the helping Ben that had pissed her off. Or, maybe that was only part of it. It was also the fact that I'd assumed what she would want me to do in this circumstance and that I had assumed rather incorrectly. Mirabella wanted to be heard. To be seen. To have a voice.

So, I supposed I still had a lot to learn about my little spitfire, and I was planning to spend every minute of her return doing just that. I wanted to romance her, to seduce her, to make her realize that I wanted more than just sex from her.

To say I was busy was an understatement. But I was already making moves to free up my calendar for her. For us. I needed Mirabella to know that she is a priority for me. That there isn't anything I wouldn't do for her. That that one day in four weeks hadn't been enough. *Fuck*. I needed to calm the fuck down.

I shook Mirabella from my thoughts because I couldn't afford to allow thinking about her to get the better of me. Usually, if I let my thoughts linger too long on her, I ended up with a raging erection, something I did not need right now. And right as I was about to make a bourbon, Sherilyn buzzed.

"Yes?" I said.

"I've just sent Akila to your office, sir," Sherilyn said, her confidence showing.

"Thanks, Sherilyn," I said before releasing the intercom button.

Just then, Akila knocked on my open door.

"Come in," I said, smiling at her. She was always so beautiful and confident looking with her hair flowing down her back in waves and her manicured hands clutching a designer bag. I wasn't looking at her *that* way. Akila was the kind of woman who not only commanded attention but was deserving of respect. So, I would have to be really drunk or high to be looking at her with anything other than professional intent. Besides, I'm fairly sure she wasn't into white guys with dead father issues. And, even if she was, it was never going to happen.

"Hi, Mitchell. How are you?"

I pointed to the couch so we could sit comfortably together in this meeting, as I walked around my desk and said, "Great, Akila. How are you?"

"Very well, thank you," Akila said as she sat on the couch across from the one I was about to sit on after she was seated.

"Are those new glasses?"

Akila blushed.

"Yes, well, I mean, I've had them for a few weeks. Thanks for noticing."

"They look great on you, Akila," I said, as she blushed some more.

"So, before we talk about the layoffs, I wanted to let you know that I promoted Clara and Cindy," I said, feeling bad for not including her in the decision, meaning she was going to have to work harder and faster to get all the paperwork done.

"Oh. When did this happen?"

"Just today. This morning. I had been meaning to do it for the past few weeks, but with everything else going on, I never got around to it. Clara is going to be Chief of Staff to the CEO," I said as Akila began taking notes, "and Cindy will be Vice President of Operations for the Executive Team. I don't know what either of them make now, but whatever it is, please give them both raises of thirty percent effective immediately."

"That's fantastic, Mitchell. Whenever I have dealt with either, they have both been professional and delightful," Akila, ever the gracious one, said.

"Also, while we are on the subject of delightful professionals, I want to promote one more individual," I said, trying to remain stoic.

"Oh?" Akila said, as she readied her pen to take down the name of the next lucky person.

"I'd like to promote you to Vice President and Global Chief People Officer. The insight, leadership, professionalism, and effectiveness you have shown throughout this crisis and when my parents and brother died has demonstrated your ability to make tough calls and effortlessly handle the resulting fallout. Your talent for being able to decipher office politics, make meaningful and appropriate decisions about organizational structures, communicate and message around difficult issues, and of course, your loyalty to and support of me were key factors in making this change. Please give yourself a forty percent raise."

Akila was nearly in tears, and her emotions were about to reveal themselves. She quickly pulled them back and offered me an appreciative smile.

"You have no idea how much it means to be recognized like this, sir," she said.

"Please, Akila. I knew from the day you asked me about protecting Black women in the workplace that you were a gem. Thank you for that, by the way," I said, remembering our exchange as if it had only recently happened. And yet, it seemed so long ago now. That was shortly after two monumental events in my life; the day I met Mirabella Castle and my first commercial airlines flight.

"Ok, well, thank you once more. I will scope out the job descriptions with Clara and Cindy and make certain you have input before we finalize and get signatures. Same for mine. Oh, and to whom will I be reporting?"

"You'll report directly to me."

Akila smiled as if reporting to me was some great feat, and that got me thinking. My dad would never have promoted Akila. Until I took over as CEO, no one had ever included Director and Manager level people in big meetings with high stakes. Only VP and above. But in Akila's case, she was serving in an interim capacity in a role she was considered unqualified for simply because she lacked the requisite number of years' experience as a director. And, while we hunted for someone to be her boss, Akila was killing it. And now, because she was amazing and I placed her in a position to be seen and heard, she was able to get promoted today.

I smiled to myself as I thought about all the changes I'd made in contrast to how my dad had run the business. Take Cindy. Dad would never have promoted her either. He would have shown his appreciation by giving her gift cards and jewelry. And because he never tasked her with anything more than being a corporate butler, he never knew her true potential.

Now, as I sat across from Akila, I was finally beginning to feel like I belonged in my father's chair as CEO of Magellan Media. I finally felt like the fucking boss. And that feeling had me wanting to celebrate by having Mirabella under me.

"Ok, great. I have the paperwork for you to sign for the terminations you asked for," Akila said, all business.

"Are we certain we can afford to lay these people off? What's the reorganization going to look like?" I asked, taking the folder she handed me for my signature on the thirty termination letters. These were people with families, bills, and obligations. Nothing could make a boss feel like garbage more than having to fire people. But a reorganization of the departments formerly under Peter Trenom was necessary, starting with the ousting of the Trenom loyalists.

I opened the folder, and looked through the names and titles of the people Akila was going to deliver the unwelcome news to.

When I looked up, Akila made an empathetic face, and said, "Need a pen?"

"I'll get it, thanks." I took the opportunity to check my phone without appearing rude.

Akila checked her phone while I was deciding which pen I liked best. After grabbing a white gel pen I'd stolen from Mira, I leaned over the desk and proceeded to review and sign the termination and severance letters. And, as I read through the documents again, I was surprised at how I was feeling right then. That I was feeling any-fucking-thing other than vindicated was weird.

Fucking Peter Trenom had betrayed my father, my aunt, and me. But these people? Most of them were unfortunate casualties of the shady shit he was involved in. Then it dawned on me that unfamiliar emotion. It was empathy. These people were victims of Peter's fucking selfishness and utter disregard for them and their families. He used them for his own fucking nefarious goals.

So, I was glad to know that at least they were all getting a six months' severance package and that they would have health insurance paid for them for up to a year or until they get another job, whichever came first. After all, they were human beings first. I refused to treat them how Peter had.

And, as I signed the very last one, I walked back to Akila, who was still reading messages on her phone, and said, "Hey, you free for lunch?"

THE EVENTS of the day weighed on me as I sat alone in my apartment in the dark with a drink in my hand. Even my one-hour after-work workout did little to shake the horrible feeling I had seeing people being laid off and escorted out of the building, knowing I was the one who was responsible. I'd had a no exceptions policy. If you had worked directly with Trenom, you were out.

The fish rots from the head expression came to mind. How the fuck had Peter Trenom gotten away with his dirty deeds for so damn long? Did Aunt Meg suspect anything?

I'd been in that chair since Mirabella texted me at two thirty am Lisbon time, and my heart leapt into my chest. I tried to seem calm, sexy even. But in truth, I was a fucking wreck. My thoughts turned to Alex. He would have been laughing his ass off at the idea that I was fucked all the way up over a woman. And for the brief few seconds that I had to wait for her text to tell me she was in fact ok, I thought I would die.

I turned the news on after Mirabella messaged. One of the main stories was about Mena's mother. She'd been president of Euro-America International Bank for six years and had held executive positions before that at Citi Group and JP Morgan Chase. And the thing that stuck with me was how toward the end of the report, they said, "She is survived by her husband and daughter."

They'd said the same thing about me when my parents and brother died. I plopped down on the couch in my living room, the overwhelming weight of everything that had happened to me since then blanketing me, crushing me, smothering me.

It was as if all the emotions I had buried somewhere deep inside me burst out from their tombs and rushed me like zombies all at once. And this time, instead of fighting, I fucking let it all out, and cried like a baby.

CHAPTER SIX

MIRABELLA CASTLE

As we taxied to the runway, I saw several cars on the tarmac as Mitchell had promised there would be. There was a blacked-out silver Bentley Flying Spur, a blacked-out black Rolls Royce Ghost, a blacked-out two-toned Mercedes Benz Maybach SUV, and a blacked-out black Rolls Royce Cullinan, Magellan wealth on display.

When the captain said we could disembark, I let everyone else go ahead of me. I watched from the window as Mitchell greeted everyone. But he looked distracted, looking past them all. He was looking for me. A smile crossed my face as my heart drummed faster the closer he got to the plane.

I watched as he scooped Christina into his arms and exchanged the biggest hug with her. They played for a while and then it was time for Mitchell to hug RayRay and his mom. It warmed my heart how much they looked like found family. Mitchell then escorted RayRay's mother to the Ghost and then RayRay and Christina to the Flying Spur. As they walked, he must have asked RayRay where I was because RayRay looked up and pointed to the plane.

"Miss Castle, is there anything else you need?" the nicest flight attendant said, as he and the other two prepared to disembark.

"No, I'm just gathering the last of my things. Thanks for everything," I said.

Mitchell gave Mena a super long hug. And when he was done, he walked her over to the Cullinan and helped her get in.

He was such a gentleman. How he treated my friends and RayRay's mother and daughter warmed my heart and stirred longing in my pelvis.

And then, Mitchell walked with purpose toward the plane. The closer he got, the damper my panties became. The wetter my panties got, the more my clit began to throb.

"Mirabella?" He called from the steps of the plane. I may have stopped breathing.

And when he turned the corner and came into view, I wanted to cry because he looked so fucking handsome. I nearly fell trying to get to him. I ran to him, threw my own arms around his neck, and pressed my body to him as I kissed him fully and deeply.

He moaned into my mouth as he squeezed me to him even more, the bulge in his pants growing bigger and harder.

He pulled away so he could look at me. The expression on his face told me what he wanted to do right then.

"I can't, Mitchell." There was literal pain in my voice.

He kissed me again.

I pulled away this time, wanting to explain and to look at him. It had been six days since I had seen him last.

"What's wrong?"

"I told Mena I would go to New Jersey with her. She doesn't want to go home alone."

Mitchell stepped out of our embrace, lowered his head, and looked out the window. The Cullinan was still there because it was waiting for me.

"When can I see you then?" Mitchell appeared wounded and rejected.

I kissed his cheek, then his other cheek, then his nose, and then his mouth. He smiled, seemingly enjoying the attention. He then kissed me back and pulled me into him again.

"I don't know. I'm probably going to stay over there. I will text or call you when I can."

Mitchell's wounded look worsened, but then changed to hopeful as if he had just gotten a brilliant idea.

"Can you ride with me, and let me drop you at Mena's dad's?"

"That would be nice, but I need to be with Mena. Her mother just died, and I think she can use a friend, especially since Dino's in Italy," I said in a tone I now regretted. Certainly, Mitchell could relate to what Mena was going through.

I cupped his face, and kissed him deeply and slowly while I pressed my body against his. Then, I pulled away, feeling bad, and said, "I missed you so much. I can't wait until we can be alone. Are you going to be ok until then?" I said, with as much tenderness as I could muster.

Mitchell looked down at the small space between us, and said very unconvincingly, "Yeah. Go be with your friend. Call me later."

We kissed again, and as much as I wanted to enjoy the moment, it was clearly not what he had planned for us. But given the somberness of the situation with Mena's mom, car sex with Mitchell was going to have to wait.

WHEN THE HOUSE was silent and everyone was seemingly asleep, I checked my phone. It was 12:30am, and Mitchell had neither called nor texted. So, I quietly crept down the marble staircase in Mena's parents' New Jersey mansion. As I walked past the kitchen, I saw a small light coming from the room. I thought I was being quiet, but I guess I wasn't as stealthy as I had intended.

"Who's there?" Mena's dad called out.

I made my way into the kitchen, and said, "It's me, Mirabella."

Upon entering the room, I was shocked to see Mena's dad and the man who I assumed was Mena's dad's lover looking all flushed and worked up.

Shit.

It was too late to turn around and pretend I didn't see them there, so I waived, pressed my lips together, and gave them a I'm-not-really-here smile.

"I'll let you have some privacy," the statuesque man said, before kissing Mr. Kathri's cheek, and making his way out of sight.

Holy shit, I thought as he snaked past me. He was young. Probably not much older than me.

Alone in the kitchen now with Mena's dad, I felt like an intruder, a witness to a most inappropriate exchange.

"She didn't mind, you know. I mean, she did at first, but she finally got over it and began to have her own affairs," Mr. Kathri said, as if he was obligated to explain his open marriage to his daughter's roommate.

"Please," I said, wholly embarrassed for us both, "you don't have to explain. I'm just here to help Mena get through this. If I can help you in any way in addition to that, please let me know. And, for what it's worth, I am truly deeply sorry for your loss."

It's what came out of my mouth as my mind raced about his boyfriend, how old he was, how they met, how Mena felt about it, and whether he had always wanted to be with a man.

"Thank you, Mirabella. Mena is extremely fond of you," he said, trying to comfort me in the middle of his loss.

"I'm fond of her as well. We've become close these past few months. I'm glad I could be here for her. For you both."

He smiled. "I'm glad she has you, Mirabella. My daughter doesn't make friends easily."

An uncomfortable silence crept into the room and landed between us. He must have known Mena had told me about his affair and marital problems.

"Well, if you don't mind, I was just going to slip out onto the back porch to make a phone call. I hope that's ok," I said, not wanting to be rude.

"Oh nonsense. It's cold out there; please, let me show you to my study."

"Ok." I followed him out of the kitchen, down two hallways, and through an archway at the end of the second hall. We stopped at a closed door, which he opened, and then stood aside so I could enter. Once inside, he followed me in, flipped the switch on the wall, and said, "Take all the time you need. Please shut the light off and close the door when you're done. And, Mirabella?"

"Yes?"

"Thanks for being here for Mena. For our family," he said, before closing the door and leaving me alone in his dark-paneled office.

I removed my phone from my pocket and dialed Mitchell's cell. As I waited for him to pick up, I walked around the office looking at all the degrees, plaques, and accolades on the walls. On his desk, a photo of Mr. Kathri, Mrs. Kathri, and Mena when Mena was a toddler sat framed in gold.

"Hey you," Mitchell said.

"Hey," I said.

"How's Mena? Her dad?"

"Mena's ok, I think. She's exhausted. They had this ritual today called a *Antyesti*. I hope I'm pronouncing it right."

"What's that?"

"It's where they wash the body in like milk and honey and yogurt and butter. They put turmeric paste on the forehead, and the family dress the body. They're going to cremate her tomorrow night after the public viewing."

"Oh wait; I just Googled it." Mitchell paused to read. "Oh wow. Did they put cotton balls in her nose and ears?"

"Yes. I've never seen anything like that before. I asked if they wanted me to leave, but Mena wanted me to stay. They had all these flowers and like rice balls positioned around her."

"It says they tie the toes together," Mitchell said, intrigue in his tone.

"The big toes, I think."

"Wow. How's Mr. Kathri?"

"Her dad? I just caught him in the kitchen with his lover," I said, starting to whisper halfway through.

"What? No way," Mitchell sounded amused.

"They weren't doing anything, but he's in the house, which is weird don't you think?"

"So, you mean if I died, you wouldn't have your lover in the kitchen less than twenty-four hours later?"

I laughed.

"And, Mitchell," I said all conspiratorial like.

"What?" Mitchell mimicked my tone.

"He's like my age. Maybe even younger."

"No shit. What happened when you saw them in the kitchen together?"

"Mr. Kathri literally started explaining to me how Mrs. Kathri knew about his relationship and accepted it," I said, whispering now in earnest.

"Get the fuck out of here."

"Yeah, and he said she was having affairs, too!"

"Shut up!"

I laughed again at Mitchell's penchant for gossip.

"He said 'affairs,' so, like, more than one!"

"Wow. Old rich people really do get up to some crazy shit," Mitchell said, and in that moment, I wondered if he was referring to his parents too.

"What old rich people do you know with crazy shit like that going on?" I asked.

"If I tell you this, you cannot tell anyone. Ok? You have to promise me that you will never tell another soul."

"Oh, this is going to be good. I promise. I won't say anything to anyone."

"You know Peter Trenom?"

"Peter Trenom on your Board Peter Trenom?"

"Yes," Mitchell said.

"What about him?"

"He's fucking my Aunt Meg. Has been for years."

I gasped. "But he's married!" I said, hating how men just cheat all the damn time.

"Yes. He is."

"And he has kids."

"His kids are adults, Mirabella," Mitchel said, and his voice sounded like he was scolding me.

"That's no reason to cheat on your wife."

"And Aunt Meg? She can do much better. She's so pretty."

"Yeah, well, if Peter goes to jail, maybe it will solve that issue."

"Do you think he will? I mean, why haven't you told me about all that has been going on with you?"

"Honestly, Mirabella? I just wanted to focus on your tour and you when we talked. It took all the stress of my current situation away. Talking to you soothed me. I didn't want you worried about me or looking at me with pity for all the shit I have going on."

"Ok," I said, feeling sad.

"Ok?"

"I just wish you felt you could talk to me, take me into your confidence. I wish you trusted me enough to tell me things. To share what's on your mind."

"You're on my fucking mind."

And now, my panties were useless.

"Mitchell, I said, "I can't possibly be on your mind twenty-four-seven. I would like you to confide in me. Lean on me."

"Mira. Bella."

"Yes," I said wondering what sexy thing he was going to say next.

"You are always on my mind, whether you want to believe that or not. Do you think about me when we're apart?"

"Yes."

"What do you think about?"

"Oh no you don't," I said. "We are not doing this in Mena's dad's office," I said, hoping Mitchell wouldn't insist.

"Just tell me one thing," Mitchell said. He sounded sexy as fuck.

"What?" I said, trying not to let on that I was turned on.

"Are you wet right now?"

Mitchell's voice was so heavy with need. He wasn't even trying to hide it.

"Yes."

"Do you want me to come get you?"

Jesus. I wanted him to, so badly.

"Under any other circumstances you know I would want you to. But, Mitchell, I can't. Not tonight."

"I want you so fucking much, Mirabella. When can I see you?"

"Are you coming to the service tomorrow? If so, you know you have to wear white, right?"

"Of course, what time does it start?"

"Well, it's from 11am until 4pm. You can come at any time."

"Do you know what you just said?"

"What did I say now?" Before he could respond, I realized exactly what I'd just said. "Oh my God, Mitchell; you are insufferable."

"You know you love it."

"I do. I really do."

We both laughed.

"I have a few things to do tomorrow, but I guess I will get there around three. Are you going to be ready to leave with me when I arrive?"

"Yes. I will. I can't wait to see you, Mitchell."

"Really?"

"Yes, why?"

"I don't know, sometimes you don't seem all that enthused."

"Seriously?"

"Yeah, like when I came to visit you on tour. I was so fucking psyched to see you, Mira. I was fucking losing my mind. And when you opened that door, I didn't know what to do. You were so fucking beautiful, so sexy. I wanted to put all my things on you, my fucking mouth, my hands, my dick, my tongue. I just wanted to give you all of me right then. But I could sense you didn't feel the same."

"Mitchell, I'm so sorry. I never meant to make you feel as if I didn't want you or that I wasn't super-excited to see you. You looked so damn good when I first saw you. I wanted you to put all your things on me, in me, or whatever. I was ready."

"But your need to fight was stronger than your need for me," Mitchell said. He sounded sad and defeated.

"I'm sorry I made you feel that way; I was wrong to do that to you," I said, wondering if I would ever be comfortable enough with Mitchell to let him see how much I needed him, how much I hated being away from him. To be one hundred percent vulnerable without being terrified of his rejection of me.

"You know what? I think all the shit happening right now and Mena's mom's death is just bringing up a lot of stuff for me that I need to work on."

"Mitchell, talk to me," I said.

"You should get some rest. We can talk tomorrow."

"Are you sure?"

"Yes. Get some rest. Take care of your friend."

"Ok but, Mitchell, I'm here if you need me."

"Goodnight, Baby."

"Goodnight."

MENA MADE it through the service, just barely. She alternated between being hysterical, stoic, or completely shut down. With just one more hour to go, I found myself excited to leave. I know that was a shitty way to feel but I was ready to spend some time with Mitchell in a meaningful way. He'd sent a beautiful arrangement which was labeled as being from *The Magellan Family*.

Some of Mena's coworkers, her friends from college, our other roommates, and RayRay had also stopped by today to pay their respects. It was nice of Iggy to come on the way to his gig which happened to be on Long Island.

"When do you think you'll be coming back home?" Shay asked.

"I don't know. I think I want to stay in Jersey for a while, spend some time with my dad and my grandparents from India," Mena said.

"Makes sense," I said, thinking briefly about the last time she had spent significant time in New Jersey. Mitchell had come over, and we'd had amazing sex all night long. The guilt of thinking about Mitchell now, with Mena's dead mom a few feet away was too much. And since the service was now nearly over, I went to call him to see when he would be arriving.

As I was walking out of the room the service was in, Mitchell walked through the door. God, that man was a vision in a white suit, brown shoes, taupe shirt—open at the collar, no tie, and freshly shaven. I wasn't sure I would have the self-control not to find a bathroom or closet to pull him into. And when he saw my face, he smirked, obviously realizing how fucking hot he looked.

Mitchell kissed me as we met in the aisle. It was the most chaste kiss he had ever given me, and I found his self-restraint very sexy. It was such a turn on being with a man who was secure, knew how to carry himself, and fully understood how to navigate social norms and expectations even when complex emotions like grief and loss were involved. Mitchell was confident and self-assured, and that shit made him incredibly attractive.

"I was just going outside to call you," I said, admiring him and smiling. "You look amazing, Mr. Magellan."

"Why thank you, Miss Castle. You look pretty fucking gorgeous yourself," he said as he quickly allowed himself the small pleasure of eyeing the cleavage spilling out of my white deconstructed blazer dress.

I grabbed his hand and escorted him to where Mena's family was gathered. He made his rounds, introducing himself, and offering his condolences and any assistance that might be needed. And when Mena's father thanked him for coming and for the beautiful bouquet of flowers, Mitchell was gracious.

But then something happened.

"Mr. Magellan, we appreciate your support of our granddaughter, Mena. She tells me you have become a friend. But we do not want a media spectacle at our daughter's funeral. We would appreciate it if you did not attend," Mena's grandmother said without adding a smile, but holding Mitchell's hand while she did.

"What my wife means is," Mena's grandfather chimed in, "We know you are going through a lot of challenges right now, and the media seems particularly interested in your whereabouts. And while our daughter is somewhat of a media figure herself, we don't want any negative attention at her funeral, no matter the source. We hope you can understand."

Mitchell seemed surprised at first but then graciously responded with, "Absolutely. I would never dishonor your daughter by making a media circus of her services. I understand completely. Please accept my deepest sympathies once more. My offer for whatever you or Mena may need stands. Sorry to have met under these circumstances," he said. And then he turned to me, squeezed my hand, and said, "You ready?"

I didn't know what to do or say, so I turned, and began walking down the aisle, keeping his hand tightly in mine. When I passed Mena, RayRay, Shay, and Iggy, I mouthed, "Call you later," and to Mena I mouthed, "So sorry."

When we exited the room into the hallway, I stopped and said to Mitchell, "I have to get my bags; I'll just be a minute."

"I'll be outside," Mitchell said, and when I looked past him, even more media had gathered, no doubt due to his presence here.

"But how will I go with you if there's all that press?" I said, panic in my voice.

Mitchell turned to look at the media, and then turned back to look at me before saying somewhat angrily, "Well I guess you're going to have to be seen with me, then. Unless it's going to draw too much negative attention for you too?"

And just then I realized Mitchel Magellan was hurt by what Mena's grandparents had said and asked of him.

I placed a hand on his arm and offered him a supportive smile.

"I'll be right back, ok?"

I think he could see the concern I had for him on my face because his expression softened and he said, "Ok. Hurry, Mirabella."

And by 'hurry' I knew exactly what he meant.

CHAPTER SEVEN

MITCHELL MAGELLAN

If anyone had ever told me that I would be banned from a fucking funeral, I would never have believed them. Well, I guess there's a first time for fucking everything. Part of me wanted to be petty but the truth is, I wouldn't want me at my funeral either. It was just as well, because I didn't have to spend another minute being somber or trying not to look at Mirabella the way I had wanted to. I no longer had to push thoughts of what I wanted to do to her out of my head.

Feeling like a kid who'd just been released from detention, I was free to let my mind think on what we were going to get up to soon and to allow my eyes roam. And, when she walked down the circular marble staircase, struggling to carry her suitcases, I nearly didn't even bother to help her because the angle created by her leaning to her left and forward gave me a perfectly delicious view of her bouncing tits.

Meeting her halfway because I wasn't a total fucking animal, I said, "Is this everything?" Grabbing one bag out of her right hand and another out of her left, I kissed her nose. She smiled a most beautiful blushing smile letting me know I'd caught her off guard.

"Are you serious? There are three more bags plus a garment bag and a makeup trunk," she said, as if she was speaking to a complete fucking idiot.

"Ok, I'll be right back then," I said. And when I got to my car, cameras flashing and paparazzi calling my name, I asked Brendan to come inside and help me get the rest of Mira's bags. I didn't want to be in that place a minute longer than I needed to be.

"Oh my God, Brendan, thanks so much for helping," Mirabella said when Brendan's beefy ass arrived to save us. Right then I realized she understood nothing about my world. People didn't help me. They did what I asked because I paid them, and Brendan makes three hundred fifty thousand dollars a year to do whatever the fuck I ask him to.

"It's no problem, Miss Castle," Brendan said as he grabbed what he could, and carried it out to the car. I picked up the final bags in one hand so that my other hand was free to hold hers, and we exited the funeral home through the front door and in full view of the media and paparazzi. And as the cameras flashed and reporters called my name and hers, I knew we were going to make front-page news.

Brendan took her remaining bags from me and put them in the trunk. As he did, I put Mirabella in the car, closed her door, then got in on the other side. When I sat down, Mirabella took my hand.

I looked over at her and said, "Are you ok?"

She said, "Yes." Mirabella stared at the crowds outside the funeral home and flinched as photographers took photos of my car while Brendan tried to maneuver the SUV out onto the road.

Just then my phone rang. It was Braxton.

I picked it up.

"Braxton, where the fuck have you been?" I said for the umpteenth time in the past few weeks.

"It's no matter where I've been. What's more important is what I have been doing," Braxton said in his peculiar way of communicating.

"What have you been doing then?" I asked.

Mirabella mouthed, "Can they see inside here?"

I shook my head.

"Are you sure," she mouthed, looking awfully concerned.

"I have been talking to Peter Trenom's friends, all of whom are ready to rat his ass out for the right motivation," Braxton said.

"Yes, I'm sure, why?" I mouthed back to her, listening to Braxton but looking at her intently.

Mirabella reached up under her skirt and began to pull her panties off.

"Braxton, hold on, please," I said and put the call on mute.

"What are you doing?" I asked, incredulous.

Mirabella stared into my eyes, and said, "Didn't you promise to fuck me in the car?"

Fuck! My cock twitched in my pants several times, my erection growing quickly.

"Braxton, something's come up. I'll call you later," I said unable to hang the phone up quick enough.

When she got her panties fully off, Mirabella looked in my eyes, handed them to me, and said, "I don't need these anymore."

Mother of God.

I reached out to her, to put my hand between her legs, but she stopped me from touching her. Still looking into my eyes, Mirabella hiked her already short skirt up to her hips. I reached out to touch her breast, but she gently pushed my hand away. And when I said, "How come I can't touch you, Baby?" she didn't respond. Instead, she unbuckled my belt, and unbuttoned and then unzipped my pants.

"Sweet fucking Mirabella," I said, my voice strained from being so turned on. Mirabella pulled my pants down so that they were around my knees. "What are you doing to me?"

Instead of answering me, she climbed on top and straddled me. And as she kept her eyes fixed on mine, she fucking moved her body slowly over my thighs until her drenched pussy was pushed up against my underwear that was struggling to contain me.

Every single time I tried to touch her; she moved my hands away. Her denial was driving me fucking wild. I was so damn into this. She was so fucking hot. And, just as I was admiring my beautiful Mirabella, she unbuttoned her dress enough for me to see more of her perfect tits. Right fucking then, I broke eye contact with her to look at her two perfectly round mounds that she had shoved into a push-up bra, her nipples straining against the thin mesh fabric.

But when I went to fucking touch her, she denied me. So, I followed my girl's lead. This was Mirabella's show now, and I was going to let her do exactly what she wanted.

She leaned forward so that her breasts were touching me, and put her hand on my chest, right at my nipple which she was lightly rubbing as she whispered in my ear, "Are you sure Brendan won't hear me if I moan out your name?"

Fuuuuck.

My breathing was so fucking loud, I thought he was going to hear that.

"No," I breathed out.

"Will he hear me when I beg you to fuck me?" she said when she moved to my other ear and nipple.

She straightened her body and put her arms around my neck, looked me in the eyes and said, "I'm so fucking hot for you, Mitchell." She then took her finger and placed it inside her. Mira moaned and ground on it a few times. And when she removed her finger from her cunt, she rubbed the wetness on my lips and then kissed it off.

I fucking moaned into her mouth like a greedy motherfucker. I wanted more.

Mirabella ran her finger onto her slick center once more, and then rubbed the wetness on my lips, and then sucked and kissed it off again.

And when I went to slide my fingers inside her, she grabbed my hand and began sucking on my fingers. When she had adequately sucked each one, she kissed and licked the palm of my hand up and down, and even though I had never thought of that part of me as an erogenous zone, my balls felt like they were about to fucking burst.

"Mitchell," she breathed out.

"Yes, Baby," I said, fucking feeling overwhelmed by not being able to touch her.

"You look so fucking good today. I love when you wear white," she said, breathy and fucking sexy.

She made me smile; I loved knowing my girl liked the way I looked.

"You look fucking amazing too, Mira."

"Mitchell?"

"Yes, Mirabella?"

"I want to come in your mouth," she said as she climbed up so that she was scrunched up against the ceiling and her pussy was in my face.

FUUUUUUUUUUUCK!

I quickly pushed her skirt up just enough for me to lick and suck on her clit. And when Mirabella started fucking my face, I knew it wouldn't take long.

So, I did what she loves. While licking her throbbing clit, I shoved two fingers slowly in and out of her, going deeper each time I inserted them. And when I reached her wall, I held my fingers there, enjoying how she gripped and clenched while pulling my underwear down to expose my aching fucking dick.

Mirabella looked down and saw my cock dripping and looking like a pole. It was so fucking rigid and engorged, pre-cum literally oozed from the tip. Without warning, she inched herself down and onto me, pushing my cock so deep we both screamed, "Fuck" when she was fully seated atop my thighs.

My girl felt so fucking good, slippery, tight, and fucking warm. We both stayed there for a few seconds loving how her body stretched to fit me. And then suddenly, Mirabella was humping and fucking me and sliding my dick in and out of her at her own fucking pace.

"Shit, fuck me just like that, Mirabella," I said.

"I was going to come in your mouth until you fucking teased me with your beautiful big cock," Mirabella said. She was talking lots of shit tonight. "I didn't want to waste all that delicious pre-cum dripping from your swollen tip," she added. And that was fucking it for me.

She must have felt that I was going to come, because she moaned loudly and fucked me even faster right then.

"You're gonna make me fucking come," I said, completely out of breath.

"I can feel you losing control for me, Mitchell," Mirabella said. "Please come for me, so I can come too."

"Fuck," was all I could manage. Like a good boy, I did what she fucking asked, and came deep inside her glorious pussy, come dripping down my cock as it ran out of her.

"I'm coming with you. Ah . . . Mitchell. I'm fucking coming with you," she said as she gripped me so fucking tight that she squeezed the last bit of cum right out of me.

Now, she let me kiss her. And even though we were both spent and out of breath, she let me kiss her slowly and deeply until we both fully came down from our orgasm highs.

Just then, Mirabella looked out the window and noticed we were not in Queens but in Manhattan.

"Does Brendan know where he's going?"

"Yeah, we're going to my apartment in Chelsea. Is that ok with you?"

"Ok," she said, which wasn't comforting.

She had that just-been-fucked-so-damn-good look I loved to see on her. When I smiled, she said, "Is there something I can clean myself with? All my stuff's in the trunk."

I reached into a compartment, and showed her its contents of wet wipes, paper hand towels, a first-aid kit, deodorant, toothbrush, mouthwash, toothpaste, dental floss, and condoms. Fuck. I didn't need her to see that.

"Can you pass me the wet wipes then? And a paper towel or two? You came, a lot," she said, and I know she saw the condoms.

"I fucking came so much, Mira," I said as I handed her what she'd asked for and took some for myself.

We cleaned in silence, but I spent most of that time thinking about how I'd officially christened the Maybach.

When Mirabella looked done, I pulled her panties out of my jacket pocket, and said, "Want these back?"

I made her smile which made me fucking smile.

"Nope!"

MIRABELLA LOOKED around my apartment as if it was *not* what she was expecting.

"Not exactly the son-of-a-billionaire nepo baby bachelor pad you had imagined?" I offered as Brendan and I carried the final lot of her bags inside.

Mirabella continued looking around, not saying a word, ignoring my comment. Every few seconds, though, she would say, "hmmm" as if she were noticing something curious or odd.

"Anything else, Bro?" Brendan said, looking around the apartment like he was shocked that I would bring Mirabella here. I assume he too wondered why I hadn't upgraded, bought an apartment befitting a man of my newfound wealth.

I leaned forward and said, "No thanks, Brother. I appreciate you," dapping him up then bringing it in for a one-armed bro hug. Then I whispered loudly in his ear with the confidence of a man who not only had a shit-ton of money but also one who was about to get laid, "And there's more than one way to impress a woman."

Brendan slapped me on the back, and said, "Enjoy, Bro, and don't forget, I have an impression of my own to make tonight. Maleko is on call if you need to go out."

"Enjoy, Brother. I'm working from home tomorrow, so, no need to worry about tomorrow morning," I said as code for "impress her all night for all I care since I don't need a driver tomorrow morning."

"Alright cool," Brendan said before turning to leave.

I found Mirabella on one of the two terraces, soaking up the late afternoon sun. I pulled her into a hug and let her lean against me, her back against my front.

"It's cold out here," I said. "Why don't you come inside and let me run us a hot bath?"

She leaned her head against me and said, "That sounds nice. Thank you."

She felt so good in my arms, and I let my thoughts run across the idea of asking her to move in together. But when she turned her body so that she could look at me, and placed her arms around my neck, I was caught off-guard, suddenly hesitant.

"What?" she said, as if she was sensing me being off my usual game.

"Nothing. I was just enjoying how good you feel. I was thinking about how nice it is to have you here," I said, which was not a complete lie. For some reason, the night we had that date-non-date in London at the Shard came to mind. That night, she was all sexy-flirty-drunk-coy and fucking insanely gorgeous. Now, here in my apartment looking up at me with those beautiful fucking eyes, letting me touch her and hold her, enjoying it even, was everything. I smiled at my girl.

She smiled, then slowly kissed me. And when she had her fill, she said, "It's so not what I was expecting."

I kissed her more, loving how neither of us was able to stop touching and kissing one another whenever we were together. And even though we had recently had massive orgasms in the car, I was ready for her again.

"What were you expecting?" I said, in between kissing her mouth, cheeks, nose, and neck. Mirabella was ticklish on her neck. And when she would giggle and squirm inside my embrace as I kissed her, it really turned me on.

"I don't know. Something . . . *different*," she said as I slipped my hand inside her dress, and gently but firmly kneaded her left breast.

She moaned and her body seemed to automatically push itself closer to me. This fucking thing we had was deep, sexy, and damn electric, and it made me feel so good to know that I could make her feel this way. That she was moaning for me. That it was highly likely that if I put my hands under the skirt of her dress and touched her pussy, that she would be dripping for me.

I moved my hand over to her right breast and did the same as I had done to her left. And, since she liked to pretend that I neglected her right breast, I took my fucking time, drawing out the delicious rubbing and squeezing and kneading I gave it. Mirabella continued to moan, only a little more loudly now, as I continued to trail kisses all over her neck and mouth and back to her neck.

I was so fucking hard as I imagined how turned on she was. And, given that she wasn't wearing panties, my mind raced with thoughts of that sweet wetness running down her legs. And just as I was thinking about this, she rubbed her thighs together.

"You ok, Mirabella?" I said with my lips against her neck.

She fucking nearly melted right then. Seeing the effect that had on her, I hedged my bets, and did it a-fucking-gain. Then, I licked her neck from just under her chin to the bottom where it met her shoulder. Every single slow and deliberate wet kiss I trailed along her neckline, from one shoulder to another and back again, made her moan.

"You starting to feel good, Mirabella?"

She moaned in response, louder this time, making my fucking cock twitch and vibrate and strain against my white suit pants.

Fuck!

Mitchell," she moaned out, straining to talk through her immense fucking need for me. "I thought you were going to run us a bath," she said, breathy and fucking needy as she pulled my face to hers so she could assault my mouth with her own.

And when she finally let us up for air, I couldn't take it anymore, and said, "I'm going to run us a bath, and we'll have some of that wine you enjoyed in London. Would you like that, Mira?"

"Mmmmmm," she moaned. "That sounds good, Mitchell. Thank you."

"You're very welcome," I said, placing my hand around her neck and squeezing lightly to see how she'd react. *Damn.* She moaned again and squeezed her fucking thighs together.

"Mitchell," she said, fighting to speak through her arousal.

"Yes?"

"I could really use that bubble bath."

And as I squeezed her neck a tiny bit harder, I licked my lips, and said, "I know, Baby. But first, I'm going to fuck you."

CHAPTER EIGHT

MIRABELLA CASTLE

IN ALL MY FANTASIES ABOUT BEING SWEPT AWAY TO MITCHELL'S apartment in Chelsea, I didn't imagine it would have been so normal. Not only was he the richest person I knew, but he was even richer now that he had inherited the wealth of his family. I believe the press had been quoted as listing his wealth as at least one hundred fifty billion or more dollars. And while his townhouse was a million times nicer than my apartment, it was smaller and far less expensive looking than I had been expecting.

The kitchen was a small galley-style kitchen that wasn't much bigger than ours in Queens. Of course, Mitchell's had top of the line Miele and Viking appliances as well as marble countertops. It even had a built-in Miele espresso machine and its own laundry room.

I continued my self-directed tour of the first floor, noticing the books in the bookshelves that flanked either side of the wood-burning fireplace thinking about how I didn't know he liked to read. The idea that I didn't really know much about Mitchell at all would not let me be. Somewhere between how he'd been portrayed in the media and how he was with me was the real Mitchell Magellan.

ALL THE WAY OUT

Sprinkled in with books by Stephen King, Andy Weir, and David Baldacci were photos of Mitchell and his brother Alex from when they were kids. I didn't see any photos of his other family members. Mitchell had books on architecture, ships, and baseball, along with some baseball memorabilia from the New York Yankees and Yankee Stadium.

On one side, Mitchell had records, CDs, and some forty-fives in a varied music collection consisting of everyone from Elton John to Guns-n-Roses, to Adele, to Jay-Z, Pearl Jam, The Police, Public Enemy, Busta Rhymes, Deftones, and EPMD. Clearly, I didn't know Mitchell Magellan *at* all.

But of all the rooms downstairs, his office was the most intriguing. In it was only a desk and a chair. On the desk sat a closed MacBook Pro.

Something about Mitchell's apartment made me want to take care of him, to nurture him, to love him. To show him how he could make his apartment a real home. A place of refuge. A place of warmth and love. And as I made my way out onto the terrace, even though it was cold, I looked around, wondering how much time, if any, he spent out there.

My thoughts turned to when I first met Ben. He'd been working for *Time Out New York*, and was temporarily assigned a music beat. So, he ended up covering one of Iggy's rare local shows, and when he couldn't keep his eyes off me during the concert, I introduced myself to him after the show. We ended up going for coffee at a diner that night. We talked for three hours doing the typical 'what's your favorite color, food, and bands' conversation like you do when you first meet someone. What we should have been talking about was intimacy and his views on sex.

Now, I was with a guy whose favorite color I didn't know, but rather, I knew how he liked his balls tickled during intercourse.

I had been going non-stop for the past four weeks overloaded with appearances and traveling on my world tour. And when I wasn't doing that, I was going on talk shows and press junkets. Having to be constantly on was exhausting. And now, being here at Mitchell's apartment, I wanted to curl up in his arms and rest.

But Mitchell had other ideas about how I should have been spending my time with him. So, when he came up to me on the terrace and put his arms around me and his body against me, all rational thoughts left me. Soon, I was overcome by my need for him and my desire to feel him and taste him. And when he told me he was going to draw me a bath but fuck me first, I surrendered to the man who knew my sexual needs and how to meet them better than I did.

As I sat in our hot bubble bath, I looked around the room at the candles Mitchell had lit for us. The bucket of ice and white wine next to the tub were a nice touch. And the rose petals in the bathtub added a pleasing natural fragrance. At first, I was alone because Mitchell had to take a call from Braxton. But when he opened the door and entered the room in only a towel covering his lower body, I nearly forgot how exhausted I was.

I didn't even mind that he caught me looking at him because when he did, he leaned over the side of the standalone tub, and kissed me gently. I smiled at him, being so happy in that tiny moment. He smiled back but his was smirky.

"You like looking at me, Mirabella?"

He was determined to embarrass me now.

"Yes," I said, a blush creeping up my cheeks.

He straightened, and then dropped his towel.

As much as I tried NOT to look down there, my fucking Judas eyes betrayed me. I instinctively reached out to touch his penis after I noticed he was becoming hard. I pulled my hand back quickly, super embarrassed.

He laughed and stepped into the tub.

"I was trying to stop it from getting hard," I said.

"Only you would think that touching it would stop it from getting hard," Mitchell teased.

Mitchell lowered himself into the tub and poured himself a glass of wine.

"Thank you for this, Mitchell," I said when he turned to me and put his arm around me.

"You're welcome."

I raised my glass to his and we clinked. After we took sips of our respective wines, Mitchell kissed me again.

I smiled and laughed, thinking this man was never satisfied.

"What?"

"Nothing. It's just you're always touching me and kissing me," I said and then regretted it immediately. I didn't want him to think I didn't like it. So, I added, "I love being the center of your attention, Mitchell Magellan."

Mitchell smiled.

"You are extremely touchable and kissable, Mirabella Castle," he said, before kissing me again. And when he was done, he put his wine glass to my mouth. I drank some, smiling at him while I did.

"What?"

Mitchell smirked.

"I love telling you where to put your mouth," he said.

"You love ordering me around."

"I have never ordered you to do anything but if you're into it, I'm happy to order you around, Mirabella."

Just then, his eyes told me he was getting even more aroused.

"I'm good. The last thing I need is you telling me what I can and cannot do," I said, seriously thinking about how sexy it would be.

We drank more wine, and for a few minutes, silently enjoyed the peace and quiet.

When I finished my glass of wine, Mitchell poured me more without me having to ask. To reward him, I kissed him on the cheek and then on his mouth, and then planted a few soft kisses on his neck. And when he moaned a little, I stopped.

"Why'd you stop, Baby?" he asked, looking at me like a lost puppy.

This man.

"I'm sorry. Do you want me to kiss you some more?"

"Yes," he said, a little breathy.

I chugged my wine, put my glass on the floor next to the tub, and then kissed Mitchell Magellan fucking deeply and slowly. And when he and I both were getting too heated, I tried calming us down by kissing him on his face and nose.

"I love kissing you, Mitchell," I said while planting little kisses on him.

"I love being kissed by you, Mirabella," he said, breathing my name out.

I smiled at him. He was so fucking handsome.

"You're so fucking good-looking, Mitchell," I said, mistakenly thinking out loud.

He smiled and tilted his head staring into my eyes.

"Thank you, Beautiful," he said, still smiling.

And now I was smiling too.

"Can I ask you something?" I said, looking into his gorgeous eyes.

"Sure."

"How much money do you *actually* have?"

Mitchell smiled even more. He looked briefly down, then back at me.

"A-fucking-lot."

"What's *a lot*? Because a million dollars is a lot to me, and I know you have much more than that."

"It changes based on the value of my assets."

"That's a total rich guy thing to say," I said, smiling at him. "Does it make you uncomfortable that people look at you and wonder how much money you have?" I asked, thinking it must be annoying to live that way. "I mean, you didn't look at me and wonder how much money I had in my bank account, right?"

He laughed.

"I looked at you, and the first thought that came into my head when I saw you sitting in the waiting area of the Magellan Media Executive Floor was, I wonder what it would feel like to have her perfect fucking lips wrapped around my cock," Mitchell said, as if it was the most natural thought ever.

I smiled, not in the least surprised or offended.

"And your second thought?"

"Sure you want to know?" he said, as a tiny panic began in the pit of my stomach.

"Yes, I want to know," I said, my smile fading.

"My very second thought when I saw you was how much I wanted to come down your fucking throat."

I gulped rather loudly, and that made Mitchell laugh.

"Just like that, Mirabella," he teased, making me laugh too.

"Was there any time your thoughts about me weren't sexual?"

"No."

"And now?"

"Same. Still all about sex," Mitchell teased. "But no, it doesn't make me uncomfortable knowing how people only care about how much money I have because in all honesty, when I meet rich people, I too wonder how much money they have."

"So, you really have no idea how rich you are?" I said. The idea was strange to me, because I knew about every single expense, expenditure, withdrawal, deposit, and fee, in my bank account.

I moved out of his hold so I could grab my wine glass and pass it to him so he could pour me some more wine.

"My parents left me everything they had. Money. Real estate. Art. Land. Cryptocurrency. Cars. Boats. Planes. Businesses. Trusts. Stocks. Bonds. Insurance policies. Commercial real estate. Jewelry. About six months after their death, my financial and legal teams finally established a value for all of it. At that time, it was valued at approximately one hundred fifty-five billion."

Mitchell poured the rest of the wine into my glass and handed it to me.

I don't know what I was expecting him to say, but it wasn't that.

"No fucking way," I said, unable to fathom that amount of wealth in general, let alone belonging to one person.

"Yeah. I was surprised it wasn't more, actually."

"Really? Why?"

"They had left about twenty-five billion to Alex. But when Alex died with them, the money and other assets were put into escrow."

It made me sad for him to think about losing his brother too. I touched his cheek and then leaned in to kiss him.

He moaned softly.

I wentto remove my hand from his face, but he grabbed it and kissed it, kissing my palm and fingers as we spoke, no doubt knowing full well it was sexy and fucking distracting.

"Why?" I said, trying not to smile or react to his kisses.

"Alex was engaged when he died. Sarah and her family are asserting a claim to Alex's inheritance," he said as if it was an annoyance he'd rather not have to deal with.

"Wow. They didn't sign a prenup?"

This man took my arm, and planted sweet, sexy kisses from my hand and up to my wrist and slowly up my forearm.

"Can't talk now, kissing my girlfriend," he said, staring into my eyes as he did.

This. Fucking. Man.

"Mitchell," I said, feeling sleepy and aroused.

"They did have a prenup. So, it's just a formality at this point. She will get a death benefit of about fifty to one hundred million."

Mitchell moved toward me and began planting kisses all over my neck and shoulders making me squirm.

"Jesus. Why so much?" I said, my voice uneven as I attempted to worm and squirm away from Mitchell. And as I did, something was very clear to me, as I enjoyed the feeling of his mouth on my wet skin. Mitchell Magellan was not going to let me go to sleep. Mitchell had one fucking thing on his mind, and it wasn't his bank account.

"Something about his lifetime income at Magellan. I don't really know the details."

Mitchell began licking my neck and applying pressure, and damn if I wasn't already wet for him.

"Then what happens to the balance?" I said, losing my battle against Mitchell's hands, mouth, and tongue.

"Well once they establish that Alex has no offspring to support, it moves to our Magellan Family Trust from which Aunt Meg, Preston, and I can draw."

"How do you get paid then?" I said, just as I successfully pulled out of his grasp.

"Where the fuck do you think you're going, Mirabella?" Mitchell said, and suddenly he seemed almost angry, like I had taken away his favorite toy.

"I'm sorry; I want to talk," I said.

"I want to fucking talk too. But I want to touch you and kiss you while we do," Mitchell said, looking at me, clearly upset. "I'm just being honest, Mira. When you fucking pull away from me, it makes me angry."

"I'm sorry. I wasn't trying to upset you."

"Are you mine?"

"What?"

"Are you mine, Mirabella? I remember you telling me how you would lie in bed wanting Ben to fucking touch you, but he wouldn't and how upsetting it was. And I know I'm not the level of fucking asshole that guy is, and here I am wanting to fucking touch you, and you pull away from me."

Just then, Mitchell looked hurt, and I felt like such a fucking asshole. The thing is, I wanted him to touch me and kiss me. I just hated how much I wanted it. I hated needing him. I hated being so into him. And if I was being honest with myself, it all had to do with the fact that I did not trust him. Deep down, I knew Mitchell Magellan was eventually going to break my heart.

"I . . . I love how much you seem to enjoy touching and kissing me. I've never actually allowed myself to be so sexually vulnerable with anyone. And if I squirm or pull away, it isn't because I don't want you to touch me. It's because I know where it will lead," I said hoping that made things better.

"And what's wrong with where it leads?" Mitchell said.

"Nothing. I fucking love being with you in that way. But Mitchell, we need to talk more. We need to get to know one another. We can't just have sex all the time, and that's all we do. I want a deeper connection with you. . . Unless you don't. Unless you don't want to know me other than sexually," I said, praying I didn't cry right then.

Mitchell seemed to consider what I said. And even though he didn't respond, I could see by his expression that he understood. And now, he looked at me like a child waiting for his mother to release him from time out. And when I leaned in to kiss his mouth, he smirked at me, and said, "I should fucking pull away from you."

"But you won't," I said, teasing him back with a huge smirk myself.

And, for a few sexy seconds, I contemplated climbing on top of him and riding him until he was coming deep inside me. But I kissed him instead and when he kissed me back, he gently pushed his tongue into my mouth, and said as he did, "You're gonna fucking get it, Mirabella."

"Yeah?" I breathed into his mouth, "And who's gonna give it to me?"

"Keep fucking with me. Keep it up," Mitchell said, his strongest warning yet.

Mitchell looked like he was planning an attack, unsure of whether to go in through the front or back door. The look on his face was so fucking sexy. I couldn't believe how far things had come between us since that first day at Magellan Media.

I smiled at him.

"You think it's funny, don't you?"

"What? I think what's funny?"

"How you have me wrapped around your fucking finger," Mitchell said, seemingly serious and pained.

"Exactly where I'd like to be right now, wrapped around your finger," I said, pushing him on purpose.

"You know what, Mirabella?" Mitchell said, a tortured look on his face.

"What?"

Mitchell Magellan grabbed me, pulled me up on top of him and plunged his fucking rock-hard cock into my pussy.

"You're gonna learn to stop running your fucking mouth, Mirabella."

"Mmmmmmmmmm," I said as I rode him the way I had thought about doing.

"What are you moaning about, Mirabella?" he said, fucking me hard and fast.

"Fucking punish me, Mitchell."

CHAPTER NINE

MITCHELL MAGELLAN

It wasn't that I didn't want to talk to Mirabella. I would have talked to her all night if she had insisted. But she was right when she said all the phone and video sex self-love over the past couple of weeks had not been enough. I needed all of her to feel fully satisfied.

For me, sex with Mirabella was an amazing pleasure-filled assault on my senses. Her smells, sounds, tastes, the feel of her skin, the bounce of her tits; everything about her was like someone had left a trail of little treats for me to explore. And that one time her orgasm was so strong that she fucking cried? I felt like a goddamn king.

And now that her tour was done and I had her in my apartment, my overwhelming desire for her was behind every decision I'd made since I knew she was coming here. I wanted everything to be perfect. I wanted to impress her. I wanted to create a space she could see herself in.

She was tired, and I should have let her sleep. But Mirabella understood her fucking power. She pretended like she didn't, but she knew exactly how to drive me to the brink of fucking need. And when she did, I had to fucking check myself over the definition of *consent*.

Mirabella Castle caused me to be totally out of control, wild, and fucking wanton. And that was only part of her allure.

Now, as we laid in my bed up on the second floor, she had been thoroughly fucked, deliciously fed, and gently bathed. Surely, she was ready to sleep. But of course, Mirabella had trouble knowing when to stop fucking talking.

"I love this bed," she said in a sleepy voice while looking at me, like she was considering letting me fuck her right then.

If Mirabella was tired when she arrived, fucking her three times since then must have left her exhausted, but she fought sleep, even as she lay on four-thousand-dollar sheets made from the highest quality Egyptian Cotton Giza forty-five.

"Maybe you should close your eyes, Mira," I said, not even realizing the warning in my tone.

She smiled a happy, tired smile.

"You never finished telling me about the money," she said.

I sighed at her insistence, but also secretly welcomed the opportunity to have her again if she was determined to stay awake.

"I have several sources of income. I make an annual salary as CEO at Magellan Media. So, like everyone else, I get paid every two weeks."

"Direct deposit?"

I laughed at her strange question.

"Yes, direct deposit."

"Is that it?"

"I also get bonuses at Magellan Media for performance. Then I get a payment monthly from my personal trust and the Magellan Family trust. I also get payments from my investments and whatnot."

I reached over and began touching her beautiful face, running my index finger along her jaw line and then under the chin and back again. She made a tiny moan, closed her eyes, and smiled with her eyes still closed.

"How often do you get bonuses?"

"Quarterly."

"Nice."

"Honestly, it's stupid. I shouldn't be drawing a salary. I don't need any more money."

Mirabella opened her eyes.

"You can donate your salary. Use it to create a scholarship for children of Magellan employees or something like that."

"What an awesome idea; I'll mention it to Akila on Monday," I said, amazed by how Mirabella came up with stuff like this even when she was dog-tired and nearly asleep.

"How much would that be then?"

"I make about one hundred eighty-eight million dollars per year now from all sources, meaning I actually receive that as cash before taxes."

"Holy shit. How much of that is from your salary as CEO of Magellan Media?"

"Maybe about sixty million? More with options."

"That's a lot of potential scholarships. You could even do ones that reflect what each member of your family was into. I read how your mother loved art."

It was both amazing and weird that Mirabella had read things online about my family.

"Yeah. It would be great if you could run it."

"Run what?"

"The scholarship fund we create."

"We?"

"It was your idea. I don't want to do it without you."

"Mitchell, I can't have anything to do with you publicly. Technically, being here right now makes me in breach of contract with Brennan Enterprises."

"That's the next thing we need to work on; getting you out of that bullshit contract."

"I like my job at Brennan Enterprises."

"I know, but it's fucking bad for my business. And if I'm being honest, Mirabella, the fact that you and Brennan Enterprises are profiting off me being an asshole makes me angry."

"You acting like an asshole makes you angry or, me having a job that pays me and which I was only able to get because you decided getting a blow job was more important than interviewing me for a job in which we could have worked closely together makes you angry?"

Mirabella was sitting up now, her fight fully back.

"Fucking all of it, Mirabella. Ok?"

I hated everything about it, and it was embarrassing, wrong, and stupid. I fucked up big time, and despite the fact that I got to have Mirabella in my life in this way, I hated that we had to hide our relationship. I hated that I had been the one to agree to it, caving at the last minute because I wanted to protect Preston from learning he was the child of rape.

"Well, none of it probably matters now that there are actual photos of us holding hands outside of the funeral home and ones of me getting into your car."

"I'm surprised Hyacinth hasn't been calling you non-fucking stop."

My phone had been ringing and dinging so much, I had to put it on *silent*. Even still, constant vibrations let me know the media was not going to stop until they had an official statement from me on the status of my relationship with Mirabella. I didn't want that for her, having to live in a fishbowl with the media and everyone with an internet connection analyzing and commenting on everything she did. And yet, that's how it had been for Mirabella since the day I canceled our interview. Only now, it was about to get way fucking worse.

"I turned my phone all the way off. I'll deal with her on Tuesday."

"Tuesday?"

"Yeah, I took tomorrow off."

I couldn't resist giving her the you-know-what-that-means look. She giggled and buried her head under my armpit like she does when she's embarrassed. The fact that my girl was still embarrassed about the idea of sex with me cracked me up. She was still so fucking innocent and inexperienced.

"Are you happy there, at Brennan Enterprises? Those pictures of us could have an enormous impact on your brand and all your licensing deals. I mean, I don't think they are stupid enough to fire you."

Mirabella peeked out from under me like a fucking turtle.

"I am happy there except for the occasional shit Hyacinth gives me about you. She'd said that if the pace of deals continues, I might make two hundred thousand dollars this year or something like that. Now? Who knows what's going to happen?"

"That would be amazing if deals continued at that pace. I'm so proud of you."

I said it even though I was concerned that perhaps something I had done, something as simple as grabbing her hand knowing everyone was watching, could ruin everything for her. And if I was being one hundred percent honest, maybe I wanted us to get caught. Maybe I'd wanted to fucking claim her in front of the world.

"Are you really?" she said, coming fully out from under me now, possibly detecting a tone of insincerity from me.

"Look, it's no secret how I feel about Brennan. It's also no secret that their success is bad for Magellan. But *your* success is good for me personally because it's good for you. I just hope my actions, being so selfish, haven't hurt your chances."

"That means so much to me. Thank you," she said, smiling. "Does it bother you that I asked about your money?" Her smile turned into an expression of concern.

"No. I'm surprised you didn't ask me sooner. But since we're talking about possible uncomfortable topics, I have been wondering about something."

Concern spread across her face.

"What?"

"How many men have you been with?"

"Two. But have only had full intercourse with one." Mirabella answered without hesitation.

"Full intercourse?"

I kept my smirk at bay for as long as I could.

"Like penetration and completion," she said all professional like.

"Oh. You said Ben couldn't stay hard long enough to satisfy you. Did he ever come inside you?"

"That's direct."

"I'm sorry but I really need to know."

"Need?"

"Ok. *Want*. I really *want* to know."

"Why?"

"Because I'm a fucking jealous asshole."

"But that was before I knew you."

I looked down, immediately thinking about all the shit I had done with women before I met her and what I would say if she finally asked.

"So yes then?"

"No. He didn't. He never came inside me," Mirabella said in a small voice.

"You didn't want him to? You didn't let him?"

The smirk was making its way across my face.

"I didn't . . . He couldn't . . . We didn't get that far."

Mirabella struggled to articulate exactly what she wanted to say.

"And you? Did you come with Ben?"

Mirabella looked defeated now, like my questions were wearing her down.

"I don't think so. Maybe. I'm . . . Not sure."

I didn't know what to say. I didn't know how it was possible to not know if you have had an orgasm or not. And for the life of me, I could not let it go.

"And this other guy?"

"Mitchell, I have only ever had an orgasm with you. I've never even been able to achieve one when I've tried touching myself."

Holy shit.

"Why didn't you tell me?"

"Because my inexperience is embarrassing, considering your past." She looked down at the milk-white sheets as if she was going to cry.

I pulled Mirabella's chin up toward me so she could look at me now.

"Embarrassing? Do you know how good it makes me feel to know that I'm the only guy who's ever made you come?"

Fuck; my dick started twitching, getting hotter and engorged.

"I feel so insecure sometimes when we're together, wondering if you talked to other girls like that, if you called them 'baby' the way you do me. If you touched them like you do me. If you had sex with them in your cars, your plane, your fucking bathtub, in this fucking bed on these fucking sheets."

And as she talked, she began to cry.

"Mira. I have never brought a woman to my home before. You are the first woman I have wanted to bring here."

I wiped her tears as fast as they fell.

"What about Cassandra Reed? I read about her online."

"So, you're Googling me now? Is this how you plan to get to know me?"

"Don't change the fucking subject," Mirabella said.

"I lived on a boat when I dated Cassandra."

"How long were you guys together?"

She'd stopped crying, and now was only sniffling.

"Like a year and a half."

Mirabella seemed to be thinking about her next question.

"Were you in love with her?"

"At the time I thought maybe I was. But I realized later that it was the stability and routine that I loved."

"Was she in love with you?"

"I think so."

"What does that mean? Did she tell you she loved you?"

"Yes," I said fucking hating to recall the pain I had caused her.

"Why'd you guys break up?"

What came out of my mouth next had to be the truth, no matter how horrible it was. If I lied to Mirabella about this, she would never trust me. And yet, I couldn't stand to see the disappointed look I knew would come if I told her what I had done. So, I didn't respond.

I'd seen the look on Mirabella's face before. It's how cops look when they question you. She watched me intently, her eyes searching for the slightest change. And when I broke eye contact for that one second, I gave myself away.

"You cheated on her," she said.

"Yes." I chose to be honest despite being fearful of her reaction.

"Thank you for telling me the truth," she said, even though I was more cowardly than forthright right then.

"How does it make you feel knowing you're with someone who cheated on his girlfriend?"

"It makes me think I would be stupid to trust you."

"It's different with us. I'm not the same person I was five years ago. Heck, I'm not the same person I was a year ago. Even nine fucking months ago."

She stared at me, expressionless. It seemed as if her exhaustion was hitting her once more, as she positioned herself comfortably on her pillow.

"Before when you asked me if I was yours, what did you mean by that?"

"I wanted to know if you considered yourself my girl?"

"What does it mean to be Mitchell Magellan's girl?"

"I want to be the man you share *everything* with. Your good days, bad days, your hopes, your dreams, your nightmares, your fears, your body, your successes, your thoughts, your failures, your orgasms."

I trailed my fingers across, up, and down her body, ghosting and blowing on her sensitive skin as I told her what I wanted.

"Mitchell..." She moaned a tiny moan when she said my name.

"Mirabella, I want to be the man who knows how to make you feel good and does it just to put a smile on your face. I want to be the one you confide in, take advice from, who listens to you."

By then, I was trailing kisses on her neck right on that ticklish spot that made her squirm. Mira put her hand in my hair, and that shit awakened all the nerves on my skin. I must have moaned now, because she smiled at me and said, "What else?"

"I want to fucking take care of you in every single way a man can take care of a woman." I lightly licked her nipple and then blew on it.

"Mitchell..."

"I don't want you to fucking hide from me. I want you to give yourself to me completely, to trust me, and believe in me. I want to dream with you. Plan with you. Build with you. And Mira. Fucking. Bella." I accentuated each of her names as I sucked her nipples between my lips. "When I want to fucking touch you..." I moved my hand down to her mound and held it there long enough to make her react the way I wanted her to.

And when she raised her hips off the bed, I slid a finger into her pussy. She arched her back, closed her eyes, and moaned some more. "I don't want to have to ask permission. If you are *fucking mine*, then you are mine to touch whenever the fuck I want and however the fuck I want."

I removed my finger from her pussy and ran it across her bottom lip. She smiled a lazy smile at me, and said, "Why'd you stop?"

I smiled back, and then licked her slickness off her bottom lip before kissing her and climbing on top of her. Using my knee to spread her legs, I found myself exactly where I wanted to be.

She moaned again, the anticipation of what I was about to do evident.

"I'm sorry I stopped, Mira. Let me make it up to you."

"How exactly are you going to do that?" She whined out, her voice full of desire and emotion.

I kissed Mirabella as I buried myself deep inside her, not stopping until I reached my destination. And, by the look on her face, she was satisfied with my answer.

EVEN SLOW, sensual, delicious sex was not enough to get Mirabella to stop asking me questions. I had mistakenly thought I'd told her everything there was to know about Cassandra and my relationship with her. But Mira seemed to contemplate what I'd said before, like there was a clue missing from the mystery of Mitchell Magellan, and she was determined to find it. Tonight.

"Why did you cheat on her?"

"Because I was a selfish and immature prick."

"And now?"

"Mirabella . . . I wish I had known you sooner. My life could have looked a lot different if we had met even one year ago. But we didn't, and I was a different person then. I had a lot of sexual encounters with a lot of different women. For the most part, they were blow jobs. I never really even kissed them or touched them. I never wanted to."

She seemed surprised and subdued by my admission.

"It goes both ways, Mitchell," she said as the weight of her statement had me thinking about the extortion looming over my head. Now was the perfect time to come clean and to demonstrate my loyalty to her.

"It does, and I am ready to commit to being all yours, Mirabella. And to prove how serious I am, there's something I haven't told you that I need to."

Mirabella sat up again, fear on her face.

"Do I want to know what it is?"

"Probably not. But, if we are really going to be all the way in, then I owe it to you to tell you the truth."

"Ok, just tell me then."

I looked down at the sheets now, attempting to build up my courage. When I looked back at Mirabella, a small tear ran down her face.

"I'm being extorted."

"What? How? By whom?"

I sighed.

"I don't know. But it's probably the same person who leaked the video of you in the lobby the day of your interview and the same person who leaked info about Peter Trenom that resulted in his indictment and subsequent arrest. They have video and audio footage of all the offices on the Executive Floor."

"Oh. Why does this not sound so bad? I mean, I thought you were going to tell me that you had already cheated on me."

"No, Baby. It's not that. This person has threatened to release footage of my office extracurricular activities," I said, doing my best to fucking sugarcoat it, but she still didn't seem to get it.

"I don't understand," she said, doe eyed. She looked so perfect and innocent that she may have even been feeling bad for me right then.

"Mirabella, they are planning to release the video of me getting a blow job from Marissa from Accounting at the very same time I was supposed to be interviewing you. I'm so fucking sorry."

It would have been better if I had kicked her in the fucking stomach. Mirabella broke in that moment, as the realization of what I'd said hit her.

"Oh my God, Mitchell. Pay the fucking money. I cannot have this video and my name as part of that narrative be released. Please. You have to pay them."

"Baby, I will but it seems they don't want money. They want to destroy and humiliate me."

I pulled her into my arms and held her as we both sat quietly lost in thought. And even though I was only indirectly responsible for her pain, I felt wholly and personally responsible for healing it.

The fact that something I did in a moment of complete selfishness and weakness when we didn't even know one another could hurt her this much made me feel like shit. And yet, if I hadn't and I had just interviewed her like I was supposed to, I don't think we would be together right now. So, it was hard to feel remorse in this moment, but it would be impossible for me to get her to see it that way.

I was so in my feelings that I didn't realize when Mirabella had stopped crying. And, when she was calm and able to speak again, she sat up and looked expectantly at me, her eyes sad and her expression one of defeat.

"Is there *anything* you did with me for the first time, Mitchell?"

Her question threw me off guard. I had already told her I had never had a woman in my apartment before. So, everything we had done here together was a first time for me. But given what was happening now, and how much I had already hurt and humiliated her, and what was to come if this fucker actually released this tape, I had to come clean to Mirabella about something else.

"Yes."

"What?" she said, sleepy, beautiful, and broken.

"I fell in love."

CHAPTER TEN

MIRABELLA CASTLE

In the forty-eight hours since my tour had ended, RayRay and Mena came to visit me in Portugal, Mena's mom died, and Mitchell Magellan told me that he had fallen in love with me. Now, as exhausted as I was after attending Mena's mother's wake, having sex with Mitchell in his Maybach, on his couch, in the bathtub, and in his bed, and with jet lag settling in, I should have been tired enough to sleep for a week.

But the looming shitstorm brewing caused by us holding hands and me getting into his car and the extortion video of him getting a blow job instead of interviewing me kept me awake as Mitchell slept peacefully beside me, completely spent. And yet, I couldn't help but notice how gorgeous he was. I found myself wondering if he was dreaming and then what he was dreaming about. As I mused and stared at him, anxiety and intrusive thoughts did their best to creep in, hoping I would allow them to fill my mind with self-doubt and fear.

The clock on Mitchell's nightstand read 4:30*am*. I had been staring into space since Mitchell fell asleep about four hours ago. And since I wanted him to get some rest, I rummaged through his closet, put on one of his sweatshirts and a pair of sweatpants. I'd intended to go make myself some tea. Between his revelations about cheating, his use of the "L" word, and my general anxiety about facing Hyacinth over those photos of us holding hands, I was wide awake.

"Mira, you in here?" he said, his voice groggy from sleep. And as he rounded the walk-in closet's door and he laid eyes on me in his clothes, he became noticeably erect.

"I didn't mean to wake you, Mitchell. I was gonna go downstairs," I said, thinking about how I could scoot past him and brush up against his erection in a subtle way.

"It's good that you didn't do that. You would have set off the alarm."

"Oh," I said, staring dreamily at this handsome fucking man, here amongst his things, the air already charging, arousal thick and buzzy all around us.

Mitchell looked so fucking good. His hair was a little messy and his facial hair was about a two o'clock shadow. I couldn't resist; I had to go to him and put my arms around his neck and kiss him. It started slowly with deep delicious kisses. Soon Mitchell's hands were all over me, under my borrowed sweatshirt, and inside my borrowed sweatpants. And when he felt only my naked body underneath, it did something to him.

In his closet, clothed in his sweats, I let Mitchell Magellan finger me until I came. When I could barely stand, he said, "I'll bring you up some tea. Get back in bed."

He began to walk away despite the giant tent in his underwear.

"Wait," I said. "Thank you."

I kissed his mouth, feeling grateful for his presence in my life right then. No one had ever treated me like Mitchell did. He was giving, supportive, and warm. He made certain I was taken care of and cared for.

I returned to bed as Mitchell had instructed me to. He went to the bathroom to wash his hands, and before he went downstairs, I called him to me. When he came, I tried not to look to see if he was still turned on.

"I can make my own tea, you know," I said, suddenly sleepy.

Mitchell kissed my nose, and began to walk away.

"Mitchell," I said as I pulled him back to me.

I must have looked needy and dumb, but I put his hand on my left breast. Mitchell's eyes nearly popped out of his head as he moaned at the feel of me.

"You need more, Baby?" he asked, desire coming out of every one of his pores.

"Yes." My voice was weak and pleading. I was thirsty for him and hungry for his attention despite what he had given me in the closet. My need for him was surprising. I never knew it could be like this. That I could be with someone whom I simply could never get enough of. Whose hands I wanted on me constantly.

"Mirabella," he said as if it was the last thing he would ever say.

I pulled him onto the bed, raised the covers up so he could get under them with me, and spread my legs for him. Mitchell pulled his t-shirt off with one hand, and it was the sexiest fucking thing. I sat up so I could kiss him. And when he turned his head slightly, it was because his eyes were wet.

"Mitchell," I said, unsure what I should actually say.

He slowly turned to me.

"Look at what you do to me," he said, tears in his eyes but too proud to let them fall.

"Mitchell . . ." I said, building up some courage. It was now or never. I was too scared to admit it before but now, I had to. I needed to. "I'm so in love with you."

"Don't fucking say it unless you really mean it." He stared at me intently.

I pulled my borrowed sweatpants down and then off. I then quickly pulled his briefs off. And when Mitchell hesitated, I pushed him into my throbbing pussy still slick from my orgasm.

"I love you, Mitchell Magellan. I need you inside me."

Just then, Mitchell moved slowly out and back in again, moaning as he did.

"Say it again, Mira," he breathed out.

"I love you," I said.

Mitchell felt so good; I was feeling heady and emotional.

Our sex was slow, sweet, deep torture.

I kissed him and rocked my body against his with such need there was no way he didn't know how I felt. There was no longer a reason to deny my feelings for this man. My need for this man. My love for this man.

IT WAS nine-thirty in the morning when I next opened my eyes.

Mitchell and I had decided to spend Monday in bed after the media camped outside his apartment. And when I finally chose to check my messages, my voicemail was full. It had four messages from Hyacinth, one from Mena, one from my grandma, several from reporters looking for a statement about the pictures of us holding hands, and two from RayRay.

My texts were not any better. Apparently, my moment with Mitchell Magellan was front-page news.

Mitchell's PR team was thrilled because it was something other than the investigation and arrest of Peter Trenom. If I'd spoken to Hyacinth, I'd know if the stunt we'd pulled had jeopardized potential new licenses or current ones for their 'million-dollar-brand.'

Starving from the near twenty-four hours of sex, we ordered breakfast in. Mitchell may have gone a bit overboard because when I exited the shower, he'd set out a spread of croissants, bagels, lox, three different cream cheeses, various butters from France, eggs, bacon, sausage, potatoes, mixed fruit, yogurt, tea, and coffee on the kitchen table.

He was already having coffee when I joined him, a half-eaten croissant, some eggs, fruit, and bacon on his plate.

"How was your shower?"

"Lonely," I said as Mitchell ran his eyes over me.

I kissed his mouth, then sat next to him at the kitchen table.

"I'm sorry, Mirabella. I needed to make some calls."

"It's ok," I said. And really, it was. I had begun to feel a little sore from all the attention Mitchell had paid to my vagina.

Mitchell prepared a plate for me and poured me some coffee.

"Thank you," I said, loving how politeness and gratitude was part of our couple culture. Just then I had to push thoughts of my shitty relationship with Ben from my mind. Ben who would never do anything for me unless I asked. And even then, he would either do it half-assed and act as if he had to move mountains to do something as simple as holding my hand.

"You're very welcome." He passed me the plate.

"I think I'm gonna text Hyacinth," I said, devouring a little bit of everything he'd made me.

"To say what?" Mitchell's tone let me know he didn't approve and the look on his face told me he was thinking, *Where does she put all that food?*

"To apologize," I said in a tiny voice with a mouth full of eggs.

"You're gonna apologize for being with me?"

Mitchell's question told me he was feeling wounded by my proposed conversation with my boss.

"Yes. Only in the sense that I should have been honest with her. She should not have found out this way. And, if she wants to fire me, I'll accept that. I should not have put her in this position."

Whatever Mitchell was going to say in response, he kept it to himself, the only sounds he made coming from him sipping his coffee. He had a block when it came to Hyacinth, and no matter what I said, he would likely oppose or take issue with it somehow.

"I hate that I have a job that puts limits on my personal life," I said.

"Come work for me at Magellan. You can run the scholarship program," Mitchell said as if I hadn't already told him no.

"If I get fired from Brennan, I may take you up on that."

"Mirabella. If you get fired from Brennan Enterprises, it will be the second-best day of your life."

"Oh? And what was the first?" I teased my sexy boyfriend.

"The day you fucking met me. And, Mirabella," he said, putting his coffee aside.

"Yes." I chewed a piece of bacon.

"Hurry up and finish eating so I can bury myself inside you."

This. Fucking. Man.

ALL THE WAY OUT

I MUST HAVE FALLEN asleep because I woke up again at 2:30pm starving. Mitchell was in bed next to me shirtless and typing on his laptop. And when I said, "Good morning, again," he put his laptop down, and put his hands on me.

"I was waiting for you to wake up."

With a sexy and satisfied smirk, he buried his face between my legs.

"I NEED TO GET BACK HOME," I said to Mitchell at 8:30pm.

"If I can't figure out how to get you out of here without the paparazzi noticing, you aren't going anywhere."

"I know you want to protect me. But I'm a big girl. I can take care of myself. I can't hide here all week."

Mitchell wiped his mouth on his napkin and pushed his plate of butter chicken forward so he could lean on the table with both elbows.

"That's what this was to you? A place to hide?"

I couldn't tell if he was upset or merely curious.

"Yes. And a place to rest. And get to know you. And yes, hide from the world so I could get lost in you. But Mitchell, I have to go back home," I said. And I'm not gonna lie, Mitchell fucking Magellan was looking at me like I was a whole free dessert.

Mitchell looked tortured, and aroused, and sad, and contemplative.

"I was hoping you would consider making *this* your home. I mean not *here* but maybe we could move in together. Get a place together. You could pick it out," Mitchell said, leaning forward and cupping my face now.

I smiled at the idea of this man. If anyone had told me I would be sitting in his kitchen talking about moving in together, sore from all the sex, I would never have believed them.

I took his hand from my face and held it in mine, hoping to connect with him on this.

"Mitchell, I love you. I want to be with you."

"But?" He pushed.

"But this is all really fast for me. Can we slow down a little? Let things settle? You have so much going on. I gave Brennan Enterprises a reason to fire me, and I have to make that right. I need to be there for Mena and RayRay and Christina. I need to find time for Jared to visit."

"You can just say you don't want to live together, Mirabella," Mitchell challenged me, not breaking eye contact with me.

I stood and moved to sit on his lap. And when he saw what I intended to do, he moved his chair away from the table so that I had room to. The way this man anticipated my actions changed my brain's chemistry. He was responsive, attentive, and curious.

I put my arms around his neck and kissed him gently and deeply. He responded by moaning, a bulge growing in his pants like we hadn't been fucking every few hours.

"I'm not making excuses. I promise. I just want us to make sure we're ok and able to enjoy it if we decide to live together."

I searched his face to see if he understood.

"Life's not gonna always be easy, Mirabella."

"I know. I just . . . need some time."

Mitchell picked me up then and carried me to the couch. The anticipation of what he had in store for me stirred in my loins, despite how sore I was feeling. And as he laid me down on my back and positioned himself between my legs, I had a feeling I was going to be even more sore than I was at that moment.

"Mitchell," I said. "I'm so sore. Be gentle."

"Baby. I just want to taste you some more. I'll be so gentle, Mira."

"Mitchell," I breathed out, his mouth such sweet delicious fucking torture. I wanted this man with everything I had. Everything I was.

"Mirabella, when I said I was all the way in, I fucking meant it. If you don't want to be all the fucking way in, then you are all the way out. There's no fucking in between. I don't want to play games. Which is it going to be, Mirabella? *All the way in?* Or . . ."

Mitchell's face was suddenly inches away from mine. I was lost in his fucking eyes, overwhelmed in that moment. Brought to tears by this man's beautiful, tortured face as he pushed his manhood inside me when he said 'all the way in,' I moaned, the pain of being sore mixing with the pleasure of him filling me.

"*All the way out?*" he said, vacating my soaked pussy. He was going to make me beg.

Mitchell held his twitching dick, then began stroking it from root to tip, pre-cum all over his hand.

I was so turned on now, I didn't care if I was sore. My vagina was clenching and my clit was throbbing. I needed Mitchell so fucking badly.

"I'm all the way in, Mitchell. I promise," I said, but he didn't put himself back inside me. So, I had to take matters into my own fucking hands.

I kissed him, and he let me. And when we both started feeling like we couldn't fucking breathe without the other one, like the only way to get the air we needed to live was to fuck? We gave in, and soon, he was back inside me relentlessly pumping hard and fast. And when he raised me up just enough to get a finger into my ass, I came from the fucking anticipation.

"I'm coming, Mitchell," I said as I exploded all over him.

And when he felt me coming on him, he came too.

Mitchell moaned his contentment and kissed my nose.

We laid there, coming down and breathing fast, tangled up skin-to-skin, the smell of sex in the air. There was so much I wanted to say to him before I left. So much still we hadn't discussed. I wanted to ask him about his past. To ask about the other women. I wanted to ask about his brother, Alexander. His fiancé. I wanted to know more about his friends. His cousin. But there wasn't time because Mitchell said, "Let's shower, and then I'll get Brendan to take you home."

I smiled a tired, sore smile, and said, "I'll shower upstairs. Your ass is showering down here."

Mitchell feigned an innocent hurt look.

"Ok, Baby," he said, "call me if you need me."

And that was just it. I needed Mitchell Magellan more than he would ever know.

MITCHELL INSISTED on riding back to Queens with me. And despite the paparazzi following our car, I fell asleep in his arms on the way there. When we arrived, the paparazzi were camped outside of my apartment too. The plan was for Brendan to get me out and shield me with an umbrella while he took me inside. He'd bring my bags in after that.

Before we exited the vehicle, Mitchell kissed me as if he wouldn't soon see me again.

"Call me later. I'm not getting out with you because I don't want to give them more fodder. Brendan will take your bags in for you."

"When will I see you again?" I said, suddenly and already missing him.

"I actually can't until Thursday, and only between eleven and two."

"Oh," I said, disappointed.

"Maybe we can make it a long weekend. Go away?"

"I told RayRay I would watch Christina on Saturday. He has to work."

Mitchell looked disappointed now too.

"Let's plan on having a long lunch on Thursday. And then maybe an early dinner on Friday," Mitchell said.

And as I kissed him goodbye once more, Thursday seemed so far away.

CHAPTER ELEVEN

MITCHELL MAGELLAN

IF I WASN'T AVOIDING THE MEDIA AND DODGING CALLS AND TEXTS from journalists and Aunt Meg, I was in back-to-back-to-back meetings through around two-thirty. I had to constantly push thoughts of Mirabella from my mind in order to be present. Not to mention how fucking exhausted I was. I was going to have to figure out a way to sleep around her. To stop fucking touching her.

After my last meeting, I checked my phone to see if Mirabella had called or texted. And when she hadn't, I texted her.

> ME: I miss my girl.

> MIRABELLA: Miss my very sexy boyfriend

> ME: He misses you too. U ok?

> ME: RayRay sent over some bouncers he knows to help me get out of my apartment. They made sure I got to work safely

> ME: Remind me to thank RayRay

> **MIRABELLA:** Can't stop thinking about you
>
> **ME:** Me too, baby

Mirabella's texts were enough to put a fucking smile on my face for the rest of the day. I had a business dinner scheduled for tonight. I was thinking of asking her if she would come panty-less to the same restaurant, sit at the table next to mine, and let me watch her eat. And then, when I was fucking ready, I would take her into a bathroom stall and feed her my cock for dessert.

If she objected to that idea, I was thinking that maybe she would sit at the table with me, and whenever I asked her to, she would lick my fingers. That she could be my human napkin. And when she had licked them clean, I would put them into her pussy and make her come, right in front of my dinner guests. And then she would lick herself off my fingers, and I would turn to my guests and say, "Where were we?"

But I had to keep my fantasies in check. We weren't exactly there yet. Mirabella didn't know that side of me. The side that wanted to do things most women only agreed to do when they were paid to.

Happy that Mirabella and I were making progress, I focused on my work, and prepared for my meeting with Akila, who seemed to sense that I was distracted more than normal.

I was practically beaming when I told Akila about Mirabella's scholarship idea, and when she said, "Mirabella Castle doesn't work for Magellan Media, sir," I was fucking pissed.

"You think I don't know that, Akila? Please just message her and work with her on this. She's got a lot of amazing ideas about programs for Magellan Media staffers and families. Maybe you can ask her out to lunch or something. Pick her brain. I'm sure the two of you will enjoy working together."

"Oh? And why is that?"

Akila was in a challenge-the-fuck-out-of-Mitchell mood today.

"Because you're both insanely smart, you both care about the impact you're having on people's lives, and you both want to see Magellan Media be an amazing place to work."

"So, you're not going to mention the pictures? Seems the cat's out of the bag officially now, huh?"

I smirked, not willing to give her more than that. Akila had managed, as far as I knew, to keep my relationship with Mirabella a secret since Christina's Gotcha Party. I should really have indulged her on this a bit more.

"Can you please just make it happen, Akila?" I said, instead, not wanting to gossip about my own relationship.

"Yes, sir," she said, taking to calling me 'sir' again, suddenly. And today in particular, she seemed to be disinterested in looking at me directly, casting her eyes down and averting mine whenever possible.

What the fuck, Akila?

Just as I was about to challenge her about whatever the fuck her problem was with me and Mirabella, both our phones began dinging and ringing with alerts and calls. Out of courtesy, we both ignored it for a minute or so. But as both phones became impossible to ignore, we both looked.

On mine was a video and a report.

Mitchell Magellan caught with pants down

Scroll

Magellan Media executive takes personal meeting to a whole new level

Scroll

Mirabella Castle deserves an apology

Scroll

Mitchell Magellan caught on tape having oral sex

Scroll

Now we know why Mitchell Magellan canceled interview with Mirabella Castle

Scroll

Another scandal rocks embattled Magellan Media

End scroll

Motherfucker! The audio and video tapes have been released.

Suddenly a knock came at the door. It was Clara, Sherilyn, and Cindy.

Akila finally looked in my eyes then. On her face now? Nothing but panic and sympathy.

I turned toward the door, uncomfortable now with how Akila was looking at me and how all three of my assistants hesitated to enter my office, as if afraid, unsure, un-fucking-comfortable like I wasn't the same person I was this fucking morning. Like they'd seen me getting my dick sucked.

"Come in. Please shut the door," I said in a solemn voice.

They all stood, rather than sitting, each with a look on her face that told me they had either seen the video or listened to the audio. Neither was considered "work-appropriate" material, not even in our divisions where erotic content was worked on.

I cleared my throat and stood. I had already prepared this speech. Already decided what I would say to my team. But now, when the day actually came, I was uncertain. I cleared my throat again, hoping doing so would provide me with the courage I needed to face the woman in my work life who have probably just witnessed a side of me I would rather they had not seen.

"First and foremost, I want to apologize to each of you. There is no excuse for my behavior, so I won't give one." I looked at Akila, wondering if she was fucking done with me now. But she hid from my scrutiny, her eyes fixed on my shoes.

Sherilyn cleared her throat. I turned my attention back to my support staff, lined up against the wall like a firing squad, waiting for the bullet.

"I would understand if any of you wants to tender their resignation at this time. I don't want you feeling as if you have to defend me or justify why you would continue to work for me. And, Cindy, I'm especially sorry for not being even half the man my father was, someone you were proud to work for," I said, meaning every single fucking word.

Clara's eyes were cast down, as if she didn't want to see me looking contrite or embarrassed. Like it was as simple as being caught with my fly open. Cindy had tears in her eyes, like she was watching the son of a dear friend self-destruct and was unable to do anything about it. And Sherilyn, she looked all together horrified. She was literally shaking.

When no one spoke, Akila rescued me. She stood, straightened her outfit, and said, "Ladies, why don't we give Mr. Magellan a moment alone to collect his thoughts and you time to collect yours."

I nodded, sorry that Akila had to step in to save me from this torturous situation I had put myself in.

The four of them couldn't fucking get out of there fast enough. And when Akila took the long way out so that she didn't have to pass me, it broke me.

And when she closed the door to my office, leaving me alone with my thoughts, they immediately turned to the only thing I truly cared about losing: Mirabella.

I dialed her. Her voicemail was full.

I texted her.

> ME: Baby, I'm so sorry. Please let me know you're OK. I will send a car to get you and bring you back to my apartment. Or anywhere you want to go. Please let me know you're OK.

> MIRABELLA: *read*

I clicked on the first link, and that is where I made my mistake. It was the audio version.

The sound of my own voice playing back to me sounded so foreign. The guy who was getting head in this audio recording sounded like me but also so unlike me. He was rough and demanding. He was fucking nasty.

"LICK THE TIP FOR ME, *lick all that fucking pre-cum off.*"

"*Let me see you wear it like lipstick.*"

"*I'm gonna put my dick so far down your throat, you're gonna gag on it.*"

"*I wish I was in your fucking ass right now.*"

"*Get on your fucking knees and open your mouth.*"

"*Come here. Let me fuck your gorgeous mouth.*"

"Yeah, suck it, just like that."

"What are you fucking doing? Are you playing with your pussy?"

"Let me fucking see you play with it."

"Take it deeper."

"You like when I spit inside you?"

"I bet you're wishing I was fucking you right now. Fucking tell me you want me to fuck you."

I SHOULD HAVE BEEN TURNED on. I should have had a outrageous hard-on the size of my fucking arm. But all that I had right then was a sick feeling in the pit of my stomach thinking about how Mirabella would feel if she heard this. And the only thing that could possibly make it worse was the fucking video.

I dialed Braxton but it went to voicemail.

I called Aunt Meg on her cell and at home and got no answer in either place.

I even called Gina Abruzzi-Torres, and got her voicemail.

When I called Anna, she picked up.

"Please meet me in my office, can you?"

"I'm already on my way," she said, and I was glad she had been looking out for me because I was about to lose my fucking shit.

I called RayRay. He picked up before the first ring finished.

"Mitchell? Don't involve me in your shit. I'm at work, and I cannot even fucking deal. So just imagine how Mirabella feels right now. Give her some space. Let her be. You hear me?" RayRay whisper-screamed into the phone.

"I just need to know she's ok," I said.

"Ok? Ok? Have you lost your whole damn mind?" RayRay sounded like he was fast model-walking.

"Yes. I need to know she's ok. I need to see her."

"Oh, now I know you have lost your damn mind. Mirabella will not be seeing anyone, especially not you. Go on with your life, Mitchell. Handle your business. Leave Mirabella alone. And if you don't, if you show up at her apartment or at her office, she will take out a restraining order on you faster than you can say, 'I'm gonna shoot my load down your fucking throat'."

RayRay hung up the phone.

Just then, Sherilyn buzzed. Clearly, she hadn't yet quit.

"Yes, Sherilyn," I said.

"Hyacinth Rose is on the line."

The only thing she could possibly have wanted was to gloat. And if I dared speak to her the way I was feeling right now, I would say the wrong thing. Then, I would be giving Mirabella another reason to be angry with me after I told her boss to go fuck herself. And since I was full up on audio of me saying and doing the wrong fucking things, I declined to speak to her.

"I'm not available. Thank you."

Braxton called me back.

"Braxton, what the fucking hell? Who released this shit and what do they fucking want?"

"Well, Mitchell, since no demands came prior to the release of the video the only thing I can come up with is this is someone who doesn't want or need money. This person is out to embarrass you. To tank Magellan stock."

"Well, FUCK!" I said.

"Have you spoken to your attorneys? Will there be an injunction to stop further dissemination and distribution of the tapes?"

"I haven't been able to reach anyone as of yet. But knowing Gina, it's already happening."

"It's not like you to leave something so important to chance, Mitchell. Are you still interested in my advice?"

I wasn't sure how to answer Braxton right then.

"Yes. Of course," I said.

"You need to focus on the important stuff. Get that injunction. If the girl won't see you, maybe it's for the best right now. Keep your head in the game. Keep your circle tight. And Mitchell," Braxton paused for effect and was about to continue when I interrupted him.

"Wait. You know about Mirabella? What do you know?"

"Mirabella? I don't know anything about Mirabella. Was referring to Marissa Canto, the woman in the video. I hear she wants to file a sexual harassment lawsuit."

"Jesus."

"Well, I'm not a lawyer but I'm pretty sure they will tell you not to talk to her, Mitchell. Don't accept any communication from her at all. Don't comment on her to the media or anyone else for that matter. Send all inquiries to Gina."

"Of course, Braxton. I want to know who is behind all of this. And I am not going to be crying in my fucking office, feeling sorry for myself. I had consensual sexual relations with an employee. There's video of our first elevator ride. Get it. She asks if she can 'see my office.' And once she's in there, she asks if she can do anything for me. If she wasn't into it, she could have said "no" at any fucking time. The audio and video are doctored. Nowhere is the conversation we'd had before or after that encounter."

"I'm on it. And, Mitchell?"

"What?"

"Why do you think she wants to claim sexual assault?"

"Because someone is offering her more money than she can ever imagine."

"No other reason?"

"Does there need to be another fucking reason?"

"Calm down, Mitchell. I'm on your side. I'm asking you if there is a reason why this woman might be feeling . . . *scorned* . . . that maybe there has been a misunderstanding about consent?"

"I'm telling you right now, the tape is doctored. What I did to her, she was one hundred percent on board with. She fucking asked me to do it. She suggested it. So, why would Marissa be feeling scorned?"

"When was the last time you had a *personal meeting* with Ms. Canto?"

I don't know why I didn't think of it sooner. The last time I had a scheduled 'personal meeting' with Marissa was the day I was supposed to meet with Mirabella. And I canceled all others after that. Even before I'd touched her, Mirabella had ruined me for all other women.

"It was the very same day of that missed interview with Mirabella Castle."

"And do you find that suspicious?"

"Braxton, I fucking appreciate you more than you know. But if I must do the fucking question asking and investigating, we will get exactly nowhere. What are you getting at? What theory are you working on?"

"You know I don't like to talk theories until I have something concrete," Braxton said, telling me exactly nothing. "Let me know about the injunction, and if I have something prior to that, I will be in touch."

Despite Braxton's eccentric nature, he got me thinking. I know for a fact what I did with Marissa was fucking consensual. A person doesn't fucking jerk off if they are being coerced. A person doesn't ask you to spit in them if they're not into it.

There was a knock at the door just as the direct office line rang, meaning the person had not been patched through from Sherilyn.

"Braxton, call me if you have any news to share,' I said.

"I will, Mitchell," he said before hanging up.

"Come in," I said, massaging my temples.

I checked my phone but there was no message from Mirabella.

But as I saw Akila walk through the door looking somber, I took the call to my office line's speaker phone while Akila made herself at home on my couch.

"Mitchell, it's Gina," Gina Abruzzi-Torres said in that I'm-better-than-you voice she always used on me.

"What the fuck is going on, Gina? Have you filed an injunction to put an embargo on the tapes?"

"Yes of course, Mitchell. But I have to be honest, between the investigation into Peter Trenom, paparazzi photos of you and Mirabella Castle, and now . . . this . . . Our office is overloaded. I have spent the last few hours on calls with Kain, Carpenter, & Maguire. This is a total clusterfuck, Mitchell. When are you going to learn to keep your hands to yourself and keep your dick in your fucking pants?"

Akila looked up at me with a shocked expression, as if she could not believe I had let Gina talk to me that way.

I shook my head.

"That's rich coming from you, Gina. Get the fucking injunction, I want this gaping fucking wound closed now." I slammed the phone down on that conniving bitch. I was not in the mood for her snarky fucking comments.

"If this is a bad time," Akila started.

"Why are you here, Akila?"

"Sir?"

"Why are you here? Why are you here helping me and supporting me? I'm clearly a fucking asshole," I stated, taking my frustration out on a woman who had become a friend over the last few months. And since I could not recall the last time I'd made a genuine friend, I should have been more fucking careful. But sometimes, I couldn't stop myself from acting like a fucking spoiled and entitled ass.

Akila sat forward on the couch.

"You know what? I've been asking myself the same question," she said giving it right back to me, only in a British accent.

"Yeah, and what did you come up with?"

"Well for starters, you supported me. So, I'm going to support you. Until or unless you give me a reason not to. Secondly, people make mistakes. It doesn't mean they don't deserve a second chance. Third, I was under the impression that we are not just colleagues, but friends. Am I wrong about any of this?"

I walked to the couch where Akila sat and took a seat next to her.

"Akila," I said more softly. "You're a bright fucking star. You have the world at your feet; I don't want you mixed up with me. I don't know how any of this will shake out."

She seemed to be considering what I had said.

"Was it consensual?" She looked me in the eyes now, her expression one of fear, as if she wasn't sure whether she had hitched her professional and personal wagons to a predator.

"Yes."

"Did she say 'no' at any time?"

"No, I fucking swear."

"Then I'm with you. All the way."

"Akila, you're a fucking amazing friend."

"You better not let me down."

"I won't."

"Well then, let's get to work."

"Let's. And, Akila? Stop fucking calling me 'sir' if we're actual friends."

"Right. Ok," she said in a very British way.

"*Now*, let's get to work," I said.

"We have had twenty-eight resignations since the tapes released. The media is saying it's the end of Magellan Media and people don't want to go down with the ship."

"Can't blame them. But twenty-eight out of twenty-two thousand isn't very much. So, let's reshape that narrative," I said, agitated due to no response still from Mirabella. "Find out where we'll need support and which roles being vacated are essential. Ask Clara and Cindy for help if you need it. Also, let's figure out if the messaging about the resignations could be tied to short tenure, poor company culture fits, etc. Make sure none of our superstars are going to fucking Brennan Enterprises. Offer them incentives to stay."

Sherilyn buzzed in.

"Sir, Anna Park is here."

"Send her in. Thanks."

"I have to have this next meeting. If you can prepare a statement for the staff, I'll read it and give it. I'll say whatever you think I should say," I said.

"Ok, great. And, Mitchell," she said, back to calling me by my name instead of Sir.

"Yes?"

"Be positive. If you don't stay focused on positive outcomes and give off an air of confidence and hope, no one else around here will."

"Thanks, Akila."

"Oh, and Legal thinks you should keep your door ajar when meeting with female staff."

Just then, Anna poked her head in.

"Anna, come in, leave the door open. Thanks, Akila. Call me later."

Anna arrived and Akila left. It was a revolving fucking door today.

I buzzed Sherilyn. "Hold my calls. Do not disturb unless it's Mirabella Castle or one of the attorneys."

"Yes, sir," she said.

"Anna, have a seat, please. Thanks for coming."

Anna sat across from me.

"I gather you know why you're here?"

"Why am I here, Mitchell?"

"To keep me from fucking punching a wall and breaking my fucking hands."

"Only you can stop you from doing that."

"Trust me; that is not the case," I said.

"What's on your mind, Mitchell?"

"With everything that's going on, all of the legal troubles and investigations, and tapes of me with my fucking pants down, the only thing I really care about is Mirabella."

"That can't be one hundred percent true, Mitchell."

"It fucking feels true."

"And have you spoken to her since the tapes released?"

"No. She won't return my calls or texts."

"Can you blame her for that?"

"No. This whole thing is my fault. I told Mirabella someone was extorting me and that they had tapes, but I didn't tell her how bad the tapes were. How out of control and nasty I was then. She doesn't know me like that. I never wanted her to know that side of me."

"Why not? Are you ashamed of the man you are sexually? Your primal needs? Sexual fantasies?"

"Because that guy is depraved. He only cares about one thing."

"And what's that?"

"Getting off."

"And the Mitchell Magellan Mirabella knows? What's he like?"

"Warm. Sweet. Funny. Protective."

"Sounds like two different people."

"That guy on the tape isn't me. It's bravado. Wild sex talk. The raunchier the better. It's not who I am. At least not now. That guy is scared, selfish, insecure, and fucking barbaric. He doesn't care about the women he's with further than what they can do to and for him."

"It's hard to look at yourself in a mirror and not recognize the person looking back at you," she said.

"I never wanted to be a superhero. I just wanted to live my fucking life out of the limelight and outside of everyone's expectations. I never asked to be here," I whined, adjusting the jacket of my custom suit.

"That may be so, and yet, here you are. And you know what? No one feels sorry for you. So, you fucked up. People fuck up every second of every day. The question is, what are you going to do about it? How are you going to be a better man tomorrow than you are today? How will you be a better man five minutes from now than you are right this second?"

"I need Mirabella," was all I could say.

"You can't make your journey to redemption and reputation recovery about Mirabella. It must be about you."

"But she may never speak to me again," I said, defeated.

"She may not. But you have to forgive you. Heal you. Love you. She can't and won't forgive you or love you unless or until you believe you deserve it."

CHAPTER TWELVE

MIRABELLA CASTLE

My relationship with Mitchell was probably the worst-kept secret in the industry. Maybe they didn't know the extent of it or how close we'd become but it was kind of an inside joke by now. But when the photos of Mitchell and I holding hands leaked, everyone went apeshit. The media began camping outside of my building. Several times a day, I would receive weird phone calls and voicemails from people wanting me to comment. The worst part was being followed into the subway by people calling my name, trying to get me to say or do something stupid so they could get it on tape.

Still, nothing compared to the isolating stares of my co-workers. Their judgmental eyes followed me whenever I worked in the office. People openly talked about me, their comments slightly above a whisper. It was as though they wanted me to know they were gossiping about me but not quite what they were saying.

RayRay had said, "Bitch. They talk and stare because they wish they were you. Look at you. Gorgeous. Classy. And you're fucking Mitchell Magellan. Let it roll off your back, honey."

But when the tapes of Mitchell getting blown in his office landed,

ALL THE WAY OUT

the whispers sounded more like screams. So, I locked myself in the bathroom on the twenty-third floor of the Brennan Enterprises building. The video that Mitchell had warned me about was out and all over the Internet. And like a dummy, I watched the unedited version in HD in between text messages from RayRay, Mena, Iggy, Shayla, Jared, Jenni, Billy, Grandma, and the man himself.

I watched Mitchell get head from Marissa from fucking Accounting. But unlike in my fantasy, it was *not* sexy. I was *not* aroused. And the way he talked to her, telling her how much he liked how she sucked it, how much he liked how she took him deep, and how he told her, "Yeah take it all, I want to feel you gag on my fucking cock, Marissa..."

I ran to the first stall and threw up. And when I was done. I threw up again.

I could not get his words out of my head. The images of him in ecstasy with her seared into my brain. The man on camera looked like Mitchell. He sounded like Mitchell. But the man I saw, that man on the video, that was not my Mitchell.

"GET *on your fucking knees where you fucking belong."*
"Touch yourself. Tell me how you wish it was me."
"Do you think about me while you're crunching fucking numbers?"
"I want to shoot my load down your fucking throat."
"I love making you fucking gag on my cock. You gonna gag for me?"
"I wish I was in your fucking ass right now. Would you let me fuck you in the ass?"
"I fucking bet you would let me do whatever the fuck I want to you."
"Rub it around. Let me see you rub my spit in and out of your fucking pussy."
"Fuck. I'm gonna come all the way down your fucking throat."

I THREW UP AGAIN, my stomach wrenching. It was far worse than I had thought it might be. And worse, I was hurt and upset and sick over something he had done before he knew me. And by the way he behaved with her, it made me think I didn't know him at all. Who was this man who spit on women? In them? Talked to them like that?

He'd called and texted me a million fucking times, but he was exactly the last person I wanted to talk to.

> MITCHELL: Baby, please answer me

> ME: *read*

> MITCHELL: Please talk to me

> ME: *read*

> MITCHELL: Please let me know you're OK

> ME: *read*

> MITCHELL: Let me come get you, Mira

> ME: *read*

> MITCHELL: Mirabella. Please don't do this. Do not shut me out

> MITCHELL: Baby

> MITCHELL: Baby. Please call me. I need to know you're ok

The thing about tragedy is when it happens to you, you do things you would normally never have. Twenty minutes ago, I would never have curled up in a fetal position on the floor of a public bathroom after puking in the toilet, holding it around. But today was a tragic day, full of not-so-great surprises. And suddenly, I didn't care about cleanliness. I wasn't thinking about germs. Rather, I sat down on the bathroom floor to consider what would become of me now. What with things between Mitchell and I in a really fucked up place, I needed to fix things with Hyacinth and make sure I still had a job.

But that would have to wait until I was done bawling my eyes out while lying on the floor with my legs pulled up to my chest and my arms wrapped around them as the physical pain of what I had seen and heard wracked through my body, mind, and soul. *How the hell did I get here?*

Soon, I was ready to vomit again as thoughts of how I let Mitchell fuck me, put his dick in my mouth, put his fingers in two of my holes, put his fingers in my mouth, lick me, suck me, make me beg him to be inside me. I'd let him make love to me. Make me come so hard that I cried.

I did things with him I had never done with anyone and would probably never do with anyone again. And the sad part about it was that as much pain as I was in, I missed him. I wanted to curl up in his arms and rest there until I couldn't rest anymore. I wanted him, the very man who was causing it, to make my pain disappear.

About fifteen minutes later, I unlocked the door so that anyone needing to use the bathroom would be able to. No longer interested in hiding, I was ready to face the consequences of what I had done. I dialed Hyacinth's cellphone number, and leaned against the far wall.

"Mirabella? Just about everyone has been trying to reach you." Hyacinth sounded way less angry than I thought she would be.

"I know. I am so sorry. I didn't want you to find out about me and Mitchell that way. A funeral no less."

"Mirabella—"

"Please; let me finish. I know I promised we would be done after London. I realize I put Brennan Enterprises at risk."

"Mirabella—"

"Whatever punishment you see fit to give me; I will accept. A pay cut. A reduction in my commission rate. Just please don't fire me."

I gulped back tears.

"Fire you?" She said in that voice of hers. Hyacinth sounded giddy, joyous even. She sounded like she would have hugged me if we had been together.

"You're not going to fire me?"

"Mirabella, are you mad? Have you seen the news? The Internet is abuzz with the goings on of a certain Mitchell Magellan in what some are calling a 'private office moment,' she said with a song in her voice that she wasn't even trying to hide. I could hear the air quotes and sarcasm in her tone. Hyacinth was stoked to see Mitchell fuck up so royally. She was gloating.

"I saw where some others are calling it a sexual harassment lawsuit waiting to happen. Do you think he will be charged with that?"

"I can tell you that it's best that you distance yourself from anything having to do with Mitchell Magellan. I know you're fond of him, Mirabella, but the woman in the video, Marissa Canto, has agreed to sue Mitchell personally and also to sue Magellan Media."

"Oh, well that's not good," I said.

"It's good for me. It's great for you."

"How so?"

"She and your friend Mitchell have done more for your brand at Brennan Enterprises than I could ever have hoped with their stellar performance."

"It's hardly something to make light of. These are real people with lives and families."

"Mitchell made his bed. He can lie in it. I won't feel sorry for him."

We were both quiet then. I wanted to imagine that there was at least some part of Hyacinth that was feeling sorry for me. And, as if she sensed this, she spoke seemingly from her heart.

"Look, Mirabella. I can't even begin to know what the nature of your relationship with Mitchell Magellan is, but I'm not completely unfeeling. I can imagine this must hurt you. And for what it's worth, I'm truly sorry for your pain."

I didn't speak because I was afraid I might cry right then.

"On a positive note, if circumstances play out the way I hope, we will have several new licenses by the end of the week totaling ten million or more upfront advances for the company and thousands for you. Mirabella, this is the best thing to happen to your brand since the day he refused you an interview," she said, and I could picture her beaming with pride.

"It doesn't feel that way," I said, not really expecting her to be sorry for me. To Hyacinth's point, this was the bed I made. And now, it was time for me to lie in it. I fell for a man I didn't really understand. A man who is older than me by seven years. Seven years ago, I was fourteen years old.

"Well, cheer up, Mirabella. Will has already got you booked on seventeen morning shows, six podcasts, and five nighttime cable network shows. Everyone wants to know what you think about your boyfriend getting his rocks off in his office when he was supposed to be interviewing you for a job."

"But aren't you worried about this blowing back on Brennan Enterprises?"

"How do you mean?"

"I don't know what I'm saying. But Mitchell said this person—whoever released the tapes—was extorting him. And the only people who stand to gain by making Mitchell look bad and me look good are the ones at Brennan Enterprises," I mused.

"Well, I'm certain Mitchell Magellan has a lot of enemies, and if I were you, Mirabella, I would stay far away from him. Nothing good can come from having anything to do with a man like that."

"I appreciate your concern, Hyacinth, I really do. But I have to figure this out on my own. I know you don't approve of Mitchell, but he cares about me."

"Mirabella, just promise me something."

"If I can."

"Promise me you are going to look after you and that you will really and truly think about what's best for you and your future."

"Thank you. I will."

"Well good. I'll have Will send over your schedule and prep you for your interviews and appearances. In the meantime, stay home. Do not go to the office."

"It's too late for that," I said. I pushed off the wall and looked in the mirror. Big mistake.

"Ok, I'm sending a car to take you back home. You can work from there indefinitely. And, Mirabella? I know what you do with your personal life is hardly my business. But Mitchell Magellan is a player. What did you think was going to happen?"

Right then, I felt so small, like a child who had done something their parents had warned them not to. And now, there was red paint all over the fucking white walls. I couldn't speak; what would I say? He called me 'baby,' or he said he loved me? He gave me toe-curling orgasms?

"I appreciate you, Hyacinth, despite how it looks. But I cannot discuss my relationship with Mitchell with you or anyone."

"So, you *are* seeing him," she said as if she had just proven a theory she'd had.

"Yes. No. I don't know. There's a lot going on," I said, sounding immature and unprofessional.

"I know you don't want to talk about your love life with your boss, Mirabella but has it ever occurred to you that he might only be interested in you because of our interest in you?"

"No. Mitchell has been interested in me since Day One."

"Wow. You're really into him," she said accusingly.

"Look, I don't want to talk about Mitchell Magellan. I will go on all the talk shows and do the press tour, but I'm not talking about him outside of that."

"Fair. But we need a new blog post and a couple of social media posts. Maisy and Will arrive tomorrow. Please have drafts on my desk by the morning. And, Mirabella, remember how you spoke from your heart and your gut about Magellan? We need that level of candor once more."

"Wait. How did you know about Marissa Canto's lawsuit? Why would Brennan Enterprises know anything about what's happening at Magellan Media to that degree?"

"We just do. I heard about it this morning, even before the tapes leaked. Does it really matter?"

"Yes, it does. So, are you saying Marissa Canto decided to sue before the tapes were leaked, and somehow you guys were made aware before Magellan was?"

"Mirabella, just get ready for your appearances and interviews and have those drafts ready by your morning."

"Ok," I said, happy the strange conversation was now over, and I was not losing my job. I wasn't going to waste my time thinking about

Marissa fucking Canto I said, shaking the image of her waltzing off the elevator that morning like she owned the fucking place from my head. She must have had carte blanche to go to Mitchell's office whenever he summoned her.

I splashed water on my face, and tried to do something with my hair that I had accidentally puked in. And when I stared in the mirror now, I looked so different from the girl who was only recently tangled up with Mitchell Magellan—getting fucked, fed, and bathed by him. I searched my purse for some of those strong mints RayRay had given me the night I ate those jalapeño peppers and onions. When I found them, I placed two into my mouth in hopes they would kill the puke smell and taste.

Mitchell had told me about the extortion, but he had failed to mention what was actually on the fucking tapes. Sure, he'd said it was from his 'encounter' with Marissa from Accounting, but he never mentioned anything about the Mitchell on that tape. And as much as I wanted to ask him about it, grill him about it, cry in his strong arms over it, I could not talk to him. I could not see him because if I did, I would not be able to resist him.

I finally escaped the bathroom, slunk through the hallway with my head down, and got on an elevator to go wait for my car. As I entered the elevator, there were three others going down. Now, they all stared. I looked at the floor and made my way to the back of the elevator so as not to draw attention to myself. Just then, I realized I had forgotten my laptop and plug.

Shit.

Oh well, I'd have to have them send me a new one, because I was *not* stepping foot in that building until things calmed down.

Newly outside and away from prying eyes, I waved at the driver standing in front of a blacked-out Cadillac Escalade, holding a sign that read *M.A. Castle* on it. He opened the door for me, and I slid in, not even paying attention. And when I saw Mitchell inside, I didn't know whether to jump out of the car, scream, hit him, cry, or kiss him.

"Mirabella, please. I needed to see you," Mitchell said as he saw the panic on my face.

"What happened to the car Hyacinth sent me?" I said, feeling tricked and trapped, and afraid of being alone in a car with Mitchell.

"I paid him to leave."

"How did you know I was getting a car home? That I would be here right now?"

"Mirabella, I have people who can find out whatever I need them to."

Mitchell looked so fucking good despite all he must have been going through. He leaned forward like he was going to touch me, then he must have thought better of it.

"Are we ok?"

I thought about how I wanted to respond; it was not my intention to drag things out for dramatics.

"I'm not ok," was all I could say when face-to-face with the man who had made me come so many times this past weekend. As I sat across from him, his stare intense, our seven-year age difference seemed more meaningful. He felt way closer to thirty than he had before. I felt entirely too young and inexperienced for Mitchell's world, so much so that he thought I'd be 'ok' after watching a video of him spitting into a woman's vagina.

I nervously stared at my hands, the images and audio of Mitchell playing in my mind right then. Dirty things. Intimate things. Things that would have made me blush. When I looked at him again, my emotions were all over the place.

"Tell me what to do, Mirabella. Whatever you want, I will do it," Mitchell said, seeming sincere.

"I don't know you. I thought maybe I did, but *clearly*, I don't."

"Mirabella, you know me. You know the real me. I didn't hide anything from you."

How the fuck dare you, I wanted to say. But my fight was totally gone. I don't even think I was angry, so much as I was in shock. Mitchell hadn't lied to me. He'd told me about the tapes. But he hadn't been exactly forthcoming either. He'd said just enough that I couldn't accuse him of lying.

"You enjoy fucking women in the ass, or at least fantasizing about it while fucking their mouths. You like when they gag on you. You like dominating and degrading women sexually and you withhold their pleasure for the sake of your own."

"Jesus, when you say it like that it makes me sound like a fucking prick."

"I think you did that all by your damn self," I said, the sass slowly returning.

"That's not me, Mirabella. You know me. That was a lot of shit talking to get myself worked up enough to come. You, you know the real me. The vulnerable me. The one who loves you. The one who doesn't need all that when I'm with you."

"I can't get those images of you fucking another woman's mouth out of my mind. The things you said to her. You spit in her fucking mouth. What even was that?"

He looked away from me just then, and I knew he was ashamed.

"It was dirty sex with a stranger. Things I would never even think about doing with you," he said, and when he did, I let my tears fall.

Mitchell reached out to touch me, and I flinched.

"Why would you never do things like that with me?" I asked in a quiet voice.

"Is that what you want from me? Someone who degrades you, and pulls your hair, and spits on you? And who fucks the back of your throat until you can barely speak and doesn't care if you're crying because you can't fucking breathe and gets off by seeing you choke on his cum?"

"Jesus, Mitchell. What the fuck is wrong with you?"

"What you saw was a transaction between two consenting adults. I told her what I wanted to do to her, and she let me."

"But *why* did you want to do that to her in the first place?"

"I don't know. I guess I wanted to forget everything. To fucking break something. To be something. Someone different for a few fucking minutes. I wanted to know what it felt like to be powerful. And now, I fucking hate myself for what it's doing to you. It was one hundred percent not fucking worth it."

I was quiet, thinking about what he'd said. I didn't even notice that the driver had pulled into traffic.

"I hate that this is out there. That people think less of you because of it. That my friends and family think I chose a fucking depraved sexual deviant who likes to spit on women and in their mouths. Fucking RayRay asked me if I let you spit in my mouth and inside me. You spit in her vagina. That there are women out there fantasizing about being Marissa. Have you fucking seen the Internet?"

He pulled a smirk back, and for a split second, I wanted to climb onto his lap and slide down onto his cock and ride it until I came all over him. I wanted to claim him for my fucking own. To bring him to the edge and leave him there until he begged to be inside me. Bring him to fucking heel. Instead, I kept my eyes on him, staring him down.

"And what if I did? What if we did, as a fucking couple? If we decided we wanted to fucking spit on one another. Whose business is it? You fucking talk about what we do? Because I'm not ok with that, Mirabella." Mitchell was suddenly angry. "What we do is between us. I don't want spectators in our fucking bed. And you know what? Don't think I can't see the look on your fucking face. Don't think I don't know you well enough to know what you fucking want right now."

I looked away, one of my fucking tells on display as Mitchell looked away too, his way of stopping himself from pouncing on me.

Both of us stubborn, neither wanting to give in, we sat in silence for a while until I realized we were in Mitchell's neighborhood.

"No. Take me home," I said, my voice panicked.

"Please stay with me, Mirabella. Let's talk through this. You told me you loved me. I told you this tape was being leaked. You—"

I cut him the fuck right off, all thoughts of possibly letting him into my pants now gone.

"You could have warned me how graphic it was going to be. How fucking dirty. You could have told me how different it was from how we are. You should have been really honest with me."

"I wanted to. I'm ashamed of how I behaved. I didn't want you to see me like that. Weak. Out of control. Desperate. It's embarrassing, and frankly, I didn't think they were actually going to release it. I thought I could pay my way out of this."

Mitchell seemed broken. Lost.

The car pulled in front of Mitchell's townhouse. I opened my door and exited the vehicle without waiting for him. I was anxious, breathing heavy, and uncertain. I knew how possible it was that I was going to vomit again.

Mitchell let me enter the apartment first, and as I did, I hated the emotions flooding me. I'd missed it. I missed being there with him.

And as quickly as I was beginning to soften, to consider staying, he spoke.

"Mirabella," Mitchell said my name in the way that let me know what he wanted, and it wasn't to *talk*.

"Yes," I said in a way that revealed how turned on I was just by the need in his fucking voice.

He stood behind me, and I could feel and hear his breathing.

"I want to touch you so fucking badly," he said.

The amount of wetness drenching my panties was insane. My nipples strained against my bra.

"Why are you doing this to me?" I asked, about to cry from the way I needed him right then.

"Because I can't fucking breathe without you. Because I'm selfish, and weak, and unable to control myself around you. Because the other day, when I squeezed your neck, you fucking loved it. And that night in your apartment when we first met, you liked it when I made you sit while I stood over you with my fucking cock in your face. And that time when I pushed my giant fucking engorged cock all over your face, the pre-cum soaking through my underwear, you were so fucking turned on."

He was wrong, wasn't he? He was fucking wrong.

"You like when I fucking dominate you, but you don't want to fucking admit it."

"I like when you take care of me," I said softly.

"And I love taking care of you," he said, making my pussy clench.

I walked away and took a seat on the couch, leaving Mitchell standing there still hard and breathing heavy.

"Why did you bring me here, to fuck me?"

"Yes. I don't want you to deny us both pleasure because you're angry at me."

"You think that's what I'm doing? Trying to punish you? You think I'm angry with you?"

"You won't let me touch you. I need you to let me touch you, please," Mitchell said, his voice even huskier. He moved over to where I was on the couch and kneeled down in front of me. He circled my knees with his arms and laid his head on my legs.

I fisted my hands to avoid putting them in his gorgeous fucking hair, like I wanted to.

"I can't be with you, Mitchell. I just can't. I need you to take me home."

"Mira, please. I love you so fucking much. Let me touch you. Let me make you come."

I was a mix of emotions, none of them fucking good. It would have been so easy to simply allow Mitchell the pleasure of my body, which would have brought me pleasure in turn. But I simply could not get those images out of my head. The sounds. How he was with her. The idea that if he had only interviewed me this never would have happened. I would not be feeling like this now. So fucking hurt. So disgusted. So ashamed. So terrified. Full of so much hatred, anger, sadness, and despair.

"I want to, Mitchell. It would be so easy to fall into bed with you. But the Mitchell I thought you were, he's the one I wanted. And now, the Mitchell you actually are, the one from the tapes, he scares me."

"It's me. I'm me. Mira, please," he said, tears in his beautiful eyes, coating his long eyelashes. I could not resist running my hand through his hair right then. He moaned.

"It's too hard for me. I'm not strong enough. I can't be that intimate with someone without it meaning something. You and I are not compatible. We want and like different things, and I don't want to feel like you're suppressing who you are just to be with me. I don't want to be thinking about Marissa Canto every time I'm with you because I am not like her. I don't want those things. And, Mitchell. I don't want to feel like you're faking it with me."

Mitchell seemed defeated now, like his fight was leaving him too. Like he had no rebuttal. The pain in his eyes nearly killed me. As if it was me who was hurting him, not the other way around.

"I just need to know that you don't think less of me now that you've seen that part of me." Mitchell's voice was small now.

"Do you think about her?"

"Not since I've been with you. It was just sex, Mirabella. Just something to get me off. I don't have feelings for her. I don't think about her at fucking all."

"Tell me how you could not be thinking about the woman whose vagina you fucking spit in."

"Do you think about fucking Ben?" He said all obnoxious like.

"Yes. But I think about what a fucking loser he was and how happy I am to be with someone like you who takes care of me and makes me feel cared for and loved and respected."

Mitchell looked fucking mad now.

"You think it makes me happy to hear you're still thinking about that fucking guy? I swear to God, Mirabella."

We were both quiet now, the energy in the room charging. Crackling. I know for a fact that Mitchell was contemplating putting his hands on me. Shoving his cock so far inside me that I would not even be able to remember I had anyone before him, let alone remember Ben's name.

"Why her? Why Marissa? I mean, she and I look very different. How can you be attracted to me after having someone like her?" I said recalling her giant boobs, long brown hair, flawless creamy skin, and Instagram-model body.

Mitchell looked at me now like he didn't recognize me, like maybe I was a puzzle he didn't have all the pieces to but still was expected to solve it.

"Mirabella. Jesus. I don't know how to show you how attracted I am to you. How sexy and beautiful you are."

I looked away for a second, needing to regain my steely composure. My confidence in myself and in this relationship was now completely shattered.

"If I asked you for time, would you give it to me?" I said, turning to face him now.

"What do you mean? How much time?"

"I don't know. I just . . . this has got me fucked up, Mitchell. It's embarrassing to have a boyfriend who acts like this and who was caught on camera acting like this with another woman. I feel so unsexy and unwanted knowing what you really like. How could I ever be enough for you? How could I ever fully satisfy you?"

"I'm so sorry, Mirabella. If I could take it back, I fucking would. I hate what this is doing to you. You are so fucking sexy and so damn beautiful. You turn me on just being near you. I wish you knew that. I wish you believed it. I don't need that shit. I don't want it. I want you. I want what we have."

"Do you want to do that with me?"

"No."

"Why not?"

"Because I don't see you like that."

"And how do you see me?"

"Mirabella, how many fucking times did we have sex when you were here?"

"I don't know, like, ten? Twelve?"

"It would have been thirteen had you showered with me before you left."

I smiled for the first time since the video and audio tapes dropped.

"Does that seem like the kind of man who doesn't find you sexy?"

He definitely had a point, but I had to do what was best for me. And, as hard as it was going to be, I told Mitchell my thoughts.

"I need time to figure out who I want to be and what I want in a relationship. I need to be alone so I can figure out what I want in life," I said. I can't do that with you looking at me how you're looking at me now."

Mitchell looked down, then slowly back at me.

"Are you leaving me, Mirabella?"

"I need time, Mitchell," I said, about to cry.

Mitchell got up, sat on the couch next to me then pulled me into his arms, and I think we both cried.

When we were both quiet, Mitchell said, "I love you, Mirabella Castle."

When I didn't respond, he said, "I'll have Brendan take you home." Then he got up and walked outside onto his terrace. I wanted to go after him, to hug and kiss him goodbye, but I knew that if I did, I would never find the strength to leave.

As I sat in the car on the way back to Queens, the conversation I'd had with Mitchell's aunt Meg played in my head. I had promised not to leave him, and she had promised to do whatever she had to if I did. And right then, I cried so hard and for so long that by the time Brendan pulled up to my apartment, my head was splitting, my eyes were swollen, and my nose was completely stuffed. It was the second time I'd cried all the way home in the backseat of one of Mitchell's fancy cars.

CHAPTER THIRTEEN

MITCHELL MAGELLAN

It was a three-week Mirabella Castle onslaught. We'd been so worried about the photos of us from Mena's mother's funeral that we were wholly unprepared for what would happen once those tapes leaked. Well, Mira and I were. Hyacinth and her team? They were on it from the minute that shit went down, almost as if they knew it was happening.

Mirabella's people at Brennan Enterprises had her on a whirlwind media tour talking about the leaked video and audio of me getting head in my office. There was hardly a mention of the photos of us holding hands except to deduce we were in some kind of relationship that was meaningful enough to negatively impact Mira.

And even though it kept the video in the spotlight longer than I would have liked and also kept the media on my ass, it was the only way for me to see her.

I was back to filling my days and nights with distractions that kept my mind off Mirabella. Yet since I had her in my apartment, reminders of her were everywhere. So, in the past three weeks, I had barely spent any time there, instead splitting my time between my parents' apartment uptown and Aunt Meg's. I didn't want to be in Chelsea if Mirabella wasn't.

Maybe she had been right about my apartment. It was nice, but it wasn't one befitting a person of my station. Maybe I needed a change.

"I've been thinking about moving," I said last week at my weekly dinner with Aunt Meg and Preston. We'd taken a hiatus after the accident and had just resumed it once Mirabella left me.

"Wonderful. Where are you thinking of moving to?" Aunt Meg said, sipping her stemless glass of merlot.

"Hudson Yard, Billionaire's Row? I was also thinking of getting a permanent place in London," I mused.

"Oh? Are you thinking of spending much time overseas again?"

"Yes. I'm thinking of opening a new restaurant and acquiring more space in the Shard."

"And how much of this is because of Mirabella?"

"Because of? No. More like despite."

"So, you're over her then?"

"Not gonna happen. We're taking a break. She was really hurt by the release of that video and audio."

"It was pretty damming, Mitchell."

"Please tell me you didn't watch it."

"I'd rather shove hot coals in my eyes. But, Mitchell, I may be the only person besides Preston who hasn't. You still seeing Anna?"

"Five days a week."

"Maybe you need to change to seven days."

"Yeah, how's Peter Trenom? Is Caroline planning to divorce his ass yet?"

"She called me."

"No shit. What did she want?"

"She'll never leave him."

"Even if he goes to prison?"

"He's not going to prison, Mitchell. Why are you so hellbent on crucifying Peter? If he's convicted, it's bad for Magellan."

"Well, one Magellan in particular," I teased. "How can you be ok with what he did?"

"Peter and I don't discuss work. We leave that shit at the office. Ours is a relationship built on trust, mutual respect, and hot sex."

"Oh God. My fucking ears."

"At least my lover isn't burning me in a public square every chance he gets," Aunt Meg said.

"Touché," I said. "But seriously, Aunt Meg, how's Peter holding up?"

"How would you be holding up if your lifelong friends and allies were all planning to testify against you?"

"Speaking of which, I have Sarah's hearing next week."

"Yeah? How do you think it will go?"

"As with anything having to do with Sarah, long and fucking dramatic."

"You never liked her."

"I liked her well enough."

"But..."

"I don't know. Call me a romantic. I wanted Alexander to marry someone he was in love with."

"Alex understood his duty. He was doing what he had to do for the family. Besides, Sarah's gorgeous. Compliant."

"Unlike Mirabella? Is that what you're getting at?"

"You would do well to choose someone more like you, Mitchell. Mirabella seems to come from a completely different background despite her Ivy League education."

It was her strongest passive-aggressive condemnation of my relationship with Mirabella yet. To punish her, I used the L word.

"That's exactly what I love about Mira. She doesn't give a shit about my money or my name."

"And look where that got you."

We ate in silence for a few minutes. Aunt Meg had made her famous lasagna after lamenting that it was the final night of Mr. Feer's vacation, so we had to fend for ourselves. And since her house was the only place I could get a home-cooked meal nowadays, I guilted her into cooking one of my childhood favorites.

Preston didn't join us then because he was in bed with a nasty stomach bug. Normally, I would have gone up to see him, but that was the last thing I needed right now. So, I FaceTimed him from the dining room table.

"Hey, Pres, you look like shit, Brother."

"Hi, Mitch."

"How are you, man?"

"Fucked. Fucked. Mitch. I'm fucked."

"I know that feeling, Pres. Just hang in there. You'll—"

"Bye, Mitch," Preston said, and hung up the call before I finished talking to him.

"It's his favorite word, you know," Aunt Meg shook her head. "He told his doctor to go fuck himself last week," she said as if that was my fault.

"Nice," I said. "There may be hope for Preston Magellan yet.

"Any news on the extortion source?"

"Nothing. Braxton has come up empty at every turn," I said.

"Odd for Braxton, wouldn't you say?"

"Well, he did say he thinks it's someone with deep pockets."

"What makes him say that?"

"No demands. Access to Magellan servers costs a lot of money."

"Honestly, Mitchell, it could be China. Who the hell knows? Did you find out how the videos and audio got leaked?"

"I found out Dad had the equipment put in five years ago. Do you know why it was there to begin with? I certainly could not have been the only person taking 'personal meetings' in their office."

"The biggest fish in the 'personal meeting' pond," she said. Aunt Meg had never given me shit about my dalliances. Not even once.

"Exactly. So why come after me? To embarrass me? Make me look bad? I have been doing that shit on my own for years. The only thing this does is fuck things up between me and Mira."

"I'm not following you."

"Who stands to gain if Mirabella and I are apart?"

"There's only one person I can think of."

"And don't you think it's odd that Braxton hasn't considered it?"

"No, Mitchell. I don't because Braxton is a smart man. He isn't blinded by love. He isn't foolish enough to try to pin something like this on Robert Brennan III without hard evidence."

"Love? You caught that, huh?"

"You aren't fooling anyone, Mitchell. Any idiot can see how smitten you are with Mirabella," Aunt Meg said, her expression sympathetic and caring. "What is it with us Magellans and love?"

"If I find out that Brennan is behind this, I'm taking him fucking down for good." I ignored her reference to her two great loves, two men who had betrayed my father.

"I would expect nothing less. I don't expect you to give Bobby an indefinite pass. I just want to protect Preston."

"And I will. Protect Preston. I promise."

It was nice to connect with Aunt Meg again in this way. For a minute, I wasn't sure we would recover from the Peter Trenom thing. But if nothing else, Aunt Meg was a company man, and her first loyalty after family was to Magellan Media. And when Mirabella left me, Aunt Meg had taken to calling and messaging me on days I wasn't staying with her to make sure I wasn't falling apart. And when she did, I held it together just long enough so that she didn't worry about me.

Surely Magellan Media kept me busy what with all the goings-on of running a business like this, but I had also kicked off new initiatives like the scholarship program Mirabella had suggested as well as a job training program suggested by Akila where junior staffers could learn to grow into managers.

But Akila had gone back to London, and I was thinking maybe I should do the same. A change of scenery could do me some good. I could hang with Emilio, check in with Shonda, and potentially offload some assets there I had no interest in.

But before I did anything, I had to sit through the mediation meeting with Sarah Crane.

AS I DID my best to keep my mind off Mirabella, I sat across from Alexander's ex-fiancé who was suing me for control of Alex's inheritance. To be fair, I wasn't exactly sure what Alex would have wanted in this instance. They weren't yet married. But the engagement was a promise of a future together. And, if Alex hadn't died in that accident, they would most likely have walked down the aisle, and she, according to her prenup, would have automatically received a shit-ton of money.

Albert Kain, the attorney who was representing the Magellan Estate spoke first.

"First, to everyone affected by the horrendous and tragic accident, we at Kain, Carpenter, & Maguire would like to express our deepest sympathies. It is with a heavy heart that we gather today under these circumstances. And, whatever the outcome of today's proceedings, we do not take lightly the pain and suffering of those involved. To that end, let's confirm both parties as present so we can begin."

Kain's father had worked for my dad for years on things relating to our personal assets, trusts, estate, foundation, etc., or as Mirabella had called it, "rich people shit." I smiled, remembering our conversation, then reined it in because no one at a death benefit hearing should be fucking smiling. Recently, I brought the firm in to represent us on the corporate side of things, not completely satisfied with the outcomes Gina Abruzzi-Torres and her team could produce.

"Mitchell Xavier Magellan?"

I raised my hand as if in school, and said, "here" despite this being the last fucking place I wanted to be.

"Sarah Michelle Elizabeth Crane?"

Coached no doubt, Sarah was too distraught to even acknowledge that her fucking name had been called. She blew her nose loudly into a tissue, and touched her attorney's arm as if to say, 'I can't. It's too difficult already.'

Her attorney offered her his fucking handkerchief, nodded to her, then said, "My client is rather overwhelmed this morning, so I can confirm this is indeed Miss Sarah Michelle Elizabeth Crane."

I wanted to roll my eyes as Sarah sat across from me in dark oversized Prada sunglasses, a Hermes scarf tied around her head, pulling tissues strategically from her Kelly Thirty with her left hand so everyone would be blinded by the fucking four hundred thirty-five thousand dollar, 8.05-carat, pear-shaped diamond and platinum ring living on her ring finger.

I didn't dislike Sarah, but theirs was a fucking arranged marriage. And now that Alex was dead, she could marry another rich guy and get even more money from him. And, while I didn't believe Sarah to be a gold digger, she was a social climber, and Alex was her ticket out of middle child hell. And for her family and mine, the union was supposed to allow us to tap into oil money and them into media, sports, and films.

So, this mediation hearing was as much of a business deal as it was a payoff for Sarah personally. Therefore, my goal was to pay Sarah as little as possible, without pissing off or seeming to disrespect her family.

"I would like to begin by pointing out that there is an existing prenuptial agreement said to govern this proceeding. And since neither party has sought to invalidate said agreement, I will read the applicable clause from it provided that there are no objections to my doing so," Kain said as he looked from me to Sarah for our objections.

I nodded for him to continue. Sarah shook her head as if it was all too much, and I wanted to tell her right then I knew she had men on the fucking side. That Alexander also knew and to cut the bullshit acting.

"No objections," said her lawyer.

Kain Jr. read the clauses pertaining to death which clearly state the prenup is to be invalidated upon either of their deaths. But this was meant to be interpreted as being applicable after the wedding. Once they were married. There was no stipulation for what would happen if they were engaged and one of them died prior to the wedding.

Then Sarah's attorney asserted that she is entitled to a cash payout from Alexander despite this and the fact that he had not made any provisions for her in his will. My guess is that he didn't provide for her in his will because she was already fucking filthy rich. Honestly, I had no fucking idea why this was such a big deal to her, getting access to Alex's money.

And, after some back and forth between the attorneys about the "right thing to do," I was getting antsy. This whole thing should never have even gotten that far.

ALL THE WAY OUT

I interrupted Albert Kain Jr., and said, "Look, Sarah, nobody here is more upset about Alexander's passing than me. He didn't put you in his will because you already have more money than God. So, let's stop with the fucking theatrics and get on with this. You're young, have no kids, and can easily marry and have years and years of happiness and love with another man who can provide for you. So, I will give you twenty-five million right fucking now. Will that work for your pain and suffering? Help with your grieving?"

Albert Kain Jr. stuttered and tried to fix what I had just said. I didn't mean for it to come out how it did, but the stress of my life at present was fucking making my tolerance for bullshit shorter than it normally was.

"What my client means to convey is that he can understand your desire to have a meaningful representation of your late fiancé's legacy, and that he is prepared to offer you something which he feels reflects the financial hardship of losing Mr. Alexander Maddox Magellan so early in the relationship and yet balance that with the bright future you could still have with another life partner should you be lucky enough to have another great love."

It was impossible to imagine Mirabella sitting here trying to get money from the Magellan Estate if I had died. And just then, as Sarah conferred with her attorney, I knew what I wanted to do.

"Sarah, I'm sorry for your loss. I know that one day you will move on with another man and probably never think of Alex again. But you were his legacy too. You were the woman he wanted to marry and build a life with, have kids with. So, I will give you the twenty-five million for yourself. You can have that, no strings attached. But I will also give you one hundred million more to create a foundation in his name that provides scholarships to underprivileged kids and helps supply books and classroom supplies to schools around the country that need it. What do you think?"

Sarah conferred with her attorney, and as they talked, I wanted to text Mirabella to tell her about my idea. To make her proud.

"Mitchell," Sarah removed her glasses as she spoke, and for the first time, it was clear that she had actually been crying real fucking tears.

"Thank you for your offer. I too am sorry for your loss, and I hate that the accident has landed us in this situation. I accept your offer and want to assure you that I will honor your family by building a foundation in Alexander's name. And, if I can speak for Alex without offending you, I know he would be happy to know this is part of how he will live on."

I teared up right then and nodded at Sarah who was genuinely grieving. Fuck. I hadn't been looking at this shit the right way. Things with Mirabella had me all the way fucked up.

"Thank you, Sarah," I said, not wanting to lose my shit in front of everyone. I didn't know when I would see her again, but I did want her to know that I wished her well because it is what Alex would have wanted. Just then, I decided to visit his grave so I could tell him how it all turned out.

I shook my attorney's hand, and then excused myself from the room. Whatever was going to happen now would be worked out by the lawyers, and when it was time for me to sign the paperwork, Sherilyn would let me know.

Now, I was back to thinking of Mirabella. About how whatever the fuck this was between us, how it was worth fighting for. How life was too fucking short to let some bullshit keep us apart. I wanted to tell her that I would spend my entire fucking life, however much of it I had left, trying to make this up to her. How I would burn the entire building down to rid memories of Marissa from it if that's what she wanted.

The thought of not having Mira in my life, not being there for her, allowing her to face the cruelty of this world alone, like Sarah now had to, it was too fucking much. I wanted to take care of her. Protect her. Comfort her. To love her.

And when I reached my office, I closed the door, poured myself a bourbon, and punched my fucking desk so hard that this time, I broke my fucking hand. And as I sat in my chair, drinking my double, feeling my hand swell, and watching the skin on my knuckles bleed, I let myself sit in that pain for a few minutes before messaging Brendan to take me to the fucking ER.

And because I'm a glutton for punishment, while I waited for Brendan, I did the stupidest fucking most impulsive thing: I dialed Mirabella.

My mind raced with ideas about what I would actually say after not talking to her or seeing her in person for three weeks. And none of the fucking ideas I'd had just minutes ago seemed remotely interesting. But time was up because after the third ring, someone answered the phone.

"Hello?"

Mirabella.

I was hoping she would answer but didn't believe she would. So, when she picked up and spoke like she didn't fucking know who was calling, I wasn't fucking ready. And now, after three fucking weeks of trying to stay busy, focus on work, and not think about her, she had given me a sliver of hope.

Everything came flooding back at the sound of her voice. I was so fucking turned on as memories of she and I came rushing into my mind's eye. The way she burrowed into my armpit when she was embarrassed, how she smells just out of the shower, how she looks with her bouncy natural curls, the feel of her perfect tits in the palm of my hand, how it feels when she's gripping on me and about to come.

Fighting through the pain radiating up my arm, the tightness of my skin around the rapid swelling, and the immense arousal taking over my body, I spoke.

"Mirabella, it's me."

I didn't even care that she could hear the desperation in my voice.

"Hi, Mitchell," she said as if she hadn't left me three weeks ago or ignored my subsequent calls and texts or crucified me on every fucking media outlet that would have her. But the moment she'd said my name, I'd forgiven her.

"Hi," I said, feeling like I was wasting precious seconds.

"I can't really talk right now," she said, crushing my fucking dreams. "Can I call you later?"

Just then Brendan texted to say he was out front.

"Ok. Yes. I have dinner with Aunt Meg and Preston tonight, so feel free to call any time after eleven. I should be back from Connecticut by then."

It was too much information in that moment, and I was too fucking eager, oversharing.

"Ok. Bye," she said before hanging up the goddamn phone.

"Bye," I said, after she was no longer on the line.

I sat back in my chair overanalyzing the call, the sound of her voice, the intonation, the fact that she answered, and what it all meant.

Fuck!

If I hadn't already broken my fucking hand, I would have put it through a fucking window and broken it again.

CHAPTER FOURTEEN

MIRABELLA CASTLE

When the whole thing erupted over the missed interview, Grandma told me to pray for Mitchell. She'd said I was wrong for what I did, and even quoted Bible verses about blessing those who curse you and turning the other cheek. After I finally told her we were seeing one another, she had taken to referring to him as 'that young man of yours' and would say things like, "I'll be keeping you and that young man of yours in my prayers."

Of all the things Grandma was great at, being a prayer warrior was at the top of the list. She not only prayed vigilantly, but inspired others to do the same. And when I would talk to her about how I was feeling, she would ask, "Are you putting in time on your knees, Mirabella?" Sometimes, I had to stop myself from laughing and thinking about how much time I was putting in on my knees for Mitchell.

I honestly felt bad knowing my grandma was praying for me all while I was having the most amazing sex of my life with the man she'd instructed me to pray for.

My brother Jared was the first person I told about the extent of my relationship with Mitchell. I came clean with him after our weekend in

London. For the most part, he was supportive, even if he was worried. He had taken to texting me any time Mitchell appeared in the news asking if I knew about this or heard about that. Mitchell couldn't shit without Mena or Jared letting me know.

Jared didn't normally have to worry about me; I was the smart one. The one with the level head. If I was doing something, I had already thought it through. Considered all possible outcomes. But literally and figuratively getting into bed with a notorious womanizer, well, how smart was that? Clearly, I hadn't exactly thought that all the way through.

My relationship with Mitchell started out with a bang. Sure, he canceled our interview, but I fired the first shot. I was the one who called Mitchell out on social media for his bad behavior. I was the one who chose to remain in my bathrobe when he'd offered me an opportunity to change before continuing. So, maybe my therapist had been right this whole time. I subconsciously went after Mitchell, and it was far too late for buyer's remorse.

So much had changed since then. And when photos of Mitchell and me holding hands and getting into his Maybach SUV together were made public, Grandma said, "So can I tell all my friends now that my grandbaby has landed herself a rich, handsome young man? And to think, this all started because he canceled his interview with you. See, baby? God always knows, doesn't he?"

We couldn't take the risk, so I said, "Yes, God always knows, and no, Grandma. You've got to keep it between you and Jesus for a little while longer." But she couldn't seem to let it go. She'd texted the next day to say what a supportive young man Mitchell was and how nice it was for him to comfort me when my friend's mother had passed. She had no idea how much *comfort* he had given me that weekend.

Of course, now, Mitchell and Grandma are good friends. He can do no wrong in her eyes. For that reason, I had avoided her calls and texts after the videos were released.

Musing over how exactly I'd ended up here while celebrating the end of my latest media tour was bittersweet. On the one hand, I no longer had to talk about Mitchell's office shenanigans on TV, radio, or at an in-person event. On the other hand, I was returning to my nine-to-five where I would spend my days in a cubicle banging out Internet and social media content, recording PSAs, drafting promotional materials, and avoiding Hyacinth.

Still feeling like a fish out of water in this role, I liked thinking about my options, options that weren't there before Mitchell refused to interview me. And in the back of my mind today was Mitchell's offer to run his new scholarship program, and suddenly, a smile appeared on my face as I let my thoughts run wild with the possibilities.

"You are a superstar," Will said, as he kissed me on either cheek. You're such a natural, Mirabella, a true joy to work with. Congratulations on completing your third tour."

"Will's right," Maisy added, smiling, then giving me a hug. You're going to get that talk show spot. I just know it."

"Thanks, guys. I could not have done it without either of you," I said, "And of course, this one," I said as Hyacinth approached. Even though we butted heads sometimes, I liked and respected Hyacinth. She was smart and strategic, and she made me believe I could achieve anything. And even though she gave Mitchell a tough time when it came to me, it was just her way of protecting her asset.

"Hey guys, can I speak to Mirabella alone?" Hyacinth said when she joined us in the living room of the suite Brennan Enterprises had rented for me to be interviewed in.

When they scurried like mice into another room, Hyacinth pulled me to the back corner of the suite.

"Is everything ok?"

"Yes. Yes. Everything's fine. Listen, I have been trying to reach Mitchell Magellan, but I cannot seem to get through to him. Do you have his cell phone by chance?"

"Is this a trick question?" I asked.

Hyacinth laughed.

"Look, Mirabella. I'm no Mitchell Magellan fan, but I do need to reach him."

"And you think I should give you his number because you ask for it?"

"I was hoping you were a viable option, yes," she said.

"I'm sorry but I can't give you his number unless I know what it's about. He's not the kind of person whose number you give to just anyone."

"Ok; I deserve that."

"Why can't you tell me why you need his number?"

"Because it's . . . *confidential*."

"What does that mean?"

"There are things I cannot disclose at the moment. Suffice it to say that if or when I must involve you, I will. Until then, I need you to trust me. Can you do that?"

"I'm going to go out on a limb here for you, Hyacinth, but if you screw me on this, we are done."

"You really love this guy, huh?"

I didn't respond.

"I hope he's worth it," she said as I retrieved my phone and texted her Mitchell's number.

Hyacinth walked away, and if I'm not mistaken, she dialed him right then. It was somewhat ironic that on the day my 'Mitchell Magellan' tour finished, Hyacinth, his sworn enemy, asked me for his contact information. And I honestly had to stop myself from running after her so I could overhear what she could possibly have to say to him.

When she left the room, I took a moment to look around the hotel suite and appreciate where I was. In one corner were two racks of clothes; next to them was an entire table of makeup. There were giant ring lights and lights with umbrellas and microphones the size of my arm in another corner. On one wall were giant posters that contained talking points and answers to questions. In the center of the room was a table with a food spread fit for royalty. Of course, there was a coffee maker and a tea station.

What had my life become? Licensing deals had exploded in the past three weeks just as Hyacinth had predicted they would. Everyone wanted a piece of me. I was the girl Mitchell Magellan loved to spurn. And how Brennan Enterprises had managed to spin that into a multi-million-dollar brand in nine months was nothing short of amazing.

My newest licensing deals included dinnerware, office and desk décor, and bed and bathroom linens. Hyacinth was convinced we would get a Mirabella Castle doll. That deal would be worth a few million upfront, from which I would make commission. It wasn't Mitchell Magellan money, but it was enough to allow me to consider potentially getting my own apartment.

Just then my thoughts turned to Mitchell again and how he'd told me he wanted us to move in together. That he hoped I would consider it. And at the time, I loved the idea. It was all very Cinderella. But now that I'd had some time away from Mitchell—his eyes, his hands, his mouth, his tongue, his man parts—I was beginning to see things more clearly.

Mitchell used to tell me not to hide from him. That he wanted to see me. But now I know I wasn't hiding from him; I was hiding from myself. I didn't want to see myself for who I was because I had no idea who I was or what I wanted. I had never set goals beyond the immediate. And when I was about to lose my apartment, my inattention to my self development was evidenced by the fact that I had allowed myself to be in that situation to begin with.

I never dared to see beyond that goal into what was really possible. And when Mitchell refused to see me that day, it was the catalyst that launched a career I may never have had otherwise. The irony of that was not lost on me. It was at first, but the more I thought about the significance of Mitchell's presence in my life, the more I realized how lucky I had actually been.

Grandma liked to say, "Everything happens for a reason, and just because we don't always know what that reason is, doesn't mean it's not important."

That day and each day since, I'd asked the Universe: Why? Why did this happen to me? Why did Mitchell have to do this to me? And what was the point of it all?

Mitchell's decision not to interview me set several things into motion starting with my social media rant, which had led to obtaining thousands of social media followers, which had led to Brennan Enterprises hiring me, and which had led to a job that was way better than the one I was trying to interview for in the first place.

And Mitchell's decision to get a blow job instead of interviewing me gave an extortionist the opportunity to blackmail him, which had further led to a second wave of significant licensing deals and increased brand awareness for me, putting me in a financial position to consider moving into my own place, getting a car, finishing school, or whatever I wanted to do. And when Mena decided to stay home with her dad in New Jersey after the death of her mother, I was in a position to pay her portion of our rent so that she didn't have to worry about bills while she was grieving.

I'm not saying that Mitchell was directly or indirectly responsible for all the profound changes in my life, but maybe he was. Maybe all of those things had to happen in order for me to be exactly where I was right then.

So, when almost every media outlet in seven countries had spent the past three weeks asking me how I felt about Mitchell Magellan's blow job caught on tape, I had to really think about my response. At first, it was incredibly uncomfortable just talking about sex openly on TV. But they wanted to talk about Mitchell's sex life and if he and I were friends, as we had appeared to be following Mena's mom's funeral, or whether I was sleeping with him, and regardless, how I felt about his behavior.

Soon enough, I learned to make jokes where appropriate, to deflect. But when pressed, I gave honest answers. One interview, however, was particularly difficult, and it was fitting for it to be the final one of my tour. I was certain the interviewer had no idea how impactful her insistent questions had been or how they would shape my subsequent actions.

It was a one-on-one interview that was pre-recorded in front of a live audience. During the early days of the tour, I worried that Mitchell might be watching, or Aunt Meg, or worse, Preston. I worried that my parents might be watching or my grandmother and her church friends.

And, when the interviewer began with, "Mitchell Magellan is the second most famous man in history for having oral sex in his office with a subordinate," I was like a deer in headlights, unsure of what to say to that presidential reference, considering my family would likely be watching when it aired. Honestly, of all the things Mitchell had been "caught doing" by the media, this was perhaps the mildest.

With Will and Maisy off-camera nodding and telling me to smile, I did what they said.

"You have made a career of hating Mitchell Magellan. Now that we all know *exactly* what Magellan was doing instead of interviewing you, how does the recent release of those extremely graphic video and audio tapes make you feel, especially considering photos of the two of you holding hands and looking quite familiar with one another leaking only days before?"

I adjusted myself in my seat, the action doing nothing to calm me.

"First of all, I don't hate Mitchell Magellan—"

"Obviously," she quipped as if she had just caught me in a lie.

I cleared my throat to regain some composure and give myself time to think about what I would say.

"When we saw one another at a mutual friend's funeral, he offered me a ride home." I didn't realize my mistake until I said it.

"And yet, you didn't go home. In fact, you went to his apartment, is that right?"

She had me. "Yes." I looked down quickly, then back at her. I was desperately hoping my thoughts about that weekend with Mitchell weren't evident.

She gave me a "that's some bullshit" look.

"And now? Now that these tapes of Mitchell Magellan are out there. How do you feel about him?"

I straightened, already having practiced how to respond to this question.

"My career focuses on supporting women who have been taken advantage of, ignored, or demeaned by powerful men. My brand isn't about Mitchell Magellan. Through my platforms and telling my story, I help give women who may have experienced something similar a voice, a sounding board, a way to express themselves, and someone to whom they can relate. Someone who made lemonade out of lemons," I said, feeling like I was disappointing her audience.

She faked a warm smile, but I knew she was pissed on the inside. She'd been expecting me to crucify Mitchell or to cry over his indiscretions. And for the remainder of the interview, she tried to corner me. And just like before, I boxed my way out with smart response after smart response. But her last question threw me. She asked, "What is the nature of your relationship with Mitchell Magellan now? Are you friends? More than friends?"

"I don't think I would classify my relationship with Mitchell Magellan as a friendship."

"How would you classify it?"

"We have mutual friends. I work for his closest competitor. We are . . . acquainted."

She looked as if she wanted to challenge me but instead, she sat forward and said, "If you could talk to Mitchell Magellan right now, what would you say?"

I hesitated, and then I worried that I had given my true feelings away. And when I was able to collect myself, I said, "Mitchell," but she interrupted me.

"Look right there, into that camera," she said and pointed to the camera that was set up to capture closeups of my teary eyes.

I turned to look where she had directed me and cleared my throat.

"Mitchell, you have an amazing capacity for change. You *can* recover from this. *Grow* from this. Everyone makes mistakes, sometimes even epic ones. Instead of seeing this as something to be ashamed of, I challenge you to see it as something to rise above. I challenge you to join me in supporting and elevating women in business and in life. Stop being a poster boy for bad behavior and endeavor to be a force for change."

After that, everything came into focus. I learned to distance Mitchell from the act that had been captured on tape because that was not the man I had come to know.

So, when next he called me, I answered.

CHAPTER FIFTEEN

MITCHELL MAGELLAN

"What happened to your hand, Mitchell," Aunt Meg said the moment she saw me.

"I broke it," I said, kissing her hello on the cheek and then following her into the kitchen.

"No shit, Sherlock," she said. "We're eating in the dining room tonight."

"What's the occasion? Preston finally get laid?" I said, joking, following her into the least-used room in her house.

"See what I have to go through, Lorelei?" Aunt Meg said as we entered the red-walled dining room we never used except for when there was company.

It was a motherfucking ambush disguised as a way for me to get to know the real estate agent Aunt Meg had hand-picked for me. Leggy, smart, ambitious, gorgeous fuckable mouth, and tits that were bursting out of her dress. I mentally chastised myself for even having those thoughts. I was going to talk to Mira later.

"Lorelei Concord, please meet my nephew, *Mitchell Xavier Magellan*," Aunt Meg said, beaming. I knew who the fuck she was. She was one of the most fuckable businesswomen in New York City and recently single after a nasty breakup with that billionaire asshole whose team won the last *Vendée* Globe race and who fancies himself a Formula 1 guy.

"Nice to meet you, Lorelei," I said, not shaking her hand.

I took a seat next to her and looked her over.

"Nice to meet you too, Mitchell," she said looking at me like she'd rather be eating me than the fucking lobster on her plate.

As I sat next to Lorelei Concord, Manhattan's third most successful independent real estate broker, I felt fucking trapped.

"So, Mitchell, what are you looking for in an *apartment*?"

When she said apartment, my brain heard "woman." I had to force my mind to focus and my eyes to look at her face when she talked. It did not help that she wore a tight blue dress that got me wondering what we might have been doing if Mira had not been in the picture. And those were dangerous thoughts for a man who hadn't had sex in three weeks.

"I don't really know," I said, looking down at my plate and then back up at her. I wasn't attracted to her. To me, she was just another woman who wanted to get into my pants, and not very subtly so.

The old me might have been all over this, giving her my list of apartment must-haves while getting blown in my car out of respect for Aunt Meg. But despite being intrigued by her, this entire look was over-Botoxed, lip fillers, and too much fucking makeup.

"Something practical? Close to the office?"

"You must have me mixed up with my brother. He was the practical one," I said, delaying her gratification.

"So, what then? What does Mitchell Magellan want?" she said, leaning forward so I could get a better look at her cleavage. Did women really think it was that easy to seduce me?

I looked at my watch, the AP that Mirabella liked. When I looked back at her, I realized that I was off my fucking game. And Mirabella had fucking put me there. Even when I dated Cassandra, I was aware of the overt flirting women would do right in front of her. Now, I barely noticed it. I truly had eyes only for Mira. But this woman had been served up on a platter for me, a gift from my aunt. I didn't even have to make an effort.

"Something ostentatious. Outrageous. Impeccable view. Unmatched amenities. Oh, and they must allow pets."

I was imagining being in a sick high-rise with an unparalleled view of Manhattan out the floor-to-ceiling window, having just fucked Mirabella, and now watching her as she laid in bed naked under the sheets, with our dog at the foot of the bed. In my two-second fantasy, I kick the dog off the bed, and get under the covers with her as she is coming down from an amazing orgasm and bury myself between her legs.

"Oh, you have pets?"

Her voice interrupted my thoughts.

"Not yet," I said, trying to shake the thought of Mirabella from my mind.

"Do you have a budget or range you'd like to be in?"

"I have no idea what things cost. So, twenty million? Thirty?"

She looked at Aunt Meg as if to say, *I thought you said he was smart.*

Aunt Meg shrugged and shook her head. Then said, "Excuse me for a minute. I'm going to go check on Preston."

Aunt Meg wasn't going to check on Preston. Preston was playing his video game and would be upset if she interrupted him. Aunt Meg was trying not to be too obvious about the fact that this was a setup.

Lorelei looked back at me like she wasn't sure this was going to work out.

"To get what you want, you need to be at least at fifty million. I recommend setting a budget of fifty to one hundred million, then being ready to pounce on something if it catches your eye. There are two apartments on the market on West 57th at the moment which are one hundred seventy-five million and two hundred fifty million respectively. Are you interested in seeing them?"

"Potentially," I said. "I don't need a penthouse or anything higher than the fortieth floor," I said, thinking about how Mirabella was afraid of heights. Since she was going to call me later, I allowed my thoughts and concerns to be of her.

"So, you don't necessarily want to stay in Chelsea?"

"Maybe. I love the neighborhood. But I was also thinking about Hudson Yard? Billionaire's Row?"

"What do you know and like about those two neighborhoods?"

I was starting to tire of all the questions. I hadn't yet signed with her. Shouldn't I have been the one asking her questions about her experience and why I should hire her? *Time to turn this fucking inquisition around*, I thought.

"You know what? Why don't you tell me about yourself? Aunt Meg never mentioned you were coming tonight," I said, letting her know I was surprised to see her.

She blushed a little, and normally I would have found it cute. Or maybe I did. But I shut that shit down.

"I graduated from Brown in 2012. Got into real estate almost immediately after because I couldn't find a job. I started out as a real estate photographer. Worked my way up the chain, then realized it was the brokers who were making the really good money. I got my real estate license, did my apprenticeship, and opened my own independent shop. Last year, I did twenty-eight million in volume."

"Wow, you were prepared," I said, impressed with her grind.

"So, you're obviously successful and smart, so tell me why I should hire you and not any of the other even more successful agents out there," I said. I took a sip of wine and sat back so that I could watch how she pitched me. It was like corporate foreplay.

"Hire me or don't hire me, Mitchell Magellan. Your Aunt Meg is the one who asked me here. But if you don't hire me, you will miss out on having a passionate, knowledgeable, hungry, and effective agent. I will make myself available to you whenever you want me to be. You will feel extremely well-cared-for."

Something about what she said felt like she wasn't just talking about real estate, and it reminded me of what Mirabella had said about me in her journal. I might be a little off my game since Mirabella, but I got the distinct feeling that Lorelei was making a pass at me.

I smiled and took another sip of wine.

"Nice pitch," I said.

"Thank you. I'm a pro, Mitchell, and I get results."

"I'm sure,' I said, briefly imagining what results she might be able to get me tonight.

"Have you considered CPW or CPS?" She said, perhaps sensing I was starting to lose interest.

"I'm happy to look on Central Park West and Central Park South if the place ticks the boxes. I honestly don't know much about Manhattan real estate."

"Do you know how many bedrooms you'd like?"

"At least five. I'll need two offices. I want a chef's kitchen and movie theater. If it doesn't already have those things, we'd need to do renovations."

"Would you consider two or three apartments renovated into one? This way you can get exactly what you want?"

"I prefer turnkey, but sure, that could be something I consider."

"Do you need parking?"

"Yes."

"How many vehicles?"

"At least six."

The truth is, I only mentioned considering moving. I wasn't thinking about interviewing agents just yet. But her questions were good ones, and they got me thinking and almost envisioning a life totally different from what it had been before my parents and brother died.

"Are you thinking family dwelling or bachelor pad?"

"I don't want something that looks like no woman would ever want to be there. I want a place a woman could be comfortable in and would want to spend time in," I said, wistfully thinking about Mirabella again.

"So, you don't currently have someone?"

"Excuse me?"

"I usually ask my clients who else needs to weigh in on the purchase or have an opinion. Some clients have spouses or significant others, mistresses, friends, or family whom they might want to involve in the decision-making or just giving their opinion during a showing."

"But that's not what you asked," I said worried now that maybe Lorelei was in on the setup with Aunt Meg.

"I'm sorry if it's a weird question. I wasn't trying to pry. I guess I was just wondering if you'd be bringing anyone else to showings," she recovered.

"Yes. On occasion, I may bring someone whose opinion I value to a showing. Is this going to be a problem?"

"It can be. Sometimes sellers of these high-value apartments and condos want only the potential buyer to come to viewings."

"Well, if I'm spending my fucking money, I will bring whoever I want to my showing," I said.

Lorelei drank her entire glass of wine and then helped herself to another.

"Will you be selling your current place?"

"I don't think so. No."

"Mitchell, have you considered what you will do with your parents' apartment uptown, your brother's apartment, and the houses on Long Island?"

"Not selling, if that's what you're getting at."

"I imagine you've had other agents inquiring about these properties?"

"Non-stop," I said, annoyed at the very idea.

"Well, if it's not too uncouth of me to say, I would like to throw my name into the hat for these opportunites."

"Noted," I said.

Suddenly Aunt Meg appeared, and said, "Sorry for being gone for so long. I hope it wasn't too awkward."

Yeah, it fucking was, Aunt Meg, I wanted to say. Instead, though, I said, "It was great, actually. Lorelei gave me quite a lot to consider."

"Yeah, Mitchell will keep me quite busy if we get to work together," Lorelei said, smiling the widest smile at me and then at Aunt Meg.

I checked my phone. It was 10:30.

"Well, ladies, I need to get going. I have somewhere I need to be.

Please tell Mr. Feer the food was delicious and it's great to have him back." I stood and reached out my hand for Lorelei to shake. "It was a pleasure to meet you. I'll be in touch."

When Lorelei shook my hand, it was the first time I had touched a woman besides Aunt Meg since Mirabella left me, and the fact that I even had that thought was concerning.

I smiled, released her hand, and then went over to Aunt Meg, kissed her on the cheek, and said, "Talk tomorrow?"

"Of course," she said, slipping me a business card with Lorelei's phone number and address.

I then made my way out of the house and to Brendan who was waiting with the Ghost. And as the time ticked closer to eleven, I got increasingly excited, anticipating Mirabella's call.

I MADE it back to Chelsea in record time from Connecticut, thinking about Mira the entire ride, trying to figure out what I'd learned over the past three weeks without her. Surely, I was in a better position to fight for us than I had been the last time she and I had spoken. And now, I couldn't wait to talk to my girl. To hear her voice.

Thankfully, traffic this time of night on a Wednesday was pretty much non-existent. As the clock read 11:11, I figured I would take a shower. For some reason, I wanted to be clean when Mirabella called. So, I showered quickly. When I finished, I hurriedly checked to see if I had missed her call. When no missed call alert showed, I began to worry.

In the few minutes it had taken me to complete my nighttime skincare routine and brush my teeth, Mirabella still had not fucking called. So, I opened Zillow and started looking at condos for sale in Manhattan. The variation in prices was huge. I could get a nice apartment for twenty million or a really nice one for eighty million. And then, there were those two that Lorelei mentioned.

Holy shit.

At eleven fifty-nine, my phone rang.

Mirabella.

"Hi," I said, trying not to sound too anxious, already coming apart for her.

"Hi."

For a couple of seconds neither of us said anything.

"How are you?" I said.

"Exhausted."

Everything in me wanted to offer to send Brendan to get her and bring her here, run her a hot bath, go down on her, and put her to bed. And, in the spirt of shooting one's shot, I did.

"Do you want to come here?"

She didn't respond at first, and I couldn't tell if she was considering it.

"I . . . I can't, Mitchell," she finally said.

"You can't or you don't fucking want to?" I said not really wanting to hear her fucking answer.

"Mitchell," she said, and I could hear the need in her voice. She wanted me. She was too fucking stubborn to tell me. She wanted to fight.

"Don't fucking 'Mitchell' me, Mirabella. Answer my fucking question."

"Stop talking to me like that," she said like she wasn't mine.

"Why? You don't want me to call you out on your shit when you're the one keeping us apart?"

"Can we talk about something else?" she said. My spitfire was against the wall, and instead of kicking me in my balls, she cowered. She hid. Fuck!

"What else is there, Mirabella?" I said, starting to fucking get annoyed.

She hesitated in such a way to indicate she wasn't at all prepared for this call. Like she hadn't been obsessing over it.

"How are you? Tell me how you are," she said. Her acting like everything was great was making me fucking mad.

"Not fucking good."

"I'm sorry, Mitchell," was all she fucking said. Not, let me come take fucking care of you or I wish I was fucking you or anything more fucking soothing than I'm fucking sorry.

"Are you, Mirabella?"

"Am I what?"

"Sorry?" I said with the biggest fucking attitude, and somehow even though I knew I was being a fucking asshole, I could not stop myself.

"Yes. This whole thing is killing me. I can't sleep. I can't eat."

Her quiet voice cut me deep. I felt like acting the fuck out. Being wild. I was out of control just from talking to her for those brief minutes.

"Fuck, Mirabella. Let me come get you. Let me run you a hot bath. Take care of you. Make you come, feed you, and put you to bed, Baby. Let me take care of you, even if you're still upset with me. Please. Tell me you need me to take care of you."

"Mitchell, I can't. I do. I want you to take care of me. But I just can't."

"Mirabella, I need to see you. Don't you miss me? I know I'm just an 'acquaintance' and all, but I can't believe you don't miss me."

The urge to be petty and remind her of how she'd classified our relationship on national fucking TV last week was too much.

"What are you doing, Mitchell? You don't sound good," she said, completely fucking ignoring me.

"I told you; I'm not fucking good."

"Maybe I should call you back when you can talk," she said even though she was the one wasting time with bullshit answers and avoidance. Stupid me, I thought we were going to make things right tonight.

"I can talk now. I have been waiting for you to fucking call me. And after everything, why today? Why did you pick up the phone this time?"

"I don't know. It felt like the right time to try talking, but clearly, I was wrong," she said, no fight in her. "I thought that if we could talk tonight, maybe we could . . ."

"We could what?"

"We could maybe try being friends instead of jumping back into how things were." Her voice was quiet, but it was as if she had fucking hit me in the head with a baseball bat.

"I thought we agreed we didn't need any more shitty friends," I said, remembering that night she begged me to come to Queens so I could fuck her.

She laughed. The sound of her voice right then got me worked all the way up.

"I miss your laugh, Mira."

Mirabella was quiet. For a brief moment, I misinterpreted her silence as hope. But then it went on way past the time it would have if she had been planning to see me tonight. To take me back.

"Mitchell . . ." My name on her tongue was like a curse, and for the first time since meeting her, I hated hearing it. She said it like she fucking didn't want me anymore. Like she was about to say, "it's not you, it's me" or some other bullshit people say when they're breaking up. She may as well have said, "Hey dickhead, go fuck yourself."

"Are you not fucking coming back to me, Mirabella? Is that what this whole bullshit fucking phone call is about?"

"Why would you speak to me like that? I didn't have an agenda. You called me, remember? This is me calling you back like I promised."

Fuck.

"Mirabella, I'm sorry. I'm glad you called me back. Hearing your voice after all this time. You sound so close but so far away. Listening to you now. It's taking all my fucking strength not to be the man you worry I might be."

"What does that even mean?"

"I'm just . . . I'm feeling out of fucking control. You want to make small talk. I just want to know when I can see you."

"I . . . I don't know. Not right now," she said, and I almost fucking lost it. I was ready to break my other fucking hand. "Mitchell. I miss you so much."

I swear to God. I was not in control right then. I was right on the fucking edge.

"So, this is what then? You miss me but you don't want me? I thought I told you I didn't want to play games."

I was about to fucking do something I could not take back. And by the pressure building inside me, I fucking felt unable to stop it.

"I just wanted to hear your voice, to see how you are."

"Because you miss me?"

"Yes," she said. I listened to her choke tears back. I was responsible for her pain. Fucking me. And yet, something about how noncommittal she was made me want to fucking push her. To punish her.

"I'm miserable. I broke my fucking hand today. Marissa Canto is suing me for sexual harassment, and my fucking girlfriend left me."

Mirabella didn't speak right away, and I got the distinct feeling she was being careful with her words. But I wasn't sure if she was trying not to cry or getting ready to fucking fight. Or worse than either of those two things, whether she was fucking hiding from me again.

I wanted to fucking punch something, break my hand some more. Smash the bones into a million fucking pieces so that it would be impossible to properly heal. To be forever physically scarred in the same way as Mira's fucking heart because of what I had done. The pain it would cause me was no less than I deserved.

I wanted to go to her right then and fuck her. I wanted to show her how much I missed her. What she was missing. To do every fucking dirty thing. I wanted to show her the man on those tapes. The one she loathed. The one she was afraid of. I wanted to let her see me this out of control.

"Mitchell," she said. Her voice was soft. I was happy she called, aroused, and fucking enraged while I waited for what she would say next. The mix of emotions was dangerous for someone like me with a propensity for excess.

I was itching for a line of coke right then, and I hated that fucking feeling.

"Yes," I said, hoping she could feel how on edge I was. That she could hear the desperation in my voice. I was hoping Mirabella would tell me that she was coming back to me tonight and save me from myself.

"I'm sorry things are bad for you right now. And despite what you may think, I didn't leave you because of the tapes. "

"So, it wasn't a break. You fucking left me."

"Yes. No. It was. I asked you for time. I needed time."

"Mira, I thought you meant like a fucking day. Seventy-two fucking hours. It's been three weeks."

"I know," was all she said.

"Then why? Why did you fucking walk out on me?"

"I left because I needed space to think and to figure my life out away from your spotlight. Away from all the media scrutiny and paparazzi."

"What the fuck are you talking about, Mirabella? I was ready to give you everything."

I hated how much and how far I had fallen for her. I'd managed to get to the ripe age of twenty-eight without feeling anything for anyone, including Cassandra. Now, it felt like I was on one of those fucking hook-up shows, hoping Mira would choose me.

"Sometimes I feel like I'm suffocating under the weight of being with you. Of trying to be what you want. Of trying to live up to what it means to be Mitchell Magellan's girlfriend."

Fuck. I was tired of this shit. My head was splitting. Thoughts of what I could have been doing with Mirabella right then instead of having this skull-splitting fucking conversation made things worse. And if I was being honest, this was one of the main reasons I didn't want or need to be attached to anyone. Fucking feelings were the absolute worse.

"Are you coming home or not?"

"Home?" She said, her denial about the location of her home pissing me the fuck off. How could she not know? Was I that damn irresponsible in dealing with Mirabella that she had no idea that her home was with me? Of all the mistakes I had made since meeting her, this was perhaps the biggest.

"Here. Home. With me where you belong," I said.

"No," she said, sealing my fate at exactly the same time as the 'no' had left her beautiful lips.

"So, we're not together then? So, this is fucking it? We're nothing to one another? You don't even want to have sex with me? I'm fucking nothing to you?"

"Mitchell."

"Fuck that. Answer me. Are we together or fucking not, Mirabella?"

"What do you want me to say, Mitchell?"

"I want you to tell me right fucking now if I have a girlfriend or not."

"You want permission to have sex with other women?"

"Yes," I said, unable to walk it back now. Not even fucking sure I wanted to. Thinking that maybe I'd fucked up by pushing back at her right then.

Mirabella didn't speak for a few long seconds. But when she did, it fucking killed me because my little spitfire was back. And she'd brought weapons. Fatal fucking weapons intended to wreak absolute fucking carnage on its victim. To turn him into someone completely and utterly so unrecognizable no one would ever want him. He wouldn't even want his damn self.

"Go fuck whoever you want."

"Mira," I said, begging.

"You don't owe me anything, Mitchell. Go fuck *whoever you want.*"

Right then, the thought of Mirabella with another man was overwhelming. If she was giving me permission to be with other women, it meant she could choose to be with another man. She could go back to that motherfucker Ben. She could go to Billy's tonight and find someone to bring home. Someone to fuck her in her twin bed.

"Fuuuuuuck!" I screamed into the phone. And then I fucking smashed it against the fucking wall. And if Mirabella was still on it, listening, all she would have heard was the sound of me getting dressed, grabbing my shit, and running out of the fucking apartment.

I flagged down a taxi about ten blocks away and asked to be taken to Lorelei's apartment uptown. And when I got there, she didn't seem surprised to see me at all.

CHAPTER SIXTEEN

MIRABELLA CASTLE

Three days had gone by since I had given Mitchell permission to sleep with other women. He hadn't returned my calls or texts. He was not interested in talking to me. He wasn't interested in seeing me. I was back to being no one and nothing to Mitchell Magellan.

It was Sunday, so I was off. RayRay asked me to watch Christina until his mom could pick her up at around noon. And, as I sat in RayRay's living room, watching her play with the toy castle that her Uncle Mitch had gotten her, my heart was breaking. I was in physical pain that radiated through my body starting with my extremities. And I was lucky Christina was too young to understand why her auntie was crying.

It had been a mistake to call Mitchell Wednesday night. Things between us were still raw and dangerous. And by the end of the call, I may have sent him into the arms of another woman. It certainly was not my intention. Rather, I had intended to talk to him. To ask how he was doing. To see what he had been up to. I wanted to tell him that I missed him but that I was not ready to pick up where we left off. I was going to ask him if he wanted to meet for lunch one day.

But whatever I said or didn't say set Mitchell off down a path that was all at once horrifying and sad. He was agitated, contemplative, combative, angry, and generally upset by our situation. And, when I didn't match that energy, it unleashed something in him. It pushed him to be destructive. So, when he backed me into a corner and asked if I was coming home, it made me fucking angry. And then when he asked if we were together or not, I assumed he wanted to know so he could fuck around on me.

So, I did what I normally do. I told him to fuck off. I told him he could fuck whomever he wanted, even though the idea of Mitchell with another woman made me sick to my stomach.

"What the hell did you do now, B? Why would you tell him he can screw whoever he wants? Are you trying to sabotage your life?"

"I don't want him waiting for me," I said, lying to myself. What I actually wanted was to erase Mitchell's past. To make it so that it had only been me for him. And it was stupid and childish and selfish, not to mention completely unrealistic.

"And why the hell not?"

"Mitchell needs . . . sex. He needs it often," I said, my mind thinking back to how often we had done it in his apartment after Mena's mom's wake.

"Yeah, and he needs sex from *you*. He wanted to have sex with *you*. He was practically begging you from what you said. Are you trying to punish him for having a life before he met you?"

How RayRay accentuated the word 'you' when he spoke pissed me off.

"No."

"Are you certain? Because it sure looks that way."

"Maybe, I don't know. I've never felt like this before."

"Because you're in love with him, Mirabella," RayRay said, empathetically and accusingly. I didn't tell him that we had said 'I love yous.'

"You think I don't know that?"

"And do you think he's in love with you too?"

"Yes. I don't know. I think Mitchell is in love with the idea of me. That he wanted me because he couldn't have me. I think he is in love with chasing a woman like me, someone who isn't lined up waiting to drop her panties for him."

RayRay looked at me askew as if I was stupid and he was going to have to spend a lot of time and effort to educate me; time he didn't have.

"You can't punish him for something he did before he knew you, B. And if there is a minuscule chance that he does actually love you, you need to fix this before it becomes unfixable."

"So, you're cool with him lying to me?" I said, near tears.

"What did he lie to you about?"

"About who he was sexually. He spit in that woman's vajayjay and in her mouth," I said, being careful about what I said with Christina in the next room.

RayRay looked at me with something like pity and frustration. "Did I ever tell you that he called me when the tapes leaked?"

"No. What did he say?"

"He was beside himself thinking about you and wondering if you were ok. His first thought was of you and how the tapes would affect you."

"Oh," I said, feeling sad about how that whole day had gone down.

"B, I'm gonna tell you something, and you are not going to like it."

"Has that ever stopped you before?"

"Listen, Mirabella," he said, "First of all, what people do in their private lives is none of your fucking business. Mitchell Magellan had a life and women before you. If you can't deal with that, then you shouldn't be with him."

"That's why I sent him away. I can't unsee that video or un-hear that audio tape. I threw up when I heard it. And when I saw him, doing those things to her, I wanted to crawl up into a ball and die. I felt dirty and ashamed for loving him," I said, letting the tears and snot fall. "The kinds of things Mitchell wants, needs, I can't give him."

RayRay shook his head, and then went to get a box of tissues from the living room.

"You're a damn mess. Don't be infecting my daughter with all of this negative energy," he said, making a circular motion with his hand as he handed me the tissues.

I laughed, even though he was right. Christina was just a little girl. She didn't need my nonsense.

"B, you tend to get scared and then you act out. And in this case, you got close to a man that maybe you didn't really know. You did things with him that you haven't done with anyone else, and he made you feel some kind of way. And then when you found out who he was before he met you, it scared the shit out of you, and now you don't know if it was all a lie. If what you had with him sexually was real. If you are enough for him. But that is all one hundred percent a Mirabella problem, not a Mitchell problem. You need to get over yourself, mature up. I know you're only twenty-one, but Mitchell is a grown-ass man. He has grown-fucking-man needs. And if you want to be with him, and I think you do, you need to figure out how to be ok with who he is."

"So, what are you saying?"

"I'm saying you fucked up ah-gain. Your insecurities and self-doubt made you fuck all the way up, and I'm not sure it can be fixed. If you told Mitchell you were ok with him sleeping with another woman, I'm guessing he took that to heart."

"So, you saw the picture of him and that woman?"

"Are you really that naïve to think there aren't women waiting to drop their panties for that man? Hell, I'm thinking about dropping mine. The broody, grieving billionaire thing is so damn hot," RayRay said.

RayRay was right. There was something so hot and mysterious and sexy about Mitchell Magellan. And when he made you the focus of his attention, that spotlight was scorching, life-affirming, and intense like the sun.

"I hate when you tell me about myself."

"Someone's gotta tell you," he said. "And, B? If Mitchell has been or is with that woman, what are you going to do? You actually gave him permission," RayRay asked a question I had no answer for. "You should call him."

"Yeah, I tried that already, and every horrible thing I felt—am feeling—wouldn't allow me to go to him, let alone take him back."

"Mirabella Castle. Call that man. Apologize. Tell him you want him back."

"I can't."

"Why the hell not?"

"For one, he isn't answering my calls. He hasn't returned any of my texts."

"He hasn't?" RayRay said, incredulously. "I just spoke to him yesterday."

"You did? I said blowing my nose.

"Yeah, I asked if he could watch Christina for a few hours today. He said he had some things to do."

"So, his phone is working, just not for me. He's choosing not to talk to me. Mitchell's all the way out," I said in a small and broken voice.

"And didn't you do that same thing to him?"

RayRay was right, I was getting what I deserved. But I was unsure how Mitchell was the good guy in all of this.

"He cheated on his girlfriend. Did I tell you that?"

"What girlfriend?"

"He dated a girl for a year and a half about five years ago." I said, in a sorry attempt to justify my feelings and my actions.

"And he admitted to cheating?"

"Yes."

"He didn't lie to you?" RayRay trapped me right then. Mitchell had been forthcoming and honest when I asked him about his past relationship.

"No."

"But he could have, B, and he didn't even though he probably knew you would judge him for that."

"I know. You know what he told me? He told me he didn't want me withholding pleasure from us just because we were fighting. He told me to take my feelings out on him in the bedroom, and when we were done, we could talk."

"Jesus. That's a sexy ass man," RayRay said, as I remembered fighting with Mitchell over his sponsoring Ben's play. Right then, I had to squeeze my thighs together remembering how good the sex was. RayRay noticed I was getting hot and bothered. He shook his head while giving me a 'you're hopeless' look.

"Did it ever occur to you that he didn't tell you what was on those tapes because he was ashamed? Embarrassed? That maybe he was afraid for you to know that about him?"

"No."

"I think Mitchell cares very much about what you think of him. He wants to live up to your impossible standards. Has he given you any reason not to trust him now, since you've been together?"

"The thing with Ben." I said it like it proved me right about my decision to break things off with Mitchell. Like I was going to win a gameshow prize.

"Is he one of those guys who ogles other women in your presence?"

"No."

"Then what's the problem, Mirabella? Do you think he's cheated on you? That he will? Is that what you're afraid of?"

"Once a cheater, always a cheater."

"Maybe. But maybe he cheated because it was the only thing he could do to find his way to you."

"What?"

"Maybe the Universe doesn't make mistakes. Maybe people make mistakes. I have seen the two of you together, B. That man would burn the fucking world for you," RayRay said, apparently with no concern at all that Christina was going to go to daycare dropping f-bombs one day.

"I'm not Cinderella. I'm not Pretty Woman. I'm not looking for a prince."

"And yet you ended up with the Prince of New York City."

"Right?" I said, living in the irony of that statement.

I blew my nose again.

"You need to call him, B. Go to him. Be with him. Talk to him. I'm gonna be late for work. Lock the door when I leave."

RayRay gave me a hug and a kiss as Christina entered the room.

"Love you. Good luck."

RayRay went to Christina, grabbed her up into a hug, and kissed her little cheek.

"Be good for Auntie B, sweet girl. Daddy will see you later."

When RayRay left, I took his advice.

I dialed Mitchell's cell phone.

Straight to voicemail.

I dialed his work number.

Unavailable.

I texted him.

Nothing. For hours.

Mitchell Magellan was ghosting me.

DURING CHRISTINA'S NAP TIME, I needed a break. It had been non-stop dolls, pretend play, and *Bluey* since her dad left.

I checked my messages.

> MENA: What the hell?

> MENA: Link

I clicked the link to *Page Six*. The headline read MITCHELL MAGELLAN STEPS OUT ONCE MORE WITH REAL ESTATE HOTTIE, *Lorelei Concord*. There were four photos of them walking together, walking together eating ice cream cones, laughing together while walking, and one of him tying the fucking shoelace on her Nike fucking Dunks.

I felt sick looking at them. Mitchell had already moved on, and it was my fault. One picture of them out was not enough to make a case but now there were more.

Mitchell didn't call me back because he was all the way out and no longer cared.

> ME: We broke up

MENA: When?

ME: 3 wks ago. Didn't wanna bother you

MENA: well now I'm bothered

ME: so much has happened since Portugal

MENA: I'll be back in Queens in a few days

ME: Really, take your time.

MENA: Thanks for paying my rent. Will pay you back

ME: Take ur time

MENA: My dad will not miss me. He and his boyfriend are going to Bali

ME: Oh

MENA: He's calling it a bereavement cleanse, he invited me. Um no fucking thanks

ME: y didn't u tell us he was so young?

MENA: cause it's fucking gross

ME: He's kind of hot

MENA: ewww

ME: they seemed really serious. Tell me more about the bereavement cleanse

MENA: Says he needs to let go of his failed marriage and my mom so he can be fully present in his current relationship

ME: Oh

MENA: What are you doing?

ME: . . .

I didn't want to admit that I was scouring the Internet for everything I could find about this woman who had been photographed with Mitchell twice in the past few days. All I could think about was what happened immediately after I had been photographed with Mitchell. That was the day he had put me inside his Maybach SUV, and I took off my panties, and fucked his face.

The thought of Mitchell being intimate like that with another woman before he met me made me sick. It was immature and unbecoming. I knew this. But the idea that he was already with someone else, a tall, leggy, fake blonde with fake boobs made me livid, and jealous, and fucking petty.

It wasn't even like I could get back at him. I didn't have guys lined up outside my door waiting to take his place in my bed. I didn't even have a dildo!

The more I read about her, the more I hated her. Hated that I had been so impulsive when Mitchell asked me directly if I was planning to come back to him. He asked me if I was coming "home."

Part of me always knew that whatever it was that Mitchell and I had was never going to work. But I was selfish and greedy. I needed him. I needed his attention. I needed to feel the things that man made me feel. It was risky and stupid to allow myself to fall in love with him. And when shit got real, I ran. I left. I couldn't face him. Even after he asked me not to do that to him again.

And now, I sat in a shit pile of my own making, regretting my words and actions in the face of photo evidence of Mitchell with another woman. I texted him.

> ME: I see you've moved on so enjoy your fucking fake Bratz doll

I put the phone down so I could start cleaning before Christina's grandmother arrived. I wiped down all the surfaces, washed the dishes, put all her toys in their proper color-coded bins her father insisted she have, and swept the floor. I even folded a load of laundry RayRay hadn't yet had time to do.

Done, feeling like Cinderella, I resolved to sit on the couch and take a much needed and well-deserved nap. I peeked in on Christina, who was still fast asleep and according to her schedule, would be for at least another hour or so. Then, I would make us lunch, and we would eat it while watching *Gracie's Corner,* if her grandmother hadn't arrived by then.

But before I could sit down, the doorbell rang.

Good, Mrs. Ellis is early, I thought as I checked the wall clock and noticed she had arrived one hour earlier than I was expecting her to. I looked around to be certain I'd tidied up all the toys before letting her in.

"You're early, I said not even looking at her, and holding the door open as I picked up a stuffy and placed it in the pink toy bin.

Just then, Mrs. Ellis said, "Mirabella," in a voice that sounded an awful lot like Mitchell fucking Magellan's.

CHAPTER SEVENTEEN

MITCHELL MAGELLAN

I WAS AMBUSHED TWICE THIS WEEK BY PEOPLE IN MY LIFE WITH opposing agendas, each thinking they knew what was best for me.

I needed a realtor, but instead of introducing me to one that would simply do their job, Aunt Meg set me up with one she thought I would be into and who would take my mind off Mirabella. When she called to ask what I thought of Lorelei and if I was going to work with her, I angrily told her to stay out of my love life.

When RayRay asked me to watch Christina for a few hours, I had to turn him down because I already had an appointment to see two apartments with Lorelei. I felt like a tool, and I didn't want to let him or Christina down. Just because Mirabella and I weren't together, didn't mean I was no longer Christina's pretend uncle. And if I was being honest, spending too much time with Lorelei was no good for my ego.

So, I moved some things around at work, took the afternoon off, and went to get Christina so her grandmother didn't have to. I had planned to take Christina to Serendipity and American Girl. I was going to uncle *hard*.

And when I knocked on the door to RayRay's apartment, and saw who had greeted me, I realized he too had ambushed me.

"Mirabella," I said as other words escaped me.

Suddenly everything came back, hard and fast. All the feelings, emotions, sounds, smells, visuals. Every fucking thing. Every fantasy, wet dream, sexual encounter, argument, that night we first met.

And then, she said my name.

"Mitchell."

I recognized the tone in her voice. She wanted me. She fucking needed me. Her panties already fucking coated in her arousal, her slit slick. Her nipples were beginning to bud and strain against her bra. She was breathing heavier, though trying not to let me see it. She was fucking aroused. And that was the thing with Mirabella. She was always hiding from me. Trying not to let me see her. To notice her arousal, her need.

The bulge in my pants fought to be unleashed on her, inside her. I fucking needed her too. But what could I do? I was not about to have sex with Mirabella in RayRay's apartment while his daughter was there.

"I wasn't expecting you," she said, breathy and fucking gorgeous, her hair in braids. I was not fucking prepared for how hot she looked right then.

"Mirabella," I said, "we should talk." In that moment, 'talk' was code for 'fuck.'

I failed to push all sexual thoughts out of my brain as images of Mira in various positions engaged in dirty fucking sex acts with me played in my head like a movie. She looked down at me like she did when she wanted to know if I was turned on too.

Mirabella became shy when she noticed that I was, and she looked down at the floor like I had never been inside her.

I entered RayRay's apartment and looked around. Like a predator, I was looking for a place to corner Mirabella.

She must have felt it, that fucking heat between us that's always been there. Like how it was when I gave her no other option but to fucking look at me, feel my needy and unrelenting gaze on her, and try to resist the desire building in her as she clenches and oozes for me while her nipples beg to be touched. And in that moment, all I wanted was Mirabella cornered and fucking dripping for me.

Because when I turned my attention to her, she backed up like she was afraid of me. And the way I was feeling right then, maybe she should have been. I played cool on the outside, but I felt rabid, out of control, and capable of doing some shit that I had no business doing.

I advanced on her, wanting to do all the things I had been dying to do with her from Day One. As she backed up even more, I used my good hand to pull her to me, against me. She started crying. But I didn't stop. She did this to me. She made me how I fucking was right then. So, I maneuvered her not-so-gently against the nearest wall.

"Why the fuck are you crying?" I said in a way that told her I didn't really care about her answer. I was done listening to her bullshit.

"I'm afraid of you right now," she said in a voice that was smaller than I remembered it to be.

"Why?" I said, knowing fully why.

"I don't want you to touch me," she said, and I wanted to put my fucking hand through the wall. I looked away, afraid she would see me for what I was, a fucking out of control lunatic. I wanted to tie her the fuck up to one of those kitchen chairs, naked and vulnerable. I wanted to punish her for what she fucking did. Mirabella had me wild as fuck, thinking about all kinds of ways to subdue her and make it so she could never leave me again.

"You don't fucking want me to touch you? Because your fucking body says otherwise," I said, breathing too hard. I put my hand just inside the band of her fucking yoga pants. I'm not a fucking idiot. I wasn't planning to really touch her unless she wanted me to. Unless she gave me permission.

"Tell me how you don't want me to fucking touch you, Mirabella, because I think you're full of shit. I think seeing me now makes you realize how badly you fucked up and now, you want me but you're afraid to admit it." I whispered in her ear.

"Admit what?" She said, tears in her eyes, her body practically vibrating with how badly she wanted me to fuck her.

"That you want me to make you come," I whispered against her.

She fucking moaned, turning her head so that her mouth was on my neck when she did, and that was my fucking permission.

I reached into her panties and kept my hand on her mound as I said, "You don't want me to touch you, Mirabella? Tell me to stop."

When she rubbed her thighs together to relieve the tension in her clit, I slipped my fingers inside her. Right then, I knew Mirabella hadn't been fucking touched since the last time we were together.

Jesus.

I felt like I was going to come just from the feel of her.

I began rubbing her very swollen clit and moving against her. I was fucking rabid.

"Mitchell," she cried, "I don't want to come," she said. "Not now. Not here."

I pulled my fingers from her tight pussy and held my head against hers as we both tried hard to come down from the frenzy that had overtaken us.

"Were you going to come, Mirabella?"

"Yes," she said not hesitating.

"I want to make you come."

"Why?"

"Because I want you to be happy. And I want to know that I can still make you come for me," I said, hating myself for being so selfish and getting pleasure elsewhere.

I stepped back slightly so I could look in her eyes.

"I want to know if you're still mine," I said finally.

"I really missed you," she said.

"I really missed you too," I said.

"Why did you leave me, Mirabella?" I whispered.

"I'm sorry," she cried some more.

"I asked you not to run. I asked you to work things out with me, to talk to me. I asked you not to punish me by withholding pleasure from us."

"I know," she said, her entire being fucking small and pitiful. "But sex isn't the answer to every problem, Mitchell."

She was right, but I wanted to tell her she was only half right. And the part of her that was wrong was very fucking wrong.

"You told me to fuck whoever I wanted," I said, realizing it had come out like an accusation, like I was placing blame on her for my fucking decisions.

She stopped crying then, and I knew what was coming next. I walked away from her, created distance between us. And that was my tell. It's how I avoided her judgement.

"Did you? Fuck someone else?" She asked the question, and I heard it and understood it. And yet, I fucking hesitated.

Then, like a little angel here to save the damned, Christina walked into the room, rubbing her sleepy eyes.

"Uncle Mitchies," she said in the most adorable of voices. I grabbed her up into a giant billionaire uncle-sized hug and showered her with tiny kisses.

And as Mirabella watched me with her precious goddaughter, relief on my face for the timely intrusion, she must have assumed the answer to her question.

A few minutes passed until someone buzzed the apartment. I watched Mirabella let Mrs. Ellis in, confused as to why both she and I were there.

When she entered the apartment, her beautiful face lit up. It was clear where RayRay had gotten his good looks. His mother didn't look a day over sixty, despite her being almost eighty.

"Christina, go see your grandmother," I said, putting her down.

"Gramma, Gramma," she said, as she ran like a drunk person and held her arms in the air for Mrs. Ellis to pick her up.

"There's my beautiful girl. How's grandma's sweet baby today? Did you have a good nap? Are you ready to eat lunch?" She said with a big smile while picking Christina up and twirling her around.

"I hungry, Gramma," Christina said.

"Ok, well let's go wash hands, and then we can see what grandma can make her baby." Then she turned to me and said, "I'm sure you and Mirabella can find something else to do this afternoon? You're off the hook."

I smiled at this kind woman; it seemed she was in on RayRay's set up too.

"Yes, thank you, Mrs. Ellis." I said, before turning to Christina, and saying, "Be a good girl for your grandma, Christina. Uncle Mitchies loves you."

Christina hugged her little arms around my neck, and for a brief second, all my troubles divided into what is important and everything else. I had planned to talk to RayRay later this week about school for her. A real school for kids her age where she can learn languages, be exposed to culture, and get a great head start in life.

"How about you go give Auntie Mirabella a hug and kiss too?" I encouraged her, taking her from her grandmother's arms, and bringing her over to her godmother.

She smiled at me and then widened the one she held for Christina. And even though we were miles apart right then, I could not stop thoughts of a future with Mirabella and maybe even kids from entering and lingering in my mind. And for the first time in my life, I felt like I could potentially have a future. If only we could get over this current rough patch.

Mirabella kissed and hugged and fawned over Christina for a few minutes it seemed. And when she was done, she collected her things, said goodbye to Mrs. Ellis, and we exited the apartment, her first and me behind her.

"Mirabella. Please." I said. "I have an appointment I have to make uptown. To see an apartment. If you aren't busy, would you like to come?"

She responded without looking at me.

"Yes."

"Can I hold your hand?" I asked, knowing that just because I'd had my fingers inside her minutes ago, there was no guarantee that she would agree.

"Please don't," she said.

We walked silently to the Suburban. I opened her door, and helped her step up. When she was fully inside, I resisted the urge to strap her in, deciding to keep my hands to myself the entire way to Midtown.

As Brendan began heading uptown, Mirabella looked at me, and said, "Is your realtor joining us?"

"My realtor?" I said, seeing my mistake only after I'd made it. She must have seen the pictures of Lorelei and I in *Page Six*.

"Yes, your fucking realtor."

I swallowed a smile at the appearance of my little spitfire. It was enough to sober me. Shit. I needed to come clean to Mira if I was to have any chance with her.

"Mirabella," I said, as the pain I was about to inflict on her weighed on me.

"What?"

"Do you still want me? Because it seemed like you might after just now."

"What does that have to do with whether your realtor is joining us?"

"Because what you say next will determine what happens from here on out," I said. "Do you want me? Are you coming back to me?"

Mira seemed like she wanted to respond but wasn't sure which of those questions were more important in that moment.

"Did you sleep with her?"

I fucking didn't hesitate this time. I fired the shot.

"No but we fooled around."

Instead of recoiling, Mirabella steeled.

"Did you ask me if you could sleep with other people so that you could sleep with her?"

"I never asked you if I could sleep with other women."

She was quiet then, no doubt, recalling the details of our brief but memorable call.

"What was it like?"

"What was what like?"

"Being with her."

"Mirabella, please. Can we not talk about this in particular?"

"I want to know, and I need you to tell me."

I hated seeing the pain in those beautiful eyes.

"Mira, it's really uncomfortable for me to talk to you about things I did with another woman."

At first, when she didn't respond, I worried I might have undone all the progress we had made today by not being forthcoming and instead, making it so she had to ask me questions I barely bothered to answer. And when she opened her mouth to speak after what felt like a hundred million minutes, I wished I had just answered her damn question.

"It's uncomfortable for me having to hear about it. To even think about it. To imagine it in great detail. To not be able to sleep. And then when I do finally fall asleep, to fucking wake up screaming in the middle of the night from nightmares about you with other women. Being sick to my stomach and throwing up in the bathroom at Brennan Enterprises because I can't fucking stop thinking about you doing to other women what you do to me. Making them feel how you make me feel. Looking at them how you look at me. Touching them how you touch me."

"Mira—"

She wasn't done pouring her heart out.

"I feel like I'm suffocating under the weight of all of this, Mitchell. I don't know if any of it was real. If anything you said to me. Did to me. If it was all in my head because no one had ever touched me like that. Looked at me like that. Wanted me like that. And if it was so easy for you to move on, the same fucking night, then what even was our relationship? Was I a fucking project for you? A toy? A fucking charity case?"

I was speechless. What could I say? I had really fucked up. And as I processed all that Mira had said, I regretted not going to her apartment in Queens that night. I should have. Even if she didn't let me up. Even if I couldn't be in the same room with her. I'd like to think she would have been able to feel me, that close.

When I made the decision not to ask Brendan to bring the car around so that I could at least try to fight for us, I'd sealed our fate. And all the fucking promises I'd made to her, like asking her to consider living with me and telling her I loved her? None of them meant anything because when shit got real, I gave up.

Fuck.

I went to Lorelei's that night with all intentions of getting my dick wet. She wanted to. Fuck. I wanted to. I let her touch me. I let her press herself to me. To feel my arousal against her. For a moment, I allowed myself to revert to the worst fucking version of myself. I used the situation with Mirabella to give myself permission to revert to the old me who didn't give a shit about anyone or anything but himself. The one who couldn't spare his own mother five minutes on the phone because he was getting sucked off by three women.

"I'm so fucking sorry," I said. "I don't think you understand how much I fucking hate myself. How much I wish I could have met you before. How much I wish I hadn't gone to Lorelei the night you told me you didn't want me and that I could fuck other women."

Mirabella looked as if hearing Lorelei's name made her physically ill. Like she was going to actually be sick just from the sound of it. And, I regretted saying it right then.

We sat in silence for the next twenty minutes, Mira staring out of her window and me staring at her, trying to stop myself from finishing what I had started in RayRay's apartment and wanting desperately to lick her off my fingers.

"Is that when you broke your hand," she said suddenly, still not looking at me.

"No."

"Tell me what happened." She was looking at me now, concern I didn't deserve contorting her gorgeous face. I hated what this was doing to her. I wanted to tell her how beautiful she looked with her hair in braids.

"To my hand?"

"No. Tell me what you did with her," she said. "Did she blow you?"

Just then, as if God himself had intervened on my behalf, Brendan stopped, and then opened my door. We had arrived at the first appointment.

"Let's finish this later, ok?" I said in a soft voice.

She shook her head, light gone from her usually bright eyes.

And when I went to her side to let her out of the vehicle, she accepted my hand as I helped her step down but held onto it when she was fully out.

Lorelei was waiting in the lobby for us. The minute Mirabella saw her, she gripped my hand tighter.

"Mitchell," Lorelei said with her reconstructed too-perfect nose turned up, "Who's this?"

"This is my *girlfriend*, Mirabella Castle," I said, in the most awkward conversation between the woman I had nearly fucked a few days ago and the woman I nearly fucked an hour ago. She and I will be viewing apartments together from now on. And in fact, she is your client now, not me. Mirabella will make all the decisions, right down to submitting offers and deciding which apartments to view and when. I'll need release paperwork for me and new representation paperwork for Mirabella immediately."

I was on autopilot, not even thinking to get Mirabella's permission. I was emboldened by her just holding my hand. There was so much hope in that one gesture. So much promise. So much fucking sexual tension.

Lorelei looked like she had swallowed ear wax. But not one to fuck with her commission, she fixed her face and extended her hand to Mirabella, who didn't accept it.

"It's nice to meet you, Mirabella," Lorelei said in a fake-nice voice.

"Mr. Magellan and I would prefer to tour the apartment alone," Mirabella said, in a surprise move reminiscent of my little spitfire.

"I'm sorry that's not possible," Lorelei said.

"And why not?" Mirabella stood her ground.

"My client doesn't allow strangers in his apartment unattended."

"Your client won't allow Mitchell Magellan to view his apartment *unaccompanied* by you?"

Fucking Mirabella enunciated "unaccompanied" correcting Lorelei's incorrect use of "unattended." Damn if my girl wasn't a fucking bad ass. All I had to do was stand there and watch her work.

"That's not what I meant," Lorelei said. "Please, Mitchell," she said looking at me.

"Lorelei, either respect Mirabella's wishes, or we can find a different realtor," I said. I'd told Lorelei the very night of my indiscretion that she should not expect anything more from me. That I was with Mirabella, and it had been a mistake for me to show up there expecting something other than her representation as my realtor.

She'd recently ended a high-profile relationship and was looking for a distraction. Not wanting to be anyone's emotional crutch, I apologized to her and left. The next day, we looked at apartments like the previous night's temporary insanity had never happened. And I wasn't even worried about the New York City gossip pool because plenty of women in it could vouch for me.

Lorelei fixed her face once more, handed Mirabella the house keys, and said, "Please return them to me at my office when you're done. And good luck. I think you're going to like this one."

And then she was gone, leaving Mirabella and I alone in the lobby.

I turned to Mirabella.

"Are you OK?" I asked.

She smiled a smirky smile.

"I can make an offer on whichever apartment I want to?"

I smiled too now, loving the way she was looking at me. That she was looking at me at all.

"Well, that was me showing off for you. Trying to impress you."

"How much is this apartment?"

"It's listed at sixty-four million," I said as casually as I would have said sixty-four thousand.

"Holy fucking shit," she said.

Her exuberance made me happy. And if it only took sixty-four million dollars to win her back, so fucking be it.

CHAPTER EIGHTEEN

MIRABELLA CASTLE

It was emotional overload from the moment I saw Mitchell at the door. Everything I had wanted to say and everything I had longed to do to him and with him was caught in my throat. My heart drummed loudly against my chest wall and my thoughts ran wild, threatening to get away from me.

When Mitchell advanced on me, seeking to corner me so that I had to face him, my body responded. I told myself it was fear, but the arousal that consumed me the closer we became was primal and barely containable.

To save myself from being found out, I lied and said I was afraid of him. But I was really afraid that if he touched me, even a little, I would come. And, if I had allowed myself to give in to the pleasure Mitchell was capable of giving me, I would be lost forever.

I clutched his hand and stood in front of the architecturally splendid building with the gorgeous black beam details and only steps away from MOMA. I rather preferred Chelsea to this neighborhood, but I was not going to give up the opportunity to see why Mitchell was interested in seeing this place.

Now, in the lobby of his potential new apartment, and with Lorelei gone, I held onto his hand, and looked around. The lobby resembled a luxury European member's only club, or at least what I imagined one to look like. We made our way to the elevators where everything was awash in brown marble. But that I could overlook. Those black beams that were on the outside of the building? They were inside too, leaning and stretching their wide girts from floor to ceiling in odd places, in some cases in the middle of a room. And this time, they were whatever color matched the interior décor.

At the elevator bay, Mitchell turned to me and gave me a worried look.

"What?" I said.

"It's the penthouse."

"What floor?" I said, terrified of heights.

"Seventy-six."

"Oh."

"And seventy-seven."

"It's two stories? Get out."

He nodded.

"We'd have our own elevator."

"No way. So, no one would be able to use our elevator?" I said, a huge grin on my face. Just then I was imagining what it could be like to actually live in this building with Mitchell. I pushed the thought from my head. We were nowhere near close to moving in together.

"Nope. Not unless they were invited up by us."

"How does that even work?"

"I have no idea. But I like it. Lots of privacy. We wouldn't have to see another neighbor like ever."

I loved the way Mitchell was smiling at me. I'd missed that. Our sudden use of 'we,' 'us,' and 'ours' wasn't lost on me. He located the elevator that led to the penthouse, pressed the key card to the pad on the wall, and the door magically opened. A gasp escaped me before I knew what had happened.

He waved for me to enter first, and then followed me in.

Once inside, he pressed the keycard to the pad inside, and pressed the button for PH76. Having let go of it earlier, I grabbed his hand again, my general nervousness and fear of heights threatening to make it so I didn't enjoy this moment with him.

"We're ok, Baby," he said in my ear. But instead of being calming, it started my loins to stir.

This. Fucking. Man.

When the elevator doors opened, I was not even halfway prepared.

Mitchell led me by the hand into the foyer of the penthouse.

"Holy Shit. The pictures do not do it justice. Who fucking lives like this?" Mitchell marveled.

There, to the North was Central Park and to the South was Downtown Manhattan in all its glory, including the Empire State Building and One World Trade Center, otherwise known as the Freedom Tower.

"These windows, how tall are they?" The excitement in my voice was amplified by the pounding of my heart.

"They've gotta be at least twenty feet. Twenty-five?"

"Breathtaking," I said.

"Very," he said in a way that made me turn towards him, but Mitchell wasn't looking out the windows. His gaze was fixed on me. I couldn't stop the smile that just happened without my permission, embarrassed that of all he could be admiring at that very moment, Mitchell chose to focus on me.

"We are definitely not in Chelsea anymore," I said, a smile still on my face.

I let go of his hand to walk to the window facing Central Park. And soon, Mitchell was behind me, snaking his arms around me. I instinctively leaned back into him, one of my favorite things to do. God, I missed this man.

"We could be so good together, Mirabella. Please give me a chance to prove it."

I turned to face him without pulling out of his embrace. I wanted to look in the eyes of the man I had missed so much over the last three weeks. The one I had cried myself to sleep over. The one I had touched myself in the shower for while thinking of him. The one who was my last thought before sleep and my first thought upon waking.

He was so beautiful. So fucking sexy. And when I was mad at him, I resented him for the way he had me in a fucking emotional vise. This man was in love with me. And instead of making me happy, that shit scared the shit out of me. Mitchell was intense. He was all encompassing. He required constant attention. Constant reassurance that I was his. And frankly, I needed the same from him.

In a lot of ways, Mitchell and I were two sides of the same coin. And in a lot of other ways, we were total and complete opposites.

"Let's go inside," I said, shaking these intrusive thoughts from my brain in an attempt to be present in this moment, house hunting with Mitchell.

Once there, I don't think either of us was prepared. A giant limestone fireplace was the centerpiece of the room that boasted one hundred-eighty-degree views.

Just then, Mitchell's phone rang, and when he looked at the caller, he seemed annoyed. For a brief moment, I worried it might be Lorelei.

"Fucking Hyacinth Rose. You don't happen to know what she wants, do you?"

"Oh. I gave her your number last week. She said she had been trying to reach you but you're never around. But I guess now we know why," I said, getting a little fight back.

"What? Why would you give her my number? And what do you mean, 'now we know why?'"

"She said it was *confidential* and she couldn't tell me but she seemed determined. So, I gave it to her."

"And the other part?"

"Nothing."

"Mirabella?"

"Now we know why, haha. Because you were out fucking other women," I said.

Mitchell got that look in his eyes. And soon, he put me up against one of those giant beams, his hand holding me there by my neck, electricity buzzing all around us, warning us of our impending combustion.

But this time, he was keeping a little distance between us. He seemed angry and sad.

"You think this is fucking funny, Mirabella?"

"No, I don't. But I was trying to lighten the mood."

"Lighten the fucking mood? You want to lighten the mood? Don't fucking make jokes about you telling me that you're ok with me fucking other women. *You* are supposed to be my fucking pleasure and my comfort. You, Mirabella. *You* are supposed to be *mine*. We were supposed to fucking be all the way in this shit. Together. You act like you can't fucking trust me. But it's me who can't trust *you*. I can't fucking trust you not to leave me when you don't like something that's happened. I can't trust you to love me when I need it. When I fucking need you."

"Mitchell," I said, not even sure how I was going to follow it up.

"No. No fucking 'Mitchell.' Let me finish, Mirabella. You want to cry? Cry in my arms. You have nightmares? Let me hold you through them. You feel like I'm the cause of your pain? Let me fucking give you pleasure to focus on."

"Mitchell," I said, emotions I could not control bubbling up and threatening to take my voice away. But he didn't relent. Instead, he increased the pressure on my neck as his eyes roamed over my lips.

"You act like I'm the fucking problem. Like I'm so toxic. So untrustworthy. The shit you've pulled? You've done it since we've been together. Your literal job is to fucking talk shit about me in the press. I have never said one negative thing about you in public or otherwise. Even before we became a thing, I defended you. I had your back. Did it ever occur to you how embarrassed or upset I was when those fucking tapes of me wilding the fuck out were released? No. You only cared about *you*. How it made *you* feel. How it made *you* look."

"Mitchell." Tears welled up in my eyes but I was too mentally, emotionally, and physically drained for them to fall.

"How could you walk out on me, Mirabella?"

Mitchell's words broke me. I didn't know how wrong I'd been, how horrible a thing it had been for Mitchell to experience the utter shame and humiliation of those tapes being released. If I was being honest, a part of me maybe felt as if he deserved to be humiliated. Shamed.

We'd said we loved one another, and yet, I'd thought I was giving Mitchell what he wanted. I'd thought I was freeing him, so he didn't have to cheat. I'd thought Mitchell wanted someone else.

"I'm sorry," I said, knowing that it wasn't enough.

"Don't fucking joke about taking your fucking body away from me and refusing to fucking come home, leaving me to my worst fucking instincts."

He looked away, an extremely tortured look on his face. When he turned to me and locked his eyes on me, there was sadness there.

"Mitchell."

"Mirabella, you want to know what happened with Lorelei?"

Before I could tell him 'no,' he spoke again.

"I went to her apartment with all intentions of fucking her. She wanted me to. Asked me to. Said she too had been through a bad breakup recently and we both seemed like we could use it."

Images of Mitchell and Lorelei together danced in my mind's eye making me shake my head in an attempt to stop my imagination from running wild. As badly as I thought I wanted to know before, I no longer did.

"Mitchell, please," I said. I didn't want him to continue but I also was so choked up, I couldn't speak those words.

"I couldn't."

"What?" My voice was small.

"I couldn't. I couldn't fucking do it." Mitchell's voice was small now too. He let go of my neck, leaving only coldness where his hand and fingers had been.

"What do you mean?"

"I told her it had been a mistake for me to go there. That you are it for me. That I don't want to fuck around but if she can be my realtor, that's all I can offer her."

Mira looked like she'd been given a new lease on life right then.

"So, you didn't have sex with her?"

"No."

"I don't understand."

"I'm fucking ruined, Mirabella. And it was you who fucking ruined me. And when you told me to fuck whoever I wanted, knowing it was *you* who I wanted, you broke my fucking heart."

Neither of us spoke for a few minutes. Mitchell ran a hand through his glorious head of hair.

"Mitchell, I'm sorry. I'm so sorry."

I reached out for him, and he moved slowly toward me.

I put my arms around his neck, and looked deeply into his eyes, and said, "Forgive me, please, Mitchell?"

"Yes," he said in a tired, small, and whisper voice. "Do you forgive me?"

"Yes," I said, even if I was apprehensive about it all. Still, something changed between us right then. Something I wouldn't understand until much later.

"You wanna look at the rest of this apartment?"

"Yes," I said, a little happier than I was moments ago.

"And, Mirabella," he said, "Please stop giving my number out."

"If you stop hooking up with real estate agents."

Mitchell shook his head and gave me a stern look, "What the fuck, Mirabella? How many times do I have to tell you about that fucking mouth of yours?"

"I thought you liked this fucking mouth of mine," I teased, easing back into our special style of banter, having been out of practice.

Mitchell swatted my ass and directed me into the all-white kitchen outfitted with white Miele appliances, two sinks, and a Wolf cooktop. I felt so small looking up at the top row of cabinets.

Next up was the dining area. Holy shit. We could eat dinner there overlooking Central Park on one side or the Citicorp building on the other side. And the area was so big; they had it set for twelve.

The rooms in this apartment had the same amazing interior structural beams that looked like decorative triangles. And the primary bathroom, which was larger than my living room in Queens, had slanted windows for walls, an incredible soaking tub, and a steam shower to die for.

Except for interior walls, this apartment was all floor-to-ceiling windows.

With every room entered, my body and mind were keenly aware that Mitchell could have made a move. I was on edge, waiting for him to. I was feeling needy and fucking aggravated by his lack of attention.

"I'd like to come back and see it at night. Can we do that?"

"We can do whatever you want," Mitchell said, ignoring another call that looked to be from Hyacinth.

"Why don't you answer it, see what she wants?" I said.

"Because I don't give a fuck what she wants. She made her bed over at Brennan Enterprises. She can fucking lie in it."

When we were done touring the apartment, Mitchell and I sat in the living area, and he read to me from his phone.

"It has a pool, gym, Pilates and yoga studio, massage studio—Did you see the service entrance, Mira?"

"No," I said, noticing we could see Central Park and the Hudson and East Rivers from our location in the living room.

"I love the limestone fireplace."

"Me too."

"It has a wine room and a media room. But if I lived here, I'd make one of the bedrooms an office. What the hell would I even do with four bedrooms?"

"That makes sense. Then you would have two spare bedrooms," I added as if Mitchell couldn't do math.

"The master bedroom is huge," Mitchell said.

"It's called 'primary bedroom' now, Colonizer," I joked.

Mitchell laughed.

"Now that's a joke," he said.

"That closet? I could fill it up," I mused, thinking of all the fancy clothes I needed. "But maybe, it could be bigger."

He smiled at me, looking so damn gorgeous.

"I like that media room. I'd love to watch movies up there, play video games," Mitchell mused now.

"We could sit up there and fool around, maybe get to second base," I teased. "And those Juliet balconies are pretty cool."

Mitchell smiled despite looking sad.

"Thanks for coming with me, Mirabella. I hated looking at apartments without you. I hated that I couldn't tell you about the ones I'd seen. That I couldn't ask your opinion."

"I hated seeing those fucking pictures of you and her."

Mitchell smirked a small smirk before saying, "Fake Bratz doll?"

"That was the nicest thing I could think of," I smirked back, despite the nausea settling in the pit of my stomach at the idea that he'd had his hands on another woman in an intimate way and that it had been my fucking fault.

"Seriously, what do you think, Mirabella? Can you see yourself here?"

That was the perfect time for me to say, "You know, Mitchell. I have been thinking about moving from Queens into an apartment in Manhattan, on my own." But instead, I said, "I absolutely love this one."

MITCHELL and I viewed apartments until seven thirty that night, stopping to get a quick bite before resuming.

We sat side-by-side in a booth at the Brooklyn Diner, feeding one another, laughing, and flirting. Beneath is all was an undercurrent of sadness edged with hope.

And when he suggested we go back to the first apartment to see it at night, we did. Whatever I had been expecting, nothing compared to seeing the New York City skyline all lit up from the penthouse. Full from dinner and not ready to say goodbye yet, both Mitchell and I were quiet while touring Penthouse 76. The more I saw, the more I could see visiting Mitchell there.

"I think this is the one, Mitchell."

I stared out the window that overlooked Central Park, recalling our first date at the Shard in London and wondering when we might have another. Mitchell came up behind me and put his arms around my waist. When I leaned back into him and placed my arms over his, I felt him smile.

"Me too."

My phone buzzed, scaring the shit out of me. It was fucking Lorelei. The spell was broken.

> LORELEI: I haven't gotten the keys yet. Perhaps Mitchell can drop them by my apartment. He knows where I live

> ME: *ignore*

I turned around to face Mitchell, and shoved my phone in his face so he could see the shit this bitch was trying to pull.

"Fucking fire her. Right fucking now."

Mitchell swallowed the smirk off his gorgeous face.

I pulled my phone away.

"I'll fucking do it."

> ME: You're fired. I will return the keys to the condo office

I deleted her number from my phone and blocked it. Then, I put my hand into Mitchell's pants, pulled his phone out, turned it toward him to activate his FaceID, turned it back to me, and deleted and blocked Lorelei. When I shoved his phone back into his pants, he pulled back a laugh.

"There's my beautiful little spitfire."

"Fuck you, Mitchell."

I walked away and headed to the elevator.

Mitchell followed me.

On the ride down from the seventy-sixth floor, Mitchell and I stared at one another from opposite ends of the elevator.

He grabbed my hand when we reached the ground floor. I let him. He dropped the keys off at the concierge desk, uttered some niceties, and before I knew it, we were sitting inside of his Ghost.

"Will you come home with me? We can . . . *talk*," Mitchell said, looking at me with a mix of sadness, hope, and now arousal.

All I could manage to say was, "ok."

The smile on his face was worth my anxiety as we rode to Mitchell's soon-to-be former apartment in Chelsea.

"So, are you going to make an offer on that apartment?"

"Do you want it?"

"Do *I* want it? It's your apartment."

"I would like it to be ours."

"Well, I had already been thinking of moving out of my apartment and getting something on my own," I said with a fucking attitude.

"So not with me?"

"It was just a place where I didn't have roommates, where I could have more privacy, space to myself."

"I really like that apartment. I love that you love it too. If I buy it, I want you to consider living there with me, even if it's only for part of the week. Where were you thinking of moving to?"

"I like Chelsea, but I'm not sure I can afford it."

"What's your budget?"

"I don't know. I need a realtor to help me with all this. Know anyone other than fucking Lorelei?"

"I didn't choose her, Mira. I was set up."

"What the hell does that mean?"

"That night, the night we talked. I told you I had dinner with Aunt Meg and Preston. Well, Lorelei was our guest, compliments of my aunt."

Holy shit. I must have been making a face because Mitchell creased his eyebrows and said, "What?"

"Nothing."

"Tell me."

"I don't know. I don't want to start anything."

Mitchell laughed out loud.

"What?"

"Mirabella Castle doesn't want to start anything?"

Now it was me who was smirking.

"What I mean is, I don't want to cause trouble."

"By all means, Mirabella. Start shit."

Mitchell was so fucking handsome.

"Your aunt. She told me that if I ever left you again, she would do what she had to do."

"What? When did she say that?"

"When I begged her to let me see you while you were on house arrest."

"What do you mean you begged her to let you see me. Why didn't you just ask me?"

"I did. I texted you. You never texted me back."

"I never got texts from you. I thought you didn't want to talk to me." Mitchell seemed confused then.

"So, I'm thinking Lorelei was a plant. A set up."

"Not much of a fucking set up," Mitchell mumbled.

"Apparently it was since you fucking fell for it hook, line, and sinker." Even though I mumbled it, I knew the minute the words left my lips that I should not have said it.

In seconds, Mitchell was out of his seatbelt, he'd quickly unbuckled mine, and before I knew what was happening, I had my yoga pants pulled down, my underwear pushed to the side, and Mitchell deep inside me, ramming me mercilessly, kissing my neck, grabbing at my breasts, and moaning his pleasure onto my nipples.

In minutes, Mitchell and I both came extremely hard. Neither of us spoke in the time it took us to come down from our orgasms. And yet, despite what he had just given me, I wanted more of him.

"What was that?" I said, still breathing heavy and wondering what I had done to get him so worked up.

"I thought I fucking told you to let that shit go and not to tease me about having to go outside our relationship for fucking sex." His tone was angry with a twinge of remorse.

I pulled up my panties and pants and put my seatbelt back on as evidence of Mitchell's punishment dripped out of me.

We'd reached Mitchell's apartment and it was time to get out. He angrily opened his door, and then came around to help me out. He was looking at me but not like he normally did. Mitchell was fucking pissed.

I followed him up the steps and into the apartment. He slammed the door behind us and came to stand in front of me.

"I don't think you understand how fucking much you hurt me, Mirabella. You have a big fucking mouth, and you talk so much shit about what other people should or should not be doing."

"I'm sorry."

"You're *not* fucking sorry because you keep fucking doing it."

"I'm sorry," I said again. "I joke around when I'm fucking hurting. I make jokes about things that bother me because it gives them less power over me."

Mitchell was silent for a few seconds. What I said seemed to have calm him a little.

"Why did you fucking do it then? Why did you tell me it was ok to fuck other women if you didn't want me to? Did you want to give me a test you knew I would fucking fail?"

I couldn't speak. I didn't know what to say. I hated that he was calling me out on my shit. But more than that, I hated that he may have been right about why I'd done what I did.

"You wanted to see me, for me to stop hiding from you? Well, this is me. And yes, I talk a lot of shit. It's how I cope, according to my therapist. But being in this thing with you fucking terrifies me. I have never felt like this for anyone. I didn't even know it was fucking possible. I hate being addicted to you. I fucking hate needing you. The whole time we were in that first apartment I kept wondering if you were going to touch me. I wanted you to so badly."

Mitchell's entire demeanor changed. He ran a hand through his hair and shook his head. He looked like he didn't know whether to put me through the wall or fuck me up against it. It was very sexy.

"Jesus, Mirabella. Why didn't you tell me? Why are you so afraid to tell me what you need from me?"

Still looking like he was contemplating his next move, he scooped me into his arms and moved his head so he could force me to look at him.

"I don't know."

"Baby, tell me."

"I'm embarrassed to need you. I haven't yet figured out how to exactly need someone in this way. I have never had a real boyfriend.

Not really. I don't know how to be a proper girlfriend. I was always walking on eggshells with Ben, trying not to be too much or too little. Every day I had to keep parts of myself hidden for fear of being rejected by him or worse, ignored. He wasn't interested in me. Trying to figure out which version of myself I should be in any given moment just so that he would notice me, see me, want me? It was fucking exhausting. And, somewhere along the way, I lost me. I lost who I am. I didn't know who the fuck I was by the time it ended."

Mitchell looked all together confused, sad, and angry. He didn't need someone as messed up as me in his life.

"Mirabella, I don't know what to say. I haven't been in a relationship in a long time. I hate hearing that you wanted me to touch you but didn't know how to ask me."

"I was afraid that I wouldn't be able to handle it. Like in RayRay's kitchen."

Mitchell hugged me now. He held onto me tightly and said, "Do you still want me? Do you want to be with me?"

"I don't like relying on anyone or needing them. I hate it when I feel deprived and starved of attention and affection. I don't want to be that girl who's always hanging on their man or begging for his attention. But Mitchell, I never stopped wanting you. I missed you so much."

"I was fucking miserable, Mirabella. What were you doing all this time that we were apart? Please fucking tell me that you didn't go back to that motherfucker Ben. That you didn't contact him."

I pulled out of his embrace, wanting to look at him. Yeah, I hurt him, but he hurt me too. And the more I thought about it, it wasn't necessarily the thing with Marissa Canto that hurt me. It was that given the opportunity to tell me about it, he chose to tell me a fairy tale version, leaving me vulnerable and totally unprepared for what was to come. He didn't protect me.

"You thought I was with Ben? Jesus, Mitchell. I wasn't with anyone else. Besides, Ben has a new girlfriend."

Mitchell looked like I'd punched him in the gut.

"So you've been keeping tabs on him? You fucking thought about running back to him?" His breathing was unsteady. He looked angry. Hurt. Jealous. Impossibly handsome.

Mitchell walked away from me. He opened the door to the first-floor terrace and stepped outside. I went to join him, even though it was chilly out and knowing that it was highly likely that we were not going to resolve our issues tonight. I remembered what RayRay had said earlier about how I view things sometimes. About how the Universe doesn't make mistakes. How I had impossible standards. How Mitchell would burn the world for me.

Then I considered what Mitchell had said, about how he couldn't trust me not to love him through adversity or trust me not to run when things got hard. And he was right. This entire time, I had been acting from a soon-to-be-victim mentality. I'd assumed, no, had been expecting that Mitchell would hurt me. I had been holding back pieces of me and not allowing myself to fully fall for him, despite feeling so in love. But in doing so, I was creating a self-fulfilling prophecy. I sent Mitchell into the arms of another woman.

I stood behind Mitchell, wanting to touch him but unsure of whether I should. He must have known I was out there, even though he didn't turn around to face me. He stood with his good hand in his pocket and his broken, casted hand hanging to his side.

"Mitchell," I said, "I want you to be able to trust me. I want to be able to get over your past. I want to be able to let your fling with Lorelei go. I want to move in with you, and I want to be all the way in. But I think we need to take things slow. Yes, we have an amazing sexual connection, but we also need to connect on a deeper level. We need to really get to know one another. We need to learn to like each other even though we love one another."

Mitchell still didn't turn around, so, I went to stand in front of him.

He looked down at me and said, "You fucking ruined me, Mirabella. I'm fucking ruined."

CHAPTER 18 1/2

MITCHELL MAGELLAN

Getting back together with Mira was going to take honesty, compromise, and lots of talking. It was going to require me to stop myself from touching her. I was going to have to really listen to her. To force myself not to get angry or to shut her up by putting my fingers or my cock in her mouth.

She was calmer now, and I was too. We had been talking for a while, and it had led us here. It was the place neither of us really wanted to go. But alas, there we were.

"I hate that you know this about me; how touch and attention deprived I've been. How I sought comfort and pleasure in the arms of a man like Ben. How I'd begged him to touch me. To hold my hand. To want me. That I felt so un-everything."

I schooled my face, forcing myself not to react to the fact that Mirabella used the words, "begged him to touch me" about another fucking man. I inhaled deeply, trying to let my fucking rage out on a slow exhale.

"Mira. You know the worst things about me. How depraved and nasty I can be. The drugs. The arrests. The cheating. *Neither* of us is perfect. But we're perfect for each other. We're two broken people. And for some reason, we ended up together. Fucking scars and pain and all. I already told you how I feel about you. What I need from you."

She began to cry silent tears. I don't think I was helping at fucking all. Still, I kept my hands to myself.

"Let me love you. Let me prove to you how heartbreakingly beautiful you are. Let me take care of you. Let me un-break you. I promise you'll never want for anything ever again."

"I'm so scared." She was shaking. I kept my hands to myself.

"What are you afraid of?" I asked despite already knowing the answer and moving toward her.

She moved back.

"You."

I ran a hand through my hair in frustration. I needed to fucking touch her. "Please don't say that. I'm so fucking into you, Mirabella. I can't stand that you're afraid of me." I moved closer, the tiger preying on the mouse.

"I'm afraid of your past. I'm afraid that there's so much more that I won't be able to handle. That the knowing will break me beyond repair. That the not knowing will eat me alive."

I stopped moving.

"Mira. Please. Come here."

"Why?" Her voice was so small like she didn't trust me.

FUCK!

"I want you so fucking badly. Let me worship you."

After a few contemplative seconds, Mira decided between feeling like shit and giving in to the pleasure I could give her. She practically ran into my arms. Long, painful sobs shook her whole body for minutes after our "talk." When she finally stopped crying, I said, "I'm gonna make you feel so good, Baby. Tell me you want me to make you feel good."

She nodded a shy nod while looking into my eyes, the need on her face undeniable.

"Tell me." The need in my voice now was also undeniable. The tone of it reverberated in my ears sounding a full octave lower than it normally was.

I ran my hand up under the hoodie of mine she'd changed into since arriving. She shivered with anticipation as I trailed my fingers lightly across her skin.

"Tell me. I need to hear you say you want me."

"Mitchell," she breathed out as I touched her left nipple gently and then the right one not as gently. Mira's body bucked from that alone.

"Tell me, Baby."

Not wasting time, I reached into her panties. She was dripping already. Coating my fingers in her sweet pre-cum, I moved them agonizingly slowly over her clit.

I was barely touching her, but Mirabella was about to come. A tear ran down her cheek.

"Fucking tell me," I said as I ran my gaze over her entire body, realizing I had forgotten to tell her how much I love her braids.

Embarrassed by her need, she turned her head away from me and said into my arm, "Please, Mitchell. Make me feel good."

Now, Mirabella wasn't the only one leaking pre-cum.

"I'm gonna make you come as many times as you can handle it. And Mira, after today, I don't want to hear that motherfucker's name come out of your mouth ever again."

CHAPTER 19

MITCHELL MAGELLAN

"I convinced Mirabella to allow me to put her name on the title of our new apartment. She now has access to about sixty million dollars in equity. That's money she can tap into to, and spend however she likes," I said sitting across from Akila and her fiancé Gerald.

"That's a nice gift," Gerald said with a huge knowing smile on his face.

"Very generous," Akila said, also smiling.

"Cheers to your new apartment. May you and Mirabella be incredibly happy there." Gerald raised his glass, signaling for us to join in.

"Thank you both, very much," I said. "So, what about you two? When's the wedding?"

"We haven't even gotten that far in our planning yet. Just trying to enjoy engagement life," Akila said.

"Well, when the time comes, do let me know if you need a venue for parties or the wedding, whatever. I own four floors in this building and a few other restaurants in London besides the two here in the Shard."

"That's rather generous, Mitchell. I appreciate the offer," Akila said, sipping her wine.

"I understand you're into textiles, Gerald?"

"I am indeed. I oversee production quality control standards for several luxury brands, actually. And, as you can see," he said, nodding in Akila's direction, "Akila approves."

Akila was a stunning woman, always impeccably dressed and professionally made up. Her style was above reproach, right down to the oversized glasses she sometimes wore and ass-length hair. I'd never seen her in anything other than designer from head-to-toe. And when Akila wore designer, every single piece was one hundred percent authentic.

"Indeed, she does," I said, admiring my beautiful friend.

"If ever Mirabella would like to come tour any of our production facilities for Hermes, Saint Laurent, or Gucci, do let me know. I'm certain she will get a thrill out of it, and maybe a bag or two?"

"Mirabella does love a designer purse. I will let her know of your offer. Thank you, Gerald."

"Now that the two of you are 'out'" Akila said, putting 'out' in air quotes, "let's bring her along next time."

"Of course, I will. Brennan's got her super busy, always on a tour of some kind. I swear they do it just to get under my skin," I said, realizing only after how whiny it sounded.

"I put nothing past them," Akila said, taking my side like the soldier she was.

"So, tell us more about your new flat," Gerald asked, refilling Akila's wine glass.

"Ah, yes. It's a penthouse apartment on the seventy-sixth and seventy-seventh floors. We purchased the apartment furnished, and since Mirabella is never satisfied with anything, we're doing renovations."

My smile gave me away. I missed my girl.

"Oh wow, it's new construction, right? Didn't you tell me that?"

"Yes, but Mirabella wanted to renovate a bit of the kitchen and add more closet space."

"Does she cook?" Akila asked.

"You know what? I have no idea."

"What?" Akila said. Her face scrunched up into an incredulous expression.

"Wait a minute. I wonder if Mirabella can even cook?"

"I guess you'll find out after you finish your renovation," Gerald said, he and Akila laughing at my expense. I laughed too.

"The kitchen renovation should be done in another six weeks or so. Then after Christmas, we are going to hire a designer to help us make the apartment reflect more of what we like."

Just then, Shonda came over.

I stood and gave her a hug and a kiss.

"Good to see you, Mitchell," she said.

"Good to see you too, Shonda. Shonda," I said, turning toward Akila and Gerald. "Shonda, you remember Akila Norris from RayRay and Christina's party? This is her fiancé, Gerald . . ." I couldn't recall his last name for the life of me.

"King," he said. "Gerald King."

"Gerald King," I said as if Gerald saying it wasn't the full effect.

"It's nice to see you again," Shonda said while she reached past me to shake hands with both Akila and Gerald.

"You should join us, Shonda. We're celebrating Akila's promotion," I said, hoping to affirm our friendship outside of work. Akila beamed.

"Oh yeah?" Shonda beamed too.

"I was just promoted to Vice President in the People and Culture organization."

"Always so formal, Akila," I said. "Akila makes it all work. All of it. The human capital, the culture of the company, inclusion, diversity, and making sure people can be their authentic selves at Magellan. And even though that's the case, tonight's more of a social thing," I said proudly.

Gerald and I were both grinning.

"That's wonderful. Congratulations, Akila," Shonda said with a smile.

"And Shonda, here, is our newest General Manager at Magellan

Restaurant Group Ltd. She's now overseeing management of all our London-based dining facilities," I said, ecstatic that I was also able to finally promote Shonda.

"Wow. That's amazing. Congratulations," Akila said.

"Let's toast to these two amazingly talented women, Gerald. Right here, right now, how lucky are we to be in such company?" I said, my smile a mile long.

"Here, here. Cheers, ladies," Gerald said, and we all said, "Here, here! We clanged glasses, except for Shonda, who had no glass.

"I'll ask Emilio to send over something old and obscenely expensive, Mitchell."

I laughed.

"Great idea," I said. "And thank you, Shonda. Oh, any new pictures of my nephew?" I said, talking of her son Lamar.

Shonda blushed, pulled out her phone, and scrolled through five or six photos of Lamar in football.

"Wow. Look at that kid. Tell him his uncle Mitch said hello."

"I will. Maybe he can see you before you leave London."

"Yeah, no problem. I would love to. Let me know. I'm leaving on Friday."

"Ok, I have got to get back to it. Good to see you, Mitchell. Good to see you, Akila and nice to meet you, Gerald. Enjoy the rest of your night," Shonda said. She then gave me another hug and kiss on the cheek, then walked briskly away.

"She's great," Akila said.

"She really is," I said.

"You're quite an interesting bloke, Mitchell Magellan," Gerald said.

"I will take that as a compliment."

As much as I was enjoying my night out, I missed Mirabella.

"Ok, back to the apartment," Akila said. Do you have any photos to share?"

"Actually, I do," I said like a proud parent.

I turned the phone in Akila and Gerald's direction and scrolled through the envelope labeled, *New Apartment*.

"My God, Mitchell. It's absolutely gorgeous," Akila said, as I landed on a photo of Mirabella standing in front of the giant limestone fireplace looking fucking gorgeous and immensely fuckable.

"Thanks. When you guys are in New York next, you *must* come and hang out with Mira and I there," I said truly hoping they'd be among our first guests.

"You should throw a house-warming party," Akila said with a look of excitement.

"We totally should," I said.

"That would give me the opportunity to thank Mirabella for her brilliant scholarship idea, which I know you said she isn't able to work on right now, but I really wish she could come run it," Akila said.

"No work talk, hon," Gerald said.

I smiled. They were really a handsome couple and seemingly in love and in tune with one another. It was nice to see good people be happy.

Just then, Emilio came over.

"Bro, you didn't tell me you were coming to London," he said pulling me up out of my chair and into a bro hug. He stopped when he saw my hand in a cast. "Ah, so you finally found out who's stronger, you or Maleko?"

"Ha! You should see the wall," I joked.

"It's good to see you, Brother," he said.

I introduced everyone while Emilio presented the wine and poured for us. I invited him to have some as well, and then we all made new toasts.

After some more small talk, Emilio left the table, and the rest of us ate our food. By the time desserts and after-dinner drinks came, it was 2:30am in London and 9:30pm in New York.

Spending time like this with Akila, Gerald, Emilio, and Shonda was like being home. The only thing that was missing was Mirabella.

FRESH OUT OF THE SHOWER, I checked my watch to find it was now eleven forty-five pm in New York. I would have called Mira sooner, but I like being clean when I talk to her. As a little treat for myself, I texted her first.

> ME: Hey Baby. You ready for me?
>
> MIRABELLA: No
>
> ME: No?
>
> MIRABELLA: -----

Shit.
I dialed my girl.
"Achoo," she said into the phone.
"Baby, are you sick?"
"I'm so fucking sick. Sneezing, stuffed nose, fever, sore throat, chills, stomach cramps, headache. It's not pretty," Mirabella said in a soft voice that made her sound like she was under water.
"I'm so sorry. Have you gone to the doctor?"
"I can't move."
"Who's taking care of you?"
"Nobody. Me. I don't know. Iggy got me soup yesterday," she said, sounding like the most pitiful baby ever to live.
Mirabella coughed for a few seconds. I kind of hated that Iggy was the one who'd gotten her soup.
"Well shit, Mirabella. Maybe you should do like a TeleDoc visit. Get some meds in you," I said, selfishly wanting her to get well in time for when I got back on Friday.
"Yeah, maybe I'll do that. Hyacinth suggested that too," she said.
Just then I remembered that Hyacinth had been trying to reach me some weeks ago.
"Mira, is Hyacinth in London or New York this week?"
"She's in London, why?"
"Because I never did find out what she wanted. I'm gonna try to meet with her before I leave. And I'm telling you, Mirabella, if it's about some bullshit, you're gonna get it when I get home," I said, teasing her.
"Why am I gonna get it?"

"Because you're the one who gave her my number."

"Oh," she said," sounding super-congested.

"Are you taking anything at all?"

"Tylenol and Motrin, alternating to keep the fever down. Mena got me some NyQuil to help me sleep."

"I'm sorry you're so sick, Mirabella."

"Me too."

"Do you miss me?"

"Yes," she said without hesitation.

"I miss you so fucking much. I wish you were with me. All this travel and being apart, isn't good for us."

"Speaking of which, Hyacinth is planning another tour, only two weeks this time."

"Absolutely fucking not," I said knowing full well there was nothing I could do to stop it.

"Feel free to tell her how you feel when you talk to her," she said, managing to be perfectly slightly snarky despite how sick she was.

"What are you wearing, Mirabella?"

"Um. An oversized t-shirt, sweatpants, fuzzy socks, and a hair bonnet. Oh, and granny panties, since I'm expecting my period."

"Fucking sexy as hell, and if I was there with you right now, I would fuck that sickness right out of you," I said, trying to turn us both on.

When Mirabella laughed at my joke, she sounded like an eighty-nine-year-old man who had been smoking for eighty years. Then, she started coughing.

"I'm sorry to made you cough," I said even though I didn't want to hang up yet. "Did I tell you how much I love you in braids?"

"You do? I was worried you wouldn't like them."

"Baby, you're a fucking knockout. And those braids? Chef's kiss."

"Thank you, Mitchell."

"You're welcome, Baby."

"What are you wearing?" She said.

"Black underwear, black tee," I said, hoping she liked the imagery.

"Fucking yummy," she said coughing a little.

"You sound horrible and sexy."

"It sounds like you have a sick kink."

"A what?"

"A sexual attraction to sick people."

"As usual, what the fuck are you talking about, Mirabella?" I said, convinced now that I was on the other end of Mirabella's fever dream.

"I took a class on Kink as an elective in college, and I learned there are people who are sexually attracted to sick people, especially those who sneeze or have fevers."

"I don't even know what to say, Mirabella."

"Would you want to fuck me right now, even though I'm super sick?"

"Is that a trick question? I literally just told you I'd fuck that sickness out of you."

"I'm serious," she said, sounding even sicker and weaker.

I sighed, thinking about the shit-talking I was doing earlier and reality.

"If you asked me to, I would definitely have sex with you while you are sick."

She was quiet now. *Did I just say the wrong thing?*

"Have you ever had period sex?" She said.

Jesus. That was not what I was expecting to come next.

"Have you?" I said, taking a page out of Braxton's book by answering a question with a question.

"Um, in the two and a half times I've had sex? Um, no."

"Can we talk about something else? Because I don't like talking about my sexual past with you. It feels disrespectful."

"So, you *have* had period sex."

"Yes," I said after she asked me a second fucking time.

"How was it?"

"Jesus, Mirabella."

"Please just tell me," she said as if she was asking me what I'd had for lunch.

"Why so you can use it to fucking walk out on me again?"

"I guess I deserve that," she said.

"No, you don't. I'm sorry, Mira. I just honestly . . . when you ask me about these things, I feel so far removed from them, like it happened to someone else. But I will answer your question. Yes, I had period sex with Cassandra. It was her idea. I was reluctant."

"Oh," she said like she wasn't expecting my response to be what it was. "So, how was it?"

"For her? She said it was amazing, relieved her cramps."

"For you?"

"It was weird."

"Weird like you suffered through it weird or weird like you were so grossed out you couldn't finish, weird?"

"The latter," I said wondering how the fuck the conversation had taken this turn. "Why? Are you into that?"

"No. But I do get super horny right before and right after my period, though."

"Good to know. Please share your cycle in a Google calendar," I said, not joking in the least.

"Lots of deep penetration prior to one's period does help with cramps," she said as if she was stating medical facts.

"Just call me doctor fucking Magellan," I said thinking about Friday, when I get home, mentally renaming it 'Deep Penetration Friday.'

"Have you narrowed down your list of interior designers yet?"

"Been too sick last night and this morning. I may have to cancel my meeting with the contractor tomorrow," she said.

"Yeah. I'll call him and let him know. You rest, Mirabella. Drink lots of fluids, ok?"

"Ok."

"I'll check on you later."

"Ok."

"Mitchell?"

"Yes, Mirabella."

"I love you."

It was the first time she had ever said it without me saying it first.

"I love you too."

CHAPTER 20

MIRABELLA CASTLE

For three days, I was so sick that I forgot to tell Mitchell that my brother Jared was planning to visit because he said he had "news." What kind of news he could possibly have, I didn't know. And, having missed three days of work, there was quite a lot to do.

With so much pressure on me to perform, I found myself wishing I'd had my own apartment. Someone was always in the kitchen or living room here, forcing me to work from my cramped bedroom or a nearby coffee shop which honestly wasn't better. Having to do most of my meeting on mute so that no one would hear that background noise my roommates made or angling the laptop in such a way as to not see anyone walk behind me in their underwear was becoming a challenge.

So, I decided to go to Mitchell's new apartment, which was technically also mine, and see if I could get some work done there, when my phone rang.

"Hey, you," I said to Mitchell.

"You sound better. Are you better?" he said exuberantly. I could tell Mitchell was moving around. It sounded like he was flipping papers or something on his desk.

"I still have a cough and congestion, but I'm cured for the most part," I said sniffling.

"I'm so glad. What are you up to?"

"I'm heading over to the penthouse so I can get some work done. I figure since they're only painting and doing finishes it might be quieter and more comfortable than here."

"Send me pictures of the progress."

"Ok," I said, stuffing paperwork, my laptop, and plug into my backpack.

"Mitchell?"

"Mmm Hmm," he said breathy but not sexy breathy. It was frustrated but not sexy frustrated. It was work annoyance.

"Are you ok?"

"Yeah, just trying to find this paper I had printed out yesterday. I may have left it in the office."

"Do you need to go so you can find it?" I was wondering what it would be like to witness Mitchell bossing at work. I on the other hand was not bossing; I owed Hyacinth a presentation that was already two days late.

"No, Baby," I'm good. I'll get it after lunch. I'm sorry I was distracted," he said.

"Ok. Well, I forgot to tell you that Jared's coming to visit tomorrow."

Mitchell was silent for a few seconds.

"Ok. When did this happen?"

"With everything going on I totally forgot to tell you. I'm so sorry."

Mitchell was again quiet, and I know he was trying to think of something positive to say.

"Tell Jared he's a cock-blocking son-of-a-bitch."

I laughed so hard it caused me to cough.

"You can tell him yourself. Besides, I'm pretty sure he will ditch us and find someone other than us to go home with."

"Where's he staying?"

Tell me this man isn't jealous of my brother.

"Here."

"In that small ass apartment?"

"Yes. And anyway, Mena's not going to be here."

"I thought she was back."

One thing about Mitchell was, he listened when I told him things.

"She is but she's thinking about moving in with Dino. They're going away this weekend and she thinks he's gonna ask her to marry him."

"Jesus. That guy's a bit of an asshole."

"Yeah, but she seems happy with him."

"I don't like him."

"Gee. Really?"

Mitchell huffed as if both Mena and I were insane.

"She can do much fucking better."

Something about his statement brought out a twinge of jealousy. And, since I didn't respond, he changed the subject with a peace offering over a fight we had just avoided.

"Are you ready to leave yet? I can send Brendan to get you."

I wanted to object but honestly, it would be nice not to deal with the subway today.

"If it's not too much trouble," I said feeling oddly like my life was changing in so many ways recently that it was hard to keep up. A few months ago, I was on the verge of being homeless, and now, Mitchell Magellan was sending his driver to pick me up to take me to the sixty-five-million-dollar penthouse he'd purchased for us.

"It's nothing. I'll text him now."

I pushed back intrusive thoughts that would have had me questioning and imagining how many other women Mitchell may have had Brendan "pick up" and take somewhere.

"Thanks, Mitchell," I said, trying to sound appreciative of his generosity rather than upset.

"You're welcome."

"What time do you arrive tomorrow?"

"I arrive around 3pm New York time," he said, a little lust and longing in his voice. "What time's Jared getting in?"

"Around 1:30."

"What are your plans?" Mitchell said. And right then, I knew how much restraint he was showing by not taking over and giving me an opportunity to decide what plans I would be making with my brother and my friends. It wasn't that he was overbearing in that regard, but rather that he liked to "help."

When I was planning RayRay and Christina's party, Mitchell had offered his enormous wealth and access to the finer things to give the two of them an adoption "Gotcha Party" befitting royalty. He wasn't one to throw his wealth around, and until recently, he'd lived a relatively modest life, despite having access to untold money. So, when he suggested I allow him to "open his checkbook," I let him.

"I was going to talk to you first, since I kind of sprung this on you." I said.

Mitchell didn't miss a beat though.

"Why don't we all go to Altro Paradiso or Morandi for dinner? We can get drinks at Parcelle before or after."

"I vote Morandi around eight thirty? Drinks at six at Parcelle?"

"Sounds perfect," he said.

Remembering the last time we'd dined at both, I was excited to return with my brother and my friends. As I allowed my thoughts to travel over what my life was becoming, I was grateful.

"How long's he staying?" Mitchell was showing the utmost of restraint. Behind everything he said pertaining to the issue of Jared's impending visit, he seemed to be trying hard not to impose on the sibling one-on-one time I had carved out for us.

"Just until Monday. He's leaving Monday afternoon."

"Can I have you on Saturday?"

Mitchell's voice was deep, husky, and full of need. He'd asked such a loaded literal question that was dripping with the implications of so much sex, it had me squirming in my seat.

"Mitchell," I said, just as needy, "I was thinking we can stay at the penthouse and Jared can stay here. He was planning on spending the day with RayRay and Christina on Saturday. Then we'd get dinner together. So yes. You get me all day."

"Mmmmmmmm. I cannot wait."

Damn, he was sexy.

"I miss you, Mitchell."

"Yeah? What do you miss?"

"Everything. But right now, I miss your mouth. I wish I could kiss you," I said, this time, needing to squeeze my legs together to quiet my throbbing clit.

"Me too, Baby. I can't wait to kiss your perfect mouth."

I had to change the subject because I was getting much too heated.

"Hey, did you ever talk to Hyacinth?"

"We're getting lunch today, meeting at my rental flat."

"Oh," I said remembering the last time Hyacinth and I had visited Mitchell in his rental flat in Phillimore Gardens.

"Lemme know how it goes," I said, chewing the last of my bagel.

"I will," he said. I wondered if he too was remembering.

"So, what about the rest of the weekend?"

"Maybe Sunday we can play some racquetball. He mentioned it last time I saw him. Told me he would, and I quote, 'beat my ass' if we'd played."

"Jared would love that. Thank you, Mitchell."

"You're welcome, Baby. It will be my pleasure to crush him on the court."

"I didn't know you were so good at racquetball."

"I'm good at a great many things, Baby. Maybe I'll show you some of them on Saturday."

This. Fucking. Man.

"Yes, you are," I said. And then I was fully thinking of Mitchell in the most delicious way.

Mitchell spoke next with a smile in his voice, "Listen; Brendan is ten minutes away."

"Ok.

"I'll send a car to get Jared from the airport on Friday. Have him text me his flight info."

"You don't have to do that."

"I know. I want to."

"Thanks for doing that for us."

"I'm sorry, Baby; I've gotta go. I'll text you when we take off tomorrow."

"Ok. I love you."

"Be careful at the penthouse."

"Ok, Mitchell."

"Bye, Mirabella."

"Bye."

THE MAGELLAN executive car fleet was impressive. Then again, I was impressed with pretty much everything I'd seen so far of the Magellans.

I'd ridden in the Rolls Royce Ghost, and it seemed to be the one Mitchell liked to travel in the most. I'd also ridden in the Maybach SUV and had sex in it. I'd ridden in the Suburban too, and I liked the seating configuration which allowed Mitchell and I to sit next to or across from one another. After having ridden in the Rolls Royce Cullinan, I much preferred the Ghost.

Riding to the penthouse in the Bentley Flying Spur, I wondered what other cars the Magellans had in their business fleet, and what happened with them when they were not in use. I didn't even know if Mitchell had his own cars or if he could drive.

Still, the idea that this is how super rich people did things was incredible. And I had a feeling what I had already seen was just the beginning. After all, I had just been named a co-purchaser on a sixty-five-million-dollar condo on Billionaire's Row. In fact, Mitchell had paid a few million dollars over asking to secure the furniture and furnishings.

I called my grandma when we were out of the Queens Midtown Tunnel.

"Hi Grandma," I said.

"Mirabella, I got the pictures you sent of Christina and the penthouse. My, my. Things are truly changing for you. Praise the Lord. God is good; isn't he?"

"Yes, Grandma. I'm on my way to the penthouse now," I said because she loved when I confirmed to her that I was not totally lost to sin.

"The church is praying for you and Mitchell. The devil never takes a day off, does he?" She said, ignoring my comment about the penthouse completely.

"He stays busy, Grandma."

"Amen. But you know, God has a plan for you, so don't be discouraged," Grandma said, strong in her faith.

"Ok, Grandma. Is everything ok with you? Did you get that last payment I sent?"

"I did, and I thank you for sending it. It was wholly unnecessary."

"I appreciate what you did for me; it's the least I can do," I said, thrilled that I was able to pay off Grandma's house after paying her back in full for all the money she had invested in me.

"But won't God do it? Just a couple of months ago you were having trouble paying your cellphone bill."

"Yes, He will."

"Yes. Yes. God is good all the time. We just have to pray and believe and let the Lord work in our lives. Here it is a man who you thought was your enemy is now your friend. God will turn our worst enemies into friends."

I tried not to laugh at her insistence that everything was the work of the Lord, and normally I would have but these days, it sure seemed like someone must have been looking out for me.

"How's work? Any more tours coming up?"

"Work's good. I think I will be going on another tour in a couple of weeks."

"And is Mitchell behaving, or do we need to pray harder?"

"He's good, Grandma."

"I didn't ask if he was good; I asked if he was behaving."

"He is, Grandma."

"Don't let that man make a fool out of you just because he's handsome and has a lot of money."

"I won't, Grandma. Mitchell loves me," I said.

"And do you love him?"

"Yes," I said.

"Yes, and . . . ?"

"Nothing; just yes."

"Ok, just be smart. It's ok to be in love. But being in love and being stupid don't go together. You tell Mitchell I expect him to call me. To keep in touch with me," she said sternly.

"You do?"

"Yes, as a matter fact I do," she said, a smile in her voice, "Who wouldn't want to get regular calls from such a handsome young man?"

I laughed.

"Are you trying to move in on my territory, Grandma? That's messed up," I teased.

"Someone has to keep you on your toes; it's dangerous to let a man like that out of your sight for even a minute, Mirabella."

"I know, Grandma." I had already been burned by doing so.

"You sure you're ok Mirabella?"

"I am, Grandma, I promise."

"Are you excited about your brother's visit?"

"Of course, why wouldn't I be?

"Not saying you wouldn't be. Just keep an eye out for him. He's in a way," Grandma said, cryptic as ever.

"What does that mean?"

"Well, I have a customer, so I've gotta go. But, Mirabella?"

"Yes, ma'am?"

"Maybe some time you can see if one of Mitchell Magellan's fancy airplanes flies to Kentucky," she said, never one to miss an opportunity to remind me how few times I have been back to see her.

"Ok, Grandma. I miss you," I said. "Love you, Grandma."

"Love you too, Baby," she said, and I fought the urge to tell her that I was Mitchell Magellan's "baby" now.

CHAPTER 21

MITCHELL MAGELLAN

Hyacinth was three hours late for our meeting originally scheduled for twelve. Lucky for her, I had cleared my afternoon.

She was quite secretive about why she wanted to meet. But I had to imagine that someone who had called me several times at work, a few more times on my cell phone and then requested an in-person meeting nowhere near her place of business at Brennan Enterprises believed they had something explosive to reveal. And yet, for the life of me, I could not figure out what it possibly could be.

It was supposed to have been a lunch meeting at my rental flat, so I ordered food in. And despite having had breakfast with Shonda's son Lamar, I was starving. At exactly three hours and twelve minutes past our scheduled time, Hyacinth rang my bell. Part of me wanted to make her sweat, make her wait out on the steps for a few minutes. But out of respect for Alex, who had liked her a lot, I didn't.

"Hyacinth Rose," I said greeting her, then looking at the time on my seven-hundred-thousand-dollar Patek Phillipe watch just to be crass.

"Magellan; sorry I'm late. I couldn't get away sooner," she said in that cold way she can say even nice things.

I moved out of the doorway to allow her entry, and took her bespoke overcoat.

"I hope you're hungry." I led Hyacinth into the living room where all the food was spread out and waiting to be devoured, I was concerned about the possible news she carried and what it would cost me.

"This was entirely unnecessary," she said as she eyed the food.

"You said you wanted to get lunch."

"I said I could meet you during my lunch break," she said.

"Ok, well, I'm starving, so I hope you won't mind if I eat *my* lunch? I ordered her Thai because I remembered we had it when we first met in New York."

She eyed me like she was surprised I had recalled a tiny detail about her that at the time seemed inconsequential.

"Please, eat. I ate already," she said.

My focus was spotty since I had no idea what Hyacinth wanted. My mind turned less to what she wanted now and more to what she had wanted the last time she was here. She'd brought Mirabella with her as a sort of gift. She had instructed us to get whatever it was between us out of our system and gave us a weekend to do it in. Clearly, that was a L for her since it backfired.

She must have sensed my mind's walk down memory lane because she seemed muted now. That night, Hyacinth had won. She'd had a prize in Mirabella, proof that Brennan Enterprises had bested Magellan Media. Now, this Hyacinth sitting across from me today had no such bravado. Rather, she had a lot on her mind. She seemed almost troubled.

I took a sip of water and dug into my Chicken Pad Thai. She's the one who requested the meeting, so I wasn't planning on asking her what she wanted. I had planned to sit there until she was ready to say whatever it was that she had come to.

Hyacinth spied the waters I set out, and said, "Do you have anything stronger?" She glanced over at the bar.

Shit. Hyacinth was about to tell me something she needed liquid courage to say.

"Certainly. Bourbon ok?" I wiped my mouth on a napkin and stood.

"Yes, thank you," she said.

I walked to the bar, and poured Hyacinth a drink. I didn't make one for myself, though it was rude to make her drink alone. I preferred my head to be right whenever she opened up so that I could act or react accordingly.

I cleared my throat and handed her the drink. Then, I took my seat on the couch across from hers and continued eating.

Hyacinth took a big sip of her Bourbon, depleting half the glass.

"I know you have no reason to trust me, Magellan," Hyacinth spoke through the burn, "but I'm here because I think we both care about Mirabella."

"Ok," I said, wishing that was not the thing she and I had in common.

"And no matter what you might believe, I really do care about her. I care about what happens to her; she's not just an asset to me. Not *anymore*."

"So, this is about Mirabella?"

"Indirectly, yes."

"Ok, Hyacinth, I'm listening."

"What I'm about to share is dangerous for me to know. So, it's dangerous for me to share. And the more people who know it the more dangerous it becomes for all of us. The only reason why I'm sharing it now is because there is little I can do about it. You are the only person I know with the resources, means, and possible interest in doing anything."

"Please do not tell me anything illegal. I am full up on insider and corporate secrets at the moment," I said, making a kind of joke which Hyacinth didn't seem to find funny in the least.

"My brother is an amateur hacker. He prides himself on hacking banks. Two years ago, he hacked twenty thousand banks from all over the world and stole three dollars from each. It was a tiny unnoticed theft. But what he discovered was the stealing wasn't hard, it was the putting back that was hard. He went to put the money back but needed to pass through different and more difficult hoops in order to deposit money," she said.

"What does this have to do with Mirabella?"

"I'm getting to that," she said, and took a swig of her Bourbon. "He wanted to practice more advanced hacking without the burden of the banking system and its quirks. So, I challenged him to hack into Brennan Enterprises. A few months later, he was in. One night in particular, he discovered Brennan's intelligence on Magellan went deeper than the things you both agreed to share. Video and audio recordings caught his eye."

"How long ago was this?"

"Fourteen months ago," she said.

"So, your brother has recordings from when my dad was alive?"

"Yes."

"I would like those files."

"He's put copies of everything Brennan has on Magellan on a virtual drive, which he has given me the login to." Hyacinth sat forward and handed me a piece of paper with codes written in red ink.

I needed to hold myself together, to remain calm in front of Hyacinth. I couldn't let her see me fucking lose my shit. But beneath my cool exterior, I was enraged.

"Thank you, but I am still not following you all the way," I said, trying to force her to say what she suspected exactly.

"Mitchell, there is a file on Marissa Canto. My brother asked me about it once the tapes got leaked. I was confused because she worked for you at Magellan Media. But our servers at Brennan Enterprises contain records of payments to her in excess of one million dollars, and there are a whole bunch of documents in the file with numbers neither he nor I understood."

"Marissa Canto worked for Brennan Enterprises?"

"That's just it, she wasn't an employee. She was listed as a private contractor, but her files and contracts were separate from where those files were stored on the Brennan server. She was found under Magellan Media."

"So, what do you think that means? She could have been a contractor for both companies. It is allowed under unique circumstances."

"But not if she was involved in any kind of financial, research, or development capacity. Right? Didn't she work in your accounting department?"

Mother fucker.

"It was a set up from the start. Marissa was sent to Magellan Media to infiltrate accounting and seduce me," I said, major migraine brewing.

"And you fucking fell for it."

"More than once," I said.

It wasn't often I felt like a fool. But in the last few weeks, it had happened at least twice. First when Mirabella told me I could sleep with other people and now. The only good thing about this, is maybe it would be comforting to Mirabella.

"So, if Marissa was a plant, that means someone knew there were cameras at Magellan already. Who would have known that? My father had them installed around five years ago."

"Someone must have known, Mitchell. Someone in your dad's inner circle must have known."

"What makes you say that? It could have been someone from the camera installation company. People spend lots of time and effort trading information and secrets for one company over another."

Hyacinth was serious. She seemed even more upset than she had been prior to drinking her Bourbon.

"Regardless, this is some serious shit. Who knows how high up it goes? This cannot blow back on my brother. You cannot tell anyone where you got the tapes and documents from," she said.

"What are you after, Hyacinth? Why are you telling me this? You could lose your job. Your brother could go to jail. You could go to jail for aiding and abetting his crimes."

Hyacinth flinched at the harsh picture I painted of hers and her brother's potentially harsh future.

"Magellan used to be my home. I loved working under your brother. That and the fact that Mirabella sees something redeeming in you. I think she deserves to know that you were set up. And you deserve to know that someone at Brennan Enterprises isn't playing fair. Someone seems out to get you personally," she said. And I believed her.

"Thank you, Hyacinth."

"You're welcome."

We sat in silence for a few minutes.

"Mitchell?"

"Yeah?"

"Why aren't you more upset about this?"

"Because I have something even more fucking explosive, and I'm going to use it to take Robert Brennan all the fucking way down. I'm tired of turning the other goddamn cheek. I'm tired of playing nice. I'm finished. And when this is over, he's gonna wish he had done more than release some fucking tapes."

"Well, that's the villain speech of speeches," she said handing me her glass so I can refill it with more Bourbon.

I took the glass, went to the bar, filled it halfway then returned it to her.

"We need to get Marissa Canto to sing," she said.

"She will never betray Brennan," I said while she sipped her Bourbon.

"Why not?"

"I'm sure they paid her handsomely."

"Well then pay her handsomer. Make it worth her while."

"You're a genius, Hyacinth. We have money. We can pay her too," I said.

"I told you that I'm a genius, but you haven't been listening."

I smiled at her, and she smiled back.

"What's in this for you?"

"I give you what you need to take Brennan down, and you make me a VP at Magellan, like your brother promised me. And of course, you keep my brother out of this. Offer him a job too. Clearly you can use it. Your digital security is rather lax." She held back a smirk, but she had me either way.

"My brother promised to make you Associate Director."

"Well, you will make me a VP because now it seems you owe me, and between the two of us, I'm the one holding all the cards. One could even say I'm the smartest in the room."

"She's going to press charges against me, Marissa Canto. She's going to say she didn't consent."

"But the tape that was released seems to have been altered. She clearly consents at least four times during the . . . *encounter*. She asks you to, spit in her woman parts."

"I remember," I said, not even fucking embarrassed anymore at this point. "I need you to be my eyes and ears at Brennan Enterprises," I said.

"No. I'm not a corporate spy. I told you what I know, and I gave you the proof." Hyacinth was firm but there was fear in her eyes.

"I need you and your brother to secure the paper trail for payments to whomever was involved, including who authorized them."

"I don't want to be involved in this, Mitchell," she said. "The only thing I want is a suitable promotion, a job for my brother, and a nice vacation out of it."

"You have my word, Hyacinth. Just promise me that if your brother uncovers anything else—"

"He'll upload it to the server you now have access to."

Hyacinth stood up a little too fast.

I ran to catch her before she fell.

"Well, that was embarrassing," she said, straightening her clothes, and stepping out of my embrace.

Just then my phone alerted me to Mirabella's text.

> **MIRABELLA:** The kitchen is GORGEOUS

I smiled at the text, and then turned my attention back to the matter at hand.

"Thank you again, Hyacinth. Are you ok to get back on your own?"

"I have a car outside."

"Mitchell, you have to take Brennan down. Nothing about any of this is right."

"Oh, don't you worry. I'm going to strip Robert Brennan III of everything he has ever fucking loved.

And as my thoughts ran over Preston and what the actions I take next might do to him, I wasn't even fucking sorry.

I helped Hyacinth to the door, helped her into her coat, and walked her down the stairs to her waiting car.

When she got in, I closed her door, and tapped the roof to let the driver know he was clear to go.

And as I went back into the flat, I wanted to punch a fucking wall.

Instead of breaking my good hand, I decided to dial Mirabella. But her phone went straight to voicemail.

> MIRABELLA: On a call. Will call when done.

> ME: Ok Baby. I have a few calls of my own to make. So, maybe we can just talk later before bed?

> MIRABELLA: K

> ME: Can't fucking wait to see you tomorrow

> MIRABELLA: Me too

> MIRABELLA: R u OK?

> ME: Yes

> MIRABELLA: Did you meet with Hyacinth?

> ME: Aren't you on a call?

> MIRABELLA: Not on camera, on mute, just listening

> ME: Yes

> MIRABELLA: Spill

> ME: I can't text it. Will talk later.

> MIRABELLA: k

I dialed Braxton because once again his ass was missing in action.

He didn't pick up either. So, as a last resort, I called Aunt Meg. I was thinking I should warn her about the shit that was about to go down. I was going to burn Robert Brennan's name and company to the ground, and I didn't want it to have a negative impact on Preston. But even Aunt Meg sent me straight to voicemail.

> ME: Can you chat for a bit

> ANNA: Sure, client in 10 mins

> ME: I'm going to do something that might hurt some people I love

> ANNA: Then why are you doing it?

> ME: To right a wrong because I don't want to turn the other cheek

> ANNA: I'm not going to tell you not to do it. I'm going to advise you to attempt to find a way to do it that doesn't hurt your loved ones

> ME: I can't.

> ANNA: There is no other way?

> ME: No.

> ANNA: Then be prepared to live with the consequences. Feel free to book a session for tomorrow. I'm free between 8-9am

> ME: Will be on a plane

> ANNA: Coming or going?

It would have been so easy to make a joke about coming, but Anna was a professional and she would not stand for that.

> ME: Coming home from London

> ANNA: Safe travels, gotta go. Patient here.

ALL THE WAY OUT

ME: Thanks

ANNA: Any time

CHAPTER 22

MIRABELLA CASTLE

After the afternoon I'd had, I was ready to unwind and spend time with my brother. When Hyacinth called on me to do something unrelated to work, I was hesitant, unsure if I could or even should. But Hyacinth was not one to mince words. She helped me see that what I was about to do was the right thing in the end, and that sometimes we need to put our personal feelings about something aside for the greater good.

And by the time Jared arrived at the penthouse, I wanted a drink. It was so good to see him. He'd lost some weight and looked tired around his yellowish eyes but otherwise he looked exactly the same.

"Wow, B," this place is amazing. You are definitely moving on up," he said, making a Jeffersons TV show reference as he looked around the penthouse.

"Yeah, I did good, huh?" I said, remembering how hard it was for us growing up.

Jared smiled a sympathetic smile.

"What?"

"Is he good to you, Bella? I mean, I saw the fucking video."

"Well, that's fucking embarrassing," I said, taking a seat at the kitchen island and thinking about how it sounded like something Hyacinth would say.

"Sorry. If it makes you feel any better, I hated every minute of it, and when I see Mitchell later, I will be judging him."

Jared made a funny face like he used to do to cheer me up when we were kids.

I laughed pretty hard.

"Dude was out of control." He shook his head and checked his phone.

"Ok can we not?"

"Sorry, B. I just couldn't believe it. I hope you're ok. That things are better for you guys. I really like Mitchell."

I gently pulled Jared's face toward me so I could look in his eyes. "I really like him too."

"Good because I think I can take him. I mean, he's not the biggest guy in the world."

I laughed again.

"Hey, are you hungry?" I said, getting up and walking to the new refrigerator, and opening it so I didn't have to look at Jared. I know he wanted to say more but he also probably wanted to give me a break.

I'd gone shopping for the basics yesterday when I was here. Eggs, milk, water, orange juice, bacon, and a whole bunch of other stuff. When I mentioned it to Mitchell, he told me to order the groceries. And now, with our new see-through fridge doors, we could see it all.

"I'm good, I ate. We're going to dinner, right?"

"Yep. Italian food."

"I didn't bring anything fancy to wear," he said.

"It's totally casual."

Just then, a text arrived from Mitchell.

> MITCHELL: Just landed. Where are you?

> ME: Home

> MITCHELL: I'm coming to Queens. I can't wait until tonight to see you

> ME: I'm at the penthouse with Jared

> MITCHELL: Oh

> ME: I can't with Jared in the house

Then, my phone rang.

Mitchell.

"Listen, I'm not waiting until after dinner tonight. I fucking want you now. So, either send him on a fucking walk, or send him to Queens. Better yet, send him downstairs to the gym. Whatever. I'm fucking coming for you."

"Mitchell, hold on a sec," I said, worried Jared had heard Mitchell somehow, even though he wasn't on speakerphone.

I looked hopelessly at Jared, then excused myself, ran up the stairs, and sat on the bed in our bedroom.

"Mitchell, I need alone time with my brother," I said.

"Mirabella, you can be away from him for an hour. He won't wither and die. I fucking need you; I haven't seen you for an entire week."

"Something's going on with Jared. Something's wrong with him. I need him to tell me what it is," I said. "I think it's something we need privacy for."

"Mirabella, I'm fucking exhausted. I need to shower. I need to eat a little something and then love on my girl. Didn't you miss me, Baby?"

I turned over on my stomach and put my feet in the air as I laid on the bed.

"Yes. I missed you so much, and I can't wait to see you."

"Then take off your panties, and wait for me," he said, making me hot and wet.

"Mitchell," I said, breathy.

"Yes, Mirabella?"

"How do you do that?"

"How do I do what?"

"Say one thing and then suddenly my panties are soaked?"

"You're already soaked?"

"Yes," I said, squeezing my legs together.

"I can't wait to be inside you. I have not been able to think of much else all week."

"I don't believe you," I said, teasing.

"Why not?"

"Because I think you've been thinking about my mouth this week too, and how you want to fuck it."

"Jesus."

"And I think you have been thinking about my hands rubbing up and down your dick," I said.

"Yes, Baby, how'd you know?"

"I know everything about you, Mitchell Magellan," I said, lying through my teeth.

"What else do you know?"

"I know how fucking hard you are, and I know you're thinking about touching yourself while we're on the phone."

"Mirabella, I'm ten minutes away. Take your fucking panties off," he said.

And then he hung up on me.

"Here you are," Jared said, walking into my bedroom, seeming winded from the walk up the stairs. "Holy shit, this is nice."

"Thanks, but can you do me a favor and wait for me downstairs?"

Jared looked apologetically at me, and said, "Sorry, Sis. I'll be in the living room."

I made my way into my bathroom and closed the door. I grabbed a washcloth, and brought body wash over to my sink. I cleaned under my armpits, under my boobs, and my woman parts. Once I dried off, I put on some scented lotion, and sprayed a light scent I'd gotten from Penhaligon's in London.

I changed into my mint green cropped Nike sweatshirt and some white linen high-waisted pants I'd also gotten in London. At that point, I knew it was going to be impossible for me to actually sit down because if I did, my wetness would stain my clothes. Still, I was ready for Mitchell, and I hope it showed.

When I went downstairs, I heard Mitchell and Jared in the kitchen. Shit, how was he here already?

When I entered the kitchen, the site of Mitchell took my breath away. And when he looked over and smiled at me, I almost lost my shit.

"Excuse me, Jared; I need my girl," Mitchell said. I stood in place as Mitchell walked to me. I put my arms around his neck, and he gave me a chaste kiss. And right when I was feeling neglected and confused, he squeezed my butt cheeks, and whispered in my ear, "Jared wants to talk to us."

Just then, Jared said, "Look, I'm gonna give y'all some privacy but I need to talk to you. Both of you, if that's ok."

"Yes, absolutely," I said, "why don't we go sit down in the living room."

Mitchell grabbed my hand to hold and led me into the living room as Jared followed.

"Jared sat first, I sat next, and Mitchell sat last. Once we were seated, Mitchell put his arm around me, the broken hand arm.

Jared sat across from us, so that his back was to the window that overlooked Central Park.

"I don't know how to say this, so I'm going to come out with it," Jared said, looking like he had swallowed a frog.

"Ok, well whatever it is, we love you," I said, while grabbing Mitchell's other hand to hold.

Jared hesitated, and then he began crying.

"I'm fucked up," he said through his tears.

I was up and off the couch and at my brother's side immediately.

I touched his face, but that made it worse. He was crying so much more now. And when he wasn't able to get words out for crying, I got really scared.

Mitchell got up, went to the bar, and came back with a Bourbon.

"Here," he said. "It will help," he said.

Mitchell tried placing the glass in Jared's hand, and said, "Come on man, you're scaring your sister. Pull yourself together and tell us what's going on." But when he noticed that Jared's hands were shaking too much to accept, he placed the drink on the coffee table in front of us.

Jared stopped himself from crying, and looked first to me and then to Mitchell.

"I have cancer," he said.

"What?" I said, incredulous.

"Stage three pancreatic cancer," he said.

"Oh my God, Jared," I said, crying now, "when did you find out?"

"Nine weeks ago," he said, calmer now."

"I'm going to have surgery next week, and then a few weeks after that, I will have chemotherapy and radiation therapy."

"I'm sorry to hear this, brother," Mitchell said, but I want to offer my resources to you, whatever you need to find the best care possible." He patted Jared gently on the back and held onto his shoulder.

I pulled Jared into a giant hug. We held one another and cried together.

Soon, Mitchell said, "I'll leave you two alone to talk. I'm going up to shower. And, Mirabella? Let me know if you need me," he said, not even the slightest hint of a double meaning in his tone.

"No; please stay," Jared said.

"Ok," Mitchell said.

Jared turned to me, and said, "there's something else, Mirabella."

"What?"

"I got a girl I'm not with pregnant."

"Wow," I said unsure how to unpack any of this.

"Exactly. Wow. I'm feeling kind of overwhelmed at the moment."

"How far along is the girl? What's her name?"

"It's Bianca, from the bank," Jared said.

"What? How?" I said.

"I flew her out; she and I have been talking. But I'm not ready to have a kid. I told her this. She wants to put the baby up for adoption. Grandma thinks we should take responsibility for our actions and raise the baby, even if we aren't together."

"How far along is she?"

"Three months."

"Are you certain you're the father?" Mitchell said.

"It's mine."

"Does she know you're sick?" I said.

"No. I was planning to tell her after my surgery."

"Is she still in Kentucky?" I needed to know how the hell he let Bianca get her hooks into him like this.

"Yeah. She wants to stay there now that she's pregnant, have the baby there, and then come back to New York."

"Are you sure she wants to place the baby for adoption?" I was rapid-firing questions off to Jared who probably didn't need that shit right then.

"That's what she said."

"Can I say something?" Mitchell said.

"Of course." Jared turned his attention to Mitchell.

"Before you agree to anything, I think you should speak to an adoption attorney in Kentucky to learn about your rights as the father, what the adoption laws are there, and also the type of adoption you want or don't want."

"I get it but this cancer diagnosis has thrown me for a loop, and I don't know if I have enough fight me for two people. I mean you would be the baby's uncle," and then he looked at me and said, "and you its aunt. How would you feel if we placed the kid for adoption?"

I looked at Mitchell, and back at Jared.

"First of all, Mitchell and I are not married, so I would be its aunt, yes. But honestly, it's your life and your baby. You need to decide what's best for you," I said as Mitchell began to brood.

Jared seemed to notice Mitchell's mood had changed, and said, "What do you think, Mitchell? I just don't think I am cut out to be anyone's father in my condition."

"I don't know, man. Anyone can get sick at any time. Look what happened to my brother. He was cut down before he had a chance to get married or have kids. So maybe you should be asking yourself, what if this is your one and only chance to have a family, have kids, be a dad?"

"Wow. Sorry, man. I didn't think of it that way. I didn't mean to be insensitive." Jared's face became sad, like he was ready to give up.

"What about you guys? Things look pretty serious between you.

Look at this fucking penthouse. If that's not serious, I don't know what is."

I smiled an uncomfortable smile, and shot Jared a look that meant, "we're not talking about us, we're talking about you, motherfucker."

"She just took me back, man. I don't work that fast."

"I hear you, Bro. My sister can be super high maintenance," Jared said, taking sides against the family.

"Ok, Fredo," I said.

We all laughed.

"We should do a Godfather marathon in the movie room," Mitchell said.

"Totally," I said, smiling at him. I'd never seen all the films in their entirety.

"Get a room you two."

"But seriously, Jared," Mitchell said, "I want to make some phone calls, and see if I can get one of the Sloan Kettering and also Mayo Clinic specialists to give their opinion on your care and treatment, and see if any would be willing to see you, perhaps perform the surgery.

"What do you mean, like not have surgery on Friday in Kentucky?"

"Yes."

"I need surgery, Mitch, like now."

"I know, brother. But give me until Tuesday to talk to some people, and if they can get your records and possibly schedule something for you the following week, maybe it could work."

"So, what do you need me to do?"

"I need you to authorize me to access your medical records so I can send them freely to whomever may want to view them. Can you do that?"

Jared made a face, as if to ask if he could trust Mitchell with his eyes.

I nodded my approval.

"Ok, I can do that. Where do I sign?"

"I'll give you something to sign tomorrow or Monday at the latest. Then I can access your records and share with experts at both hospitals."

"And what makes you think they'll accommodate your request and see me?"

"Not to be an asshole, Jared, but I'm *Mitchell Magellan*."

When Mitchell said that, it brought a huge smile to my face.

Just then, Mitchell excused himself to go shower.

And when Jared and I were alone, we fell back into a familiar pattern that I had missed more than I realized. We spent the next hour or so laughing and goofing around, and when we thought we had reached the end of things to talk and laugh about, one of us would remember something from our childhood or recall something stupid someone did or that someone said, and it would start a round of giggles all over again.

"Oh, you know what? I forgot to tell you something Mitchell had told me to tell you," I said.

"Oh yeah? What's that?"

"He said you're a cock-blocking son-of-a-bitch."

"What the hell? What did I do?"

"We've been apart for a week. Today was his first day back from London," I said wistfully.

"Oh shit, B. I'm sorry. Why didn't you tell me to get lost? Like, make me go jog around the block for five minutes?"

Jared waited for me to get his 'five minutes' joke, and then when I did, we both busted out laughing.

"That's fucked up, Jared."

"I'm just messing with you, Sis."

"I know."

"But B, you really seem to be in love with this guy," Jared said. "Just make sure he treats you right. The money is awesome. I mean. This fucking apartment. It's easy to ignore shit when you're way up here. Make sure he treats you well. Don't settle because he's broody and rich and possessive."

"You forgot hot. He's hot and sexy."

"He's not my type."

"Thank God. Imagine if you came here and stole Mitchell from me?"

We busted out laughing again.

"B?"

"Yes?"

"Thanks for being there for me."

"Where the hell else would I be, Jared?"

"I mean it," Jared said, with tears in his yellow eyes.

"I mean it too. We're gonna beat this thing, Jared."

"You think so?"

"I know so," I said, trying to be positive for us both. "Are you gonna tell everyone at dinner?"

"No. I haven't told anyone except mom, dad, grandma, and now you and Mitch."

"Well let's keep it that way then."

"Let's just go out and have a good time," Jared said.

"Let's," I said, thinking that now would be the perfect time to start praying.

CHAPTER 23

MITCHELL MAGELLAN

It wasn't the homecoming I wanted, but it was the homecoming I got. And if sacrifice and suffering meant I got to be with Mirabella, it was all worth it to me.

Since Mirabella and I began seeing one another, we had done the whole integrating lives thing. As a new blended friendship circle, we worked. Her circle accepted me, and mine did her. So, when she told me her brother was coming to visit, I was happy for her because we hadn't seen him since Christina's Gotcha Party.

Mirabella's brother Jared was an upstanding guy. He had a fantastic job, handled his business, and never gave anyone a reason to worry. I also understood him to be a bit of a ladies' man, which I could certainly admire. But when he came to New York to see his sister and their friends, no one was expecting him to drop not one but two bombs upon arrival.

So, when I got to the penthouse looking forward to kicking his ass out and getting tangled up with my girl, he surprised me. The minute he dapped me up in the foyer, I knew something was wrong. Jared began quickly telling me his news before he had even told his sister. I barely had minutes to digest the information before Mirabella entered the kitchen. And I hoped she couldn't see the hopelessness I felt beneath my excitement to see her.

She may have sensed something was afoot by the way I greeted her. Had we been alone, I would have scooped her into my arms, kissed her with all the intensity and need I had for her then put her up on the counter, and licked and sucked at her pleasure center until she begged me to put my dick inside her.

Instead, not wanting to have a raging boner in front of her older brother, I kissed her rather chastely, gave her gorgeous ass a squeeze, and tried to prepare her a bit for what was coming. I didn't even allow myself to acknowledge the fact that, according to the feel I had just copped, she was not wearing any panties.

But when Mirabella started drinking shortly after Jared had revealed his cancer diagnosis and his having fathered a baby with a woman he was not with and nor did he want to be with, I had a sneaking feeling that I was not getting laid tonight. And right then, that thought made me feel like a right prick.

Around 4:30, I excused myself to the bathroom so that I could shower, and the siblings could be alone. And by the time I had returned, they were already laughing and giggling like kids. It was beautiful to see Mirabella like this, free, completely herself, and happy, even if for a few minutes. And as I went to the kitchen to grab a cold water from the fridge, I heard her say, "You don't have to worry, Jare, I'll be there for your surgery next week. I won't let you go through this alone. And please *do not* worry about the medical bills. I can cover whatever you need. I just want you to be healthy and to take care of yourself."

"Thanks, B," he said, the love between them so obvious and pure.

Right then, my thoughts turned to my own brother, Alex, and I allowed myself to mourn him silently. I would not wish this upon Mirabella. I couldn't stand it if she had to endure this fucking pain. So, I decided in that moment to make sure Jared had the best care, surgeon, and treatment, no matter where he had to go to receive it. What was the purpose of all this fucking money if you don't use it to help the people you love?

I walked into the living room and interrupted them.

"I need to go make some calls. Mirabella, it's five. If we want to be at *Parcelle* at six, we need to leave in about forty minutes."

"Ok," she said, not even looking at me. And when I didn't move until she acknowledged me with her eyes, she must have felt it, that pull we have because she turned her head in my direction, and gave me the saddest, sexiest smile. "I'll come up in a few, Mitchell," she said, and it felt like the promise of so much fucking more.

IN PREPARATION for next week's surgery, Jared couldn't drink. So, in telling herself she would do so for the two of them, by the time we reached *Parcelle*, Mirabella had already had two glasses of wine and a shot of tequila. By the time we left at seven thirty to head over to *Morandi*, my girl was already singing Harry Styles songs with her fucking friends, and then passing me the hand she was using as a microphone when it was time to sing the *ooohs* and *aaahs*.

RayRay opted not to join us because he was going to see Jared tomorrow. Tonight, our party included Iggy, Shayla, Jared, Mena, Jenni, Mirabella, Maisy, Will, and I. And since Will and Maisy were heading back to London tomorrow, Mirabella had tacked that on to the occasion and reasons to get piss drunk.

I got called away to an impromptu meeting with Braxton during dinner, and when I had given Mirabella my Black Card, she pushed it away, and told me, "I've got this, handsome," with a fucking gorgeous and reassuring smile. Right then, the feeling that Mirabella didn't need me hit me hard, as I made my way out onto the street to take a meeting with Braxton in the Escalade.

I shook Braxton's hand, then led him to the waiting Escalade I'd instructed Brendan to bring around. We got in, and I turned the interior lighting on, and waited for Braxton to tell me what was so fucking important that he had to intcrrupt my dinner to tell me.

"Mitchell, sorry to disturb you tonight, but I thought you would want to hear this immediately and also from me," Braxton said, looking somewhat worn out despite being impeccably dressed in a navy suit, no tie, shirt open at the collar.

"What is it, Braxton," I said, as fear temporarily gripped my heart. It had been Braxton who first told me about the death of my family.

"Peter Trenom is taking a plea deal."

"No shit," I said upon hearing the unexpected development. "What do they have on him?"

"It's not what they have on him, it's what I found out."

Fucking Braxton was going to make me ask him, that dramatic motherfucker.

"What did you find out, Braxton?"

"Well," he said like his information was gossip and not hard-won investigative material with the power to change all our fucking lives. "Robert Brennan III knew Peter was practicing insider trading. It's what your Aunt Meg and mother had been talking to him about in the photo I showed you. Robert Brennan was threatening to reveal dirt on your father and Peter Trenom who was his number two."

"I'm gonna kill that motherfucker with my bare fucking hands," I said. The blood boiling in my fucking veins felt hot and stifling.

Nodding at my broken hand, Braxton said, "perhaps you should consider attempting to keep your anger in check?"

I rolled my eyes and shook my head.

"What else, Braxton?"

"I don't know what Brennan had on your dad, but in order to get Brennan off his back, Trenom gave him access to the video and audio your father had installed in all the offices on the Executive Floor."

"You have got to be fucking kidding me. Fucking Peter Trenom sold me out to save his sorry ass?"

"It's worse than that. Brennan has been privy to every conversation you have had in your office, and your father before you, for about fourteen months. And, when your father died and whatever he had on him no longer held relevance, he turned his attention to you."

"So it was that motherfucker who released the tapes to the media."

"I presume so. But it was also Brennan who sent the tapes of Peter Trenom to the feds. Peter's been practicing insider trading and corporate espionage. The timing of the stock dumps was co-incidental, it would seem."

I sat with this information for a few minutes, Braxton letting me stew in it and process all that it might mean.

Mirabella fucking texted me.

> MIRABELLA: Everything OK?
>
> ME: Yes, Baby. U OK?
>
> MIRABELLA: I miss you
>
> ME: I miss you too, Baby. Am I getting laid tonight?
>
> MIRABELLA: If you don't spend all fucking night with Braxton
>
> ME: Working, Baby. Will be in there in a few

"I want Trenom charged with corporate espionage," I said.

"It's a third-degree felony, a federal charge. It only carries more weight if it had been in support of a foreign government."

I Googled it.

"It says here that the charge could include trade secrets, data theft, stealing secret or patented formulas or designs, utilizing surveillance and key sniffer, etc. Sounds a lot like exactly what Brennan was doing."

"You want me to pass this to the attorneys or would you like to handle it?"

"No, you pass it over. Do not copy me on the email, as usual. I found something else you might think pertinent," I said wondering if I should tell Braxton what Hyacinth had told me.

"Are you going to tell me, or will you make me guess?" That was rich coming from Braxton since he did the exact same fucking thing to me.

"A hacker contacted me last week with proof that it was Brennan behind everything, and get this, Marissa Canto was a fucking plant. She was a double agent, hired by Brennan Enterprises. They paid her over one million dollars for her consultative services."

"You trust this guy? This hacker?"

"Yes, it's a credible source."

"We may not be able to use it if it is a backdoor into Brennan, since that would mean we have someone hacking them back."

"Let me get with the lawyers, and then get back to you. Also, Mitchell, I'm going to need another deposit."

"Sure. How much?"

"With the NTSB report scheduled to be released in the next few weeks, no evidence of foul play in the tragic accident that has befallen your family, and Peter Trenom about to go to federal prison, tying up loose ends should be about two hundred thousand."

"Oh, you're not getting rid of me that easily, Braxton," I said. "I'm about to go after Robert Brennan, and I will need your help." I said, wanting to add, "we ride at dawn" to the end of that statement. "I'm going to need some people willing to do some underbelly shit. So, if you want out, let me know now," I said, wanting to be certain he knew we might have to bend some rules and even break the fucking law.

"Mitchell, one day, I will tell you about my exploits with your father. Perhaps when you're older. Or when I am."

I laughed.

"What, like a deathbed confession?"

"Exactly like that, Mitchell."

I sat forward, and shook Braxton's hand.

"Thanks, Phillip. I appreciate you."

"You're welcome. I'll be in touch."

Then I opened the door for him to exit before me, and for a not-so-brief moment, I considered texting Mirabella and telling her to get her ass out here. And because of this, I had to fucking sit in the Escalade a few minutes longer and think of unsexy things in order to calm the fuck down.

I AWOKE Saturday morning to an empty bed and the sound of our espresso maker, very much aware of my morning wood and the fact that I had not gotten laid last night. The fucking thought of her sent heat into my pelvis, making me feel sexually ravenous and frustrated at the same time. Luckily, Jared went to Queens last night with Mena, Iggy, Shayla, and Jenni, and would be spending today with RayRay and Christina. That meant I had Mirabella all to myself today, and I planned to reacquaint myself with her body all fucking day long.

After washing up and brushing my teeth I practically skipped down the fucking steps and into the kitchen. And if it was possible, I was getting harder the closer I got to laying eyes on her. And when I did, I was treated to a fucking site that had pre-cum dripping out of my tip. Fucking Mirabella was standing in our newly renovated kitchen in a new silk robe with nothing on underneath, cleaning the espresso machine's milk frothing arm by literally stroking the phallic-shaped metal appendage up and fucking down.

I advanced on her, pushing my full weight against her so she could feel my erection and body heat. And then, I slipped my good hand into her robe, the feel of her skin making my dick twitch and jump against her.

"Good morning, gorgeous. You going to touch me like that?" I said into her ear.

She responded immediately but didn't turn around. Mira's body betrayed her as a tingle went up her spine, causing her to shimmy inside my embrace and causing her ass to wiggle against my fucking cock.

Fuck.

Mirabella managed to turn herself to face me, straining against the hold I had on her. She wasn't fucking going anywhere.

She smiled the most tired, sexy, smile, trying to hide her own arousal from me as she sipped her flat white.

"Why is everything about sex with you?"

"Mirabella," I said in the sexiest fucking voice, "I'm done waiting."

The surprise on her face was delicious as her mind must have registered that she was about to get fucked.

When she didn't speak fast enough, I said, "You can either finish that coffee in the next few seconds, or I will fuck you while you drink it," I said.

"Mitchell, I—"

"Don't fucking 'Mitchell' me," I said, taking the coffee mug from her, grabbing her by the hips and placing her on the kitchen island. "You can say my fucking name when you come on my cock."

I stared at her for a moment, so fucking happy to be with her in this apartment that we're planning to make into a home for us. She looked beautiful and sleepy and turned on. I spread her legs, so I could see her, but she tried to close them. And when I spread them again, she tried to close them again.

"What's wrong, Mirabella?"

"I get embarrassed when you look at me like that," she said.

"You don't want me to look at you? I wish you could see yourself."

"Why?"

I rubbed my fingers slowly from her clit to her opening. She fucking arched her back and pushed into me, trying to get my fingers inside her.

"I wish you could see how drenched you are, how you're fucking dripping onto the countertop and pooling on it. You're so wet, Baby."

That seemed to loosen her up a little. I had just enough room to push two fingers inside her vagina, and when I did, she gripped them so fucking hard I wasn't sure I would be able to get them back out.

"That feel good?" I breathed out, already so fucking turned on by her. It made me feel good to know I could make her react like that.

Her response was a moan, and when she slowly began to release, I inched my fingers out and back in again before moving my mouth to her soft, throbbing clit, taking in the scent of her arousal, and enjoying the fucking taste of her.

With only one good hand, I was unable to touch myself the way I'd wanted. I took my mouth off Mirabella, straightened, and said, "Baby, do you want me to finish licking your pussy and fingering you, or do you want my cock?"

Just then, Mirabella did something I was not expecting. She slid down from the countertop, put her arms around my neck, and began to lick her juices off my lips. Totally unprepared, I could barely control myself. Suddenly, my good hand was everywhere I could put it. Her hair, her cheek, her neck, her fucking tits, her mouth, her cunt, her ass. I kissed Mirabella so fucking long and hard and deep, it was like I was trying to taste her fucking throat.

"I need to be inside you, Mira," I breathed into her fucking sweet mouth while my dick twitched and pre-cum ran down from the tip.

My girl ignored my plea. Instead, she got on her knees, looked up at me from down there, put her mouth on me, and took me slowly and deliberately all the way to the back of her fucking mouth. She gently palmed and rolled my balls, sending my head back and eliciting a deep unexpected moan.

She stared at me and blinked timidly, like she was preparing us both for something and then slowly brought her mouth up to my tip, licking and sucking off the pre-cum. Then Mira twisted her hand around the base and began to lick all over my dick. And when she sucked on her own fingers, still wrapped around my cock, I fucking began to shake.

Heat crawled up my spine. My balls tightened. I extended my hand to balance myself against the countertop.

Mira took me deep again, and even though it had only been a few minutes, I was about to lose my fucking shit.

"Mirabella. Fuck. You feel so good. I love when you do me like that," I managed, always wanting to praise her for how good she was at taking my cock, how much she seemed to enjoy it. There was something about her slow and deliberate movements that made me want to shove deeper and harder into her mouth, to take over. She was trying to control me when I wanted to be out of fucking control.

Right as the last bit of resolve left me, I gripped her face like I did when I was about to come deep in her fucking throat.

"Fuck, I'm gonna come, Mira."

But instead of coming in her mouth, she popped me from her swollen lips, and rubbed my dick between her fucking gorgeous breasts as streams of cum shot onto her skin while she held her mouth open and tongue out to catch whatever she could.

Mother. Of. God.

As I looked at my Mirabella, covered in my cum and with satisfaction in her eyes, I wanted to never let her go. I wanted to tell her right then that she was it for me. I didn't want or need anyone or anything else, ever.

I helped her up.

Mirabella had sleepy doe eyes, afraid to ask me for what she now needed. After what she had just done, Mirabella had quickly reverted back to the shy girl who was afraid to ask me to pleasure her.

When we were both standing, I kissed her for a few seconds, hoping she knew how grateful I was for what she had just done for me.

"Let's go to the living room so we can be comfortable," I said, taking her by the hand and leading her to the couch by the fireplace, which was already on.

"Where do you want me?" She said, timidly.

"Come here," I said, as I laid down in front of the fireplace. Mirabella?"

"Yes?" She remained standing, suddenly shy.

"Baby, come sit on my face."

CHAPTER 24

MIRABELLA CASTLE

When Mitchell told me to sit on his face, I almost died. Aside from the face fucking I'd done to him in his Maybach after Mena's mom's funeral, we'd never done it like that before. But since I had just let him come on my tits, I guess today was a day for sexual firsts. Now, straddling him on the floor of our living room surrounded by floor-to-ceiling windows on the seventy-sixth floor of our new penthouse, this man had me fucking his mouth and fingers on my way to one of the most intense orgasms he had ever given me. And when I exploded all over his mouth, gripping the three fingers he had inside me, Mitchell didn't let any of my cum go to waste.

He helped me lower myself to lie on top of him, and I was surprised by the fact that he was hard.

"Thank you," I said as I kissed my juices off his mouth.

"Was that good? Did you like it like that?"

"Yes, Mitchell. You are incredibly good at your job," I teased while planting kisses all over his beautiful face.

"Mmmmmm," he said. "My job, Mirabella?" The sexy tone of his voice seemed to match the erection that was growing as I lay across it.

Still slick from my orgasm, I began to rub myself against him. It reminded me of how I used to dry hump pillows, trying to jerk myself off when I first discovered arousal at the age of fifteen.

"Yes. Your job." My voice was breathy. I moved against him in a way that had me trying to satisfy us both, allowing the fire that burned between us to overtake me.

Mitchell was humping me too. And as simple as our movements were, they felt very erotic. When I looked into Mitchell's eyes, he seemed lost in the delicious feeling of our bodies coaxing pleasure from the friction.

"And what exactly is my . . . *job*?"

"To *fucking* please me."

My own voice sounded foreign to me. I wasn't confident in my sex appeal, and yet there was something about having Mitchell beneath me that had me worked up and not joking in the fucking least.

Mitchell must have really liked that because he moved against me more ferociously now, and claimed my mouth as his.

"Mirabella," he said so softly, I thought maybe I had imagined it.

Mitchell was about to come undone beneath me, and in that moment, I felt powerful and sexy. I wound my hips in a circular motion and ground against him while kissing him. But then, I stopped and rubbed my finger on my clit. I pulled some wetness from my folds then put that finger into his mouth.

"See what you do to me, Mitchell?" I stared into his eyes as I spoke, our connection unbelievable.

He fucking sucked on my finger as I said, "that's right. Let me see you suck it for me, Mitchell," while feeling my pussy soak us both.

Mitchell suddenly turned me over onto my stomach. And when he raised me up just enough to get his hand beneath me, he finally answered my question.

"Yes, Baby." Mitchell was all breathy, turned on, and determined. "I see what I do to you. And when you show me like a good girl, when you don't hide from me, Mirabella, it makes me feel like a goddamn king. I want to be your fucking king. I want you to show me your world. How it feels to be touched by me. Kissed by me. Fucked by me."

Fuck!

Mitchell began moving his fingers over my slick clit in slow teasing ghost motions, causing me to moan and thrust forward in an attempt to get him to really touch me.

Soon, he tortured me some more by teasing my opening with his cock. He wanted me to beg.

"Mitchell, I need you so fucking much. You are my *fucking king*. Touch me. Put your cock inside me. Give it to me how I like. Please, Mitchell. Make me—"

Before I could finish, Mitchell buried himself deep inside me. He rubbed my aching clit and thrusted in and out at a pace that was both delicious and frustrating.

"Baby," Mitchell said, and I knew exactly what he had wanted to say.

"Oh God. Right there," I said not wanting him to stop hitting me like that. Whatever Mitchell was feeling, I was feeling it too. My pussy clenched him, my pelvis tightened, and my arousal dripped onto his hand.

"Fuck, Mira, right here?" Mitchell had somehow managed to push just a little more inside me RIGHT FUCKING THERE.

And then he stilled. This was it. Neither of us was going to make it past this delectable moment.

"Fuck!" Was all I could say. I was lost in this man. In the way he made me feel.

"Mira. Fuck, you're making me come!"

"Mitchell, I'm coming too. It's so good."

He stilled inside me again, pushed my hair aside, and kissed my shoulder. He gently removed himself from my vagina, and then turned me over onto my back. He smiled down at me before giving me a deep appreciative kiss. And when he pulled away, I made a face. He smiled at me, and said, "What's wrong?"

"I want to kiss you some more."

I snatched the smile off his face with a deep kiss in which I pushed my tongue into his mouth and challenged him to resist kissing me back. Sucking on Mitchell's tongue was one of my favorite things to do. And when I had my fill of it, I moved my mouth to his neck and kissed him all over it before sucking on his Adam's Apple. Soon, Mitchell was moaning with his eyes closed.

Now it was me who pulled away, and asked, "What's wrong?"

Mitchell opened his eyes, and said, "Mira. I fucking love when you pay attention to me like that. I love when you kiss me, Mirabella."

This fucking man was so handsome; all I could do was smile.

WE MUST HAVE FALLEN asleep because the sun was lower and there was a blanket covering us. Mitchell's casted arm was like dead weight across my stomach, and when I tried to move it so I could pee, he pulled me even tighter into his sleep-induced death-grip.

After a few minutes, I had managed to shimmy and shake my way out of his hold and sneak to the bathroom. When I returned, I got back under the covers, causing him to awaken. When his eyes met mine, his sexy sleepy smile did things to me.

I kissed his cheek. But it didn't feel like enough, so I turned his head to face me and kissed his mouth some more.

Taking my time and loving on Mitchell felt so good. He tasted so damn delicious. The stubble on his face and neck was bristly, and still, I kept my mouth and tongue on this man because I had missed him and had not yet had my fill of him.

Mitchell said, "Is everything ok?"

He repositioned himself on his side with his good arm placed under his head like a pillow.

"Yes, why?" I mimicked his action and then snuck in another kiss to his glorious full lips.

He smiled again.

"You were different today," he said. "And I am no way complaining. It's just you've ... Never kissed me like this before. Licked me like that. You let me come on your tits."

I pulled the blanket up around my neck and moved away a little, his words making me embarrassed and anxious. I had done my best to be sexy and adventurous for him. To show him that I could be like the other women he'd had.

"Yes."

Mitchell's expression was contemplative then. He outlined my chin with his finger and looked lovingly at me.

"I wanted to give you something different."

"Yeah?"

"You seemed to like it," I said, my confidence coming back slowly.

He smiled.

"Mirabella, I liked it *very* much. But not because it was different, I liked it because it was you."

"But you still fucking liked it, and don't even think about denying it," I teased.

"Yes, Baby. It was *very fucking good*," he said, and when he smiled, I could tell he was getting aroused again.

This. Fucking. Man.

"Can I ask you something?"

"Um-hm." I was feeling rather lazy and in love.

Mitchell ran his thumb across my bottom lip, his gorgeous green eyes following the movement, and his touch sent a shiver up my spine.

"Did you give Ben head like that? Did you let him come on you?"

"Why?" I said, feeling super inexperienced and unsure of myself again. I didn't want him to think of me that way, but I also didn't want to lie to him. I really didn't want to talk about Ben, especially since it was Mitchell who'd warned me that he never wanted to hear me say his name again.

"Yes." I said in a small voice. "I mean, I gave him head. I tried to. To get him hard. But it didn't work."

"What? What the fuck does that mean?"

"I tried to do it, but he wasn't getting hard. He said that I wasn't doing it right. He said I should watch porn to learn how guys like it."

"And did you?"

"Did I what?"

"Watch porn to learn how to give head?"

"Why would I do that when my best friend is a resident expert?"

"Ahhh. Remind me to thank RayRay."

MITCHELL WAS asleep next to me when I checked the clock to see that it 4:44pm. The man was beautiful even when he slept. Staring at him while he was so still and peaceful, I felt happy, full, and content. I looked around our new bedroom, and even though it was not decorated to our tastes, it felt like home.

I slipped quietly out of bed to find my phone so I could text Jared. Unable to find it upstairs, I looked downstairs. When I found it on the kitchen counter, it was plugged in, something I didn't recall doing. I smiled to myself thinking about how attentive Mitchell was and how he took care of me in all things. It was a simple gesture but the level of thoughtfulness and consideration it exemplified made me smile.

Looking around the living room and admiring the views out of its windows, I dialed Jared's phone.

"Hey, B. How are you feeling today?" He said like he did whenever we got shitfaced.

"I was a little iffy last night, but I actually woke up feeling great. Mitchell said he knew I was done for when I started singing One Direction!"

"You were fucked up, B. I'm glad you had a good time. You deserved it."

"What about you? You seemed to be having fun."

"Yeah. I felt like shit for lying to everybody, but once I realized that was probably the last time I'll get to hang out for a while, I snapped out of it."

"That karaoke place couldn't believe their luck having a celebrity in the midst."

"Oh my God, B. Mitchell actually has a good voice. I was scared for a minute."

We both laughed.

"Right? Like is there anything this man can't do?"

"He works all the time like that? I mean, when he left to go take a meeting and didn't come back for like forty minutes. What was that? Is that normal?"

"He works really hard, Jared. Sometimes he has to step away from social things."

"Are you sure that's what he's doing, B?"

"What do you mean? What else would he be doing?"

Neither of us said anything then as the implication of Mitchell dipping out to see a woman sat silently between us.

"Jared, I don't think he's doing that."

"I'm just saying. He's always been kind of a playboy. I'm just looking out for my favorite sister."

"I'm your only sister," I said, despite the fact that we now had a stepsister. Jared remained quiet like he did when he didn't want to talk about something for fear of us fighting.

"You should make an effort to see Mom and Dad, B."

"Why? They make zero effort to see me."

The anger, snark, and bitterness in my voice was not unlike me whenever Jared tried to talk me into spending time with my parents, each of whom had entirely new families.

"You haven't even seen grandma. Maybe you can make some time. Especially for Mom. She gets so excited when you text her back."

"I know. I will. I promise. Mitchell and I were thinking of having a housewarming party. But well, we're not sure when it will be. Maybe in January when you're back on your feet or something."

My voice trailed off, not wanting to think about Jared's surgery too much.

"Well, whatever you guys decide, I'm sure Mom and Dad would love to come."

"Oh, did I tell you that Mr. Tate's dog died?"

"No way; Sparky died? That's horrible. I loved that little three-legged dog. Oh man."

"Yeah, they found him in the backyard after he had been missing for like four days."

"Oh no! Poor thing."

"Yeah. But listen, some of us were talking about charades tonight in Queens."

"What time?"

"Maybe around nine?"

"Is everyone on their own for dinner? Do you want to eat with Mitchell and I?"

"I'm kind of beat, B, and I'm in a little bit of pain, so I think I'm just gonna chill in Queens and try to turn in early. But I'm gonna have brunch with you guys tomorrow, and I promise to whoop your boyfriend's ass in racquetball."

He sounded so tired and weak.

"Ok, well maybe don't overdo it."

"We did a lot of walking today, that's all."

"How are you gonna play racquetball tomorrow then?"

"These pain meds work really well."

I was so sad right then. I hated seeing my brother in pain and suffering.

Just then Mitchell joined me in the kitchen. He kissed my head, and then got a water from the fridge.

"So, you want us to come to Queens or you don't?"

"You know what, B?" I think maybe I'll just see you guys tomorrow. Is that ok?"

"Of course, whatever you want, Jare. Just be ready tomorrow by eleven so we can have brunch. Bring your stuff with you so you can stay over here Sunday night. Ok?"

"Ok," he said.

"Call me later, you know, when you get settled and stuff."

"Ok, B. Talk to you later."

"How is he?" Mitchell asked when I put the phone down.

"I don't know. He sounds tired. He says he's in pain. Maybe you guys won't be able to play racquetball tomorrow if he's like this. He has pain meds, but I don't know."

Mitchell pulled me into a hug. I wrapped my arms around his neck, and we stayed like that as I leaned against the counter.

"Mirabella, I made some calls about Jared's doctors and medical records. On Monday, we should know a lot more. His surgery is scheduled for Friday, so we have a little time. If it makes more sense to have him at Sloan Kettering, we can."

"Do you think that's advisable given the advanced stage of his condition?" I said refusing to say the word.

"That's just it. My father knew the Chair of the Department of Surgery and the Hospital President. I'm sure either can recommend a great pancreatic cancer specialist. I have already left a message for both of them who, at my father's funeral, told me to let them know if there was ever anything they can do for me. And I know people say that at funerals, but now is the time to call in those favors."

"Thank you, Mitchell."

"You're welcome."

I checked my phone. It was 5:15pm. I yawned, sleepy from the late night and all the sex.

"I made a list of things I want to talk to you about while you were away," I said, hoping not to sound too weird.

"Should I be worried?"

I smiled.

"No. I just want to talk."

"You don't have to make an appointment to talk to me, Baby. Just tell me what's on your mind."

"I'm gonna make a fruit bowl with some yogurt. Should I make some for you too?"

"I can help you make it," Mitchell said.

"Thank you, Baby."

"I like when you call me that," Mitchell said.

"I like calling you that," I said and smiled.

He smiled back, and then got the yogurt, strawberries, grapes, blueberries, black berries, and kiwi from the forty-eight-inch glass door Sub-Zero fridge. Mitchell stopped in his tracks after putting the food on the countertop.

"I have no idea where the cutlery is."

"That's because we don't have any," I said. "We're using plastic until we can decide which cutlery to buy."

"Ok, where's the plastic knives, cutting board, and colander?"

I laughed.

"We don't have a cutting board. Maybe let's just wash the fruit, cut it up with a plastic knife on a paper towel, and call it a day."

"Very practical," Mitchell said.

"That stuff is in the second draw over there," I said, pointing.

"So, what are we talking about?" He said, as he washed the fruit.

"Well, stuff like that. We are eating off paper plates, using plastic utensils, and using paper towels as cutting boards. We literally are starting from scratch."

I dried the fruit as Mitchell washed them.

Mitchell smiled at me, and said, "Mirabella, order whatever you want for the apartment. I won't have an opinion mostly. I like certain things, and when I have an opinion about them, I will share it with you. Otherwise, please use my card, and get whatever we need. Whatever you want. There is no spending limit. Just buy it, have it delivered."

I understood where Mitchell was coming from, but I wanted him to be involved. It was his house too, and I didn't want him to be just a spectator here. I wanted him present, and to me, that meant helping me make choices about what to purchase for our shared apartment.

"Why don't I just add you to my card?"

"I'm not sure that's necessary. I can buy things with my own money, Mitchell. Like last night, the bill was two thousand five hundred six dollars at dinner. I didn't need your help paying. I appreciated the offer, but it wasn't necessary."

"I can't believe you left a fifteen-hundred-dollar tip."

"What good is having money if you can't help people with it?" I said, feeling especially grateful for my life right then.

CHAPTER 25

MIRABELLA & MITCHELL

MITCHELL MAGELLAN

Sometimes I forgot that Mirabella is only twenty-one years old. She is wise beyond her years and limited life experience. I know people three times her fucking age with no clue about a goddamn thing, and these people continue to fucking fail up and get rewarded by life. And when I see someone like Mirabella who is smart as a fucking whip, emotional intelligence off the charts, and with a good heart, it leaves a mark. And, from the day I met her, I knew she was going to have a profound effect on my life.

Mirabella had been sheltered from most of the pain of life by her grandmother who, God bless her, either blamed the devil or attributed everything that happened in life to God's plan. As a result, Mirabella most likely never considered that she could be any different than she was. How could she if it was God's plan for her to be that way?

When Mirabella told me that what she thought was her un-sexiness and inability to please a man made her feel like there was something wrong with her, I wanted to fucking wrap my hands around that motherfucker Ben's neck and squeeze the life out of him right fucking then.

Thinking about my girl pushing all sexual thoughts from her beautiful head for years, thinking herself unworthy of amazing sex with a partner who adores her and only cares about her happiness in bed, means she went running into the arms of guys like fucking Ben who never deserved to be looked at by Mirabella, let alone to receive the pleasure of her attention or her body.

If she had been with a guy who was worthy of her, even in the same fucking place as her intellectually, full of emotional intelligence, and remotely fucking hot and it didn't work out? "Ok," I would say, "well, that shit didn't work out." But fucking Ben is a scourge on my fucking soul. He is a mouse of a fucking man, and for the life of me, I cannot let it go. Whatever the fuck he did to her, to her psyche and sexual self-esteem is unforgivable. Watching the damage he inflicted play out in my bedroom, it's no wonder she reacted how she did when she learned Magellan Media was a sponsor for his fucking bullshit stage play.

These fucking guys who are weak and broken, these are the type of guys who make women like Mirabella, who are too fucking good for them in the first place, feel low and unlovable. And, while I went into this knowing she's too fucking good for me and that every minute she allows me to be in the same fucking room with her is a minute to be treasured and made the most of, these fucking assholes who are addicted to porn or whatever other vice they worship, have a false sense of importance they use to cover for their utter lack of fucking self.

So, women like Mirabella, try to please them, to be more of this or less of that or to be what they think these fuckers want, until they become so lost in self-doubt, they end up as a shadow of who they are or who they could be. And now, Mirabella is inhibited to the point of denying herself the immense pleasure I can give her. She has trouble being vulnerable with me because she fucking thought so little of herself to wait for the right man.

I'm not saying I'm the right man for her. I know I don't fucking deserve her. But I wanted to be the right man for Mirabella. I wanted to earn her love. I wanted to invest in her. I wanted to be the man she not only needs but wants. I denied myself some of my most dark and depraved tendencies, in an effort to be worthy of her. And when she fucking left me, I had no one to reel me in.

So, I had become very attuned to Mirabella. How she reacted, the slight ripple of current up her spine when she began to feel aroused by my touch. How she looked away when faced with the truth of soaked panties, her body coming to life under my gaze, talked to her in a certain way, or touched her. How her nipples ripened and strained against her clothing, always peeking at me from beneath whatever top she had on like a fucking beacon calling me to her. The little goosebumps that covered her skin which she attributed to being chilly? She didn't even recognize it as one of the first signs of her need for me.

Mirabella probably wasn't aware of her sexual tells. But when I saw them, I took them as permission, as an invitation, as an unspoken request. So, when she asked me "why is everything always about sex" with me, I didn't know what to say. I fucking loved sex with her. I loved the idea of sex with her. Every time we were together, I discovered something new about her. I'd find new ways to give her fucking pleasure. Mirabella has altered my entire brain chemistry. Anna said, I had replaced one addiction with another, and you know what? I didn't even fucking care.

Mirabella grounded me. She comforted me. She made me believe I could do anything. She made me want to be good. Fucking, great even. And when I made her come and she looked at me in that fucking way, when I made her look into the eyes of the man who made her feel like that, I felt like a fucking god.

So, when I went to London, I did so reluctantly. Of course, business had to be done but it was also a good way not to feel so tortured by the fact that Mirabella and I were fucking struggling. My indiscretion with Lorelei and those tapes, even though she didn't mention them, were on her mind.

She was willing to try again, but I was going to have to work even harder to get her to trust me, to want to be with me.

Since it was clear that Mirabella neither cared about my money nor did she fucking need it now, I had to be more than just some guy with a lot of fucking money and a dark past. That shit's for the romance books, not real fucking life. I needed to step the fuck up and earn her.

So, the time in London put distance between us. It also gave us time to really talk and miss each other in a way that would make getting to see one another more meaningful than just delicious sex. But when her cock blocking brother planned to visit, I fucking had to check myself. I had to push past my fucking need to be with her, to get lost in her because her brother needed her. And when he revealed to me what was going on with him, I needed to be there for Mirabella in a way that I hadn't been before. That she would need me to be a man who can take care of her outside of the fucking bedroom.

I couldn't shake the feeling that the Magellan curse was rubbing off on Mirabella after Jared revealed he not only had cancer but also an unwanted pregnancy with a girl with whom he was on-again and off-again but mostly wanted to be off-again with.

It would have been super easy for me to swoop in, throw my fucking money around, and take over. I wanted to; it was the Magellan way. If there's a problem, throw money at it, and watch it disappear. But when I had offered my resources, connections, and money, both Mirabella and her brother had seemed to exhibit cautious optimism.

What was supposed to be an amazing reunion weekend in my new apartment with Mirabella had turned out to be tinged with sadness, pain, and fucking downright upsetting and unsettling news. I wanted to help her through it all but that was in direct contrast to all the other things I had wanted to do with her, to her, and for her.

Mirabella once told me that we could not solve all of our problems with sex. And while that was true for sure, sex with the right person, or even the wrong one sometimes, could make us forget the pain temporarily. If we were able to give ourselves over to another person completely and trust them to give us pleasure without worrying about what it meant or who would think oddly of us, we could get lost in one another and forget the world and all its fucking pain.

And with so much on her fucking mind and so much uncertainty about how she'd split her time between the penthouse and her apartment in Queens, adjusting her schedule so that she can help Jared through his surgery next week, and the state of our relationship, I was shocked when Mirabella switched things up in our fucking bedroom. The girl I experienced until now was vastly different from the one who fucking put my hand on her pussy and instructed me to do my fucking job.

Now, in the kitchen preparing a snack of fruit and yogurt and planning to watch a movie in our theater room, Mirabella said she'd had a list of things she wanted to talk to me about. It took all my fucking strength not to tell my new boss that I wanted her to fucking let me work overtime.

MIRABELLA CASTLE

OF ALL PEOPLE, it had been Hyacinth who'd helped me see the light. We hadn't developed a friendship outside of work. And when the video and audio tapes of Mitchell with Marissa Canto were released, my concentration at work was fucked. How could I put the tapes behind me when my actual job was to talk about them every damn day?

The cat was now out of the bag about Mitchell and me. The fear we'd all had about damage to the brand if anyone found out had all been for nothing. Millions of people all over the world had taken to supporting our relationship likening it to a phoenix among the ashes. Some had begun calling me "the girl who made lemonade out of lemons." Others had celebrated me for subduing Mitchell Magellan, calling him to heel like a rabid fucking dog. The creativity of the Internet was unmatched. And when Hyacinth suggested we create a fictional version of my story as a Young Adult novel, I hated the brilliant idea.

I could often feel Hyacinth's judgement and hear it in her tone whenever she talked about Mitchell, but on one night in particular, she offered to take me to dinner. And when your boss offers to take you to dinner, you accept, no matter if you're in the mood to be lectured or not.

Sitting across from her, I was grateful to have someone like her in my life. She seemed to genuinely care about me, and as a result, she was willing to give it to me straight. Being older, her advice seemed wiser and better suited to the situation I had found myself in. And in the ill-lit booth in the back of the restaurant away from nosey New Yorkers, we talked in a way we had never before done.

"How are things with Mitchell?" She said on the day after I had given her his phone number.

"Are you asking as my boss who wants to protect her asset or as my friend?"

"Would you be affronted if it was a little of both?"

I looked down at my plate of pasta, feeling a sudden freedom to speak candidly about Mitchell.

"Can I speak freely without worrying that what I say will be repeated at work?"

"Yes, of course. I would never betray your confidence, Mirabella. And despite what it seems, I don't have it in for Mitchell Magellan. He is a means to an end in terms of my job and career trajectory. If not him, then someone else, really. The two of you just so happened to create the perfect storm of opportunity, and I pounced on it."

"Makes total sense. It's brilliant, actually. If I weren't the one in the middle of the shitstorm, I'd be on the sidelines cheering you on."

"And you aren't now? Cheering me on?"

"I am. I am. It's just sometimes I can feel you judging me."

Now it was her turn to look down at her pasta. She looked up again, seemingly thinking about her next words.

"Can I speak freely too, Mirabella?"

"Of course." I stiffened in my chair.

Hyacinth put her fork down, sighed, and looked sincerely into my eyes.

"I feel protective of you. As a young Black woman in an entanglement with a rich, powerful, egotistical, white man, I worry about you."

I didn't know how to feel about what she'd said. Mitchell and I had never discussed race. He seemed to have more Black friends than I did. And when I suggested the scholarship idea, he didn't flinch. He was all over it. I didn't even know what his political views were. His parents seemed to be liberal leaning, according to the causes they had been known to support.

"Would you be concerned about me if he was Black?"

Hyacinth took her time assessing my question, considering it.

"Yes. But his whiteness *is* a fact, is it not? Just like his wealth?"

"Yes," I said, appearing to confirm whatever the hell she must have already been thinking about my relationship. She made a knowing face. I guess she had been wondering about this for some time, holding back in the office despite the questions and comments she had already made.

"The circles he runs in, the people he engages; they are not all like him, I presume. Not everyone will be thrilled about your place in his life."

"I know." I looked around the restaurant to be sure no one was watching us or listening in or taking photos.

"Mirabella, I hope you know I'm not trying to hurt you or attack you. I have noticed a change in you since the tapes were released, and it isn't a good one. You seem . . . *broken*."

Don't cry. Don't fucking cry.

"I feel broken," I said in a small voice. "I feel insignificant and inexperienced and not enough."

Hyacinth gave me a sympathetic look then reached out to take my hand, but I pulled my hand away and placed my hands in my lap. She lowered her eyes, and said, "I hate that this man has made you feel like less of you."

In that moment, I wanted to defend Mitchell. I didn't want anyone to think he was a bad person. I loved him, and that was the reason why the videos hurt so much.

"It isn't that Mitchell has made me feel this way. I have always struggled with . . . things in the bedroom," I said, then immediately regretting saying it.

"Oh," she said.

"Is it a medical thing or is something more intangible, like maybe you are just unsure of yourself?"

"Ok, since we're speaking freely, I'm just going to say it. Is that ok?"

"It's perfectly fine."

"I have only ever had intercourse twice. Maybe three times."

I could tell Hyacinth was doing her best not to react. I bet she was thinking someone like me with the mouth I had could not possibly have been so inexperienced.

"Ok, and how were those three times?"

"Oh, wait, I meant before I met Mitchell, I had only had sex three times. Mitchell and I cannot keep our fucking hands off one another," I said immediately regretting that too.

Hyacinth smirked and said, "I should hope you're having lots of sex with that beautiful man."

Her words elicited a surprised smile from me.

"What? I'm not blind, Mirabella," she added with a devilish expression.

I think we might have giggled.

"Those tapes though, they showed me a side of Mitchell I didn't recognize. And when I saw them, all of my insecurities came rushing to the surface. I didn't know he wanted those things. Needed those things. We certainly had never *done* those things."

I was fully embarrassed now.

"I dated a man who was much more experienced than me. It can definitely bring out our insecurities."

"And how did you cope? Because I cannot get my own intrusive thoughts out of my head. And now, I can't unsee the video or un-hear the audio. It's so hard to be around him without those things fighting for room in my headspace."

Hyacinth reached out for my hand once more, and this time, I took my hand from under the table, and placed it in hers.

"You have to beat that shit at its own game," she said.

"What? How?"

"Be a fucking vixen."

"What?" I said, laughing at Hyacinth's use of an f-bomb.

"Mirabella, you don't strike me as someone content to allow others to walk all over them. So why are you allowing these tapes of Mitchell before he even met you ruin your life, or worse, your sex life?"

"We have amazing sex, not to be crass, but it is so good with him."

"I'm sure Mitchell Magellan knows his way around the bedroom. But, Mirabella, what if your sex with him could be even better?"

"I don't know how that's even possible."

Just then the waiter returned.

"Can I get you ladies anything else? More wine? Dessert menu?"

Hyacinth said, "We are going to need another bottle of wine," then made a face like we were about to get into some delicious girl talk.

And when the waiter left, we giggled again.

"So, tell me," I said, ready to learn how to have better sex with Mitchell and rid myself of the voices of self-doubt in my head from the person I could never imagine would be the one to teach me.

"I don't want to offend you, Mirabella. But I too saw the video, much to my dismay. And what I saw? It was a man who likes to dominate women, someone who likes his partner to be subjugated. But what if it's more complicated than that? What if Mitchell Magellan is looking for a sexual counterpart, an equal, and he acts the way he does in order to see who will actually challenge him?"

Right then and there, a lightbulb went off in my head. It was like that cartoon I used to watch when the one kid told his friend, "I know what we're going to do today." I was going to fucking dominate Mitchell Fucking Magellan. I was going to own my power in the bedroom. I was going to make him beg to be inside me.

CHAPTER 26

MIRABELLA CASTLE

When Mitchell took a call from Aunt Meg and Jared retired to the guest bedroom, I seized the opportunity to shower. The pressure of feeling like I had to entertain Jared and fill every minute of his visit with something to do was never greater than it had been.

As I stood in the steam shower alone for the first time that day, I let my mind wander wherever it wanted. I thought about how much I liked our primary bath but also how much I didn't *love* it. And now that the kitchen had turned out so well, I wondered if I should ask Mitchell what he thought about remodeling it.

I didn't realize how tired I had been until late Sunday night. Freshly showered and in a t-shirt that fell midway over my ass, I finished my skincare routine and stared in the mirror at the puffiness in my face. Alcohol did that to me for some reason, and so now, I would have to detox with much less wine and much more water.

I didn't even notice that Mitchell had been standing in the doorway and was watching me. And when I did see him, the look on his face was fucking feral. Mitchell Magellan saw something he liked and was about to pounce on it. There was no denying what that look did to me, and as I stared back at him from the mirror on my vanity, he didn't move.

"Mirabella," he said from over there, "bend over."

I had to squeeze my thighs together to calm the throbbing in my clit. Evidence of my arousal ran down my legs. The anticipation of what Mitchell was going to do to me had my nipples crushed up against the cotton of my shirt.

And, as I considered how to respond to his explicit order, I made a split-second decision that would change how I interact with Mitchell in the bedroom from now on. I threw my towel into the dirty clothes basket, rubbed my bare ass against the tent in his sweats as I attempted to ease past him, and said, "bend me over your fucking self."

I had planned to slip past him, lock the bedroom door, and jump into bed before he could recover. But Mitchell grabbed me by the waist as I finished saying the word "self." He quickly maneuvered me against the bedroom wall with my back to him. The sound of Mitchell's heavy breathing and freeing himself from his clothes was so sexy, I nearly orgasmed from the anticipation alone.

Fuck.

But he didn't keep me waiting long. Mitchell plunged himself into me harder than he had ever done so before. He then pulled out all the way and leaned forward as he slammed into me so hard that my body banged against the wall. After he pulled all the way out again, he teased my entrance with his cock, and it was like he was deciding what to do next. Just when I thought I would have to beg him for more, he slammed into me again.

"You want me to fuck you, Mirabella?" Mitchell said against my right ear as my pussy clenched. Then, he moved his head over to my left ear and said, "Just fucking ask me."

Mitchell ran his hand from my ass, up my back and across my shoulders. I leaned my head back as he plunged into me once more and said, "Don't walk around with no panties on and your ass uncovered."

All I could do was moan.

"Are you listening, Mirabella?"

He reached his hand around, wedged it between the wall, and

grabbed both breasts in his hand, squeezing and twirling my nipples between his skillful fingers. *This. Fucking. Man.*

When I didn't move or respond to his words, he must have known how close I was to coming for him. Mitchell reached up and put his middle finger into my mouth.

"Suck it, Mira. Get it nice and wet for me."

My pussy clenched again for this man. A hiss left his lips as he pulled his finger out of my mouth and said, "Good fucking girl."

"Mitchell," I moaned against the wall.

He eased the finger he'd had in my mouth into my ass and slid slowly out of my pussy simultaneously. The feeling of being emptied and filled at the same time threatened to send me over the edge.

Mitchell moaned into my ear, his breath all over the skin of my neck and shoulder. He shoved back inside me hard and deep, stilling until he felt me grip him again.

His cock twitched against my wall, as if knocking to be let in just a little deeper, back where it's super slippery, hot, and fucking tight.

Shit.

"I'm coming, Mitchell."

"Fuck. Mira, I'm coming with you. Fuck!" he said as he plunged even deeper into my dripping center.

Mitchell kissed my neck, gently removed himself from inside me, and then turned me to look at him. He was so damn handsome, sometimes I could not believe he was mine. And as I stood there staring at my beautiful boyfriend, his cum was running down my legs.

"Let's get in the shower," he said despite the fact that I had only just taken one.

"Mitchell," I said with a smirk knowing that whenever we had taken a shower together, it had always led to sex.

He gave me a devilish smile, and said, "Let me clean up the mess I made."

Mitchell turned on the shower using the remote, one of the cool features of our primary bathroom. I went to pee and Mitchel got us wash cloths from the linen closet.

I opened the shower door, stepped in, and Mitchell entered after.

He wet a washcloth and wrung it out several times over me, paying special attention to dripping the water over my breasts. Not gonna lie, the hot water felt good on my skin.

"Can I wash you?" I said smiling at him.

"Of course, Baby," he said before he kissed my mouth.

MITCHELL TOOK a call from Sheldon in London, something about whatever it was that couldn't wait until Monday. And by the time he exited the bathroom, I was nearly asleep.

He got into bed beside me, and I brought myself over so he could hold me as he did some things on his phone. Whatever the call was about seemed to agitate him. I listened as his phone made haptic sounds in response to his gorgeous fingers and their commands.

"When do you get the cast off?" I asked.

"Next week."

"Good," I said, sleepily, pulling him up under me some more.

"Excited for me to have two hands for you?"

"Ummm, Yes."

Mitchell laughed.

"Me too."

I must have fallen asleep because I woke to Mitchell saying, "Mira. Hey."

He pulled me up to look at him.

"I got a response from the Pancreatic Cancer specialist at Sloan Kettering. He can see Jared Tuesday morning at 9:15. He's going to look over his scans and lab work and confer with his colleagues. He asked if I would like to confirm the appointment. Well, his assistant did."

I sat up now, awake and alert.

"Really? Let me ask Jared."

I pushed the covers off me and grabbed my robe from the chair next to the bed.

"Mirabella," Mitchell said, but not how he usually said it.

I put my robe on and tied it.

"Put some clothes on before you go down there."

"Mitchell; it's just Jared," I said about to ignore him.

"Mirabella," he said again, angry this time.

"What?"

"Put some fucking clothes on before you go down there."

The look on his face was somewhere between anger, frustration, torture, and arousal.

"Ok" I said.

And to fix his attitude, I removed my robe, dropped it on the floor then bent over with my bare ass out to find sweatpants in the bottom drawer.

"Did you find something to put on?" He asked, from bed.

"Almost," I said, continuing to dig in the drawer that contained only two pairs of sweats, giving Mitchell a full view of my pussy and ass at the same time.

But when he didn't move from bed, I grabbed some white sweats and put them on. Then, I put my bathrobe on, tied it, and looked back at him to see why he was still in fucking bed and not all over me.

Mitchell was touching himself under the covers. And now, it was me whose attitude had been adjusted, watching this gorgeous man jerk himself off while watching me.

"Hurry the fuck up," Mitchell said, "or I'm going to come without you."

"What the fuck did you just say?"

"You fucking heard me, Mirabella," he said, continuing to stroke himself.

I slammed the bedroom door shut. Took off my fucking robe, then began walking toward him while taking off the rest of my clothes as I approached. When I reached his side of the bed, I said, "show me."

"Show you what?" He said, looking up at me through his dark fucking lashes and a fucking sexy ass look on his face.

"Show me how you touch yourself," I said.

Mitchell turned the covers back and showed me how he rubs his engorged cock.

"You are insanely sexy, Mr. Magellan," I said, fighting the urge to touch him.

With his breathing getting faster, he took my nipple into his mouth and pulled me closer with his broken hand.

"Let me know when you're close to coming," I breathed out as I ran my hand through his hair.

"Why?" Mitchell was tugging faster now, periodically closing his eyes and then looking at me while kissing and sucking on my tit.

"Because I want to swallow for you."

"Jesus," he said. "You do?" Mitchell stopped handling himself, and slid a finger in my pussy.

I put my hand in his hair, and said, "Mitchell, I want to suck you off," meaning every word.

And, when he made me come, I began to rub him up and down. And when he said he was close, I covered his cock with my mouth and said, "Come in my mouth, Baby."

Mitchell immediately responded, and only a few seconds later, he did. And because of the awkward angle, I gagged a little.

"Fuck, Mira. I love when you gag on me."

I licked him up good, getting everything that had spilled. And when I was done, I kissed him, all over his face and mouth and neck.

He smiled, and said, "Thank you, Baby."

"I love you, Mitchell." I was overwhelmed with emotion right then.

"I love you too, Mirabella. Let's wash up, and then we can talk to Jared together."

In the bathroom, while we both freshened up, I caught Mitchell looking at me as he caught me stealing glances at his naked body.

"You fucking like what you see, Mirabella?

I pulled my sweatshirt over my head, pulled my panties on, and then my sweats.

Then, I walked over to my extremely handsome boyfriend, and said, "If I didn't like what I saw, you wouldn't fucking be here."

I then swatted his ass with my towel, flung it into the dirty clothes basket, and went downstairs to see my brother.

ALL THE WAY OUT

"SO, I can see the specialist on Tuesday? I was supposed to be back at work on Tuesday, B."

Mitchell knocked on the open guest room door, and I turned to look at him as he strode into the room and gave me a sly smile.

Jared must have noticed.

"I don't want to intrude on your space, guys."

"Nonsense, Jared. You can stay with us for as long as you like. Right now, the key is to get you seen by the specialist, and then we can go from there. And when you're ready to go back to Kentucky, I'll make sure you get out on a private jet. You don't have to worry about commercial air travel right now."

"Thanks, Mitch. You really don't have to do that," Jared said, always hating the idea that he might be a burden or a freeloader.

"It's no problem," Mitchell said.

I smiled at Mitchell and then at Jared.

"I took off tomorrow, and I can take off Tuesday too, if need be," I said.

"Do you want me to go with you on Tuesday? Should I fly Grandma or Bianca in?"

"Grandma, yes. If she can make it. Bianca, no."

No one said anything for a minute.

"Jared, I hope you don't think I'm overstepping, but with your diagnosis, maybe you should consider telling Bianca. Maybe you guys aren't together but until she places that baby for adoption, she is the mother of your child. She deserves to know what's going on with you."

I shot a displeased look at Mitchell, wondering about the advice he had just given. I didn't agree with it. It was wholly Jared's decision who he decided to tell or not about his cancer. I didn't think he owed Bianca anything.

"You know what? You're right, Mitchell. I'm being selfish at least not telling her about it."

"I don't know about being *selfish*, but certainly you shouldn't feel obligated to tell anyone anything. You had sex, made a baby. That does not make you obligated to tell her personal information if you don't want to," I said.

"It's ok, B. I know you're always looking out for me despite me being the older brother. I appreciate it. You know I do. But Mitchell has a point. So, as soon as I hear what the specialist has to say, I'm going to talk to Bianca about it."

"Right, so we have a plan. Specialist on Tuesday. No surgery on Friday unless he says go to Kentucky and have the surgery."

"Thanks, you two. You guys are like a fucking power couple," Jared said, smiling a tired grateful smile.

I kissed him on his cheek and hugged him.

"Goodnight, Jare. Get some rest. Ok?"

"Goodnight, B. Goodnight, Mitch," he said.

Mitchell let me out first, and I walked past him into the kitchen.

"You want me to take off tomorrow?" Mitchell said when he grabbed a bottle of water from the fridge.

"I'm going to sleep in tomorrow, a little. Then I think we're gonna have lunch with RayRay at Bergdorf's, maybe do some shopping. So, unless that's your thing, I don't think so. Maybe you can come home early though?"

Mitchell walked over to where I sat at the kitchen island and ran his finger from my ear down and across my jawline, then placed it on my lips for me to kiss. And right then, despite everything that had happened, was happening, and had yet to happen, I was one hundred percent head over heels in love with Mitchell Magellan.

CHAPTER 27

MITCHELL MAGELLAN

"Thanks for meeting me, Aunt Meg," I said, sitting across from my aunt in a diner uptown.

"You call, I come. Don't make it out to be like this is an oddity, Mitchell."

"Snippy. Snippy," I said. I needed her pliable.

She smiled that classic smile, and I think she already knew what I was going to say, but out of respect for me as the head of the family, she let me say it.

"I'm just going to come out with it."

"Fine," she said.

"I'm going after Brennan. It's time."

"What do you have on him?"

"Is that a trick question?"

"You're going to need something more than what we have because I don't want Preston involved."

"Well, there is no way to keep Preston out of it. He's the key to me destroying that motherfucker."

"Mitchell, I don't want Preston involved. Find another way."

"We have corporate espionage, extortion, and sexual assault."

"Can't you get him on just the other charges?"

"I won't use it unless I have to, but I think we need to. I think we need to declare Preston his son. He has an heir clause in his operating agreement. Preston is his only actual heir. That means, Preston has a full right to Brennan Enterprises at fifty one percent ownership. With my five percent, we will own fifty-six percent of Brennan Enterprises, and that will give us the ability to sell it, break it up, do whatever we want with it. We will control it."

Aunt Meg have realized that this was the only way. Hearing it laid out like that, however, seemed hard to take. Now, the world would know about Preston.

"I don't want reporters in his face, digging around in his business."

"His business?"

'Yes, Mitchell. His business."

"What kind of business are we hiding from the press about Preston, Aunt Meg?"

She said nothing, rather she sipped her coffee and avoided eye contact.

"I'm not kidding, Aunt Meg. What don't we want the media to know about Preston?"

"Well for fucking starters, Mitchell, that we kept the assault that made him a secret because it was bad for business to expose it. That your mother abandoned Preston when he was born and left him in private foster care until I adopted him. Don't you think that's damming? Don't you think that will hurt Preston when it all comes out?"

"Preston doesn't know?"

"Of course, he knows Brennan is his biological father; he sees him once a month," Aunt Meg said as if I was fucking stupid.

"What the fuck did you just say?"

"I said he sees his father once a month." Aunt Meg doubled down.

"You take Preston to see the fucking man who raped my mother?"

I almost put my fucking good hand through the window at that moment.

"Why the fuck would you do that?"

"Calm down, Mitchell, and watch how you fucking speak to me," she said, like I gave a fuck about how I spoke to her right then.

"No. I think you need to fucking watch what you fucking say and how you say it to me, Megan," I said, calling her that for the first time in my life.

Her eyes nearly popped out of her head when I called her by her fucking actual name.

"Why would you focus on making Preston have a relationship with that man? He is not a good man."

"Preston deserves to know his father. Brennan deserves—"

"Don't you fucking dare finish that goddamn sentence. Don't you fucking dare."

"Mitchell, I promise you; you aren't looking at this the right way. Brennan is his father, whether we like it or not. He is the only father Preston has ever known. If you take that away from him, then what will he do?"

I sat across from one of two of the only family I had left, wondering if I ever really knew her at all. And now, faced with the idea that I would be responsible for taking Preston's father away, I stewed in anger and disbelief while staring into my bowl of Italian Wedding Soup.

IT WAS ALL-HANDS on deck as I sat in the conference room with the attorneys from Kain, Carpenter & Maguire, one paralegal from Legal, two legal assistants from Legal, and Clara. The only person missing, was Braxton, who was by now, ten minutes late. And even though he wasn't an employee, I liked for him to join these meetings.

"I have been told that the charges against Robert Brennan III will be as follows: Two counts of extortion of a federal government official—

"Wait, who is the federal official?" I asked Gina.

"Peter Trenom and you. All officers are official U.S. government consultants. Were you not aware of this? We also have several federal contracts in the broadcast and Internet spaces." She said in that snarky-ass tone.

"I had no idea. But does that count?"

"We're certainly going to bring the charge. If it doesn't stick, it doesn't stick."

"Ok, sorry to interrupt, please continue," I said.

"Fourteen hundred counts of corporate espionage, representing the number of video and audio recordings he stole from Magellan Media, and numerous counts of theft, fraud, and some other minor charges. He's facing as much as twenty years in prison."

"When do we expect these charges to be filed?"

"Within the next two to three weeks," Kain Sr. said.

"Gina, we need those affidavits by the end of this week then," I said to Gina who was on the call from London.

"They'll be in your inbox tomorrow midday your time," she said.

"Thank you. I may be out of pocket until around noon tomorrow. Please send directly to Clara, and she'll make certain I get it."

"Will do," Gina said.

Next, Kain Sr. Spoke about the nuances of the evidence we have, the legality of its usage, and what we can and cannot do.

Mirabella texted.

> MIRABELLA: Hey handsome

> ME: In a meeting, baby

> MIRABELLA: I miss you

> ME: Miss you too

> MIRABELLA: Come home for a quickie

> ME: Where's Jared?

> MIRABELLA: Out

> ME: In a meeting

> MIRABELLA: COME HOME

> ME: Working

> MIRABELLA: you have work to do at home

It was all I could do to concentrate on this fucking meeting. I had to sit forward and cover my lap with a folder to keep from revealing my growing bulge at the thought of Mirabella being four blocks away, missing me.

About thirty minutes later, the meeting ended.

As the room cleared out, I asked Clara to stay.

"Is anything the matter, Sir?"

"Clara, can you please get all the quarterly reports from Magellan for the past fourteen months and also get my Brennan Enterprises reports for the same period and do a competitive analysis on the two? No that's not right."

"No, it isn't," she said.

"We need Brennan's for the last six months of last year, and ours for the first six months of last year in order to see how our reports impacted them, if in fact they were privy to privileged information from illegally obtained recordings."

"That's exactly right."

"Also please get me any Brennan reports that mention Mirabella Castle."

"Yes, Sir. Anything else?"

"I'll be working from home for the remainder of today. Please ask Sherilyn to reschedule my morning tomorrow until 1pm."

"Ok, Sir."

"I need specs and pricing on the Rolls Royce Defender, and I want to remodel the executive floor. Can you please get Cindy started on sourcing an architect? Please get Mirabella Castle added to my Black Card. I'll have her text her details. I need a housekeeper for the penthouse. Please ask Cindy to secure someone by week's end. She can talk to Mirabella about what she's looking for. Please ask Cindy to find out which space is available in the Shard. Please make me a private appointment at Tiffany."

Clara looked from her handheld device where she had been making notes, as if to say, 'is that all?'

"I think that's it, I said. "Thanks."

"Are you all moved into the penthouse?"

"No but I need to do that. Can you ask Sherilyn to find a mover for me? I'm moving clothing and personal items. No furniture. Some furnishings."

"When would you like to move, Sir?"

"Wednesday," I said.

"This Wednesday? The day after tomorrow?"

"Yes. Is that a problem?"

"Of course not, Sir."

"Great. Thanks, Clara," I said.

"Sir, will you be having a housewarming party?"

"You know what? You're the second person to ask. I'll check with Mirabella."

"What about Thanksgiving? It's a week away."

"I have no idea where I'll be spending Thanksgiving."

"Alright; if there isn't anything else for now," she said.

"Nothing more right now," I said, grateful for her thoroughness.

"Fantastic. I'll keep you posted on my progress, Sir. Enjoy the rest of your afternoon."

"You too, Clara, and thanks for everything."

I ARRIVED at the penthouse about an hour and a half after Mirabella had texted. I should have called her on the way over because when I got home, the penthouse was empty.

> ME: where r u?

> MIRABELLA: —

I heard her phone buzz and ding from a distance.

I ran upstairs to find her asleep in bed. She looked so peaceful and beautiful. I guess I had missed my window of opportunity. Smiling to myself and thinking about how next time my girl summons me home for a quickie, I'm going to be much better about getting there. So, I showered, and then did some work at the desk in the bedroom.

The lunch with Aunt Meg and the meeting with my attorneys weighed heavily on me.

When Mirabella began stirring, I joined her in bed.

"Hi, Mitchell," she said all groggy and sleepy.

"Hi, Beautiful," I said, running a finger across her cheek. "You ok?"

She kissed me.

"You look, tired. Are *you* ok?" She said, reading me so well and pulling a Braxton by answering a question with a question.

Mirabella sat up in bed now, looking at me with concern. When I didn't respond, she pulled me into her arms, and ran her fingers through my hair to soothe me.

Soon I was on top of her, kissing her ferociously all over her neck and then down to her breasts, her stomach, her mound, and then up and down both legs. She moaned for me as her body began to come alive with need. And when I made it back up to her panties, I kissed her clit through the thin fabric, then kissed my way back up to her delicious mouth.

She had her hands in my hair again, which caused me to moan too, as she wiggled beneath me. I wanted it deep and slow today. Fucking missionary. I wanted to see her, to watch her respond to me. To love all over her. She was my sanctuary, my calm, my fucking shelter.

Fuck. I was feeling emotional in that moment, and when she shimmied out of her panties, her way of telling me what she wanted, I fucking did not hesitate. I pulled my pants off, freed my aching cock, and shoved inside her soaked cunt as slowly as I could, torturing us both.

The look on her face when I entered her was so unbelievably sexy. She clenched me fucking immediately, closed her eyes, and then turned her head slightly to the side.

"Look at me, Mirabella." No matter what came out of her gorgeous mouth, it had always been her eyes that told me everything I needed to know.

Something about us looking at one another brought us both to our knees. Mirabella became noticeably wetter, and her eyes began to water. I think she was going to cry.

I kissed her slowly and deeply.

"I love you, Mirabella. Do you love me, Baby?"

"Yes," she breathed out as tears fell.

"Say it, please." I was nearing release, and our pace became quicker. But she moaned instead as she was building too.

"Tell me," I said, barely able to speak then.

"Mitchell, I love you."

We both came in a delicious orgasm that had both our emotions in a fucking vise.

As we came down, I kissed her all over her wet face before laying on my side so I could still look at her.

I wiped her tears and stared in awe at this amazing woman who had come into my life quite by accident.

"Next time I ask you to come home, I need you to come home."

"I know, Baby. I was in a meeting I couldn't leave. I wanted to come home to you so badly. I didn't mean to make you wait."

I kissed her mouth, and we made out for a few minutes.

"Did I make you feel better, sweet baby?"

She smiled a shy smile, giving me my answer.

"I told you how horny I am before and after my period."

"Horny Mirabella is my favorite Mirabella," I said nuzzling her neck.

She swatted me in my good arm.

"I'm at your service, ma'am, whenever you need me. I will be your fuck boy."

I must have said the wrong thing because Mirabella began to get out of bed. I gently pulled her back.

"Wait. Wait. Wait. Where are you going?"

"I need a shower, and I want to change the sheets."

"Please tell me what I did or said. Don't fucking walk away from me. Not after just now."

She shook her head at me like I didn't understand her at all.

"I don't like when you joke about us like we're casual, not even together in a real way." Mirabella was about to pick a totally unnecessary fight. My little spitfire was scared out of her mind now, after what we had just shared. And now, those tears she held in? She was going to allow them to fuel her anger.

"Ok, I won't do it again," I said, trying to diffuse her because fighting mad Mirabella was my least favorite Mirabella. I kissed her, and she let me. And when she went to take a shower, I remained in the bedroom, in case she wasn't having it.

CHAPTER 28

MIRABELLA CASTLE

"Would you like me to go with you tomorrow?" Mitchell asked on the evening prior to Jared's appointment with the specialist. We sat in front of the fireplace, Mitchell with a glass of Bourbon and me with a glass of red wine.

"You don't have to; I know you have a lot going on at work."

"Don't be polite, Mirabella. Either you want me there or you don't because if you don't, I'm not offended. I plan to go to Chelsea tomorrow and pack up my shit."

"Definitely do that, then. I will call you when we get done," I said, wondering what Mitchell was planning to bring with him from his old apartment.

Despite telling me he wouldn't be offended, Mitchell looked hurt.

"How did your lunch with Aunt Meg go?"

Mitchell massaged his temples, closed his eyes, and tilted his head back as though in pain; something I had seen him do a lot lately.

"Mitchell, what happened?"

"This thing with Brennan is a clusterfuck."

I sat forward and placed my wine glass on the coffee table. He rubbed my back then. I smiled at him as I sat back and curled up under his arm.

"I still can't believe you're working with Hyacinth," I said.

"She really came through. Without her and her brother, we'd have no case at all."

"She thinks you're hot, you know," I teased.

"And she's one hundred percent fucking right," he teased me back. "She's a beautiful woman," Mitchell said.

"She really is."

"We talked about you," I said, immediately regretting it.

"What the fuck does that mean?"

"Nothing. Finish telling me about Brennan," I said.

Mitchell eyed me suspiciously but let it go, even as his breathing quickened. Something wasn't right.

"Robert Brennan is most likely going to spend the rest of his life in prison."

"Oh. It's that bad? Not a smear campaign?"

Mitchell stood suddenly, and walked over to the bar to refill his drink while chugging what was left of his current one it down. When he came back, he didn't sit down. He seemed especially agitated to the point where, I began to get anxious. He looked out the window toward Central Park and downed half his drink before turning in my direction and saying, "Smear campaign? No. This motherfucker is going all the way down. And if I can figure out how, I will take Brennan Enterprises from him. He will fucking have exactly *nothing*."

He swallowed back the rest of his bourbon.

Mitchell was visibly angry, a wrinkle in his brow. I tried to calm him with what I said next.

"Releasing those tapes was a dick move. But the damage done was minimal, I mean, look at us. We made it out the other side."

Instead of neutralizing him, I lit the fuse.

"Fucking minimal? It broke us up. And spying on your competitor is fucking illegal. Breaking into your competitor's servers is fucking illegal. Recording your competitor is fucking illegal. Using information you stole to better your business advantage is fucking illegal."

He was getting madder and madder. I got the impression there was something he wasn't saying. Something he didn't want me to know.

"He was nice to me when I met him. Gave me advice. Wished me good luck. He's just an old man with too much money," I shrugged, trying to demonstrate to Mitchell that he was expending too much energy on some old rich guy.

Just then, something snapped in him.

"You fucking met Robert Brennan III?"

"Yes. The day you attacked him we were all in a meeting about the subpoena you served on me," I said, making it sound like Mitchell was an asshole, but it wasn't what I meant.

"Don't fucking glorify that douchebag," Mitchell spat.

"Mitchell what is going on? What are you not telling me?" I stood now, unsure of whether to go to him then.

He had anger and fear and hatred in his eyes.

"That motherfucker raped my mom. Preston is his son."

I went to him immediately, and tried to put my arms around him, but he pushed me off of him and said, "I'm going for a walk before I do something we'll both fucking regret. And when I come back, you had better not say one kind word about Robert Fucking Brennan because I'm going to take everything he fucking has, *including you.*"

Holy shit.

I had never seen Mitchell so angry.

Jared came out of the guest room and walked into a minefield.

"Go back in your room, Jared."

Jared looked from me to Mitchell and then back to me.

"What the fuck is all the yelling?" He said to Mitchell.

"Go back in your fucking room. This doesn't concern you," Mitchell said his angry eyes on me.

"Are you good, Mirabella? Did he hurt you?"

"What? No, Jared. We are . . . Please. Go back in your room. I'm good. Mitchell's good."

"Call me if you need me," Jared said, then went back into his room and closed the door.

"Mitchell," I said. "No leaving, remember?"

I went to him and tried once again to put my arms around him, but he just stood unmoving, rage on his face.

"Don't touch me, Mirabella," he said.

I reached up to put my arms around his neck and run my fingers through his hair.

"Why don't you fucking listen, Mirabella? Why? Why do you always have to make shit so much fucking worse?"

"What am I doing? I'm trying to comfort you!"

"Comfort me? You fucking work for the man who raped my mother. You glorify him to me. I know you resented me when I went there and knocked him the fuck out, and you never once asked me why I had done it. You just assumed like everyone else that I was out of fucking control."

"I was worried about you," I said in my defense.

"You have a funny way of showing concern," he said. "I asked you to come work for Magellan. You fucking refused me like nothing at Magellan was good enough for you. You didn't want to be an assistant? I would have made up a fucking job for you. I would have let you do whatever it was that you wanted."

"I told you I didn't want to be your assistant," I shot back. In that moment I should have told him what I'd done for him, but I knew he would be upset about it, mad even. Maybe even embarrassed.

"Why the fuck not? It's the job you were originally interviewing for."

"I didn't want to work that closely with you after I got to know you. I didn't want to be sleeping with my boss."

"So, you take a job with my fucking enemy talking shit about me in the fucking media," he said, and it was an accusation.

"Mitchell, I thought you were fine with it."

"This motherfucker is making millions off you and paying you pennies on the dollar of what he should be fucking paying you. But anytime I say something, you fucking tell me how great Brennan is and all they are doing for you. So now you know this isn't about them getting the upper hand or me being jealous."

It was a lot to unpack. I sat down on the nearest couch and let it sink in.

"Why can't I touch you?" I said looking up at him.

"Because the way I feel right now . . . I'm angry. I don't want to touch you when I'm angry."

"But you're not angry at me, are you?"

"I think I am," he said, his voice a little quieter.

"But I had no idea about any of this. You never told me."

"Would you have quit if I would have? Or would you have told me you don't really work for Brennan himself. I know you, Mirabella. You would have found a way to justify it."

He wasn't wrong.

"Mitchell, please sit down."

"I'm not fucking sitting down," he said.

"Then will you go upstairs with me?"

Mitchell looked down at me with a tortured look on his face. He was angry, yes, but he was also aroused. And in a few moments, I would know which of the two would win him over.

I walked up the stairs, and changed into a sexy nightgown I had been saving for a special occasion.

Mitchell came into the room and closed the door. The look on his face scared me. He looked me over, and the brief acknowledgement of my change of clothes gave way to something else. He was still angry.

"Come here," he said.

My breathing quickened. It felt like I was playing a dangerous game with a man who was exercising great self-control.

I remained standing near the far corner of the room. I was not going to let him subjugate me.

"I fucking said, come here, Mirabella."

"I heard you." I kept my eyes on him and he kept his on me.

"Then why the fuck aren't you listening?" Mitchell began to stroke himself through his pants.

"Because you fucking work for me," I said. Mitchell pulled his budding smirk back.

I sat in the chair near my side of the bed, and spread my legs for him. He was slowly fucking melting before my eyes.

"You want some?" I said, not taking my eyes off of him as I ran my finger over my clit and began to pleasure myself. Why the fuck was I so aroused?

Mitchell put his hand inside his pants and began to rub and tug at his cock.

"Yes." He said, nearly subdued.

"Are you going to be a good boy?"

"Yes," he said without hesitation.

"Then come to me and take what you want."

Mitchell walked over to me, and lowered his pants and underwear enough so that his cock was fully out. He was so erect, I found myself feeling bad that I had let him get like this, despite all the sex we had been having. Mitchell was the kind of man who not only needed lots of sex but allowed other feelings like anger and sadness to feed his arousal.

He continued to stroke himself while watching me sitting in the chair with my legs wide open. I had stopped touching myself because I didn't want to make myself come. And then something I wasn't expecting happened.

Mitchell came all over me. And when he finished, he pulled his underwear and pants up, and said, "I'm going for a fucking walk."

When Mitchell left, I showered, and changed into pajamas while replaying everything that had happened on repeat in my head. I threw the nightgown out. If I were dramatic, I would have burned it in the fireplace. I replayed everything that had happened a thousand times in my head. Just like I had done with Mitchell when those tapes released, he was blaming me for something I had no idea about. And as far as the angry sex, now I know why he said he didn't want to touch me when he was angry. Mitchell had left me sad, confused, and fucking horny.

I stared at the clock on my phone. Mitchell had been gone for two hours already. It was one thirty in the morning.

As I lay in bed, intrusive thoughts made their way into my troubled mind. Was he with Lorelei? Were he and I done? Preston is his brother.

And now, there was no way I was going to fall asleep. I needed to know if he was coming back tonight.

> ME: Where are you?

> MITCHELL: --

> ME: Please call me

> MITCHELL: --

> ME: I love you. I'm sorry.

> MITCHELL: I'm at my apartment

> ME: This is your apartment

> MITCHELL: staying here tonight, gotta pack

> ME: Please call me

> MITCHELL: --

Hell fucking no. He was not running on me.

I ordered an Uber to Chelsea and left a note for Jared.

On the way to Mitchell's apartment, I thought about all I had wanted to say to him. What I had wanted to do to him. I wanted to scream at him. To punch him. To fuck him. I wanted him to fuck me. To take his pain out on me in the bedroom. Isn't that what we had agreed to? Or was it all bullshit? Weren't we supposed to be all the way in on this? Because him running away to fucking Chelsea felt a lot like him being all the way out.

Mitchell was on the steps of his townhouse with a glass of Bourbon in his hand when I arrived, and he didn't seem surprised to see me.

"You should be home with your brother," he said, all obnoxious like.

"You should be at home with your girlfriend," I said equally obnoxious.

Mitchell stood and walked up to the door.

"Are you coming in?"

I shook my head and rolled my eyes before climbing the steps to his apartment.

"You should have asked Brendan to bring you here."

"Then you would have known I was coming."

"I already knew you were coming."

"What? How?"

"I can see when you leave the penthouse."

"Oh," I said remembering the cameras in the foyer.

"It's not safe riding in fucking taxis alone this time of night," he said.

"Then maybe you shouldn't have fucking left," I said.

Mitchell looked enraged.

"You should'nt have come. You should not have followed me."

"If you don't want me, just say so. If I had wanted to be treated like a piece of shit, I could have stayed with Ben."

Mitchell's look hardened before softening.

"You think I don't want you, Mirabella? Cause I'm pretty sure I don't hide in the bathroom watching porn and jerking off while you're in bed waiting for me."

I should have never compared him to Ben, but it was too late now. I fired a shot. He fired back.

"Sure seems that way."

"Why does it seem that way? I fucking stood there in our living room like an asshole with a giant hard on for you while I told you that my mom was raped, and that Preston was my fucking brother. I couldn't fucking even control my need for you then. Do you know how much of an asshole that makes me? You text me in the middle of a meeting, and then I have to fucking cover my lap with a folder to keep anyone from seeing how turned on I am at the thought of you thinking of me and wanting me to come home to you. We have so much good fucking sex, I don't know how you can say I don't want you."

He looked wounded and sad and angry and annoyed and miserable.

"You left me with my legs spread and my pussy dripping for you. You punished me by withholding pleasure from me."

"You know what, Mirabella? Just taking a page out of your fucking book."

"I'm sorry."

"Well, I told you I was a selfish asshole when we first met. I don't know why you're fucking surprised," he said, swallowing all of the bourbon in his glass.

"Mitchell." I regretted being there then.

"Mitchell, what? What do you want, Mirabella? You want me to fuck you? Is that it? You came all the way down here so I could make you come? You could have fucking done that yourself." He was looking at me like I was the one hurting him.

Tears fell down my face.

"Here come the waterworks now." Mitchell mumbled to himself, shook his head then poured himself more bourbon. When he was done, he chugged the entire thing down in four gulps. He was very drunk.

I watched my entire life fall apart before my eyes, and all I could think about was how much I was losing as I watched Mitchell spiral out of control and take his pain out on me.

There was no way I could imagine how he was feeling. Losing his parents and brother a few months ago could not have been easy. And yet, when Mitchell was tapped to take over the enormous family business, he did it with grace, humility, and a tremendous amount of pressure on his shoulders. Finding out his mother was raped by Robert Brennan, the man I work for, an act which produced Preston, whom he thought was his cousin but is his half-brother, could not have been easy to digest. And then I upended his life.

"Why did you say you were going to take everything from Brennan including me?" I said, almost at a realization about how Mitchell might have been feeling about me.

"Because you fucking belong to me," he said, "And the thought that this motherfucker has you under contract, that you are his property fucking kills me." For some reason, his words comforted me. He wasn't leaving me.

I went to him, and put my arms around him. He stiffened, and didn't hug me back.

"I'm so sorry, Mitchell. I have been so selfish. I had no idea all you have been going through."

"You're not the only person in this relationship with feelings, Mirabella."

"I met her, you know," I said quietly.

"Who?"

"Your mom," I said.

"What? When did you meet my mother?"

"Last year, around Christmas. She came into the store looking for a gift for a friend. She was nice and kind. Beautiful. I helped her pick it out."

"Mira, why are you just telling me this now?"

"I don't know. It never seemed like the right time. I didn't want to upset you," I said.

"I love that you met her. That she met you."

Mitchell looked even sadder now despite a smile slowly making its way across his face.

"Please forgive me? I have been so focused on me and what I need. I love you so much."

"I love you too, Mirabella, but you can be very self-centered, and I let you get away with that shit. I spoil you because I know what you've been through. But this time, I need you to focus on me. To care for me. To be there for me."

"I am. I will be. Whatever you need."

And the thing is, even though I was making promises, it was obvious to both of us that I had no fucking clue as to what Mitchell needed. Now, those intrusive thoughts pushed their way to the forefront of my mind reminding me how inadequate I was and how I could never keep a man like him.

"Mirabella, I need you to stop trying to be what you think I want in bed and just be yourself. Be the girl I fell in love with," he said.

"What?"

"I said, I need you—"

"I heard what you said but I don't understand why you're saying it."

Mitchell seemed to have leveled out a bit, no longer angry and not as drunk as he appeared to be earlier. Now, he seemed more contemplative and less combative.

"I don't give a fuck about lingerie. You can wear a fucking box, and I will be just as aroused and turned on by you. It's you Mirabella. Not some fucking gimmicky crotchless panties or wild sex talk or whatever it is you think I need. I need *you*, Mirabella. Just *you*. *You* are all I need."

I was embarrassed then. I had thought Mitchell liked the new sexy vixen persona I had created for us. Had I been wrong? Surely, he liked it. He sure seemed to respond differently at times. There's no way I was wrong about this. He must have sensed my confusion right then.

"You want to be equal with me in the bedroom? Then love me like I love you. Need me like I need you."

CHAPTER 29

MITCHELL MAGELLAN

I had just finished bringing in the rest of the boxes from my apartment in Chelsea when I found Mirabella in the kitchen making herself a coffee. She had been to the specialist with Jared, and I wanted to know how it had gone. But sometimes, things don't always go as planned.

"Hey, Babe," I said just as Mirabella finished spraying canned whipped cream into her coffee. Then, she took the nozzle into her mouth, and moaned.

"Hey, Babe," she said just as fucking nonchalantly as she hadn't just done what she had done.

The smirk on my face now was almost as big as the bulge in my fucking gray sweats. This woman knew exactly what she was fucking doing. And as she put the can back in the fridge, I said, "Um, did you just suck on the fucking whipped cream can and moan?"

Mirabella looked surprised and embarrassed.

"No. I licked it."

That was not better, and it did nothing to calm me down.

She must have realized what she said, because she smiled at me, with the most devilish but innocent smile.

"You know what, Mirabella? I think I'm just going to start spanking you when you misbehave."

"What? You wish I would let you spank me."

"Yes, actually I do. I can't even begin to count the number of times I've wanted to spank you since we met."

"I thought you said I was your good girl?"

FUUUUUUCK.

I moved toward her, stalking her like prey. Things were still touch and go after last night, but I wanted her on me. And if I recall, I owed her a fucking orgasm.

As I approached, she picked up her coffee and licked the rim of the mug to catch some of the cream that had seeped out of the opening.

Fucking, Mirabella.

I went to grab her by the waist.

She put her hand out and said, "Stop."

I pulled my hand back, unsure of what to do next.

"You can't corner me like this every fucking time I do something you think is sexual but is actually normal," she said.

I breathed a sigh of relief when I realized she didn't intend to tell me that I couldn't touch her. But I kept my hands to myself in case.

"Can't I though? This is *my* fucking apartment."

"*Our* apartment."

My little spitfire smirked in my fucking face, challenging me.

"This is *my fucking kitchen*." I backed her up against the cabinets, put my hand flat against the wall next to the door.

"Ours." There was a trembling in her voice. Mirabella was shaking.

"This is my fucking pussy."

I put my hand inside her panties, and good God, the girl was fucking soaked.

"Fucking say it's ours, and watch how fucking fast I make you come."

That shut her right the hell up.

But Mirabella was being spiteful. She was totally silent, totally still.

Not grinding against my fingers or moaning for me, and that shit pissed me the fuck off.

I leaned closer to her so that the only things between us were my hand and my erection. I planted slow wet kisses along her neck from the bottom up, as I kept steady pressure on her clit with my palm and moved my fingers in and out of her.

"Mirabella, I need you to come for me. Tell me what I have to do to make you come on my fingers?" I said softly into her ear.

She fucking moaned.

"You want to move on me? Go ahead. Fuck my fingers."

"No," she said, and pulled my hand out of her panties.

Now I was the one who was stunned into silence. I thought I had her nearly there.

"What's wrong, Baby?"

Mirabella looked wild and horny and sexy and frustrated.

"Take me upstairs," she said.

"Take you upstairs?"

"Yes," she said, softly.

"What do you want to do when we get up there?"

"I want you to worship me."

Sweet. Beautiful. Mirabella.

"DO you think he can hear us?" Mirabella asked me while we showered.

"I don't think so. But I can ask him man-to-man if you're too embarrassed."

"I will ask him, we're not weird like that. He tells me when he gets laid, and with who and what they did."

"Are you serious?"

"Yeah, he'll tell me some girl went down on him or he ate someone out, but it's not creepy, I don't think. We're just comfortable with one another."

"Do you talk to him about us?"

"Not to that level. I told him when we had sex for the first time. And then later he asked me about you, and I told him we were sleeping together. He asked if it was exclusive. Stuff like that. But also, he saw the fucking video, and he asked me how I felt about it."

Mitchell made a sour face.

So, is there a reason why you have yet to tell me about his doctor visit today?"

"Because it isn't good."

"What did they say?"

"It's spread beyond the pancreas. It's in the liver and has already spread to his lungs. It's why he's so winded now."

"Jesus, Mirabella. I'm so sorry."

"They're going to operate on him on Friday, as planned, only not in Kentucky. It's going to be an extensive surgery. They are not sure whether it has spread to his lymph nodes. Tomorrow, he has pre-surgical bloodwork. We have to be there at eight," she said.

The more she told me the worse it got. Jared was probably going to die. She didn't say it, and I didn't ask for his prognosis, but Mirabella was likely going to lose her only sibling too.

"Listen, Mirabella, delete your fucking ride app. Use Brendan. If he can't drive you, then Maleko can. In fact, maybe we can make Maleko your permanent driver."

"Oh," she said, seeming distracted, listening but not hearing what I was saying.

"And you need an assistant. There is no reason why you should be forced to manage all of this yourself. And what about work?"

"I'm done, Mitchell. I will break my contract with Brennan, if they sue me, my rich boyfriend will get me off," she said, not even realizing the double entendre in her statement about her rich boyfriend getting her off. I wanted to stop the smirk that appeared on my face but couldn't. The idea of it, sent heat down my pelvis.

"Mirabella, thank you," I said, shutting off the water.

We stepped out of the shower, she in the towel I'd put her in and me au natural. She sat on her makeup stool and watched me as I took my time dressing because sometimes, my girl needed a reminder of who she was fucking with.

"I'm flying my grandmother out on Thursday. She needs time to get someone to cover her shop."

"Do you need a jet for her? Airport transportation? Why don't you let Sherilyn handle all of this for you? You don't have to do it yourself."

"Yeah?"

"Yes, Baby. Please let me help you get through this at least by taking the burden of logistical planning off your plate."

"Thank you, Mitchell."

I didn't know how to comfort her or how to prepare her for what's coming. The pain. The grief. The why did it have to be him and not me questions. The guilt of surviving. And in that moment, I wished I could fix this problem with great sex.

"MIRABELLA, I NEED TO TAKE THIS," I said, still completely naked and loving the way she was looking at me.

She smiled then went ahead with her nightly skincare routine. I grabbed a towel and put it around my waist.

"Hey, Kain, what's up?"

"Mitchell, Marissa Canto recalled her statement, and has dropped charges, and in a stunning reversal, she is willing to testify against Brennan. We got that son-of-a-bitch. She can corroborate payments he made to her, being hired to frame you. We got him! This lands tomorrow. Get your PR team and be ready to make a statement.

I nearly fell over listening to the exuberance in Kain's voice.

"That's amazing. Thanks for letting me know."

I almost ran into the bathroom to share the news.

"Hey!" I said, a pep in my step. This was one less thing hanging over our relationship progress.

"Hey," she said seemingly unhappy that I was now wearing a towel.

"Fucking Marissa Canto recanted her statement. Dropped all

charges against me. She will be holding a news conference tomorrow about it all and how Brennan paid her to set me up."

"So, the plan worked? That's awesome."

"What plan?"

"Shit. She didn't tell you."

"Tell me what?" I said, getting pissed even though I had no idea what Mirabella was talking about.

"Hyacinth came to me with a plan to get Marissa to recant her statement and drop the charges."

"Hyacinth came to you? Where's my fucking phone? I don't give a shit what time it is in London."

Mitchell, wait. Stop," she said but it was too late.

All fucking bets were off. No fucking promotion. No job at Magellan. No fucking job for her brother.

"She had no right to involve you in this. To ask you to ask the woman who gave me a blow job for any fucking thing."

Mirabella stood and grabbed my good arm. She took my face in her tiny hands, and said, "Mitchell. Please look at me."

I stopped, for her.

"Can you please calm down? I want to tell you what happened. Then if you're still upset, I will let you break your other hand and ban Hyacinth and her entire family line forever from Magellan Media so that even her great-great-great-great-great grandchild will be turned away at the entrance."

I shook my head, laughing at her attempt at a joke.

"Ok," I said, for her.

She took my hand, and led me to the bedroom, and for a moment, I wished she was telling me this story while I was buried deep inside her. Then, I would be able to handle whatever news she had.

When we sat on the bed, she had tears in her eyes.

"Hyacinth met with Marissa. I think you already know that."

"Yes. Braxton met with her too. We thought a woman would be able to appeal to her, so we asked Hyacinth. And when that didn't work, I decided I wanted to win this with the truth which we had video proof of."

"I know. I didn't watch but Hyacinth told me what was on the original tape."

I looked away, unable to meet her stare. I hated that this hurt her.

Hyacinth thought you wouldn't approve, but she said we had to try, and at first, I said no. There is no way I wanted to be in the same room with Marissa."

"What changed your mind?"

"You. You changed my mind. I knew the only way I would be free of the power that tape had over me was to meet her and talk to her and appeal to her sense of right and wrong."

"You did this for me?"

"I did it for you, for your family name, for us. I love you, Mitchell and when someone hurts you, they hurt me. And when someone hurts me, I fucking hurt back."

"Oh boy do I fucking know that," I said as I grabbed her into a grateful hug.

I was overwhelmed by the selflessness of Mirabella's gesture. Putting herself in a position to ask Marissa Canto to help me must have been extremely hard for her.

"I love you too, Mirabella Castle."

CHAPTER 30

MIRABELLA CASTLE

Jared's surgery was supposed to be three hours minimum. At the two-hour mark, I became antsy. I'd spent my time pacing, sitting, getting up, checking my emails and texts, holding hands and praying with Grandma, lying in Mitchell's embrace, and drinking many cups of coffee. About ten minutes ago, Mitchell, RayRay, and Grandma went to the cafeteria leaving me with Mena, Iggy, Shayla, and Jenni.

I didn't have time to be exhausted and neither did Mitchell. The Marissa Canto press conference started a new round of media inquiries and requests for us both to comment. And the most ironic thing to happen since all of this started is the fact that I was now looking for a personal assistant.

The news stations kept replaying the Marissa Canto press conference as if there was nothing more pressing happening in New York City. I must have had a sorrowful look on my face because Iggy came over and gave me one of his own.

"I'm going for a walk, Mirabella. Wanna join?" Iggy said.

"You know what, Iggs? I think the walk will do me some good."

I grabbed my purse and phone, and asked Mena and Shayla to let

Mitchell, Grandma, and RayRay know I would be back in about twenty minutes.

Outside with Iggy, we finally got a chance to talk.

"How are you holding up?" He asked as we decided in which direction we would walk.

"I don't know. Hopeful. Nervous. Scared?"

"All of those make sense, I suppose," he said.

"Do you have any local shows coming up any time soon? I'd love to bring Mitchell out to see you."

"Mitchell Magellan at one of my shows?"

I laughed.

"He has a varied taste in music."

"No fucking way, Mirabella. No suits allowed."

I laughed now too, picturing it.

"He wears sweats mostly, when he's not working."

"He seems so different from you. So buttoned up," Iggy said.

"Mitchell would hate that someone thinks of him as buttoned up," I said.

"Does he make you happy?"

I looked at Iggy now, wondering why we had never talked like this before.

"What?"

"I didn't know you cared about my happiness."

"Honestly? Maybe not so much before but this guy seems like, I don't know. Seems like he comes with a lot of fucking baggage," Iggy said.

I thought about it.

"Yeah, I guess he does."

"He makes you happy? I mean he must since you're living with him and all," Iggy said in kind of a sad voice.

"You miss me or something, Iggs?"

"Yeah, I have no one to eat all my fucking leftover Chinese food."

Iggy was referring to that night Mitchell came by, and we ate his leftovers.

I swatted Iggy's arm.

"That was one fucking time," I said, laughing.

Iggy flipped his hair. He was looking at me in a bit of a different way than he had before.

"I just want you to be happy, Mirabella," he said.

I hugged him.

"Thank you, Iggy."

He checked his phone.

"Oh hey. Your brother's out of surgery. They've been trying to reach you."

"Oh shit," I said, pulling out my phone. "Dead battery," I said waving the useless device at him.

"Ok, come on," Iggy said, taking my hand in his.

When we reached the floor of my brother's surgery and exited the elevator into the waiting room, the first face I saw was Mitchell's. His expression fell as he noticed Iggy and I holding hands. I let Iggy's hand go immediately as Mitchell approached.

I don't think it was a matter of Iggy not liking Mitchell in so much as not trusting that he will treat me well enough for Iggy's liking.

At any rate, I needed an update.

"Thanks, Iggy. I'll take it from here," Mitchell said to Iggy as he took my hand and led me to a place where we could talk.

He kissed me when we were shielded from the eyes of everyone in the waiting room. It was just what I needed.

"I'm not even going to ask why you were holding hands with Iggy," Mitchell said his eyes suspicious and his expression angry and annoyed.

"What's happening? Where's my grandma?"

"She went down to the Chapel with Mena."

"What did the doctor say?"

"Mirabella, maybe you should sit down."

"Just tell me," I said.

Mitchell looked like he was trying to be strong, but I can tell his heart was breaking for me and my family. He spoke slowly and chose his words carefully.

"It's in his lymph nodes. It's already spread to his peritoneum, liver, and lungs. The cancer is taking over his liver, and he will most likely be in final stages of liver failure in the next couple of weeks to months. He will not go home today. He is going to be touch and go for the next twenty-four to forty-eight hours."

I felt dizzy, faint. Everything was going black.

"Jared, can I see him?"

"He's in recovery and will be for a few hours. The doctor recommended we go home, and someone will call you if or when he is able to see family."

"Can you take me to my grandma?"

"I think you should sit down," Mitchell said, pulling me toward the nearest chair.

But I was determined. I shimmied out of his grasp, and began briskly walking toward the waiting room as things continued to go in and out of focus. I held onto the wall, and then someone grabbed me.

Mitchell.

I don't know what happened after that.

I WOKE up in my bed at the Penthouse.

"Mitchell?"

I sat up too quickly because I got super dizzy.

I checked my phone for the time. It was two thirty in the afternoon.

I dialed Mitchell.

"You up, Baby?"

"Where are you?"

"I'm coming up."

I was so confused, and hot, and exhausted.

Mitchell opened the bedroom door, entered the room, and walked toward me. He had the saddest eyes.

"Are you alright?" He said, sitting next to me in bed, leaning on the headboard, then pulling me to lie down on his chest.

"I can't keep my eyes open. Why do I feel like this?"

"You had to be given a sedative."

"What? Why?"

"Well, after I told you what was going on with Jared, you fainted, and then when you came to, you were inconsolable."

"How's my grandma?"

"She's trying to be strong, but she's torn up. She asked me to send for your parents. They'll be here tomorrow."

"You don't have to do that," I said, trying to keep my eyes open.

"It's already done."

"Mmmmmm," I said, listening to the rumbling sound of his voice through his chest.

"Is there anything I can get you?"

"Can you just stay here with me?"

"I can."

"Can you get under the covers with me?"

"I can."

I watched as Mitchell took off his shirt and pants.

He smiled and said, "I thought you couldn't keep your eyes open, Baby?"

I smiled a lazy sleepy smile.

"Thank you for taking care of me, Mitchell."

'You're very welcome, my little spitfire."

"Your what?"

"My beautiful little spitfire. I've been calling you that since the day I met you. You were all fire and combative and sexy."

He kissed my nose. I stared into his amazing eyes, loving that he had given me a proper nickname he'd kept to himself all this time.

"Is there anyone else here besides us?"

"Just us. You need me to call someone for you?"

"Can we take a bubble bath?"

"Ok. I'll start the bath."

Mitchell left the door to the bathroom ajar, so I could hear him in there getting everything set up.

When he returned to the bedroom looking fine in just black underwear that was snug in all the right places, I wanted him.

"Mitchell, can you get in bed while we wait for the bath to be ready?"

He didn't respond, he just got into bed, and tried to get me up on his chest again. But instead, I kissed his pectorals and his nipple, his arm, and shoulder.

He moaned.

"Mira, are you sure?"

"Yes, but I'm also super groggy."

"Leave it to me, Mirabella. Just relax and close your eyes. I will take care of everything."

Mitchell kissed me all over my body, getting me ready for him. He ran his tongue across my jawline, then across and up and down my neck while he planted little kisses as he went. He kissed and licked at my breasts and ran his tongue expertly over my nipples, making me so fucking hot for him.

He continued kissing me all over my belly and mound. Every now and again, he would add some tongue. He especially got greedy licking my obliques and squeezing them as he admired my body.

"You smell so good," he said as he made his way between my legs.

"I'm ready for you, Mitchell."

"Me too, Mira."

Mitchell pulled his dick through the hole in his briefs, and I nearly came watching him handle himself so expertly. He stroked it and held onto the tip for a few seconds before moving his hand up and down some more.

His phone rang just then.

He looked over at the nightstand.

"It's your grandmother. I'm gonna answer it. I'll put it on speaker phone."

"Grandma Wright, how are you?"

"Hi, Grandma," I said, trying to pretend like I was not about to get fucked when she called.

"Hi, Mirabella. How's my sweet girl holding up?"

"I'm good. Just woke up. Still feeling pretty groggy though. How are you doing? Do you need anything?

Mitchell put himself back together and then went to check on the bath water.

"Don't worry about this old lady. I've been praying and reading my bible. I have everything I need. Plus your friend Mena is staying with me and making sure I'm not alone."

"Have you heard anything from the hospital yet?"

"That's why I'm calling. They said he will not be able to see anyone tonight. They will call us when he can and for us to get rest because it will probably not be until tomorrow morning."

"Do you want to come here with Mitchell and me? We have plenty of room."

"Oh no, sweet girl. I would never intrude on you and Mitchell's time together. But I would like for us to return to the hospital tomorrow at 8am, is that too early for you?"

"Not at all, Grandma."

"I'll send a car to get you at 7:45, Mrs. Wright," Mitchell said when he came back from checking on the bath water.

"Thank you, Mitchell. You're such a kind young man. Please get rest, both of you. And, Mitchell?"

"Yes, ma'am?"

"Please take care of my granddaughter."

"I will. I just ran her a hot bath, and I'm going to feed her and put her to bed."

"You hear that, Mirabella? Listen to Mitchell. Let him take care of you."

Mitchell and I both smiled when she said that last part.

"Yes, Grandma. I love you. You get rest too."

"I love you too, Mirabella. Stay strong."

"Goodnight, Mrs. Wright," Mitchell said.

"Goodnight, God bless," Grandma said before hanging up.

Mitchell fixed his sad expression on me.

"Are you sure you're up to this, Mirabella? You really look like you can't stay awake," he said.

"You felt so good before."

"But you're falling asleep."

"I'm sorry. It's not you. You are extremely sexy and everything you do is hot."

Mitchell laughed.

"Well, that's good to know. Get some sleep, Mirabella. I'll be in the living room if you need me. Either use the intercom or text or call me. Do not try to go downstairs."

I nodded slowly, trying to recall his instructions. "No downstairs. No sex."

Mitchell laughed at me again.

"You want some sex, Baby?"

"Yes."

"Will it make you feel better?"

"Yes."

"Will it help you sleep?"

"Yes."

"Ok, Baby. I will give you some sex," he said in a soft comforting voice.

"What kind of sex would you like? Sunny side up? Over easy? Raw? Hard boiled?"

"How do you manage to make eggs sound sexy?"

The man winked at me and smiled. Jesus, that's a sexy fucking man.

"Do I have to choose? Can't you give me all the sex?"

"Mira, not tonight. You're exhausted. How about I lick your pussy tonight?"

I frowned.

Mitchell laughed.

"You don't want that?"

"Well, I do but not just that."

"Ok what else do you want?" Mitchell said, removing the sheet from atop me.

Now, Mitchell was no longer looking at my face. The look on his face was one of extreme arousal as he trailed his fingers across my body, his eyes following that path as he went. My breathing quickened, as those light swirls and touches made my body come alive with anticipation. He looked back at me with those lazy bedroom eyes beneath his beautiful dark lashes, causing a gush of wetness from me.

Mitchell was barely touching me, a move so fucking erotic, I was beginning to awaken under his touch and gaze. My nipples ripened without even being touched directly. And when he did touch them, first one and then the other, his touch was so light, my body shivered in response. Mitchell licked his lips just then, his eyes so full of desire.

He freed himself from his briefs fully, but this time he didn't touch himself. Instead, he climbed on top of me, spread my legs with his knee, eased a finger inside my core to see if I was ready, then quickly sunk his penis inside, moving at a slow and glorious pace.

He looked down at me, his hair falling into his face, and said, "Is this ok?"

I shook my head in acceptance, and said, "it's so good," all breathy and sleepy and aroused.

Mitchel grabbed my arm and raised it above my head and held it there as he kissed my mouth and trailed fiery wet kisses down my neck. And because I was ticklish there, my body automatically shimmied and shook beneath him, my tits bouncing up and down even more than usual.

But something was wrong. I wanted Mitchell and I was into what was happening. But I was too distracted by what my brother was going through to allow myself to enjoy it.

"Mirabella, we don't have to do this," Mitchell said when he noticed I was out of it. He gently pulled out and lowered himself beside me, coming to lay on his side.

"I want to," I said.

"I know, but maybe we can try again later."

"Are you sure? What about you?"

"I can finish later too, with you," Mitchell said.

"Well, that's not fair."

"Go to sleep, Mirabella. When you wake up, we can try again." He kissed me gently, then got out of the bed. When he pulled his clothes back on, he took a seat on the oversized chair next to me."

I could hardly keep my eyes open, but something was still alive in me, a need for Mitchell that wouldn't let me rest. So, after a few minutes of watching that beautiful man make eyes at me, I got up from the bed, bringing the blanket over with me. He pulled me onto his lap, and held me in his arms like a baby, bringing the covers up to my neck. We stayed like that for a few minutes until he snuck his fingers between my legs.

His movements were slow and deliberate. And when I responded, he gave me more of what I liked. Slowly, Mitchell built me all the way up to that sensation I get right before I come. Then suddenly, he removed his fingers and put them into my mouth, and said, "Taste yourself, Mirabella. Doesn't that taste so fucking good?"

I moaned, more loudly than I had intended too but Mitchell Magellan had me in a fucking pleasure vise, and the second he put his hand on my clit again, I fucking came.

"Thank you," I said, as I kissed him.

"Baby," he said. "Your mouth tastes like pussy."

CHAPTER 31

MITCHELL MAGELLAN

Now that Jared was temporarily out of the woods, Mirabella allowed herself to sleep in this Saturday morning. She'd spent no less than eight hours daily with him over the past three weeks that followed his surgery. And, while his prognosis was about six months or less, Jared was in remarkably good spirits and fighting hard.

Mrs. Wright, Mira's grandmother, had taken to coming to the Penthouse and cooking for us. It was how she showed her love and appreciation. She would say, "There's no need in you spending all your hard-earned money on me, Mitchell. But since God has allowed you to bless me and my granddaughter and grandson, let me bless you with some of my good old soul food. It'll put some meat on your bones."

She always made too much. The number of containers of collard greens, sweet potatoes, and macaroni and cheese in our freezer always made me smile, and it reminded me that I was going to miss her kindness, catch phrases, and beautiful smile when she returned to Kentucky.

So, when she suggested that I do something to surprise Mirabella because of how much she loves Christmas, I didn't hesitate to hire a designer to decorate the penthouse for Christmas since Mirabella and I had no time to do it. It had been harder and harder to put a genuine smile on my girl's face since her brother was diagnosed with terminal cancer. And, when Mirabella came downstairs, I could not have been prouder of the surprise that awaited her.

"Mitchell?" She said. "What's all this?"

"Good morning, beautiful," I said despite it being nearly one. She was more beautiful than she had been even just the night before.

"It's amazing. When did you have this done?"

"This morning, while you slept. It was Grandma Wright's idea, actually."

The look of bewilderment and joy on her face, made it all worthwhile.

She tried to give me a chaste appreciative quick kiss. And normally, I would have let her do it, knowing I would get my fill of her later on. But this morning, I wanted my girl. So, I pulled her to me just as she was about to skip away.

"Do you like it, Mirabella? I asked, need in my voice. I had been letting Mirabella sleep a lot, caring for her and denying myself the pleasure of her. And from the chaste kiss she gave me, I was worried she was getting used to not getting fucked well or often.

"You and my grandma conspiring," she said as she put her arms around my neck and ran one of her hands up into my hair like we both loved.

I moaned uncontrollably, a fucking pitiful puddle at the slightest attention she paid me because on this particular day, I had not had her for three days.

"Christmas is next week, Mira. I didn't want you to stress about it."

"Thank you, Mitchell."

Mirabella kissed me fully now, her tongue brushing over mine.

My desire for her was urgent, and I needed her to know.

"Mirabella," I said, barely able to speak.

I needed skin-to-skin contact. I needed to feel her against me. I needed her hands on me. I needed to put things into her mouth. To rub my fucking engorgement across her perfect lips. I needed to know she wanted me, that she needed me and missed me too. I needed to feel her body respond to my touch. I needed to feel her desire on my fingertips. I needed to be inside her.

"Yes," she said, turning to look around at all of the Christmas décor, rubbing me in such a way as to send me over the edge. I held her to me, and there was no way she did not feel evidence of what I felt for her.

I wanted to say, "Merry Christmas, Baby. Can I come down your chimney?" Not sure how Mira would take it though, instead I crooned, "I want to make love to you," remembering how she had made a distinction between fucking, having sex, and making love.

One night in my apartment in Chelsea, after an evening of dinner out, a movie, and amazing sex, we talked all night about just about everything. She'd even asked me if I wanted kids. The more I thought about that night, the more I was certain now that it was love we would be making.

Mirabella turned back to me, the look on her face crippling me emotionally. In that moment, I would have done whatever she asked of me, including abstaining for yet another day. But she didn't ask me to wait. She kissed me deeply, needfully.

I couldn't fucking take it. All of my plans to go slowly and to seduce her went out the fucking window. My self-control was completely fucking gone. I was so deeply lost that it was now abundantly clear that if she were to leave me now, I would not survive it.

I walked her back, not taking my hands or mouth from her, happy that my cast was now off, and I could resume my expert handling of her body and give her all the things she craved and needed from me.

She pulled me down to her once we reached the couch, but kept her legs closed. So, I leaned down and kissed her some more on her mouth and on her neck like she liked. Then, I waited and watched as the hairs on her skin came alive and the strain of her nipples against her shirt was obvious. She opened her legs slightly but only to adjust her position on the couch. I sat next to her, still kissing her, and now, palming and kneading her left breast, my favorite of the two.

Soon I began to kiss her through her clothes, all over her body. I'd missed being this close to her, so in sync with her. And this Mirabella was Shy Mirabella, and Shy Mirabella required more foreplay and direct stimulation of her clit and tits. I reached a curious hand inside her sweats, only to find my girl wasn't wearing panties, something she did when she was especially horny.

I moaned when I touched the skin of her mound, so fucking soft and warm. I felt her clench in response to my touch. But instead of touching her further, I pulled her pants down and buried my face between her toned legs. Soon, Mirabella was fucking my face. I opened the lips of her scorching, slick vagina with my middle and index fingers then gently slid them inside my girl.

"I missed you so much, Mirabella." As if in agreement, she gripped my fingers hard with need.

"I missed you too, Mitchell." She was breathy and needy.

I could not get enough of her with her hair in fucking braids down her back. I moved up toward her and maneuvered her flat on her back. She pulled me down on her again to kiss her. It was a if I had poured my soul into kissing her, deeply and with immense feeling.

But it seemed I wasn't as close as Mirabella wanted me to be. And when she opened her legs and said, "Make love to me, Mitchell," I was lost in her. Lost to myself. Fully and wholly in fucking love.

She had her hands in my hair, which caused me to moan, as she wiggled beneath me. I wanted it deep and slow again today. I needed to see her, to watch her respond to me. To love all over her. She was my sanctuary, my calm, my fucking shelter.

It appeared that those three sexless days had made her virginal again; she was so fucking tight. So, when I entered her, we both gasped and then moaned a long fucking moan of pleasure. I was sure that Mirabella's body was made for me, to fit me, to heal me, to fucking break me. And, as our pace quickened, our bodies collided in delicious unison, reaching, and striving for release. Every minute of every day we'd spent kept from one another by a need to sleep, eat, and be by her brother's side, had made us both ravenous and united in our goal to come together.

"Fuck, Mirabella." I found myself wishing I could convince her of how good it was to be with her like this. A delectable feeling settled in my lower pelvis, heat traveled up my back, and my balls tightened, letting me know I was close. I squeezed her right breast, and she turned her head to kiss the arm I had beside her head.

She brought my mouth to hers once more, like she could not get enough of me. Like I was the air she needed to breathe.

"I love you so much," she said looking at me with this expression of love, arousal, gratitude, pleasure.

I stilled inside her, trying hard not to shoot my load just then.

But my girl, she understood. She knew I was waiting for her.

I put my palm on her mound with my fingers pointing toward me, and gently pushed down as I rubbed my thumb across her clit. Just then, the look on her face, took me all the fucking way out.

"Mitchell, I'm gonna come. Fuck," she said, coming so hard on my cock that I came right then, harder than I knew I could.

As we came down from our euphoria and our breathing returned to normal, I hated myself for thinking how upsetting it was going to be when she returned to the hospital this afternoon to spend hours with her dying brother, once again leaving me to my own devices and without her warmth and attention.

AUNT MEG WASN'T one to count her chickens before they hatched, but she seemed excited when I suggested that she and Preston join me for dinner at the penthouse, perhaps taking it as a peace offering.

After a tour of the apartment and some dinner that had been made my Mirabella's grandmother, Aunt Meg and I sat at the dining room table while Preston sat on the couch watching his tablet.

"It's a stunning apartment, Mitchell."

"Thank you. Mirabella plans to remodel the primary bathroom."

"I guess you two have the renovation bug, huh? First the Magellan Media Executive Floor now this lovely penthouse."

"Seems that way," I said continuing to make small talk so as to avoid mentioning anything about Peter Trenom or Robert Brennan III. But as

Aunt Meg sat there, looking at me like she disapproved of Mirabella's design decisions, I went for it.

"Don't you think it's weird that Peter Trenom and Robert Brennan III, two of Dad's closest friends ended up being his worst most back-stabbing fucking enemies?"

"Well, Jesus was friends with Judas, so, it's not a new concept," she said.

I wondered how long she had waited to deliver that line in defense of two indefensible fucking men.

"My only solace is that those two fuckers got what they deserved. Both in jail and neither coming out any time soon," I said. "And Meg? I don't want Preston visiting that motherfucker in prison. You tell him his father died, and let it go."

Aunt Meg's sad expression fell on me, and for a moment, I regretted speaking to her so harshly for the second time.

"You're becoming just like him, you know," she said, in a failed attempt to hurt me.

"Good, because now I finally realize that I cannot trust *anyone*," I said lobbing one back at her.

"We are all we have left, perhaps we should spend that time on more productive endeavors rather than fighting?"

"I wouldn't have to have fought with you had you not done what you did, treating Robert fucking Brennan III like he's some father of the year and fucking around with Peter Trenom."

"Says the man who literally sleeps and lives with the woman whose job it is to speak in the press about all of his shortcomings."

"Don't talk about Mirabella," I said slamming my hand down on the table. "*She* is off limits to you. Besides, she's done with Brennan. She quit."

"Careful, Mitchell. You don't want to break your hand again, being impulsive."

I shook my head in frustration. This was not how it was supposed to be. Aunt Meg and I had always been on the same team, or so it seemed. She always had my back. This could not have been about Trenom. He not only betrayed his duty to Magellan Media but his allegiance to our family, including her.

"What is all this about, Aunt Meg?"

"You don't need me anymore, Mitchell. You don't need Aunt Meg anymore. You need a shrewd business partner who will call you out on your shit and support you when you need to make the hard decisions, the tough calls," she said. It was silly for her to act as though we were no longer related by blood, but now only by money, power, and influence. "You have a partner now in Mirabella. She will give you the feel goods. I will give you the truth."

I considered what she had said, and it made a lot of sense. She talked to me now in the same tone as she had my father.

"Aunt Meg," I said about to go into a "you don't have to do this because we're family and nothing is stronger than family" speech like in *Fast and Furious*.

"Mitchell, you were right the first time, 'Megan' or 'Meg.' No more 'Aunt Meg' bullshit. I may not clean up after you or tell you how you can do anything if you put your mind to it anymore, but you will never ever have to wonder about where my loyalties lie."

"So, you're breaking up with me, is that it? No more Sunday dinners in Connecticut? No holidays? Thanksgiving? Birthdays?"

"You will always be welcome at my home as my nephew, but the Board's duty is to the company, its shareholders, and their various interests, and we are not going to support you acting on your personal vendettas."

"Lucky for me, I own sixty percent of Magellan Media, more than any shareholder."

"Yes, but you need my fifteen percent in order to act without Board approval."

"Are you saying I shouldn't expect you to give your approval because we're related?"

"Yes. And, if you can handle that, which I'm starting to wonder about, you and I will be fine."

"Ok," I said, looking at her and thinking about how she copes.

"Can I ask you a question?"

"Sure."

"Have you been to visit Dad since he died?"

"I visit his grave weekly on Sundays."

We'd had plenty of Sunday dinners, and yet, she hadn't mentioned this. I was beginning to consider all the things Aunt Meg was getting up to and not sharing.

"What do you do there?"

"Talk about you mostly."

"Can I go with you tomorrow?"

"Of course, Mitchell. I'm sure he would love to see you, hear all about your exploits."

I WAS on my way to meet Aunt Meg at the ridiculously ornate and large Magellan mausoleum on Long Island. Mirabella was at the hospital with Jared. When I told her where I was going, she offered to go with me. And as much as I wanted to bring her to meet my family, I had to do this first visit alone.

For some reason, I was nervous. In the back of my mind was my father's judgmental stare, questioning if I was dressed well enough in a black linen button down shirt and black linen pants. There's nothing on the Internet that tells you how to dress for visiting dead family members. So, I had to wing it, having relied on Mirabella to assure me that I was presentable.

Brendan opened my door, and I stepped out into the winter sun. My nerves were shot. How could I be this fucking nervous? I really should have taken Mira up on her offer to join me. I shook hands with Brendan, he patted me on the back, and smiled a solemn smile.

"Thanks, Brother," I said, and put on my sunglasses.

When I reached the crypt, Aunt Meg was already there.

I kissed her cheek despite the shit that went down yesterday.

"Hey, Pres," I said, and pulled him into a bro hug.

He wasn't wearing his headphones today.

"What happened to your headphones?"

"I called mommy a 'fucking bitch-ass hoe,' and she got mad," Preston said, then walked away.

I busted out laughing, unable to stop myself.

"Very mature, Mitchell. Don't encourage him. I found him listening to a song about wet pussies."

"He's a fucking forty-year-old man. Let him sing about wet pussy, for crying out loud."

Aunt Meg shook her head in frustration and said, "Shall we?"

"I'm going to go in by myself, if that's ok."

She looked surprised.

"Perfectly fine. I'll go wait in the car with Preston then."

"I walked inside, looked around, then stood in front of Alexander's name. What a fucking morbid existence. White marble and travertine with gold accents with fancy lighting, and full temperature control.

Jesus.

"Alex, there you are, been looking all over for you," I said trying to make a joke. "You'd be proud of me, Brother; I settled all family business." It was a reference from our favorite film, The Godfather Part II. Part of me waited to hear his laughter at my shitty joke. "But you know what? The thing you would be happy most about? I met someone. I think you would like her. Her name is Mirabella Castle. And, get this, Bro: I'm fucking in love."

CHAPTER 32

MIRABELLA CASTLE

Looking down from the Juliet balcony from RayRay to Mena as they sat on the couch waiting for me to come downstairs, I don't remember what I was thinking when I was considering getting an apartment on my own and away from Mitchell. This penthouse was the perfect place to entertain my friends, who looked to be just as on edge as I was.

Mitchell had just left to go to the gym in the building, something he only did if Maleko wasn't available to work him out or he intended to do only a small workout so he could get quickly back to me. But today, Mitchell had a lot of work to do. He had a huge meeting next week and had planned a conference call for about an hour from now.

I didn't expect him to be gone long but it was just long enough to have my friends here for what I had to do.

"Well, are you going to tell us what was so important that we had to stop here before our movie? Why do you look like you've seen a ghost?"

I joined them in the living room and stood in front of them now, hoping they would see how upset I was as I held the Duane Reade bag in my hand.

"B, what's wrong?" RayRay said.

"With so much going on, I hadn't been keeping track of my cycle," I said in a soft voice. "I think I might be pregnant."

Mena and RayRay looked at one another and then back at me.

"B, are you sure?"

"No, I'm not which is why I asked you guys here. I need to take a test." I walked over to where they sat and emptied the bag on the coffee table. "I bought all these tests and a morning after pill."

"Oh, Mirabella. When was the last time you had your period?"

"I think maybe five weeks ago?"

"You don't keep track? You can keep track on an app now," RayRay said.

"How the fuck do you know about that?" Mena said with a smirk.

"I know more about that shit than the two of you, obviously," RayRay said, a satisfied smirk on his face.

We all laughed, the tension easing only a little.

"I can't be pregnant. Not now."

"When would be a good time, then?" RayRay said, his tone a bit condescending.

"Never? I don't want to be a mom right now. I can barely take care of my fucking self. Can you imagine me with a kid? And RayRay, it's no slight against you. You're amazing at being a dad. But you're also older than me. I'm too young to be a mom."

Neither of them spoke. They eyed me now with suspicion and maybe a bit of empathy.

"What about Mitchell?" Mena said as she picked up two boxes from the six that lay about the table. She turned them over and read the instructions for both.

"Oh, God. I couldn't do that to him. Not right now."

RayRay picked up a box too and began reading instead of responding to me. And then after a few long minutes, he said, "Have you guys talked about it?"

"Talked about what? That I might be pregnant?"

"No. Have you talked about kids? Have you asked him if he wants kids?"

"Not in so many words. I mean I did but it was all theoretical. I asked him if he had ever thought about getting married, settling down and having a family. It wasn't like in relation to us. I wasn't asking about us."

"It says you should take first thing in the morning, B," Mena said, still looking at the box. "It's already 11:30!"

RayRay swatted Mena's arm for interrupting.

"So, what did he say? And, B. Sit down. You're making me nervous."

I sat because I needed RayRay to be calm and to be able to think this through with me.

"He said he should not be entrusted with small humans or house plants."

"That sounds like a frivolous response."

"Yeah, plus we had been drinking."

Mena looked up from her boxes and said, "That sounds like something Mitchell would say, but it's not much of a response."

"Yeah but look how he is with Christina. He may feed her ice cream for lunch, but he's great with her," RayRay said.

I was remembering that video of Mitchell and Christina that RayRay showed me during my wrap party in Portugal. Then I started thinking about how he was with her at RayRay's apartment when we were broken up. I smiled despite the tears that began running down my face.

"He's great at being an uncle," Mena added.

"He really is," I said, as the two of them gave me sad looks.

"I bought like six tests."

"Um. It only takes one," RayRay said, as if he has had to do this before.

We all laughed again.

"So, what are you waiting for, B? Take three of these and go pee on each one," Mena said. "Want me to go with you?"

I shook my head.

"I just need you guys to take it with you. I don't want Mitchell to find it no matter what the results are."

"What are you talking about?" RayRay said.

"The tests. Can you take the bag and boxes and test results with you? Discard them outside when you leave?"

"Absolutely fucking not. I will not help you hide this from Mitchell. He deserves to know, Mirabella." RayRay only called me by my full name when he was upset with me.

"I just need time to process, and then I will tell him."

"Mirabella, so are you going to tell him that you had a scare if the test is negative?" Mena said, a weird look on her face.

"I don't know."

"Maybe you should in case it helps open up the conversation. Don't you want to know where you stand if you do end up pregnant? You said you guys are having a shit-ton of sex, right?" RayRay said.

RayRay gave me a disapproving look.

"Yeah. I don't know. I just . . . I don't think Mitchell and I are ready for that conversation. So, if it's negative, then I don't feel like there would be a reason to discuss it now. I don't want him to think I'm bringing it up because it's what I want. You know?"

"I don't know, B. I think he deserves to know regardless. And anyway, what if you are? What will you do?" RayRay's expression was equal parts hard and incredulous.

"I have no idea. I just know I'm not ready to be a mom to anyone or anything. A pet. A plant. A person. Not ready."

Mena looked from the boxes to me and said, "Well, only one way to find out, right? Go pee on those sticks."

I stood, and then Mena and RayRay each handed me their boxes.

I shrugged and said, "I guess it's now or never. Thanks for being here, you two."

"Where else would we be, Mirabella? Just go. Hurry because we have to leave soon," Mena said.

"Ok." I took the boxes then went into the bathroom to pee on the sticks contained in each one.

I walked on jelly legs to the first-floor powder room, my heart beating thunderously against my chest. The idea that Mitchell was downstairs and could come up and catch me at any time scared the shit out of me.

When I reached the bathroom, my hands were too shaky to grip the door handle and to hold the three boxes. I dropped two of them.

"Shit!" I said as I scrambled to retrieve them from the cold marble floor. When I bent over to pick them up, I dropped the third one. "Fuck!" I screamed, the fear and frustration making it hard to do anything in that moment.

"Are you alright, B?" Mena's voice echoed in the hallway behind me.

I turned to see her standing there, looking at what a fucking mess I was.

She moved quickly to help me, and said, "Mirabella. It's ok. Do you want me to get Mitchell?"

More tears fell now as my mind turned to the first time Mena told me that Mitchell was in our apartment in Queens.

She nodded at me, no doubt knowing exactly what I was thinking.

"I bet you never thought we'd end up here that night, huh?"

I laughed then.

"Or the next day. Remember he took me to Le Monde Du?"

"Took you, he fucking opened the restaurant for you," Mena teased.

"I love him so much, Mena. I don't think . . . I . . . I can't be pregnant. Not now. It's too soon."

"It's ok, B. Whatever it is. Whatever happens. You will be ok. Look at how much you two have already been through."

Just then RayRay appeared in the hallway.

"Everything alright?"

"I'm just a fucking *klutz*."

"Come on. Go pee on those fucking sticks. Stop fucking around, B. Once you do it, you'll know."

Mena and RayRay gathered the boxes and put them into my shaky arms. Mena leaned forward and opened the door for me. RayRay motioned with his head for me to go inside.

"Go. We'll be right here."

I looked lovingly at my friends, thinking about how I could not do this without them. Inside, I closed the door and began opening the boxes. I laid the sticks out on the counter and folded the boxes in half. Then, I pulled my sweatpants down and balanced my ass in the air. The first stick I grabbed fell into the fucking toilet.

"Shit!"

"You ok?" RayRay said from the other side of the door.

"Ugh. Yes. Just dropped one test in the fucking toilet."

"B, calm down. Relax. Go slow," Mena said.

I grabbed the second one, peed on it, then set it on the counter. Still squatting and with shaky hands, I did the same to the other one. Then, I wiped, grabbed some toilet paper, and pulled the one that had fallen in out of the toilet.

Gross.

I yanked my pants up and then threw the toilet water one in the trash. After washing my hands, I heard talking.

Mitchell.

I grabbed everything and threw it into the trashcan with the fucking see-through plastic bag in it. Then, I took the hand towel hanging on the wall and wrapped all of that in the towel. It was going to have to be enough. When I opened the door to the bathroom, Mitchell was leaning against the wall looking handsome as fuck. And, when his gaze landed on me, I gulped so loudly that he smiled a devilish panty-soaking smile.

"Hey."

"Hey, how was the gym?" I said holding the towel and its contents behind my back.

"Good but I missed you, so I came back early."

"Oh, you just wanted to see me," Mena said coming up behind Mitchell, making her eyes big like she was trying to figure out how she was going to sneak past Mitchell and get the contraband from me.

She marched past him, elbowed him, and said, "You can't hog her. Get out of the way and let me hug my friend. Jesus, Mitchell. You guys live together. You can give her five fucking minutes with her friends."

Mitchell shook his head and laughed, and said, "Five minutes. Then you're mine, Mirabella."

"Ugh. Get a fucking room, you two. So gross," Mena joked, her eyes on me now, searching for the answer to her unspoken question of, "Well? Are you fucking pregnant, or what?"

CHAPTER 33

MITCHELL MAGELLAN

Mira's friends were over. She'd surprised me when she told me they were already on their way when I announced I was heading to the gym in our building. They had been trying to convince her to go to the movies with them all week, but Mira was being cautious, not really wanting to leave the house except for work in case something happened with Jared.

She didn't say it but since she had been avoiding her parents and making excuses about why she didn't have them over, despite having Grandma Wright over, she must have figured if she didn't socialize at all, her parents wouldn't feel as slighted as they probably already felt.

With the big partners conference next week, I had a shit ton of work to do to prepare. And so, I had scheduled a meeting with my team for this afternoon. I headed down to the gym to blow off some steam since I hadn't yet had Mira today. She'd been sleeping a lot lately, falling asleep at odd times and for short periods. So, when she slept in this morning, I let her. God knows I had my fucking way with her last night.

Thinking about it now had me feeling like I wasn't going to make it until after my meeting, so I headed home earlier than I said I would, hoping she was awake and in the mood to get tangled up with me.

When I opened the door to the apartment and heard the alarm alert say, "Front door open," I heard what sounded like the rustling of plastic bags and talking. What the fuck?

In the living room, RayRay and Mena sat on the couch looking at me like they had seen a ghost. They looked busted and found out. Caught in the act. Mena held the bag I heard and when she saw me eyeing it, she put in inside her giant Burberry bag.

"What are you two up to? Where's Mirabella?"

"Fucking hello to you to, Mitchell," Mena said all fake annoyed.

"Didn't I fucking just see you when you arrived?"

"Whatever. It's rude to be all like where's Mirabella like we don't fucking matter."

"Ok. Hi, Mena. Hi, RayRay," I said, accentuating each name. "Is that better?"

"Yes. And Mirabella's in the bathroom. She has an upset stomach."

RayRay elbowed Mena while keeping his eyes on me.

Was I not supposed to see that?

I shook my head and then made my way to the bathroom to look for Mira.

"Baby? You ok?" I called her from the other side of the door as I heard water running and more rustling from the bathroom.

Mira opened the door and stood in the threshold.

"Baby? How fucking original. Sounds like something you call someone whose name you can't bother to remember." Mena added extra annoyance and disdain to her voice and shoved past me and hugged Mira. And if I'm not mistaken, Mira passed Mena something else to put into her giant Burberry bag. They hugged; Mena shoved past me again. Minutes later, she and RayRay were hugging and kissing Mira like they were never going to see one another again before leaving and not even saying goodbye to me.

Mira walked past me and into the kitchen, and I was not having that shit. What the fuck was going on?

She went straight to the refrigerator, pulled out a water, opened it, shut the fridge, and then chugged a little. She wasn't looking at me. What the fuck?

"Hey," I said.

"Hey," she said in a way that made me think even more that this whole thing was fucking weird.

"You good? Mena said your stomach was upset."

"Oh. Yeah. I was feeling nauseous before. Lightheaded. I think I'm just a little dehydrated. How was your workout?"

I moved toward her, and for a brief second, I watched her body which normally responded to me with need, recoil.

What the fuck?

"Mira, why don't you go lie down. I'll bring you up some tea."

"I think I'm better now. I was just really out of it for a bit."

When I was in front of her, my girl smiled at me.

Thank God. It was my imagination.

I pulled her into my arms.

"You feel good, Mirabella," I said, heat running up my back, an erection growing. "Why can't I get enough of you?"

She smiled some more, and said, "Didn't I tell you I would take care of you so well you wouldn't be able to do without me?"

Mirabella put her hand inside my sweats.

Fuck.

"Yes, you did," I breathed out.

"You're so hard, Mitchell," Mira said as she stroked me through my underwear. And when she reached the tip and found pre-cum seeping through the fabric, she closed her eyes and moaned.

"I can't control myself around you," I said, pushing her up against the refrigerator.

"Let's go upstairs, Mitchell," she sighed, her expert treatment of my cock making it so I was nearly ready to come in her hand.

She went to remove her hand, but I grabbed it and said, "Don't stop. Fucking. Don't stop, Mira."

"You don't want me to stop?" she said in the sexiest voice, while looking into my eyes.

But I couldn't respond. All I could do was close my eyes, hump her hand, and feel her. My sweet, beautiful baby. Shit. I was going to come. I was going to make a fucking mess all over myself.

"Mitchell," her voice snapped me out of it. She'd stopped stroking. I looked down at her.

"Mira, what's wrong?"

"I want you to come in my mouth. Fuck my mouth, so you can come down my throat."

Jesus. Yes. Fuck. God.

Suddenly, Mirabella was on her knees, taking me quickly out of my pants and underwear. I grabbed my dick and held it to stop it from twitching off the fucking rails. When she looked up at me, I ran my cock across her mouth, coating her lips in my pre-cum. She licked her lips, keeping her eyes on me, and said, "Make me gag, Mitchell."

Fucking. Bloody. Hell.

I pushed my dick into her mouth, my head falling back, eyes closing as she wrapped her luscious lips around me. I forced myself to open my eyes and lower my head so I could watch her take me deep and fucking break me.

Mirabella kept her eyes on me as I fucked her mouth like she asked me to. And even though she moaned and gagged, she took hit after hit at the back of her throat, until she did the thing that took me over the edge. Mira looked into my eyes, reached under me, took my balls in the palm of her hand, and pushed her thumb up under the space between my balls and anus.

Fuck Me. I'm gonna come.

"You ready, Baby? Fuck, I'm gonna come, Mirabella. Shit."

And when she nodded, giving me permission to shoot my load down her glorious throat, I couldn't hold back. Hot spurts of cum shot down Mirabella's throat, making her gag even more from the force and amount of it.

And when I was done coming for Mira, she wiped her mouth with the back of her hand and smiled up at me. She put me back together before I helped her up, and in that moment, looking at the woman who had just given me perhaps the best orgasm I had ever had, I was so fucking in love that I was speechless.

"You ok?" She said, looking at me with a satisfied yet curious expression.

When I regained a bit of composure, I said, "What was that, Mira? Jesus. Baby, that was so fucking good. Thank you."

She smiled some more then kissed me, prolonging my euphoric state and forcing me to do the only thing I could. I crushed my mouth to hers, trying to claim her, own her, fucking become one with her. Everything I wanted was tied up in that desperate, grateful, and erotic exchange as I reveled in the taste of my own cum in my gorgeous girl's mouth.

Soon, I had my hand inside her panties. It wasn't long before she was fucking my fingers on the way to her own amazing release. She moaned her pleasure into my mouth, causing me to moan, and fuck if I wasn't getting aroused again.

I removed my fingers from her hot, slick center and then hand from her panties so I could run my fingers across her sexy mouth before she had a chance to protest.

"God, you taste delicious," I said, as I licked Mirabella's taste off her lips and then kissed her. She moaned some more, and I smiled while keeping my lips on her as I thought about how she had no fucking idea what I was about to do.

"Mitchell," Mira managed to breathe out. "Touch me."

I pulled away so I could look at her. I mean, really look at her. Mira was flushed with arousal, her tits ripe and budding. There was a little quiver to her lips and a pleading in her eyes.

"I'm going to take care of you, Baby. You ready?"

"Ready for what?"

I slipped my hand back into her panties and ran my fingers across her clit. Fuck, it was so soft on the outside but hard and engorged too. Mira moaned.

"Mitchell, that feels so good."

"Yeah?" I slowly inserted a finger inside her.

"Shit." Mira began humping my finger. I let her move at her own pace, and she didn't even seem to notice I was also moving against her and getting hard.

I added another finger, and kept steady pressure on her clit which was now throbbing and humming as she clenched me and drenched my fingers in her pre-cum.

"Mira, you feeling good?"

She moaned into my neck now, her breath hot on my skin.

I reached into the back of her pants and listened as her breath caught in her throat. I pulled my fingers out and stopped rubbing her clit while slowly inserting a finger in her asshole. And when I had it in her ass as far as it would go. She rocked back onto my finger.

Fuck.

I then pushed my two fingers deep inside her dripping cunt, loving the feeling of her right then, filled up with my fingers. And when I began to rub on her clit, my baby said, "Oh, Mitchell, fuck. Oh God. Mitchell. Fuck. Mitchell. I'm gonna come."

Just then, Mira came on my fingers, my name on her fucking lips.

Mira was spent, and we could both have used a shower, so after I put her back together and washed my hands, I said, "You want to shower, or do you want a bath?"

Mira responded by taking my face in her hands and kissing me. When she had her fill of me, she said, "Thank you. That was so good."

I smiled then, loving how it made me feel to know that I could make her so happy. But I knew Mirabella well by now, and if I was being honest, she needed more. We both did. What we had just done was only enough to take the edge off. To cool the sexual tension between us, not to quell it entirely.

And, because I wanted to explore what the hell was happening with Mira when I arrived home earlier, I suggested we take a bath.

"Why don't you go upstairs? I'll lock up down here, and we can get a bath."

"Ok," she said before kissing me again.

I patted her on the ass and then watched as she walked away. When she was gone, I went to shut the light in the hallway bathroom and noticed the hand towel was missing. I leaned down to get a replacement from the cabinet under the sink where Mirabella kept them. There was a piece of paper on the floor, so I picked it up. I was about to fling it into the trash when I realized there was no trash bag.

I shook my head in frustration wondering why there was no towel and no trash bag, thinking I would ask Mira when I got upstairs. I carried the piece of paper out to the kitchen with me and without thinking, flung it into the trash can there.

Just then, Mira's phone dinged. I picked it up, and read the text from Mena that appeared on the screen.

> MENA: That was fucking close. Does Mitchell suspect anything?

Motherfucker. What the hell is this shit about?

Suddenly, like in one of those fucking Christopher Nolan films, shit was coming back to me in slow motion.

When I came home, Mira was in the bathroom. When she opened the door and saw me, it looked like she was holding something behind her back. I had cast it off then because I wanted to throw her friends out and get tangled up with her. But then Mena shoved past me, and for some reason, I didn't think much of it. It was Mena being Mena. But also, not because both she and Mirabella seemed nervous. Like I had caught them doing something. Something they didn't want me to know about.

I ran to the trash can, and picked out the paper I had just thrown away.

Instructions for a pregnancy test.

It was like someone had kicked the wind out of me. I sucked in a shaky breath, locked up, and climbed the stairs two at a fucking time.

CHAPTER 34

MIRABELLA CASTLE

Jesus Christ. That was close.

I searched frantically for my phone before realizing I'd left it downstairs. When Mitchell came home earlier than expected, I had to ditch the pregnancy tests and pass them off to Mena. I was not ready to talk to Mitchell about it. How would I even start? Remember that night in my apartment in Queens when I told you I was on the pill and had been for some time and it was ok for us to have sex without condoms? And when he said, "yeah why?" I would say well remember you asked me if I was sure, and I said yes? Well, I'm pregnant.

I rushed out of the door and ran smack into Mitchell who was running up the stairs.

When I barreled into him, the phone he had been carrying, my phone, dropped to the first floor.

"Shit," I said, as I tried to move past him to retrieve it.

"I'll get it," he said, grabbing my arm and placing me against the wall.

I watched him run down the stairs, pick up the phone, look at the screen, shake his head, and then glare at me as he made his way back up to where I was.

"Here," he said not even really stopping to be sure it didn't fall again.

"Hey," I said, pulling him by the arm and turning him toward me, noticing he hadn't even broken a sweat from the running and the stair climbing.

"Thank you," I said looking into his eyes. Something had definitely changed between us since we had been in the kitchen.

"You're welcome," he said before pulling his shirt off with one hand, running a hand through his hair, and unnerving me with how gorgeous he was.

He kissed me quickly, then took my free hand and walked me into the bedroom, and for a minute, I nearly forgot about all the shit I was panicked about before he came home. But when he went into the bathroom and could be heard peeing, I checked my phone. There were no messages from either RayRay or Mena. No calls.

Shit. Their movie had already started and would likely not finish for at least another hour. I plugged my phone into the wall, and then joined Mitchell in the bathroom.

"You want a drink?" Mitchell said as he washed his hands, despite the fact that we were about to get in the tub.

Shit. If I don't drink like I normally do in the bubble bath with Mitchell, he might think something's up.

"Yes. Do we have any Moscato?"

Mitchell went into the hallway closet that we had converted to a wine fridge. When he returned, he handed me a cold glass of Moscato and held up his glass of bourbon and said, "Cheers, beautiful." We clanged glasses, and Mitchell took a sip of his drink. I pretended to take a sip of mine, as I stepped into the tub.

"Good, Baby? I think we might need to order more soon," Mitchell said as he put his hand on my lower back as I eased myself into the bath. I nodded, smiled, and then pretended to take another sip.

I made the mistake of turning just as Mitchell lowered himself in across from me so that my face ended up right near his junk.

Mitchell laughed.

"Want some more, Mirabella? Cause I can give you some more if you didn't get enough of me in the kitchen."

Mitchell's voice was deeper than normal, husky. He was aroused, even if his penis didn't fully yet show it.

"You wish, Mr. Magellan," I teased, a seductive smile on my face, as I put my wine on the side of the tub.

The look on Mitchell's face right then? I could have eaten him alive. He was all together handsome. So fucking sexy. Flirtatious. Smug. Aroused.

"Don't make me come over there and take what I want, Mirabella Castle."

Fuck.

"You wouldn't."

Mitchell put his bourbon down, and it was a warning.

"Come here, Mirabella."

"Mitchell," I said, totally unsure of why. I think maybe part of me was nervous about the change in his demeanor. Maybe it was all in my head. It had to be. I didn't have any messages or calls on my phone. There is no way Mitchell had any idea about what was going on earlier.

I moved slowly over to Mitchell. He kept his hungry eyes on me, raking the parts of my body he could see above the bubbles with his intense gaze. It was as if he hadn't had me yet today. Like he hadn't had me nearly every day since we'd gotten back together. As though what we'd had downstairs was but the appetizer, and Mitchell was now ready to fucking eat.

My movements in his direction were slow and intentional. I wanted him too. I wanted to feel him against me. Inside me. So, when I reached him, I sat on his lap and put my arms around his neck and my hands in his glorious fucking hair. Jesus, this man was something.

He closed his eyes at the feel of my fingers on his scalp at the base of his neck.

"I love when you run your fingers through my hair, Mirabella."

I smiled then. "I love doing it. Are you going to cut it soon?"

"You want me to cut it?"

"No, I like it longish."

I turned Mitchell's head every which way, partly because I love touching him and playing in his hair. He smiled a lazy, relaxed, sexy smile. I hated lying to him. I hated that I felt I couldn't tell him what was happening with me. I hated how deep my feelings for him ran. And yet, I kissed him. I don't think he was expecting that. He moaned into my mouth. We kissed one another, our kisses sweet and deep and insistent.

And, when I pushed my tongue into Mitchell's delicious mouth in search of his, he eagerly gave it to me, using his to dance with mine, each of us taking turns licking and sucking on the other.

Mitchell sat forward, placed his hands under my ass and pulled me closer to him and then suddenly, his tongue was moving and twisting even deeper into my mouth. And now it was me moaning my pleasure. He reached between us and eased inside me slowly and deliciously.

Shit.

"Mitchell," I said because he felt so damn good. He moved in and out of me so slowly and deliberately, one hand still under my ass. The water sloshed all around us as Mitchell pumped in and out. I met his thrusts while holding on to him, keeping one hand in his hair and one on the edge of the tub for balance.

"Look at me, Mirabella."

But I was looking at him.

"Look at me, Baby."

I was. I am. Mitchell. I was looking at him.

"Fuck. Mira. Look at me," Mitchell said.

Shit. Mitchell broke eye contact. He had tears in his eyes. He lowered his head onto my shoulder and then turned his head so that he could kiss my neck his hair falling onto my shoulder blade.

"Mirabella," Mitchell said in my ear as we were both about to come.

Fuck. Mitchell came first and then I came, and it was beautiful and sad.

Mitchell held me now, arms around me, face in my neck, breathing heavy.

"Mitchell, what's wrong?"

I took his face in my hands and pulled it up so I could look at him. "Are you pregnant, Mirabella?"

MITCHELL MAGELLAN

It wasn't that I was mad at Mirabella. We both had trust issues. But if Mirabella was pregnant, it hurt me that she wouldn't tell me, even if it had only been a scare.

Scare. Fuck.

I'm almost thirty years old. Maybe it was time to start thinking about my future. What would that even look like? Until I met her, I had never considered that I would want to one day have kids. I mean. I don't want kids. But Mira. God. If she was pregnant. Fuck.

Maybe she wanted to be sure first before talking to me.

Maybe she didn't know what to say what she had to say, so she asked her friends for help.

Maybe she was planning to have an abortion.

Fuck.

In the few seconds that it took me to process the text on Mira's phone, I had to actively decide not to put my hand through the nearest wall.

Everything I had ever felt about my own inadequacy came to the surface in that moment. Thoughts of Alex. The hearing with Sarah. The idea that she was supposed to be his legacy. They were supposed to have kids. But he died instead. I thought about Mom and Robert Brennan III. Preston was her first son. But she couldn't even raise him. She didn't seem to want to. Or, she put her desires aside to appease Dad. Then there was Aunt Meg. She couldn't have kids.

But Mirabella. She might be pregnant with my kid.

My kid? Jesus.

Nothing good could come from Mirabella having my kid. How could someone like me be a parent?

Maybe she didn't confide in me because she knew what a shitty father I would be.

I thought I could let it go. That I could allow Mirabella not to tell me what was going on. That I could be mature and say that she would tell me in her own time. But the more I thought about it, the more I fucking couldn't stop thinking about it. The more I couldn't stop thinking about the possibility that she could be pregnant, the more aroused I became. The more I fucking wanted her.

Being inside her right then, my mind was full of non-sexy things. For some reason, my thoughts turned to the past few weeks and all that had happened. Through it all there was one thing that remained constant, and that was my desire for her. To be near her. To see her. To be the one to make her smile. Make her laugh. To give her toe-curling mind-numbing pleasure. To hear my name on her tongue as she's coming undone for me.

And sometimes, I wasn't fully able to articulate everything I was feeling for or about her. Sometimes, she made me so angry that I wanted to fucking hurt something. Other times, she frustrated me with how fucking brilliant she is and how she's able to make so much damn sense, obliterating my arguments and rebuttals. Then, there were times when my frustration stemmed from my disbelief at how such a smart girl could make such dumb decisions, like hiding in the bathroom from me.

There were times when Mirabella could be doing something as simple as reading a book, and the most intense need would elicit an erection that would overtake me and stop me in my tracks. It was like a full body hard-on, like my entire body was on fire for her.

Normally, I was happy and content just watching her sleep. When Mira's mind was still and she was at peace in bed next to me, a slight snore escaping her gorgeous lips, it felt as if God himself was blessing me, like I was the luckiest motherfucker in the world.

And on those nights when my girl dreamt about me, woke up soaked because the Mitchell in her dreams did things to her, she'd reach for me, going right for the thing she wanted, and would climb on top of me and fuck me all sleepy, rabid, and sexy like? I was a fucking king because even in her dreams, Mirabella wanted me.

I came thinking about how she made me feel, the warm water splashing against my skin, the feel of Mira's fingers on my scalp, how warm and soft she felt against me, and my absolute terror about whether I was fucking a pregnant Mira right then took me over. All my hopes and dreams rested upon what Mirabella would say next.

She pulled out of my embrace, took my face in her hands, and asked me a simple question. "What's wrong, Mitchell?"

"Nothing. I just love you so much; that's all," sat trapped in my mind.

What came out of my mouth was, "Are you pregnant, Mirabella?"

In the few seconds it took her to process what I had asked, it felt like someone was squeezing the life out of me, like I couldn't breathe.

Mira's face contorted.

Shit.

She grabbed me, pulled me against her chest and cried long drawn-out sobs that shook her entire body and mine. I held her tightly, hoping I hadn't broken her.

"Mirabella, please. Just tell me. Are you pregnant?"

I held her still, even as she continued to sob and shake.

"Mitchell," she finally said. "I'm so sorry. I don't know."

Mirabella pulled out of my embrace. She was sniffling and shaking and snotting all over. Her eyes were swollen and bloodshot. My girl was a fucking gorgeous mess. I grabbed a washcloth from the ledge and dipped it into the water. Then, I ran it gently over Mirabella's face, first on the left side, then the right, then across her forehead, nose, and then her chin. When I was done, I planted a kiss on her nose.

Then, I grabbed the sprayer and opened the drain so we could soon get out. I sprayed Mirabella down, getting all the suds off her skin.

After quickly rinsing us both, I stepped out of the tub and snatched a towel for Mira out of the towel warmer she had insisted we buy.

I helped her out of the bath and then cloaked her in the plush towel she loved. Then, I retrieved a towel for me and wrapped it around my waist.

"Talk to me, Mirabella. What's going on?"

Mirabella began to cry silent tears. The water simply ran down her cheeks as though it was being chased out of her eyes. "Come on," I said, bringing her into her dressing area, pulling out a fluffy robe and putting her in it. Then, I walked her over to the chair in front of our bed and sat her down. I dressed in a white t-shirt and white briefs, the ones Mira liked. When I was done, I sat next to her and said, "Baby. Please. Tell me what's going on with you."

Just then her phone rang. Mira sprang from the chair like her ass was on fire. She grabbed her phone, read the text, and then began crying all over again.

I jumped up, practically breaking my neck getting over there, and grabbed her phone out of her hand. On it was a text from Mena.

"You're not pregnant, B. Sorry. Call you later. Going out with Dino."

Attached to the message was a picture of results from two pregnancy tests.

Mira dragged me into a hug. I hugged her back. And I would be lying if I said I wasn't a little bit disappointed in the results of those tests. As Mira cried what I assumed were tears of joy and relief, I think I cried too.

CHAPTER 35

MIRABELLA CASTLE

"Mirabella, you're one of the strongest people I have ever met," Mitchell said when I finally stopped crying and we were able to talk.

"How can you say that when I was afraid to face you, afraid to tell you that I might be pregnant? Afraid of what you would say?"

"Mirabella. We have to talk to each other. We have to say whatever needs to be said no matter what. If you and me are going to be committed to each other, there shouldn't be anything we can't discuss. Anything we can't tell one another, even if it hurts. Even if it makes us angry. Mira, that's what being in a committed relationship means. I don't want you hiding from me. And I certainly don't want you lying to me and enlisting your friends to cover shit up that you're afraid for me to know."

"I don't want you to feel obligated to stay with me. I didn't want you to do something stupid like propose to me because I was pregnant or thought I was."

Mitchell looked wounded then.

"I'm serious, Mitchell. I don't want to be with someone who's only sticking around for a baby."

"I'm not father material, Mirabella. But when I thought you might be pregnant, for a brief second, I thought maybe I could be. I considered whether I wanted to be. I thought about what it would be like to have a mini me to take care of. A mini you. Jesus; I would be twice ruined."

"You thought about having a child with me?"

"Yeah. I thought about killing you for not telling me too. How long did you think you were pregnant for?"

"I don't know, maybe like a week? I only bought the tests two days ago."

"Why didn't you tell me?"

"I wasn't sure how I felt about it yet. I wanted to take the test and then think about it. Think about how I felt or would feel if I was actually pregnant."

"Did you see a doctor?"

"No."

"So, you're not pregnant and also you haven't gotten your period yet?"

"No."

"Do you think something's wrong? Like medically?"

"I don't know."

"Maybe you should see a doctor."

"I will; I guess. But I think it's just stress."

"Has this happened before? That you've been this late?"

"Yes."

"Recently? Since we've been together?"

"Yes."

"Oh?" Mitchell looked disappointed.

I looked away then.

"Yes."

"Wait. You thought you were pregnant before?"

"No. My period was late."

"But you didn't think you were pregnant?"

"Every girl thinks she might be pregnant whenever her period is an hour later than it should be. But it came one or two days later, and it was fine. But this time, it's been two weeks."

"Mira, I really think you should see a doctor. Are you having other symptoms?"

"I've been really tired. Haven't you noticed me falling asleep at odd times?"

He seemed like he was just now putting two and two together. "Yes. I just figured you were under a lot of stress with everything going on. Mira. You need to go to the doctor."

"I will, Mitchell. I will. If it doesn't come in the next few days, I will see a doctor, I promise."

"Don't blow this off." He looked like he wanted to say much more. Like he was holding back.

"What?"

"I want to go with you."

"What? No. You are NOT going with me to the gynecologist."

"Why not? I have a right to know what's going on down there."

"Well, the fact that you refer to my reproductive system as 'down there' is indication number one that you should not be in attendance."

"Promise me you'll make an appointment, and you'll go, and when it's done, you'll tell me what the doctor said."

"I promise."

Mitchell was quiet then, contemplative.

"You look like you don't believe me."

"So, what was your plan, Mirabella? Were you going to never tell me? Have an abortion?"

"I'm not ready to be a mom. I'm just barely an adult."

Mitchell looked away from me. He seemed agitated like he wanted to hit something. Break it into a million little pieces.

I went to him.

Before I reached him, he turned back to me with an expression that was somewhere between sad, angry, and confused and said, "Mirabella. I'm not ok with this."

His words stopped me in my tracks.

"What are you not ok with?"

"All of it. You not telling me you thought you might have been pregnant. You not telling me you had taken a pregnancy test. You thinking you might like to have an abortion without giving me the benefit of talking to me about it."

Collecting my thoughts right then before I responded, I considered Mitchell's feelings and his rights in this situation. It reminded me of our conversation about Jared's baby. How Mitchell had asked Jared to consider that his child with Bianca could be his only chance to have a family.

I positioned myself on my knees in front of Mitchell who was still sitting. Like he had done to me when I sat on the couch in his apartment in Chelsea and asked him for time, for us to have a break. I wrapped my arms around his knees and looked up at him from below.

"I'm so sorry, Mitchell. It wasn't my intention to leave you out of the conversation or to disregard your opinion."

He looked down at me, brushed my cheek, and then said, "What do you want Mira? You don't want to have kids?"

"I. I don't know. Not now. Do you?"

"No. I don't want to have kids now. But, if it had turned out differently, if it had turned out that you were in fact pregnant, I would have liked to have had the option to consider it. To consider and discuss it with you than have you hide it from me. It takes two of us to make a baby. Don't you think we should talk about what to do in case? Make that decision together?"

I took Mitchell's hand from my face and kissed it. He closed his eyes when my lips touched his skin.

"That's not fair," he said in a lazy voice.

I smiled at him then.

"Neither is that," he said as he put his other hand on my face and stroked my cheek. And when he was finished, I took his other hand and kissed it in the same way I had the first one.

"I love you so much, Mitchell. I was afraid you wouldn't want a baby, and that if I was pregnant, you wouldn't want the baby or me."

"I love you too, Mira. But aren't you the one who told me that I shouldn't assume what you would want and to ask you?"

"Yes."

"Can I please have the same courtesy? Especially when it's something as monumental as whether I will get to be a dad or not."

I got off my knees and sat in Mitchell's lap, so relieved, ashamed, and in love at that moment.

He welcomed me into his arms with a small smile that let me know he was glad this hadn't turned into a full-blown fight.

I kissed his neck, making him moan. Right then, I thought about how come I don't kiss his neck more. He seemed to like it. And I liked it. A lot. I kissed his neck again just as I noticed Mitchell was getting hard and his breathing was getting faster.

"Mirabella," he said, turning his head toward mine and attempting to capture my mouth in a kiss.

I put a finger up, and shook my head to stop him.

"Mitchell," I said, staring longingly into his beautiful green eyes.

"Yes?"

"Let me kiss you."

I leaned in and kissed his neck again. God, he smelled good.

"Jesus, Mira," he breathed out, getting heated from that little bit of attention I was paying to his neck. Soon, I had my hand in his hair like he liked and was basically making out with his neck, chin, and cheek, loving the feel of the stubble that had gathered there.

"I love when you kiss me, Mirabella," Mitchell breathed out. And, to reward him for the praise, I gave him my mouth, tongue and all.

We both moaned now, getting worked up some more. Then Mitchell rested his hand on my lower belly. He pulled away to look at me.

"Mirabella."

"Yes?"

And even though I was interested in what Mitchell had planned to say, I was also interested in kissing him some more. God, I loved this man. I loved kissing him. Loving on him. Giving him the attention he craved and that he deserved. Soon, I'd forgotten that Mitchell was about to say something.

Mitchell was intoxicating. He was the kind of man that made you feel like the only woman in the world. Like your lips were the tastiest treat. Mitchell could spend an hour licking and sucking on my tongue if I let him. This man liked to make out. And when Mitchell made out, he made sure to give ample attention to my mouth, lips, and tongue.

But when Mitchell was especially into it, he liked to give me deep, slow, and deliberate kisses while snaking one hand around my throat and placing the fingers of his other hand deep inside me.

When I was wrapped in the taste of him on my tongue and the feel of his lips against my skin, I was so distracted that I hadn't yet noticed that he'd slipped his hand inside my robe. And when I sucked in a shaky breath, already turned way the fuck on, Mitchell smirked.

"You good, Mirabella?"

Mitchell opened my robe, exposing my boobs. This man's face was enraptured as he took me in. It was like every time he saw them was like the first time. Soon, he leaned down and cupped the left one, kneading and pinching in the most delicious way. He licked his fucking lips, making me moan.

"What are you moaning about, Mirabella?"

Shit.

"I want you to kiss me there," I said, feeling shy.

"Where, Baby?" Mitchell took my hand and put it on my breast. "Show me where you want to be kissed."

Jesus. His sexy voice and the look on his face were having an effect on me. This man knew what he was doing.

I was so shy now, and I didn't know what to do.

While I hesitated, Mitchell surprised me by putting his hand between my legs and pushing a finger inside me, pulling it out and then putting it into his mouth.

"Good. So good."

He pushed a finger inside again. And when he brought it up to my mouth, he said, "Where are my fucking manners?" before placing his finger into my mouth for me to suck. And when I did, he leaned in to kiss me and suck my juices off my fucking tongue.

"Mitchell," I moaned. I pushed my breast up in his direction. He smiled a little and then took my nipple into his mouth, his breath hot against my skin. I moaned loudly now, as Mitchell did the same thing to the other one.

"Shit," I said, accidentally aloud. But then I was so hot and bothered, I needed something else from Mitchell.

I wiggled out of my bathrobe and pulled him on top of me.

"Mitchell. Please. Fuck me."

"You want to get fucked, Mirabella?"

Mitchell angled himself between my legs, but he didn't give me what I wanted, not right away. Knowing Mitchell, it was because he asked me a direct question which I had not yet answered.

"Yes."

After I had given him the courtesy of a response, Mitchell slowly slid inside me.

"Fuck, Mira."

I was out of control with need at that moment. I couldn't wait for Mitchell. I pulled him deeper into me and began to move on him, holding his ass with both hands.

"I need you, Mitchell."

"I'm right here, Baby. Take what you need."

CHAPTER 36

MITCHELL MAGELLAN

I got garbage sleep last night. Even though Mira and I had come to an understanding about her pregnancy scare, I still didn't feel settled. I wasn't sure I could fully let it go. There was something not right with the whole thing. Something still as of yet unresolved. As Grandma Wright would say, my spirit was restless.

I'd never been in a relationship, serious or otherwise, with someone as young as Mirabella. She'd only recently turned twenty-one, and for all intents and purposes, was a senior in college. Frankly, it had never bothered me until now. Until I thought Mira might have been pregnant. My words to her brother Jared crept into my mind like unwanted guests. And throughout the night and into the morning, they played repeatedly in my head.

Fuck.

What was good for the goose was certainly not good for the fucking gander. In this case, I was the fucking gander, despite wanting desperately to be the goddam goose.

Mira was terrified. She did not want to be pregnant. On a basic level, I understood it. But my fucking insecurities plagued me causing me to wonder if maybe she didn't think I'd be a suitable father. I'd had a shitty relationship with my parents. What did I know about being a dad?

To be fair to Mirabella, I had given her no reason, other than how great an uncle I was to Christina, to make her believe that I would not ruin any kid. Look at me. I was not exactly the poster child for well-adjusted children.

Still, I couldn't figure out why I was so affected. I didn't want to be a dad. I had no desire to have kids. Where would we even put one? Despite having a four-bedroom apartment, this penthouse wasn't screaming 'kid-friendly.' Besides, didn't kids need room to run and play in like a backyard and such? A high-rise building in Midtown Manhattan was no place to raise a child.

Fuck.

The alarm went off at 9AM. I pried my eyes open long enough to turn off the sound and notice that my bed was missing one gorgeous lady. I dragged my sorry ass out of bed, peed, brushed my teeth, washed my face, and went to look for my girl.

When I reached the bottom of the steps, I heard his voice. She had RayRay on speakerphone as she plated some pancakes she'd made.

"I don't think Mitchell would mind. You guys should come by. He has a meeting anyway."

"You don't think Mitchell would mind what, having Judases in my fucking apartment?" I said, thinking about Mira hosting her co-conspirators so soon after they all conspired to keep me from knowing about the pregnancy tests.

"It was one hundred percent Mena's doing, Mitchell. You know I would never have agreed to that shit," RayRay said, throwing fucking Mena under the bus as I smiled at my girl, pulled her into my arms and kissed her good morning, making certain to be loud about it.

"Gross. Get a fucking room, you two," Mena's voice came from the phone.

"I'm gonna fucking kick your ass when I see you, Mena," I said, not even joking. She's been a thorn in my side from Day One. Since the day

I showed up at their apartment demanding to see the spitfire who'd told me to go fuck myself.

"I've said it before, I'll say it again. Fuck you, Mitchell."

I had to laugh. That Mena never backed down. She was just as much a spitfire as Mirabella. Too bad she wasn't nearly as hot, I thought to myself as I squeezed Mira's ass cheeks before reaching behind her, grabbing a few blueberries, and popping them into my mouth.

"Ok, see you guys in a bit," Mira said. I pressed the "End" button for her, happy to be rid of them for a moment."

"Is this alright?" Mira said in a ridiculously cute and innocent pleading way.

"What do I get out of it?"

"I made us breakfast."

"I can see that, Baby. Thank you. But I can get food from anywhere," I teased.

Mira put her arms around my neck how I like. Jesus. I was fucking obsessed with her. No one could accuse me of taking it easy on her. One could accuse me of being addicted. Anna had said that I simply replaced one addiction with another.

But what did she know about it? She'd only ever met Mira that one time. She hadn't seen us together in real life, like day-to-day. All she heard was how into her I was. And in many ways, as much as I hated to hear Anna trivialize my feelings for Mira and try to make it out to be unhealthy, the more I became convinced that my feelings were changing and morphing into something so unrecognizable that no one would be able to relate or understand.

"What does my baby want?" she said in the sexiest fucking way as she closed the tiny space between our bodies. When she felt my hunger for her, she smiled.

I should have been angrier than I was. But a full day of talking to Mirabella and having sex with Mirabella did wonders for my attitude. So, when she asked if I had an issue with RayRay and Mena coming over, I was fine with it. Besides, I had work to do, and that would keep me off her long enough to achieve that. Still, I reserved the right to steal her away from her friends for a quickie if I got antsy.

And that was how we negotiated it. And since Mirabella was in a negotiating mood, I pulled her to me, finding another use for the whipped cream and the honey she had intended to use for the pancakes.

MIRA SAT in the room with Jared who was in and out of sleep today. He'd lost a shit-ton of weight and was even more pale and gaunt than the last time we'd seen him, two days ago. Mirabella was doing her best to be strong, bolstered by the fact that her parents had already left, probably understanding that the awkwardness of them all being in the same room being too much unnecessary negativity for Jared's recovery.

"Jared," Mira said when he opened his eyes.

"Hey, Sis. Mitch." Jared whispered and then rested his exhausted and nearly lifeless gaze to Mira and then me.

"Hey, Man," I said.

Jared smiled a slow smile, then tears streamed down his face.

"It's ok, Jare." Mira's voice was shaky despite her best efforts to seem assured.

"I don't think so, B. I don't feel good at all."

"I know. Just rest."

Jared fell back asleep just as the nurse entered the room.

"Oh, I didn't know you both were here."

"How's he doing? He was just awake for a few minutes. Why is he so tired?" Mira said.

"Well, he had a lot of company today," she said as she checked his machines and then his pain and hydration drips. "He was up for some time before I had to get everyone to leave so he could rest. He had a good day."

"Thank you for telling me that. He just looks so pale. His skin is so dry." Mira looked sad and frustrated.

"Yes," was all Ms. Heartly said.

"We should have come earlier, Mitchell."

"It's fine. We're here now. He knows we're here. Let's just sit with him for a while. I brought his book. I'll read to him."

"Thank you" she said, a grateful smile on her gorgeous face.

She took a seat on the chair on the right side of the bed near the machines. I took a seat on the other side, opened the book, and began to read to Jared.

About thirty minutes into my story, Jared opened his eyes.

Mirabella immediately went to him to bring him some ice water, grabbing the water jug and bringing the straw to his lips.

"Thanks, B. But I can get my own water." Jared's smiled a sleepy tired smile and reached a shaky hand from under his covers. Mira pressed the dial on his bed to raise it up so that he would be sitting instead of lying down. I stood and helped Jared adjust his pillows and blanket.

"Will you guys stop fussing over me? I'm not an invalid."

"Aren't you?" Mirabella said, fucking annoyed that Jared wouldn't let us help him. Just then we all laughed so hard. The whole thing was stupid and comical at once. Jared was only recently a healthy, strapping, man. Now, this fucking cancer had reduced him to a shriveled up, always cold, yellowy, little person.

Just then, Mira apparently remembered she'd snuck some liquor in her purse along with three shot glasses. She pulled them out, and filled each with a tiny bit of tequila, the one he liked.

When she nodded toward the open door, I shut and locked it to keep the nosey nurses out.

And when I practically ran back over to join Mirabella and Jared in a toast, looking like a little boy sneaking a cigarette from his grandmother's purse, I smiled at Mira and accepted my shot glass.

She handed Jared his, and raised hers in the air, and said, "Fuck cancer."

Jared smiled at each of us and said, "Fuck cancer" in unison with me. Then we all downed our shots.

Right as we finished, a knock came at the door, and someone jiggled the door handle.

ALL THE WAY OUT

We giggled like goofballs. Mirabella collected the shot glasses, stowed the alcohol back in her bag, and I ran to unlock the door.

"You need to keep this door open and unlocked at all times," the nurse said, eyeing us suspiciously.

We all stifled giggles, even Jared.

Jared pounded on his chest, the burn of the tequila no doubt hitting him.

"Yes, ma'am," Mirabella said as me and Jared busted out laughing.

"B! You're gonna get me kicked out of here."

"Believe me, as long as Mitchell keeps paying and flirting with those nurses, you aren't going anywhere."

I made a face. What flirting? I was *not* flirting with nurses.

Jared eyed Mirabella with suspicion, "What are you not telling me, B?"

"Nothing. It's nothing."

"Mirabella. You have only two flaws. Otherwise, you're perfect," Jared said, a sly smile on his face. "You're a shitty singer and you're a worse liar."

He looked at me. I shook my head and raised my hands as if to say, "Leave me the fuck out of that shit."

Mira was being strong for her brother and for herself right then because Jared saw right through her weakening façade. If you caught Mira at just the right moment in a smile or laugh, you could see the cracks that threatened to break into a million little pieces she would rather die than have anyone see.

Today, in addition to the fact that her brother was clearly losing his battle with cancer, Mirabella thought only a few hours ago that she might have been pregnant.

She slowly cast her eyes in my direction. She was going to tell him.

"If I tell you, you can't tell anyone. Not Grandma, nor Mom, nor Dad."

"Oh shit. You knocked up?"

Lowering my eyes as Jared turned his face to me, I shook my head.

"No. It's. Well, I thought maybe I was. But I'm not. We're not"

It was as if someone had stolen Jared's heart because he stopped breathing. The only sign that he was still alive was how he stared into Mira's eyes, the two of them engaged in some sort of sibling mind exchange.

Finally, Jared said, "Mirabella Alexia Castle, you would be an amazing mom. Oh man. Fuck."

"What's wrong?" she said, concern all over her gorgeous face.

"I'm not going to be here. I won't get to be an uncle to your kid. Little fucking Magellans."

"Yes, you fucking will. Yes. You. Fucking. Will," Mira said, grabbing her brother into a huge hug while crying her eyes out once more.

And as Jared hugged her back, crying too, he and I made eye contact. In that moment, I made him a silent promise to take care of his sister.

"You are not going to leave, Jare. I refuse to be all alone in this world."

But she wasn't alone. And I was going to make it my business to make sure Mirabella never felt alone ever again.

EPILOGUE

MIRABELLA CASTLE

Snow blanketed Central Park on this brisk Christmas Eve day. From the Penthouse we could see snow topping the trees and covering the ground, as it fell at a lazy but constant pace.

We had so much to be grateful for during our combination housewarming, welcome home 'temporarily' Jared, Christina's christening, and Christmas Eve party. I was finally free of my Brennan Enterprises contract. Mitchell and I had turned a corner in our relationship.

Even though Jared remained in hospice, they allowed him to spend the day with us thanks to Mitchell's rather sizable donation.

Marissa Canto had officially dropped charges against Mitchell and recanted her statement. Robert Brennan took a plea deal and was remanded to federal prison where he was expected to serve a minimum of ten years, but his max could have been fifty. Peter Trenom was awaiting trial and also incarcerated.

The penthouse was alive with family, dear friends, and co-workers, and it was a sight to see.

Emilio was in a corner cozying up to RayRay, as Christina played in her Christening dress at RayRay's feet with the dolls Uncle Mitchies had given her.

Will, Maisy, Hyacinth, and Christopher, Hyacinth's brother, were over by the bar doing shots.

Jared sat in a wheelchair, covered in a blanket, and attached to an oxygen tank as Grandma, Dad, and Bianca hovered.

Mom, Mena, Iggy, and Shayla had a game of *Cards Against Humanity* going at the dining room table.

Shonda, her son Lamar, Mitchell, and Maleko looked to be watching the football game.

Brendan and Braxton stood in a corner being anti-social together.

Cindy, Sherilyn, and Clara and her wife Evelyn stood together near the fireplace, as if awaiting Mitchell's order, seemingly fully unable to turn off their work brains in his presence.

Aunt Meg, Anna, and Akila seemed deep in conversation about Preston.

Akila's fiancé, Gerald and Dino, Mena's boyfriend, were talking about how amazing the views were from the seventy-sixth floor.

We'd started the party at three so that our guests could get the full effect of the penthouse at daytime, sunset, dusk, then at nighttime. Against the backdrop of New York City, Mitchell and I mingled amongst friends and family, each of us making sure to check on Jared, who would ask to be taken to his room and then brought back after a bathroom break or a power nap.

Mitchell was so gentle and caring with Jared, and it was heartwarming to witness. Throughout the night, I watched as Mitchell and my family engaged one another, and whatever I was worried about in terms of whether they would gel, no longer mattered.

My dad was the most awkward of all our guests, not really fitting in with any of the cliques that had formed.

Around eight o'clock, after dinner had been served and people were thinking about dessert, Mitchell texted me.

> MITCHELL: let's go upstairs, baby

> ME: now?
>
> MITCHELL: right fucking now
>
> ME: ppl will notice we're gone
>
> MITCHELL: i want to lick your pussy for dessert

I looked around to be certain no one had read my messages.

His text reminded me of that night in London when Mitchell had said he would put me on the menu and how hot that had made me. It was also the night I had thrown myself at him in a drunken attempt to seduce him. Mitchell had looked so good that night, and we'd had such a good time. But so much had happened since then. In a way, it was a much simpler time in our lives together when we were still playing cat and mouse.

I looked up from my phone at him now, and he was looking at me every few seconds while talking to Shonda and Lamar. Then he fixed his hungry eyes on me, and hunted me from across the room. Various people stopped him to chat him up as he made his way to me. I watched as he spoke and waved, like a politician making his way through a crowd of supporters, as he remained on his mission of reaching me. And when Mitchell finally did, he kissed me deeply, crushing his tongue against mine and claiming me.

I pulled away, and looked at him as if to ask if he was aware we had guests. He pulled me to him and kissed my neck. This man was so fucking handsome and so fucking sexy. The way he touched me and handled me in public like he didn't give a fuck who was watching was such a turn on.

"Mitchell," I said. "People are looking at us."

"And whose fault is that?" He smiled a devilish smile, and whispered in my ear, "I need my girl right now."

Without waiting for my response, Mitchell took me by the hand and led me upstairs, and I could feel everyone's eyes on my back. Once inside our bedroom, Mitchell shut and locked the door. He seemed to be studying me.

"What are you doing?"

"Looking at my beautiful girl, he said.

"Don't just stand there gawking, Mitchell. Come put your mouth on me like you promised."

"There's my little spitfire," he said with a smile. Within seconds, I had my hands in Mitchell's hair as he ate me out, fingered me, and made me come. And when he came up for air, I kissed my fluids from his mouth. Mitchell stood up and pulled his pants and briefs down, and when I got on my knees for him, he moaned, and said, "Take me deep, Mirabella. I want to feel you gag."

WHEN WE RETURNED to the party, everyone pretended as if we did not disappear to have sex upstairs. Mitchell went to instruct the servers to give everyone champagne so that he could propose a toast. Once everyone had a glass of bubbly, Mitchell stood in front of the massive fireplace, and tapped the side of his glass with a fork to get everyone's attention.

Just then, he caught me looking at him, and smiled at me like he forgot we weren't alone.

"Everyone. Can I have your attention, please? And, Mirabella, can you please join me?"

I made my way over to Mitchell, and took his hand.

He looked over at me, and smiled before kissing me, and whispering in my ear, "I love you, Baby."

All eyes were on us now, and standing next to Mitchell Magellan as his girlfriend in our penthouse felt surreal.

"Thank you all for coming to our home. Mirabella and I are so grateful for all of you and could not be prouder to share our home and food with you all on this momentous occasion. This year has been full of difficulties, great and not so great surprises, video tape releases . . ."

Everyone laughed at Mitchell's ability to laugh at himself, even me. He looked at me to be certain I was ok, even though he'd told me in advance he was going to make said joke.

"In all seriousness, this year has taught me about the fragility of life. And, that if you are lucky enough to find someone to love, make your best efforts to love them with all you have, and do not let them go. Thank you all for your love and support at home and at work, and thank you for standing by us and loving us. On this Christmas Eve, we want to wish you all a very merry Christmas." Mitchell raised his glass, and said, "Cheers."

Everyone returned his "Cheers," and then we all drank. And when I finished my sip and Mitchell had finished his, I kissed him. And if I'm not mistaken, Mitchell Magellan was blushing.

IT WAS CHRISTMAS MORNING, and Mitchell and I had plans all day. We had a volunteer shift to serve the homeless from ten in the morning until one. After that, we planned to spend some time with Jared in hospice care, and then we would have dinner in. Mitchell catered a variety of things we both liked, and I for one was looking forward to pigging out and just having some alone time with him since our last guests, Emilio, Mena, Dino, Akila, and Gerald left our party last night at three forty-five in the morning. And even though Mitchell and I had snuck away for a quickie during the party, Mitchell was ready to go first thing this morning.

"Merry Christmas, Baby," Mitchell said when I opened my eyes.

"Merry Christmas, Mitchell." I said, excited to open my gifts. "When do you want to open presents?"

Mitchell reached under the covers, and copped several feels before saying, "I'm going to open the best one now."

He was tickling me while also rubbing me in all the right places, getting me prepared for him. He trailed kisses all over me too, slipping under the covers to get to the hard-to-reach places that he liked so much. Then he made his way back up to my face, and started kissing me passionately as he massaged my aching clit. I moaned for him.

He moaned in response as he rubbed his penis against me.

"I love you, Mitchell."

"I love that you love me, Mirabella," he moaned against my neck as he massaged my tits, both with one hand. He humped me then, his cock feeling so good against me.

My vagina clenched as it pushed arousal liquids out, preparing for him to enter me. I moaned again then, the anticipation of what was to come so great, I nearly grabbed him and slid him inside me myself.

"Mitchell, I need you," I said, looking at him and hoping my eyes conveyed the desperate need I had for him to fill me up with his engorged cock, and fuck away the need. Fuck away the emptiness. Fuck away the urgency.

"You want me, Mira?" Mitchell said in the lazy voice he used when he is aroused and comfy and warm.

"I need you inside me, Mitchell."

"Didn't I eat you out good last night?" He said as he reached between my legs to massage my clit some more.

"Oh, God, yes."

"Then why are you so needy this morning, Baby? Should I have fucked you last night too?" He said as he pushed a finger inside me and rubbed the wetness over my swollen and throbbing clit, making my vagina clench again, a few times.

He turned me over on my side.

"I can't get enough of you, Mitchell," I said, spilling my truth to this man. I moved my ass cheeks on his dick enjoying the feeling while doing so at the same time as he was rubbing my clit. Mitchell put his other hand over my mouth, held it there for a few seconds, and then placed it firmly around my neck.

"Mmmmmm. I love when you tell me how I make you feel."

"Mitchell, please. I need you," I said begging him to fuck me.

"I'm going to put my cock in you, Baby. Tell me how you like it," Mitchell said. "Tell me if it feels good." He grabbed my hips with both hands, and raised my ass in the air slightly so he could get better access.

Sex with Mitchell was a full body experience. The deeper I fell for him, the more emotional our love making felt. I was so taken with Mitchell, and our connection was so deep that I was able to feel not just with my body, but with my soul. My senses heightened with each touch as the smell of him and our sex permeated the air around and between us. The heat from Mitchell's mouth torched my skin, kindling a desire so deep and all-consuming that all I could think about was loving him with my body until I had nothing more to give.

Soon enough, Mitchell was inside me from behind, the sweet pressure of his urgent and deep thrusts maddeningly pleasurable. Mitchell held onto and put pressure on my mound with one hand while rubbing my clit with his other hand. I covered the hand he had on my mound with my own hand, gripping my fingers around his.

And when I took that hand and put his index finger in my mouth to suck, I felt my vagina become slicker, tighter, and hotter.

"Fuck, Mirabella," Mitchell said against my neck, his dick twitching and jumping against my pussy wall.

I could not hold on any longer.

"Mitchell, I need to come. You're gonna make me come."

"Come for me, Baby," he whispered against my skin.

"Mitchell," I moaned out as I came so fucking strongly, I thought for sure I had squeezed him much too tightly. But then, Mitchell came, telling me he was doing so by whispering in my ear.

"Don't move; just stay here like this with me for a few minutes," Mitchell said against my neck as he held me in a warm embrace while his penis slowly returned to its flaccid state.

"Mirabella," he said, as he pulled slowly out of me, and turned me toward him.

"Yes?"

"Are you happy?"

"What?"

"Are you happy? Are you happy with me?"

"I'm so happy but I'm also scared."

"What are you afraid of?"

"Nothing good lasts forever. You of all people should know that," I said, regretting it the moment it left my lips. "Jared is so sick; he's dying. You just lost your family. You found out Preston is your brother, and that is a fact you cannot even fully enjoy because of how it came to be.

Your father's best friends betrayed him, and will spend the rest of their lives in prison."

Mitchell looked down and away from me briefly, shielding his teary eyes from me.

"And yet, against all odds, we found one another. We fought to get to this point through so much fucking pain."

"Mitchell, what's wrong?"

He hesitated.

"Mirabella, I need to know that this, what we have, is enough for you. That I'm enough for you," he said.

I kissed him then, softly and gently.

"You are everything, Mitchell Magellan," I said with a loving and sincere smile.

Mitchell kissed me then pulled on his Christmas tree pajama pants I'd made him wear. "Wait here, he said with a smile as my phone rang. "Don't answer it."

I smiled at him, as he got out of bed and retrieved something from his dresser and held it behind his back.

"What is that?"

My phone stopped ringing then started ringing again.

"One of your Christmas gifts."

I wanted to see what it was so badly, but I also wanted to look at my phone to make certain it wasn't about Jared.

"Don't answer it, Mirabella, Mitchell said, as he came over to my side of the bed, holding the gift behind his back still.

I sat up in bed and pulled the covers up over my boobs, securing the sheet by placing it under my armpits, the anticipation of what Mitchell had gotten me growing.

My phone stopped ringing, and my nerves calmed a bit. *If it was an emergency or important, they would call back or call Mitchell's phone*, I thought as I pushed my anxiety aside so I could enjoy my first Christmas with Mitchell in our gorgeous penthouse.

Mitchell smiled at me, then got on one knee just as his phone began to ring. Now, both our phones were ringing.

Tears welled up in my eyes. Something was wrong.

"Answer it," Mitchell said, standing.

And when I looked to see who was calling, Mitchell had a look of hopelessness on his face.

"Hello?"

"Mirabella Castle?"

"Yes?"

"This is Marianne Heartly from hospice. Come quickly. I don't think Jared has that much time left."

ALL THE WAY SERIES

Miss them already? Mirabella Alexia Castle and Mitchell Xavier Magellan will return!

ALL THE WAY IN: November 3, 2023

ALL THE WAY OUT: December 22, 2023

ALL THE WAY Book 3: April 26, 2024

ALL THE WAY Book 4: September 6, 2024

Loved this story? Please leave a review!

ABOUT THE AUTHOR

Hensley Amethyst Park is a New York City native who loves centering her stories there.

PLAYLIST

- Love and War, Max Drazen
- Lose Control, Teddy Swims
- Starlight, Muse
- Talk, Khalid
- Love Like Rockets, Angels & Airwaves
- I Just Wanna Love Ya, Jay-Z
- Sorry, Justin Bieber
- Satellite, Harry Styles
- My House, Flo Rida
- Locked Out of Heaven, Bruno Mars
- Falling Away from Me, Korn
- Feeling This, Blink-182
- Unsteady, X-Ambassadors
- High, Stephen Sanchez
- Close to You, The Cure
- Crazy for You, Madonna
- Stay, Rihanna (feat. Mikky Ekko)
- R U Mine, Arctic Monkeys
- When I See You Smile, Bad English
- The Link is Dead, Deftones
- You Are My High, DJ Snake

ACKNOWLEDGMENTS

I would like to thank all the readers who bought, borrowed, and read ALL THE WAY IN. You've changed my life, and I am forever grateful.

Once more, thank you especially to *Ann*. Without your insight, feedback, comments, and encouragement, I would NOT have been able to bring this story or its characters to life.

I would also like to thank Brian, Cindy M, and Tiffany for your amazing feedback as I embarked on telling what happens next with Mirabella Castle and Mitchell Magellan. This story is better because of your critique, feedback, and support.

Thanks, Sariah for making awesome social media content. Thanks, Liso Reads for helping me learn about Hindu death and funeral rituals and customs.

Thank you to every single person who has messaged me to ask questions, offer support, and express their love for Mirabella and Mitchell, etc.

Finally, if you have posted about ALL THE WAY IN or ALL THE WAY OUT, posted a review, shared a post, a story or a real, followed me, commented on any of my social media posts, participated in a giveaway, or engaged with me in any way, however large or small, THANK YOU.

I sincerely hope you love ALL THE WAY OUT as much as I enjoyed writing it. Please consider leaving a review on your favorite review site or on social media.

I appreciate you!

DELETED SCENE

Miss them already? Mirabella Alexia Castle and Mitchell Xavier Magellan will return soon!

To tide you over, here's a deleted sex scene you might enjoy! It takes place the day after Jared's visit when Mirabella and Mitchell spend some much-needed time together. Mitchell has been in London for a week.

MIRABELLA **CASTLE**

"Please fucking tell me you didn't waste this fucking mouth on that fucking guy." Mitchell stared only at my mouth now. He seemed to be concentrating really hard.

I didn't know what to say. Before I met Mitchell, Ben had made me feel like the most unsexy and incapable sexual partner to ever live. And my other sex partner treated me like a means to an end.

"Mirabella," he said, still staring at my mouth but now pushing his thumb farther into it. I ran my tongue across his thumb, the same thumb he had rubbed my clit with earlier. It tasted salty.

I didn't mean to, but I moaned and closed my eyes lazily, starting to become aroused by the taste of my own taste, proof that Mitchell Fucking Magellan was doing his fucking job.

And then before I knew it, Mitchell was out from under the covers, on his knees, and moving his dick across my lips.

"Tell me what you need, Mitchell," I said, reaching up to touch my left breast, trying to give it the attention Mitchell should have been giving it. And that thought empowered me.

I stood then and put my left nipple to his mouth.

"While you're thinking about what you need, suck on me," I said.

Mitchell's eyes almost popped out of his head, and his reaction emboldened and aroused the fuck out of me. I leaned down to kiss him, as he was still on his knees, rubbing himself now.

"Mirabella." He was completely out of breath when I broke contact with his gorgeous mouth.

"Yes, Baby." I watched him stroke and tug his cock slowly and deliberately.

I grabbed his hand from his dick and put it on my clit, and said, "do your fucking job."

Mitchell moaned, his sexy expression full of such arousal and need. He began to finger my vagina and rub my clit, and I was unable to stop myself from grinding against him.

The buzz from the concierge downstairs was an unwelcome intrusion. I instinctively crouched down and pulled the covers over me. Mitchell kissed me on the nose, smiled, and said, "It's ok, Baby. Wait for me in bed."

"Are you sure?" I held onto his arm and trailed kisses on it making him smile.

"Yes, Baby."

I stood and wrapped the blanket like a towel around my naked body. He squeezed my ass and nodded in the direction of the stairs. Planting a kiss on his luscious mouth, I smiled and said, "Hurry" before heading upstairs.

More than a few moments later, Mitchell joined me in the bedroom.

"What did Candy want?"

"Our grocery delivery arrived. They're on their way up."

I was suddenly starving.

"Are you thinking what I'm thinking?"

"You should know by now not to ask me what I'm thinking, Mirabella."

I got out of bed, walked over to Mitchell who was fully dressed, I assumed, because a delivery person was on their way up. Fully naked, I wrapped my arms around his neck, and said, "Let's get some lunch. I'm, starving."

"Mirabella," Mitchell said before placing a kiss on my nose, "If you think I'm letting you leave this apartment today, you are sorely mistaken. You are mine all day, and I have until seven o'clock before I have to share you again."

I pouted.

"Don't pout, Mira. Here," Mitchell said as he handed me his phone. "Order us whatever you want, and when you're done, I'm going to bury myself inside you until we both fucking come."

This. FUCKING. Man.

Made in the USA
Columbia, SC
20 March 2024